A Pale Horse

Angels are always among us.

A Pale Horse is a work of fiction. All References to persons, places or events are fictitious or used fictitiously.

ISBN: 978-1-952474-01-9

Cover design by Jonathan Grisham for Grisham Designs

Published by WordCrafts Press
Cody, Wyoming 82414
www.wordcrafts.net

THE ARC SERIES
VOLUME 1

A PALE HORSE

MICHELLE A. SULLIVAN

WordCrafts Press

To my husband, Jason, my greatest supporter and love. I could not have started this adventure without you. To *all* of my family, thank you for all of your positive feedback and loving support. Finally, thank you to the friends who allowed me to bounce ideas off you—without you, all of this would not have been possible.

Chapter 1

And I looked, and there was a pale green horse. The horseman on it was named Death, and Hades was following after him. Authority was given over a fourth of the earth, to kill by sword, by famine, by plague, and by the wild animals of the Earth.

Revelation 6:8

"Very good. Peter, can you hear me?" The doctor hovered, slightly hunched, inches from his face, speaking softly with a sure calmness.

"Yes," Peter breathed, a relaxed exhale in the affirmative.

"Good. I'm going to count back from three to one. When I say 'one,' you will be aware, calm, and have full recollection of what we discussed during our session. Do you understand?"

"I understand."

Dr. Phillips backed away slightly and rose to her full height. A statuesque yet slender woman, the sweet tone of her voice did not match her confident, at times stern, demeanor, but it did serve to calm her patient and make him more susceptible to the much-needed hypnosis therapy.

"And 3… 2… 1. How do you feel, Peter?"

The young man lying on the couch opened his eyes, looking bemused. He blinked twice and then oriented his gaze on the smiling doctor, sheepishly returning her pleased look.

Peter Deveraux was used to the gurgly feeling he got in his gut when someone like Dr. Jo looked him in the eye. He wasn't good around attractive women and sneaking furtive looks at pretty girls, never looking them full in the face for fear of death by embarrassed mortification, was all he could manage most times. Like now. He found himself looking—no, *staring*—at the incredibly attractive psychologist. She understood and withstood his gaze knowing how hard it was for him to look at her at all. Peter couldn't help himself, and he drank her in as one would a priceless work of art that has only become more precious throughout the ages. He thought about how perfect she looked. She was an enigma to him, like all other women. He was still trying to get used to the fact that he could speak openly and confidently to her. Dr. Jo was not like other women. She didn't embarrass easily, or at all, really, and she was easy to talk to. He felt safe with her. He knew he was in good hands. She was trying to help him.

"So, doc? What do you think? I think that was one of the best we've had. Man, I feel like I have had the best night's sleep ever." He punctuated that last statement by stretching and swinging his legs around, so his feet touched the floor.

Dr. Jo just smiled. "I will lob that one back over the net to you. What did we learn during this session?" She drifted casually over to the white oak bookcase behind her marble top desk and grabbed a bottle of Maker's Mark. She took a cloth, swiped at the inside lip of a rocks glass, and deposited two ice cubes.

Peter watched and smiled at the *clink-clink* the glass made.

"More than I knew I had forgotten, that's for certain."

She motioned to him an offer of his own drink and he nodded. She crossed back to him and offered the bourbon, taking a slow sip of her own as she sat. "Tell me."

He stood and tested his feet, still feeling a bit confused by what he was feeling and by what he had remembered.

He raked his hand through his sandy hair, sipped his drink, and started, "Well, I was having a conversation…" He stopped as he tried to process what he would say next.

"And who was the conversation with?" she prompted. "It's alright, Peter. It's just us. You know you can talk to me. Just continue with what you remember."

He felt a little relief, as he always did when she spoke to him. He pressed forward, deciding that the best way to proceed was to simply tell her what he remembered. He laughed softly and looked her in the eyes.

"It's crazy, and I know it can't be right, but it was Michael. The archangel."

He shook his head and felt ridiculous saying it, but he knew without any doubt that he had spoken to the angel, and more importantly, that the angel had spoken to him. Other than a slight widening of her eyes, Dr. Jo showed no other emotions at this pronouncement. It seemed as if she were expecting something along the lines of what Peter had proclaimed and was greatly relieved to hear it.

"Did you hear what I said?" Peter asked her, trying to get some sort of reaction.

"I'm right next to you. Of course I heard what you said." She took another slow sip from her glass, stirred her ice slowly with her slender index finger and said, "What did Michael say?"

Peter blinked. "He asked me about that day," he started. "It was just the two of us standing out front of my uncle's place in Hammond, but then, all of a sudden, I was there, reliving everything."

She caught a hint of panic in his voice, and she willed a new wave of calm to assist his recitation. "Go on," she said soothingly.

Peter felt a slight warmth and peace wash over him, took a deep breath and continued. "July 4th weekend, 2006. My uncle Mike threw a big party at his house in Hammond every year." His eyes took on the glazed look of a person who was deep in thought. Dr. Phillips noticed his blank stare and wondered briefly if he was truly free of his earlier hypnotic state. She let him continue, silently vowing to stop him if he became distressed. "Uncle Mike told us that the cottonmouths were moving around pretty good because it was mating season, and we were to stay on the dock at all times. My cousin Emily had a friend from school staying with her for the weekend. Stephanie..." he recalled the girl, then paused like he was considering his next words. "There were five or six of us at the end of the dock, doing nothing. Just goofing off. I remember

Stephanie not wanting to get close to the edge of the dock because she couldn't swim. My cousins got a little rough near her. They were arguing over who was going to feed the fish the last of the food my uncle gave us." Peter took a deep breath and continued. "Steven pushed his brother into Stephanie. I tried to grab her, but she toppled into the water, and went under. I took my shirt off, kicked off my shoes, and hit the water. She resurfaced a little further out flailing and screaming. I didn't think about the danger. I had been swimming there since I was little. I just thought ther was a girl who might drown."

"What happened after you jumped into the water, Peter?"

He looked up at her and took reassurance in her calm demeanor. Recalling the terrified girl, he continued. "I swam to Stephanie. She was gurgling and crying as she came up. Her arms and hands were everywhere. She was so out of control and scared. I was able to hook my arm around her chest and pull her to shore. She stopped thrashing around when I started to swim with her. I knew everything would be okay after that."

Dr. Jo smiled at him, but his countenance clouded over, and he furrowed his brow.

"She had lost one of her shoes, and she kept saying that she would get in trouble with her parents. I figured since I knew where she fell in, I should be able to find it." Peter continued, strained. "Turns out I was right about finding the shoe, but when I got to the shallows, back near the dock, I stepped into a mating ball. It was so sudden and violent..." Peter trailed off, and a lone tear escaped down his face. "I was bitten so many times, and all I remember is pain. It really hurt, and I was scared." He looked at Dr. Jo, searching for the words to describe his nightmarish experience, fully reverted to his 13-year-old self.

Dr. Phillips closed the distance between them and laid a warm hand on his shoulder. The effect was immediate, and he continued his account.

"All of the adults were on the bank and witnessed the snakes writhing around my legs and biting me. I didn't remember this, but I was told afterward," he shrugged. "The pain was crazy. They tell me that I got out of the water and collapsed. I remember being so weak. And blood. There was blood everywhere, and it just didn't stop," he recounted, horrified. Peter was working himself into a panic with the retelling of his story. Dr. Phillips willed him to continue, silently comforting him with every breath, hurting for him all the while. This was too important to not see through to the end, she reminded herself.

"What else do you remember, Peter?" Dr. Jo asked him.

Peter looked over at her with a puzzled expression. "Up until today, nothing. Now, I remember reaching the emergency room. Lights, voices. Lots of movement; being moved to one table, then another," he said. "I remember pressure, shouting, and then—the pain faded, like someone slid a dimmer switch. I remember seeing a single light hanging above me, but it wasn't the operating room light you see on TV. It wasn't super-bright. It had a warmth to it. It didn't hurt my eyes or scare me or burn me. The light got bigger and more pleasant, warmer, as the pain went away. I could still hear the doctors, far away, doing… something. All I could think about was the light. I wanted to see the source of it, to know where it came from. The more the pain went away, the further away the voices got, and the brighter the light became. It was all I could see." Peter seemed mesmerized, reliving his fascination with the light. He blinked and shook his head. "Just light… it's all I remember." The patient stood, a bit shaken, and took another pull from the drink he held.

The doctor said, "Peter, sit back down. I'm going to try to put you under again, okay? Stay where you are right now, don't leave the light for anything." She muttered something quickly and placed a solitary finger on his forehead. She knew that this wasn't the right way to do it, but she didn't have time to do it the right way, so it was the Other Way, for now. "Peter, when I count to three, just like last time. 1, 2, 3. Tell me about the light, Peter. Can you see it?"

She stepped back and got a good look at his face. By the glassy eyed expression and calm demeanor, Dr. Phillips knew that he was there, again. He could see, feel, hear, and most importantly, remember and process everything from that moment. "Peter? You're there, aren't you? In the light? What do you see? What is there with you?" Things were getting intense, and the waves of calm pulsated so steadily and rapidly from the doctor that they were almost audible.

"Yes," Peter continued, "I see a man. A man? No, that's not right. Something else. An angel? It? No—he. He has wings. Wings. Are you an angel?" Peter asked, remembering.

"Peter, is he saying anything? The angel?" Dr. Jo asked.

"He's smiling; happy. Laughing at me. Michael, like from the Bible… in Sunday school. He says I'll be fine." Peter's voice broke with sarcasm, "Fine? Weird to tell someone who's dying that they'll be fine. I want to be okay, believe me." he said, frustrated, still entranced.

"Is he saying anything else other than you would be fine?" the doctor asked him, expectantly.

"He says I'm special and that I'm not supposed to die. I'm going back. And something else—about my selfless actions." Peter looked surprised, and swallowed hard. "My actions were selfless and have earned me a special honor," he said with a small smile. "I've been chosen," he stated in an excited voice. "Chosen for what?" Peter asked, confused.

That was enough. She had done it. She touched his forehead again, impatiently. "Peter? Peter. Look at me."

The glazed look left his eyes, and Peter zoned in on the pretty doctor. "Doctor Jo? What? You heard all of that, right? I remembered it all this time. Weird dream. I never got to the angel speaking part, though. Until today. Usually, I just died on the table in my version. What does it mean? What did *he* mean?"

At that moment, the smartphone on the doctor's desk buzzed. She looked down at her watch. "I'm afraid we went a bit over, and that will be Ms. Anders letting me know my next appointment is here," she told him. "Please, Peter, remember to write any new information in your journal so that we can discuss it in the next session." She gave him a smile and a brief nod.

"Can you tell me what all this means?" Peter asked her.

"I'm afraid I don't know that yet, but we are unravelling the mystery, aren't we?" She was elated at their breakthrough, and her face showed it. She was positively glowing, and she gave his shoulder a slight squeeze as he picked up his journal and started for the door. She assured him, "Peter, we are further now than we have ever been, and yet not nearly as far as we will go. I am here to help and guide you in your progress. Do you trust me?" she asked, searching his eyes.

"I do," he told her. "I will let you know if I remember anything else, doc. Thanks."

As the door opened, Peter turned and gave Dr. Jo one last smile and felt a sense of calm wash over him when she smiled in return. "You have my number. Call anytime," she told him, then she turned to the older black man waiting in the waiting room. "You can come back, Abe. It's nice to see you." she said to him, and smiled warmly as if greeting a dear friend.

Abe brushed past Peter on his way into the office and gave him a friendly nod.

"See you next week, Peter?" the lovely receptionist asked Peter when he reached the door.

Peter stopped with his hand on the doorknob, his heart beat wildly and his throat closed up, "I... I..." he stuttered and looked at the floor. "Yes," he said quietly. He turned the knob and walked away without looking back. He didn't see her warm smile.

Peter opened the door to the afternoon heat, and he could hear the bedlam of the New Orleans French Quarter from a distance. The Quarter was too much for many, even on the tamest of days. Peter knew well that leading up to and preparing for Fat Tuesday could be just as loud, chaotic, and frantic as the actual event. The city, *his* city, had a special place in his heart, which is odd for an introvert, he thought. Most large cities try to put their best foot forward—stately gentlemen, dressed to the nines and ready to wine and dine you with class and dignity and get you home at a proper hour—when tourists come to call. New Orleans? A crazy uncle who shows up unannounced in your driveway on a Friday afternoon in a hot red Jag that will whisk you away to a memoir-worthy adventure fit to make any of the big-city visitors blush. When Mardi Gras was in full swing it was NOLA's best foot—the best the Quarter would be all year—and every raucous second would be a write-home-about-it moment for those involved, an ear-splitting, pandemonious, carnival affair with plenty of debauchery and drinks—lots and lots of drinks.

Peter would be making some final preparations for shutting himself away for the next two weeks. He did *not* like Mardi Gras.

Chapter 2

The sun was high, the Quarter was sweltering, and Peter groaned inwardly. Even though he loved his ancestral home on Governor Nicholls Street, and living in the old part of the Crescent City normally suited him well, he did not partake in the festivities. Many New Orleanians didn't, sort of like a native of Las Vegas shunning the Strip unless company from out of town has come to see the sights. Being a shut-in was much preferred to being engulfed by the massive sea of drunken revelers that would wash over the area's already barely-tolerable party streets for the next two weeks. Loud music, even louder people, and no sleep.

Eh, it's not like I really sleep all that much, anyway, thought Peter. *It gives me more time to work… so there's that.*

Peter's home, the building at 529 Governor Nicholls Street, had been in his family for seven decades, ever since the 1936 state constitutional amendment that afforded the VCC power to go about preserving and protecting the Quarter's history and landmarks. His grandfather, Pierre-Jacques Devereaux, a diplomat and, from what Peter knew of him, a master negotiator that would make today's heavy-hitters look like dilettantes, spearheaded the effort and cut himself a sweet deal on some of the properties left when the French Creole moved to the University district. The house at 529 was what was left to Peter, and he loved his grandfather's legacy. The bottom floor had always been a business, rented to a friend or relative of Grandpa's, up until a few years after Peter was born. Since he was six years old, the lower part had been occupied by La Cuisine Ouverte, owned and operated by a sweet family who made, in Peter's opinion, the best food in New Orleans. Rose Manette was the current occupant, and when not serving her customers, she was serving the Quarter's single residents as matchmaker. She seemed to have a particular mission to find a mate for Peter, much to his chagrin. Peter loved Rose like another mother, but wished she would leave well enough alone. She knew he had a painful shyness that dogged him where the fairer sex was concerned, yet she refused to relent. The dates she arranged for Peter usually only lasted long enough for a cup of coffee and an awkward, mumbled conversation, many times followed by Peter spilling something or getting the hiccups. That was if he even showed up. Normally, he couldn't muster the courage.

Although Peter loved women, he lacked whatever the thing was that allowed a man to talk to them. It was nearly impossible for him to even approach a girl, let alone have a conversation. The lone exceptions in his life currently were Dr. Jo, his assistant at Guardian, Tammy Pryde, and Momma Rose. Other than them, he couldn't think of a recent time when he was able to put more than two sentences together. Luckily, Peter thought, Rose was older and matronly, in a nice way. If he couldn't talk to her, he would starve to death.

As he walked down Canal, he was lost in his thoughts and did not see the couple being ushered out of The Saint Hotel by the stick-like doorman. Motion to his left caused him to flash back to reality, and he noticed the woman first. She was exquisite; athletic, bronze, redheaded, and shimmery—and rapidly coming towards him. He made a move to sidestep the lady and was startled by the blast from the horn of a waiting taxi. He jumped, and as would be his luck, he ran right into her, knocking her backwards. The man, who had stopped to say something to the doorman at the Saint, only frowned and shook his head.

Peter gathered himself and awkwardly reached out to help the women steady herself, but she brushed him away as if he were a bothersome insect. He could tell from her manner that she was a *very* independent person and would *not* be requiring his assistance—his or any other man's for that matter. She gave Peter a haughty look.

"Excuse you." she said in a disdainful way.

Peter, a little stung by her reaction, attempted to speak, but then he fell into the most striking set of eyes he had ever seen. The woman was quite a bit shorter than his six-foot frame. He stood there looking down at her and tried to think of something to say.

Words, thought Peter. *Say words.*

"The polite thing to do is apologize for almost knocking me over," she prompted.

Peter found his voice finally and muttered, "I'm sorry." *Well, two words*, he thought. *Yay.*

"Yes, I can see that." she said in a cold voice, then sighed noticing his discomfort. "You should be more careful. A fall in these," she pointed down to a pair of deathly-spiky, peachy-colored high heels, "could have ruined them—and me." They looked torturous, in his opinion, which was in keeping with what he was imagining to be her personality.

"They look dangerous to me, and sort of impractical."

"Well, they can be," she admitted. "But they *make* this outfit, don't you think?"

Peter looked at the stunning woman, who did seem to be perfectly color coordinated, right down to her jewelry, and only then realized that he had spoken his thought aloud.

He gulped and pressed on, "I think they are lovely, and if you are planning to go into the Quarter in them, a big mistake."

"Jimmy Choo's are never a big mistake," the woman said, feigning an offended tone, yet her eyes gave him the impression she was attempting to be playful, and he thought he recognized a teasing glint. She was making sport of him, nothing more. Just then the handsome man returned for her.

"Poydem lyubov?" he asked her in what sounded like Russian to Peter.

"What? Oh, Max, you know I have a hard time with Russian."

She pouted prettily. She answered Peter's questioning expression, "Maxim wants to know if I am ready to go." She smoothed her dress, adjusted her sunglasses, gestured broadly to the late afternoon street and said, "Have a grand evening, Mr…?" she prompted.

"Devereaux. Peter Devereaux. And you are?"

"Magdalene Preston, but my friends call me Maggie," she said with a wink.

"Maggie. A pleasure." Peter backed a step from the couple, taking the measure of the large Russian as he did, and addressed them both. "Hope you two have a fun evening." He turned back to the pretty redhead, adding, "Don't let the shoes kill you." He thought and added, "I think I would have chosen something…" he paused as if thinking of an alternative. "Pragmatic," he finished with a smile. "At any rate, have a good one." He turned and continued down Canal Street, whistling as he went. He watched her reflection in the window as he walked and saw her looking at his retreating figure with a piqued expression.

Maxim noticed her gaze follow the local man toward wherever he was going, and took exception to the fact that her gaze was not on him.

He looked at the retreating Peter and asked, "Would you like I hurt him? He knocked you down, almost."

She smiled up at Maxim, "No. He was just an aggravation. Let's not spoil our evening." She leaned in and kissed him on the cheek, then she lay her delicate hands atop both of his broad shoulders and shook him, as if to wake him up. "Let's go have some fun." She gave him a flirtatious smile, and they got into the cab that would take them into the quarter.

Peter was stunned. He had *talked* to her. Whoever *her* actually was. *What kind of name was Magdalene, anyway?* He wondered why he wasn't discomfited at any point in their conversation. *This is big.* he thought. Giddy at this new ability, he stopped walking. *I was able to talk to her without swallowing my own tongue. If I could talk to a stuck-up, rich tourist girl, maybe I can talk to a nice girl the same way.*

It had been a red-letter day as far as Peter was concerned. He picked up the pace of his walk, and he let the late afternoon sun wend its way down his face as he considered his multiple triumphs. First the return of the memory of his dream with Michael, and now his encounter with this mystery woman—both breakthroughs happened in one day. Peter was elated with his progress and wished that he could tell Dr. Jo. She would understand how important it was, and she would commend him on his bravery.

For 13 years, Peter had been fighting a losing battle with his inner demons, Doubt and Fear. He remembered all too clearly his accident and the trauma and pain it brought him. He could not let himself be near any of the girls in high school because, as Dr. Jo put it, he associated the pain from his snake bite and near-death experience with a girl. Girls utterly paralyzed him with fear.

As it turned out, this ended up being a good thing for him. Less/no girls meant no distractions and no sidetracking from his ambition to become an engineering student. He was to be an engineer, just like his father had been. Along the way, though, he gave in to what turned out to be a very lucrative impulse. Peter had always been interested in movies and comic books with sci-fi and fantasy themes. From the time he attended his first Comic-Con, he had been fascinated by the world of cosplay and replica design. Peter didn't have the courage to actually *be* a cosplayer, but his company had developed a reputation for being the finest outfitter and replica weapons and equipment designer in the world. They had done work on the highest grossing films and most successful TV shows of all time, all while developing new technology. Peter was well-known and quite wealthy, and he had done it while mostly not having to talk to women.

But today he had. Maybe this was the breakthrough that Peter had been waiting for. At that moment a group of young women on their way to the Quarter overtook Peter from behind. As they walked past, a very pretty blonde stopped the group amid some animated conversation. Peter stopped as well, watching this play out, just out of earshot. The blonde turned to walk back towards him, with the giggles of her group following her. She walked up to him with sparkling blue eyes and a thousand watt smile—and he couldn't breathe.

Oh, no, he thought. *This has to be a mistake. It's happening again?* Peter couldn't believe that the old fear had engulfed him so quickly and completely, but here it was, big as day, and apparently here to stay.

She didn't notice his petrification as she asked him, "Are we going the right way to get into the Quarter?" happily awaiting his response, unaware that he was fighting the urge to turn and run.

His throat tightened, and his chest felt heavy. He felt the blush creep its way up his face until he was sure he was as red as a beet. He couldn't talk, only raise an arm and point in the direction the pedicab just took.

The blonde looked from him to the direction he pointed, and with a disappointed look motioned her friends to join her in the direction Peter pointed.

He heard one of her friends say to her, "Oh my God. That guy was so rude. They don't even speak to girls here? Brooke, you're such a loser magnet."

Peter helplessly watched Brooke and her gaggle of squawking friends walk down the street. A little further on, the group elicited a catcall or two from some younger boys. That activated some giggles from the girls in response, and it seemed to be more the reaction they were looking for from the local men. Feeling at a loss again, Peter decided that walking home through the Quarter was not as pleasing a prospect as when he started. He hailed a pedicab to take him home.

"Governor and Decatur, please," he said limply. Once seated, he leaned back as far as the seat would allow. He watched as he passed the same group of girls, giggling and dancing their way to the festivities. The partygoers were coming out of the woodwork, and soon the Quarter would be impossible for anything other than foot traffic. The parade would start soon, and the beads would fly from those on the floats and from those men who would like to see more of the pretty ladies on the street. Peter felt sickened by the spectacle that was his beloved NOLA at Mardi Gras, but he also knew how the neighborhood and the city would be benefiting from this debauchery. This was, after all, the most profitable time of the year.

Peter's cab passed Jackson Square and was approaching the French Market. The smells on this side of town varied from fresh bread and beignets to the overripe smell of the Mississippi River. The pedicab came to a stop at a two-story white building with a wrought iron fence surrounding an upper balcony. It was bordered with hanging flower pots on the railing and a few selective flower arrangements outside a quaint restaurant. A lovely older woman was just coming through the front doors with a broom in hand to sweep the non-existent trash from the café area out in front of the building. She looked up as Peter emerged from the pedicab.

"*Mon chou (Sweetie.).*" she said with a motherly smile, and rushed to greet him in a quick embrace, her broom knocking his elbow. "How was your appointment today?" she asked him.

Peter smiled warmly at the older woman, who he thought of as a second mother, rubbed his sore elbow, and said, "It was excellent." The pronouncement once again lightened Peter's mood. "I think I made a breakthrough today, Momma Rose," he told her excitedly. "I remembered part of what happened after my accident, but that's not all that happened, I had a conversation on my way home…" he paused for dramatic effect, "..with a lady." He finished with a flourish. He grabbed her broom as if it were a guitar and gave it a triumphant strum. He bowed as he handed it back to her, but she let it clatter noisily to the ground. Rose was clearly stunned. Momma Rose's eyebrows had nearly reached her hairline, and she had to sit on one of the vacant chairs.

She looked up at him and smiled, "Thank the Maker for this blessing." she said, "I was beginning to think this day would never come. Your folks should have been the ones to receive this happy news, *mon chou*," she said, a little sadly.

Peter frowned and asked her, "Which part?"

She smiled at his serious expression and answered, "The part where you remembered your accident. *Mon dieu. (Heavens.)* It has been almost 13 years, and you could not remember anything except jumping into the water. Your poor mother…" She trailed off.

Peter's mother never stopped hoping that he would come to terms with what had happened to him when he was a child, and she never stopped believing that the nightmares would stop. She was always his biggest fan, and right now, he missed her terribly.

"I never had a doubt that you could talk to a woman." Rose's statement snapped Peter back from his mother.

"Is that so?" he asked. "How could you be so sure?"

"Because you have been talking to me for years. And you talk to Jeanne." There was no nonsense in her tone, or her statement for that matter.

"I know, Momma Rose," he started, "but you know it's not the same thing." Peter raked his hair and looked uneasy.

She smirked. "How so? Are we not women, Peter?"

"Uhm, yeah—yes. Yes, you are, but not in the—same way." Peter fumbled the statement as the blush rose to his face. "I have to go, Momma. I think I hear the phone upstairs." He turned and fled into the open door of the kitchen and the stairs leading up.

"*Petit menteur. (Little liar.)* You haven't had a phone upstairs in years," she laughingly scolded his back as he went. She shook her head, picked up the broom she had laid aside, and started to sweep the sidewalk and eating area. She said a silent prayer of thanks on Peter's behalf and chuckled at his earlier embarrassment. She always thought Peter would make some lucky woman a fine husband, and she knew when he found the right one he would have *no* problem communicating with *her*.

Chapter 3

Dr. Jo watched Abe wave as he walked out of the door. She smiled and waved back to him, then looked at Bonnie, her receptionist, and said, "Please call my afternoon appointment and reschedule. I will be indisposed the rest of the day. Today was big."

Bonnie smiled and said, "Yeah, he almost talked to me today."

Dr. Jo smiled at Bonnie's enthusiasm. "I'll be in my office." She turned and walked into the session room and went to the door in the far corner. As she reached the door it started to glow, turning the modestly lit office bright white. Jo opened the door and stepped through. Gone was the pencil skirt and smart, tailored blouse she wore to the office. In its place was a flowing gown of lightest pink. As she walked swiftly down the brightly lit hallway, the changes kept occurring. The glasses, the jewelry, and tight updo—gone. She gave her head a shake and let the wheaten tresses fall against her wings, laughing.

I really love being an angel. she thought joyously. As the *Beauty of God*, she most embodied the world's idea, born of her prolific involvement in the Renaissance era, of the classic angel that appeared in art throughout the ages. Those wings, too, had materialized once she left the earthly realm, and as she moved, they gently brushed the floor. She was particularly fond of her wings—they were airy and gossamer and the lightest shade of pink on the ends. To her, it seemed only yesterday that she was hurrying down the same hallway awaiting news from the Master. As she moved, she retraced silently gliding to a massive set of doors at the end of the hall.

That's where she found them; a group of warriors all huddled together, a captive audience anticipating the start of a play. They waited anxiously outside a set of massive doors that were 40 feet tall and solid gold, the finish a gilt mirror reflecting the light given off by the luminous floors and walls. Periodically, a colossal floor-to-ceiling window let in rays of light that cast everything they touched with warmth and brilliance. Only a moment passed and the doors parted swiftly and silently with otherworldly ease. A lone silhouette appeared, awash in the yellows and oranges pouring through the windows. He stopped when he noticed the amassed group, visibly steeling himself, he took a breath, squared his shoulders, and walked toward his companions. Upon his arrival the questions started.

"Well?" the largest of the six asked, expectantly. He was a brute; barrel-chested and expansive breadth, a behemoth of a form. He had a furrowed, sooty brow, chiseled yet dirty features, and a long beard which wove itself up the side of his dark face to a fastidious top knot of dark hair. He gripped the hilt of a scimitar which was currently sheathed and roughly half his formidable length. "What did He say?" he asked.

"He was alright with most of it, Gabriel, but it'll be a long road to redemption for Sam."

Gabriel huffed, not completely satisfied with the response, and offered, "Surely—with a subject that is not always so willing to cooperate."

"Can we help, Michael?" The words came clear and loud from a figure almost as large as the first, with a long chestnut mane that moved with the force of his words. Michael turned and looked at Raphael, the newest speaker.

"No, not directly, anyway. We are forbidden to help Sam. He must learn this on his own." Michael went on, "We will be able to direct others into his path. They'll be able to choose whether or not to help and in what capacity," he finished. "We must allow them to choose. It's the Master's will that the spirit must move them to help—no outside interference."

Raphael looked at Gabriel, then back to Michael. "What will humans be able to do for him?" he asked Michael. Raphael had a less-than-optimistic view of man's capacities and capabilities, and he was certain that the plan would be in jeopardy if left solely to them.

Michael thought for a moment and answered, "They'll be instruments in his redemption. Some will steer, some will work behind the scenes."

"So, we can't be directly involved with Samael, but *they* can? We're going to be useful—how?" asked Gabriel.

Michael faced Gabriel and put a comforting hand on his arm. "Relax, friend. The Master's granted us some leeway here. We can be involved in the lives of the humans chosen to help. We choose the humans for the mission."

"How does that work, exactly?" Gabriel asked, more ponder than query.

Michael smiled and answered, "The Master will reveal them to me in their time. My job is to make a connection with them and assess their willingness. Once that is established, we can get them ready." Michael dropped his hand from Gabriel's arm and turned back to the group. "You will have your choice of humans from the Line of Kings; those without the taint. Pure." He emphasized the last, accompanying it with a knowing glance to his companions. Raphael and Gabriel looked puzzled by this cryptic announcement.

Gabriel scratched his beard and cocked his head to the side, quizzically, "You are going to have to elaborate."

"They are the true descendants of Shem," Michael told them. "They are his personal descendants."

"Marvelous." Gabriel said, clearly exasperated, and sarcastically chucked Michael on the shoulder. "There are only, what? Seven million or so? How will we choose?"

"I'm glad you asked." Michael said with a grin. "They will have already proven themselves worthy."

"How?" This query came from the back of the group. The others parted slightly so Michael could see the questioner—a stunning creature of humanly impossible beauty, perfect in form, with no flaw or blemish. Even among angels, no beauty rivaled Jophiel. She cocked an eyebrow at Michael and asked again, her voice a soothing singsong, "How will these humans have been proven worthy to help our cause? While I'm thinking about it, will they know they are helping us? If so, will we be allowed to help them and teach them in return?"

Michael's smile broadened. "Right to the point," he chuckled. "The Master will allow us to put together a team of Noah's youngest son's descendants who have suffered in a selfless act, up to the point of death. Some have seen Eden and chose to return to live earthly lives for us." Michael turned to Raphael. "That should narrow the pool a bit."

Raphael grinned. "So, we'll be able to interact with these humans?"

"Yes, although some of them will be quite young and will need guidance until it is time to reveal our need," Michael told them.

Jophiel cleared her throat. "Gentlemen, please." The clamor died down and she continued, "Just exactly how long will we have to do this?" she asked Michael.

Michael's countenance clouded. "Jo, it will take a couple of millennia—" he trailed off at the astonished looks on the faces of his fellow angels.

"A couple of millenia." shouted the smallest of the group. She bustled to the front, by all appearances a young girl with red hair in a brilliant teal tunic. "You're not serious?. You *can't* be serious. I can't keep up with the damage they are doing now. I have been busting my wings trying to keep the Earth together since the flood, and now I have to keep it together for another two thousand years?" she continued.

"Please be calm, Ariell," Michael rubbed his tired eyes. "The Master requires patience from us right now, and although I know that you have dominion over the resources of Earth, please think about the end game here. I have the assurance from the Creator that these humans will be able to further our cause if given the proper help. And He has assured me that you will do a wonderful job of making their world last."

Ariel, though small in stature, was fierce in nature and was protective of her Earthly charge. "Will these *special* humans help with the protection of the land while we are ministering to Sam," she asked, "or will I have to do everything?"

Michael took a deep breath and chose his words, carefully metered and precise. "The humans chosen for this task will be willing. They will be committed to ensuring that the mission goes forward and no harm comes to any other living beings if it can be helped." He paused and looked at Azrael, the last of his small contingent. "This fight will be long, Brother, but the prize. Oh, the prize will be the victory in the final battle. Surely, you of all of us can see the end?" Michael said with a searching look.

Azrael, the final of the friends, looked at Michael with a sympathetic eye. Azrael did not cut a mammoth figure like Gabriel or possess stunning beauty like Jophiel, nevertheless, he commanded the respect of his friends. He was not one to talk in excess, so when he decided this was his chance to show Michael his support while unsure of the outcome, it was as if he had spoken with the voice of the Master Himself. Azrael looked kindly at each of the friends in turn and gave Michael an understanding smile.

"He knows that you will do what you believe you cannot, Protector." He turned to Gabriel, saying, "His message will forge your bond with humanity, Messenger. Joygiver," he said, addressing Jophiel, "you will keep order during the most trying of times." He turned to the others present, "I agree with Michael. This time will fly like martens, so we must prepare. You all know what will happen if we fail." On that ominous announcement he turned and walked out the adjoining door to the hallway.

The others who had fallen silent during his short speech, looked to each other for support.

Michael, who had been watching this interaction, smiled and told the others, "The Plan is in place. You each have the Master's leave to do what is necessary. We will succeed. Go. You will be called to use your gifts soon enough. He wills it." The band, hopeful and resolute, dispersed through the door that Azrael exited through earlier. Michael felt a presence and turned to find Jophiel. Michael took a deep breath, "What more can I say?" he asked.

Just as in her memory, Michael turned and was waiting at the end of the hall. He smiled warmly and waved her to him. Jophiel looked at Michael, visage as strong and sure as it was breathtaking. She smiled, took Michael's strong hand in hers, and punctuated each word with a slight shake. "It *has* worked, Michael, this plan," she asserted. "We have had a breakthrough. Only today he remembers," she hesitated, squeezed the hand she held and added, "you." She smiled slightly, "Peter finally remembers you, and now we can move forward with the Master's plan."

Michael's smile widened and he pumped his fist in the air. "Woohoo, that is excellent news. We must tell the others and get them ready for the coming trials. Each one has a part to play, and they will need to be on the watch. The Earth is not the same as it was a millennia ago. The monsters are amassing a plan, and we need to be ready for it."

Jophiel nodded her head in agreement. "Yes, I have been working with Abe, he will be a great asset in this cause. They met today briefly. I will tell the others to let the hosts know as well as their humans." Jophiel turned and walked back toward the door, she stopped and looked back at Michael. "This *will* work. We will be able to defeat them this time. We all have faith." As she turned back to the door her heavenly visage fell away, and in its place was Dr. Jo Phillips. Michael heard her sigh as she walked back through the door.

"I hope your faith is enough," he whispered. He looked toward the golden doors for reassurance. He felt, rather than saw, the light flow down the hallway into his body. Michael felt the sense of peace and purpose the light gave him. He shook slightly, which caused his giant wings to agitate behind him. He stretched and unfurled to his full span, resplendent and glorious. His wings outstretched toward the light, he lifted his head and quietly, but solemnly, gave his pledge to the Master who had entrusted him with this mission. "I will not fail you."

Chapter 4

Maggie had been to New Orleans a handful of times, and she had always enjoyed the sights and sounds of the French Quarter, but not this afternoon. She was cramped, hot, nervous, and over it. Cramped, because Max took up the majority of the available room in the small bicycle cab, hot, because the sun continued to bake them even through the canvas awning they were under—and you couldn't buy a breeze in New Orleans as far as she knew—nervous, because she rode with the powerful son of *the* most powerful crime family in all of Russia, and over it… well, just because.

Maggie bore the ride through the quarter like a high school detention, busying herself in her current miserable condition by studying the people they passed. She saw a troupe of mummers, a very talented saxophonist, and a group of college men all in the span of two blocks; and although the experience was interesting to say the least, she didn't believe that she would be able to live in the chaos that surrounded this place on a day-to-day basis—or the heat, for that matter. They rounded the corner on to Decatur and were making their way towards Jackson Square when Max spoke to the driver of the pedicab.

"Where are you taking us?" he asked. Maggie turned to him, a quizzical look on her face. She had thought that he had ordered the driver to a specific location when they first entered. All of her instincts told her she should be on alert, and she paid close attention to their exchange.

"You will know when we stop, yes?" came his flat response.

She hadn't noticed it before, but their driver was not attired like the others she had seen, and his accent was not French—it was

Russian. Max's father was pulling the strings, even here, over 10,000 miles away. Lev Avatov had a reputation for maniacal precision, demanding perfection and efficiency from all of his men, along with his penchant for vindictive brutality. He did not trust his son alone, therefore, he was not alone. Ever. From the look on his face, she could tell Max had realized it as well

Max let an audible growl escape from him. He threw his great frame back in the seat, irritated and not bothering to hide his displeasure at the driver's attitude.

She snuck a furtive glance at her companion—as massive and imposing a figure she couldn't recall ever having been associated with in the past. He really fit to a tee the great Russian bear trope, although without the brutish roughness. Max was handsome, and he was more angular and classic than fur and girth. She looked at him again and caught his eye. His irritated look relaxed into the easy smile she had come to know in the last few months. Maggie was used to getting into situations that require finesse and a bit of acting to navigate. This was no exception. She was becoming quite attached to Max, and that, she decided, was definitely dangerous considering who his father was.

"Where are we going anyway, Max? You promised me some fun tonight. Are you going to have another boring meeting?" While she still sported a pout teeming with rehearsed disappointment, she was actually observing Max's reaction to her last question very closely.

"We will have the promised fun, but we need to make a small stop to see an—associate. Please, lyubov." Max took her hand in his, a gesture meant to placate his date and allow him the leeway needed to conduct his organization's business without risking a displeased Maggie to show for it. His expression willed her to not be angry with him for this small detour, and he doubled down in his quest to make her happy. "We will go to get dinner after this and we will have the rest of the night to have fun," he told her.

She was amazed at his eagerness to please her or escape her

well-worn disappointed expression. She had been in this place and situation countless times before, but it had never been this hard on her to manipulate her mark. Maggie had a great affection for Max that she couldn't deny—he was no thug. He was refined, caring for those smaller than himself, had a strong sense of duty and family, and he was funny and cultured. Yes, she cared for him. And he would never, ever know it. She would make certain. She brushed aside reality and slipped back into the pretend world she knew so well.

"Well, it's not going to be long, is it? The last time I had to wait a whole hour by myself in a smelly lobby reading a magazine that was four months old." She considered briefly, then decided to try a different tack She sidled up to him and, pout at the ready, gazed up at him with a look that was both doleful and expectant. "Can I stay with you this time, Max? I get so lonely." She leaned in to him a little, hoping he would relent and let her stay with him.

"I am sorry, kiska, but you would be bored. My business would not be interesting to such krasivyy tsvetok," he finished with a smile and a soft caress of her cheek.

Max, 1–Maggie, zip. This wasn't going to be easy.

She came back at him. "What does that even mean? Are you calling me dumb?" She raised her voice in a defensive tone. Max could quickly see his evening turning sour.

"Please understand, kiska—this business is not with a man I know. I must be alone, but I will be brief. I am sorry." Max frowned down at her and gave her hand a dismissive pat. Maggie knew when Max was at an immovable point, and she surmised it was best to change the subject.

"Max, I get it. I just want to know more about you, and that includes what you do. You understand, right?" she said cheerfully.

"Yes, I do, and I am eager for you to know me as I long to know you, myshka. In time," he replied.

"Max, what does that mean?"

"What part?" he asked her with a mischievous grin.

"Kiska and krassy—whatever that other thing you called me was?"

Max let out a quiet chuckle and shook his head. "Krasivyy tsvetok. kiska means *kitten* and…" he gently grabbed her chin between his massive thumb and index finger so she was eye to eye with him, as if what he was about to say carried great significance, "krasivvy tsvetok means *beautiful flower*."

"Oh." she blushed, and she was taken aback by the genuine sweetness in his comment. Maggie gently removed his hand from her face and guided it back to his lap. "Thank you," she replied and then returned her gaze forward hoping he didn't see the flush she knew was invading her complexion at that moment.

As they progressed through the quarter, Maggie witnessed architecture and establishments that ranged from quaint to eccentric to positively stately. The pedicab came to a stop at the edge of the river outside the oddest store Maggie had ever seen. It was a two-story shop, painted a garish light blue, almost neon, with what looked like a stuffed vulture in the window. She thought, *Wow. This is definitely one for the books.* Like many of the businesses in the quarter, the second story had wrought iron fencing surrounding the balcony, but it was also redone in the same obscene color. The paint, unlike the coatings adorning most of the other Quarter buildings, looked fresh.

An adjoining warehouse could be seen rising behind the weird old shop. Maggie was no Rembrandt, but she recognized erratic brush strokes and uneven paint when she saw it, and both the shop and the outbuilding wore the same colors. They were painted recently and in a hurry, and she wanted to know why.

Max lit from the back of the pedicab after her, gave a curt nod to the driver, and turned back to face the bright blue store. He gave a quick sidelong glance at either building on the left and right, then readjusted his gaze and set it squarely on the ugly blue door facing him. Maggie fell in beside him, and they approached.

Just as they reached the door to the shop it opened, and Maggie looked into the coldest eyes that she had ever seen. She took an involuntary step back behind Max's shoulder. She looked up at Max and noticed that his face had transformed to a block of stone. The warmth that she had seen only moments before had disappeared.

"Mr. Avatov?" came a voice that Maggie could only describe as unctuous. The features weren't much better in her estimation: the man was tall, thin, had a hook nose like a beak, and a sallow complexion. He was balding on the top of his sort of pointed head, but had long stringy hair that went almost to the middle of his back.

Tons of hair in back and none on top, she thought. *I'd call that a 'skullet.'* She smiled slightly at the term, but quickly stopped and froze under the uneven gaze of the oily man. He regarded her for a second, and then one fuzzy eyebrow cocked as he looked at Max.

"Yes," came the abrupt reply.

"Narcisse Olivier. Come in." He stepped aside to allow Max to enter. Maggie got the distinct impression that he was judging her as she stepped past him, and what he found obviously appealed to him. He dismissed the driver with a wave of his hand, gave one last look to the right and left, turned into his shop, and closed the door. Maggie tried to get her bearings, but really didn't know where to look. The shop was dark, and layers of dust covered the floor. The display cabinets were crowded along either side of the room and slunk low, displaying their contents in poor light and smeared glass. The glass was oily, as was the proprietor. Overhead, Maggie noticed all manner of items suspended from exposed beams and ductwork for an ancient central air conditioning system. The place was filled, not with treasures, objet d'art, or even amusing curiosities.

It's mostly touristy crap, thought Maggie. *Not what I would expect, given our business here. Why* is *Max here?*

She saw nothing of value, and she knew that the area they were in would be prime territory for the purchase of something rare and valuable, mostly from what she had heard on the street. Most of the shops and businesses on the Mississippi in New Orleans did a booming trade. Late at night. In the dark and in secret. That's what she figured; whatever they were here to get or see was something that should not be seen in daylight. She turned back to the wares displayed on the massive wooden shelves and in the bookcases and displays that seemed to spring up, not according to any planned layout, but seemingly right from the piles of dust on the well-worn wooden floor.

She saw shrunken heads, dunking birds, cheap street magic tricks, wood carvings, magnets, bumper stickers—it really was disappointing to her to see such obviously cheap garbage. She wondered if the same sorts of goods were housed in the massive storage facility attached to the back of the dilapidated old store. She very much doubted it. Maggie was willing to bet that the shoddy front did a very effective job at hiding the valuable things that passed into and out of the back.

She turned and looked to Max who had walked directly to the far side of the store as if he knew what he was after, not looking around or even breaking eye contact with the back of the old shopkeeper's mottled head. She was taking in the shelf of voodoo dolls that said "*Made in Taiwan*" on them when Mr. Olivier's voice brought her back to the filthy shop.

"Now, I believe we have some business to talk about. If you would like to browse, my dear," he said, turning to Maggie, "we will only be a moment. If you see anything you like I'm sure we can come to an equitable arrangement." Maggie shivered in repulsion. She was not sure if she felt better knowing that he would be leaving the room in a moment or if she really would rather someone remain in this little shop of horrors with her.

Max leaned over and whispered to her, "We will only be a moment, kiska. Why don't you try looking around?"

Maggie gave Max a small smile and a nod. He dropped his hand from her cheek and turned on his heel to exit the room. Maggie watched him go, then turned to look at the stuff surrounding her, no longer really interested in what she may find. Her gut was telling her to direct her attention elsewhere and to try to keep an eye on the two men as they conducted their business. She reached her hand out to the closest shelf and picked up an object without inspecting what she held. She watched their progress towards the back of the store from the corner of her eye as they went through a red painted door in the back. A light flickered on, and the door closed, but not completely, and light shone through the small crack they left. She glanced briefly at the object she had been holding, a Super Bounce Ball, and returned it to the shelf. She inched her way through the room towards the door where she could hear what they were saying without being seen.

"Now, Mr. Avatov, what is it that I can do for you?" came the same oily voice from before. "I'm assuming that you are after something for your father, am I right?"

"You assume correctly," came Max's reply in the same abrupt style. "I am searching for relics that were stolen from us. I believe they have found their way to you."

"And what makes you so certain that I have these relics?"

Mr. Oily, Maggie thought. *Come on, Mags. You can do better.* Only, Mr. Oily really *did* suit him the best, so she shrugged to herself and leaned in further to hear what was next.

"We have people who watch for these things, and our sources are *never* wrong." Inflection on the "never" part was not lost on Olivier.

"Well, as it happens, I was able to purchase a few items in the past few months that have garnered a lot of attention. From interested parties." He didn't try to contain his meaning, or his glee, with the last sentence. Whatever Mr. Olivier was holding on to, he knew it would make him a handsome sum, and he sounded like he already had it spent. He started, "What exactly can you offer me? The offers have been attractive, but I knew your father would be sending someone to me, and I did not want to disappoint, no?" he finished, and Maggie could picture him cocking a single slick eyebrow. "What does your father offer?"

"We can offer you many things, Mr. Olivier, not the least of which is your life. No one steals from us. I trust you know that," Max said, his voice passively ominous. "How about we start with the relics and where and whom you purchased them from?"

"Ah yes, straight to the point I see," said Olivier.

Maggie thought she still liked *Oily* better, and they sounded a lot alike, so she decided to keep it.

"Well, let us discuss things then."

She heard him walk a few steps and rifle through some papers, all the while clicking his tongue against the roof of his mouth. Maggie jumped a little when he slammed the sheets down on what sounded like a metal table.

"Yes," he exclaimed, and then started to speak quickly in an excited, hushed tone. "The skeleton of the beast that holds your father's fascination, purchased by me and in my possession since its arrival on land. No one else has seen it or knows of its existence, not even the crew of the barge that delivered it. Anyone involved with the transport has been dealt with, per your father's instructions."

Max, sure of Olivier's methods, winced and clenched his ample hands into tight fists. The old crowish man seemed to enjoy this reaction and dug in a bit to twist the revelation's knife.

"Did your father tell you? It appears not." The man's footfalls put him apace from the origin of their conversation, and close to what sounded like a large, metal door. Maggie slid around another counter to improve her eavesdropping position and slowed her breathing as the oily man continued. "I will sell the relics back to you for the price I paid for them, in return for a favor to be repaid at my convenience," he stated. "The other information I am afraid you will have to pay for like everyone else. Your father knows my prices, and he knows my other clients, so the fees shouldn't be a problem or a surprise."

Price paid plus a favor, Max thought. *I know your proclivities and the types of favors you ask my father for, you devil bastard.* Max's rage bubbled a bit over the top, and he crossed quickly to Olivier, grabbing him and shaking.

"You take liberties with my father's generosity, old man. Be certain that I will not be as generous when you deal with me."

Olivier, his breathing metered and calm, started to chuckle slightly while Max fumed, incredulous. The old man knowing, at least at this point, he was valuable to Lev Avatov, and therefore untouchable even by his progeny, continued to build that chuckle to a throaty, unctuous laugh. A laugh filled not with mirth, but malice. Maggie suspected that this man had never genuinely laughed at anything.

The greasy black marketeer cleared his throat, and stated in an unaffected, almost aloof tone, "Maxim, we are not at that juncture yet, are we? You are a whelp, running the wolf's errand, and though your bark be impressive, little Max, you're as impotent and unimportant to me as a shed feather to a mighty raptor. Remove your hands, Mr. Avatov, and see that you keep them to yourself in the future, or your father will surely hear about it."

Max, infuriated and dejected at his words and his own feeling of impotency, complied. Olivier dusted the front of his shirt, adjusted his collar, and glared at the younger man.

"Just make sure that they are younger this time. The last lot were all around 17, and although they were beautiful, they do not fetch the highest price."

Maggie had to swallow the bile that had risen to her throat. He was talking about *children*.

"How many will you require?" Max asked him, disgustedly.

"I think that 13 is a good number for the information and items your father requested. Ask your father, I believe my offer is very fair."

Maggie who had been backing away from the door found herself near the window, her heart pounding wildly in her chest, until her back came up against something hard. She looked up and over her shoulder right into the beady eyes of the vulture she saw in the window earlier. She gave a startled squeak and promptly knocked over the umbrella stand near the door. Umbrellas and walking sticks went all over the floor with a loud clatter. Maggie froze and heard the men get quiet. She bent over and started to tidy up the floor when they came from beyond the red door.

Mr. Oily proceeded up the aisle in a fury with Max behind him.

"Stupid girl," Olivier shouted and moved with his hand raised as if to strike her. His arm met with the vice-like grip of a very angry Russian who proceeded to fling him to the ground.

"You dare raise your hand to her?" If Maggie thought his voice cold before, it was well below sub-zero now. He bent his frame to her and asked, "Are you okay, kiska?"

"I'm fine," she said in a timid voice. "The bird startled me, and I tripped over the stand."

"Some of these items are priceless," came the oily reply from the heap on the floor. The withered man gained his feet once again and brushed off the front of his shirt. "I would think you would be more careful."

Maggie couldn't help it; she started to laugh. *Priceless. The only priceless thing in this store, other than what was apparently kept out of sight, was the preposterous statement that had just escaped the old man's lips.*

Max joined her, and soon they were both having a good chuckle, not caring in the least about the offense. Olivier stood, an indignant look on his face, but impotence in his stance—he knew he could say or do nothing.

"Can we leave now, Max?" Maggie asked him hopefully.

"Yes, we are leaving." He turned to Mr. Olivier. "I will contact you tomorrow regarding our business; you will have your answer then. Keep everything as it is today. For your sake." With that, Max accepted Maggie's arm and escorted her out the door and down the walkway to the street.

Maggie glanced back to see Mr. Oily standing in the door with a cold expression on his very angry face. As they got further from the oddity shop, Max's demeanor changed. He went from steel to relaxed in the space of a couple of blocks. He started to notice the night life a little more. It was at this point that Maggie felt it was safe to talk with him.

"Why was Mr. Oily so mad about me knocking over the umbrella stand?"

He laughed. "Mr. Oily?"

She smiled and blushed a little. "He was not a nice man, Max. Skeevy and kind of oily, you know? Unpleasant."

Max's grin grew broader as he looked at her, and he said with a straight face, "His name is Olivier, but I like Oily better."

Maggie let out a laugh and grabbed Max's hand. "He does *not* like women, kiska, and you are never to be alone with him."

At Max's pronouncement a shudder went through Maggie's body. "I don't think you will have to worry about that. I never want to see that shop again. Let's go have some fun and forget this little adventure," she told him as they walked towards the French Market.

As they walked, Maggie thought about the different people who lived in this city and the odd culture the city imposed on those willing to seek its thrills. This led her back to the strange man she bumped into earlier, Peter. He seemed to her to be typical of the city; mostly kind and helpful, with maybe a bit of a sarcastic bent.

And fashion challenged, she thought. *Definitely fashion challenged. He was right about one thing, though—these shoes are killing me.*

Chapter 5

Peter finished brushing his teeth, put his toothbrush neatly in its holder, and turned to go into his bedroom. A clamor out on the street and Momma Rose's loud reprimand delayed Peter's crawl into bed and brought him to his balcony to observe. He watched as Momma Rose drew every inch of her five-feet-tall frame up against a very drunk, very large, young man and his giggling girlfriend. Peter could hear Mamma Rose berate the man for knocking over one of her outside tables in his inebriated state.

The man, not knowing how to handle the small spitfire currently squared up to him, backed up with his hands in the air and promptly knocked a second table over in the process. Peter smiled as he watched Momma Rose walk up to the unfortunate fellow, grab him by his ear, and pull him up off the floor. Peter winced in sympathy for the guy, remembering the times he was on the receiving end of that treatment, and laughed when Momma Rose started telling the man off in French as he stood helpless in her grip. His lady friend had retreated to the street and as she stood giggling at the sight, she stepped into the light of the street lamp. Peter recognized the woman—Maggie, the one he had run into earlier this afternoon.

So, Peter thought, smiling, *the man on the other end of Momma Rose's treatment was the Russian. What did she call him—Max? Yes, that was it. Max.* Peter leaned out the window of his upper story apartment and called down to Rose, "*As-tu besoin d'aide (Do you need help)*?"

To his surprise, the big Russian looked up at him and answered his question. "Yes. Please help me by getting this little ona d'yavol, this she-devil, off of me." Max answered, barely managing to hold Rose at arm's length with a massive hand placed precariously in the middle of her forehead.

Peter laughed and shouted, "Momma Rose, if the big man pays for the damage, will you let him go?"

"Oui, long as he leaves directly, mon chou. My dishes can't take any more of his bumbling," Momma Rose said indignantly, mourning the small collection of broken plates at her feet.

Maggie had walked up to Max as he dug out his wallet, "Here, allow me." She took his wallet out and proceeded to pull out five hundred-dollar bills and handed them to Momma Rose.

"This should take care of the dishes," she said as Max looked on, stunned.

Momma Rose took the money and released Max so she could turn from the massive figure and stuff the bills into her ample bosom. Maggie noticed the little woman's gesture, reminiscent of something her grandmother would do, and decided immediately that she liked her very much.

"I will take Max home now, Momma Rose." Maggie told her. "*Desole pour le derangement (Sorry for the inconvenience).*" Momma Rose noticed how the girl slipped easily into perfect French as she apologized for the inconvenience.

The young woman seems not at all cowed by the big man, Rose thought, and smiled. *She's got him on a short leash, but he's chasing parked cars.* She laughed to herself at the thought and turned once again to face the giant Russian. She sniffed in disdain and watched as Maggie led Max, who was still rubbing his injured ear, away by the arm.

Momma Rose looked up at Peter with a smile and spoke with authority, "Thank you for your assistance, Peter. Shouldn't you be in your bed?" she asked.

"I was headed there when I heard your dulcet tones uttering profanities. I couldn't miss the excitement, now could I?"

Momma Rose smiled at Peter and waved her hand dismissing

him as she proceeded to clean up the mess Max had made in the café.

Peter stuck his head back in the bedroom and closed the window to keep the street noise to a minimum. He walked over and sat on the edge of the bed and chuckled at the look on the big Russian's face when petite Rose grabbed his ear and pulled him into a stooped position to make herself clear to him. Peter laid down in his bed, pulled his covers up to his chin, and fell into a deep slumber.

"Peter. Hey, champ. C'mon, son—I know you can hear me. You're going to be fine."

The blips and beeps of various machines came to him amid his father's voice, trying to sound calm but scary to him just the same. He was aware of a cold surface underneath him and the smell of something mediciney, as well as many frantic voices shouting orders. Peter could hear everything that was happening and feel the hands that poked and prodded his legs, and he knew that many people were involved. Trying to—what, exactly? He couldn't remember anything, but he wasn't aware of any pain. It sounded like they were trying to—save him? If he wasn't in pain, why did he need saving? A door opened and fast footsteps to his left, then a low, calm voice appeared at his side.

"Peter, my name is Dr. Lambrough. You can call me Ty. How's your holiday?"

Peter wanted to tell the doctor that he was fine, he wasn't in any pain, but when he tried to speak he found he couldn't. In fact, he couldn't move his legs or arms, and he couldn't, no matter how hard he tried, open his eyes. He felt strangely detached from himself.

"Listen, son. I'm going to need you to just hang out here and let us do our job of helping you. Can you do that for me? Can you relax? It helps everything go smoother, it really does."

Dr. Lambrough again, Peter thought. He knew he would like the man, if he could see him. He was calm-sounding enough, but

Peter could definitely feel a lot of movement around him; sense that many different people and hands were busy very close to him, the doctor's included.

He started to panic. *Am I going to die? Why can't I feel anything? I'm only 13!* He felt a subtle shift in the tension of the room and heard several of the machines start beeping in a frantic staccato.

"We're losing him—" shouted one of the people in the room.

"Peter." He heard his mother's fear and wanted desperately to tell her he was okay.

A new voice shouted "Get her out of here, and get me the crash cart, stat."

"Absolutely not. She stays right here. Mrs. Devereaux, if you could just stand over there, please." The doctor, sounding slightly less calm, suddenly appeared very close and clear in Peter's left ear. "Son, this is not what you promised me. I didn't come in here on a holiday weekend for nothing, Peter. Work with me. Work with me…" Dr. Lambrough's voice trailed off in Peter's ear, and then disappeared altogether, replaced by a low hum and the sound of…

Water? Not water, exactly, Peter thought. *The beach? Waves? And light—warm, like sunlight.* In fact, Peter found himself floating—or flying.

Floating? Or flying? Either way, this is the coolest thing ever, he thought. Down towards a narrow stretch of sandy beach that reminded him of the coast near his parent's beach house in Madeira Beach. They hadn't been back to Florida since last year, but he remembered it clearly.

Peter looked back over his shoulder into what should have been the clear, bright sky, but instead he saw his body laid out, lifeless, and he could see everything that was going on in the emergency room. He watched as the doctors and nurses tried in a chaotic frenzy to keep him alive. Peter found himself cheering for them. To him, this was almost like one of those doctor shows on TV. Peter turned back toward the stretch of beach and found he would rather be walking and gamboling in the surf than be anywhere else at the moment, including fighting for his life in the emergency room of St. Xavier's Hospital.

Peter heard a man's voice call to him from the shore.

"Hey. Quit messing around up there, Peter. I need to talk to you. Can you come down here, please?"

Peter looked down to see where the voice was coming from and was surprised to see a young man, not much older than himself—maybe 15? He touched down and his feet sank into the warm sand. The guy that had called to him approached calmly, and he seemed friendly enough. He was dressed in a pair of jeans, flip-flops, and a vintage t-shirt with the Superman "S" emblazoned on the front.

"Hey, Peter. So cool to meet you, my man." The guy extended his hand, grabbed Peter's hand as if to shake it, and instead pulled him in for a tight hug. Peter felt a warmth and relaxed in the man's embrace, and he thought he could faintly hear the blips and beeps subside and a cheer from many voices. "Yeah, you just helped them out a lot, but I don't have a lot of time to chat now, so you gotta listen up, okay?"

The boy made eye contact with Peter, and he found himself looking into the clearest golden eyes he had ever seen. He also noticed a similar hued light that was present right over the guy's right shoulder. It was warm and welcoming, and Peter knew that whatever was in that light was wonderful.

Peter was confused. He knew that the light came from a place he wanted to go, but the word of the boy stopped him from moving forward. In fact, he couldn't move at all.

"Who are you, and why can't I move?"

The kid smiled again reassuringly and told him, "Relax, Peter. My name is Michael. This is gonna sound weird, maybe, but maybe not, given the fact that you're on a beach in the middle of a hospital operating room, but I'm an angel, and I need your help."

Now Peter was really confused, "My help? You *do* know I'm only 13, right? Hell, you can't be more than 15 or so yourself."

Michael chuckled. "Yeah, Peter, I get it. It's blowing your mind.

Take a second to process—just know I don't need you right now." Michael looked back over his shoulder at the silvery light, then turned back to the boy, smiling.

Peter looked back around at the chaos in the emergency room and at his parents tear stained faces outside the emergency room doors. "That's good, because right now I won't be able to help anyone. I think I'm dying."

Michael laughed again and put his hand on Peter's shoulder. Peter thought this was very strange considering he couldn't really feel his shoulder.

"Wait," Peter said. "It's Michael, right? You said you are an angel? Why do you look like a surfer dude?" A note of skepticism had worked its way into Peter's words.

Michael raised an eyebrow, and before Peter could blink Michael had grown three feet. Gone were his t-shirt, jeans, and flip-flops—replaced by a white robe and wings that, although furled, drug the ground behind him. Around his waist was a scabbard with the golden handle of a gigantic sword sticking out.

Peter was terrified of this new apparition, but as quickly as he saw this *other* Michael, it was replaced by the young surfer. Peter, whose reflexes were slower in this place, took an instinctive step back. "Whoa," Peter swallowed audibly. "Asked and answered. Michael, please don't do that again."

"I thought you might prefer this to that," Michael laughed. "Don't feel bad. I would be pretty freaked out by me if I were you. Why do you think that we are always having to tell people, *don't be afraid,* and *do not fear,* when we show up on the scene? We're intense, bro. Peter," Michael continued, "each of us in life has a purpose, a job that we have to do before we are allowed to move on. What you see behind me—that's where my Master is, and you're not meant to be there yet." Michael took a step past Peter toward the stretch of beach behind Peter, heading back in the direction of the chaotic hospital, and he beckoned Peter to follow. Michael continued as he walked, Peter next to him. "Now, there are some very special people who have a higher calling, it's a really important place to be and a big honor." Michael paused, gauging Peter's reaction to his statement.

"You mean, like superheroes?" Peter asked in a skeptical tone and looked at Michael's t-shirt bearing Superman's logo.

Michael looked at his own shirt, smiled, and said, "Yeah, in a manner of speaking. Peter, you come from a very distinguished ancestry. Your ancestors came from the line of Shem." Michael said the last sentence with a bit more excitement than Peter seemed to think it needed. Blankness returned Michael's excited expression and he couldn't believe it required further explanation. "Peter. Shem. You know—*Shem.*" Michael spread out his hands in front of him, as if to embrace all of the air surrounding them, but Peter still didn't get it.

"Shem doesn't sound like a heroic name. Shem sounds like a sheep," Peter said.

Michael, momentarily speechless, gave his head a little shake and continued, "He was Noah's youngest son."

"Like the Ark? Noah and the Ark, with all the animals and stuff? I always wondered, why were mosquitoes allowed on the Ark?" Once again, he had interrupted Michael's tale with a childlike curiosity and exuberance, and Michael matched him.

"Yes. The Ark. All the animals, and what else can repopulate fast enough so bats have something to eat?" Michael said without missing a beat. He took a deep breath and continued. "Here's the deal: you come from this line, so, yay you. On top of that, because of your selfless act earlier, you have been chosen."

"Um, chosen for what?"

"To help. Us." At this, Michael grasped Peter's shoulders and looked him excitedly in the eyes. And this time, Peter felt the angel's hands. Faintly. He also began to notice tingling in his legs where before he had felt nothing.

"Help with what? Do I get superpowers? I always wanted a cape—" Peter was really becoming excited with the prospect of having super powers, but Michael also knew he was not going to have much more time with the boy, and he had to keep him focused.

"No super powers. I need you to help an angel. Not me," Michael added, answering the question from Peter's eyes before it escaped his lips, and he concluded, "You can wear a cape if you want to, but I wouldn't advise it." Peter stopped thinking about flying and laser vision and blinked.

"I'm supposed to help an angel?" Peter asked, a bit overwhelmed at this new information.

"Yeah. He's in trouble and needs a little help," said Michael rocking back on his heels.

Peter stopped and watched as the doctors zapped his body with paddles he knew were designed to get a stopped heart beating again. He started to feel a tugging sensation deep in his chest, and pain in his legs. He flinched, and then looked at Michael in question.

"We don't have much time Peter; the doctors are going to pull you back in a minute, and I really need to know you're on board with us," Michael pleaded with him. He looked a little nervous and Peter felt as if his answer would change his life forever.

This is too much, he thought. *I am lying dead, or dying, on a table at St. Xavier's. I am on a beach with an angel, and he is asking me to trust him, so I can be a superhero. What is happening? I'm only thirteen...*

He got scared and took a step back from the young man in front of him. Michael reached out and steadied him, then pulled his face close to his so they were eye to eye, emphasizing the gravity of the words he was about to say.

"Peter. You've got to focus. Brother, there is so much I want to tell you, and I know you have a million questions, but now isn't the time. Don't worry. I'll be there. It'll be you and me over the long haul to get this done. I can't answer everything for you now, but just know there's nothing I would ever do to hurt you, screw up your life, or jeopardize this mission. It does come from Him, after all," Michael said, smiling at the last.

Peter could see the insistence, almost desperation, in Michael's golden eyes, and he got serious.

Peter said, "What can I do? How do I help?"

"Grow up. Finish school. Live life. In time, you'll remember our talk. And along the way we'll have others—you'll remember those, too. You'll learn to believe in yourself the way I do," Michael told him with sincerity.

Peter asked, "If I say no, will I die?"

Michael cocked an eyebrow, and smirked. "No." Michael smiled and again put his hand on Peter's shoulder.

He could really feel it this time, and the pain in his legs was worse, but Peter also felt a sense of peace flow through him, and he knew either answer would be okay with Michael.

Michael went on, his hand still on Peter's shoulder, and his expression still joyful and sincere. "You will live a great life, Peter. I'm not promising you'll be rich or always happy, but you're going to do some incredible things for yourself and for others. You won't remember me until you're ready. That's okay," Michael added when he noticed Peter's sorrowful expression. Michael liked the boy, and he could tell that the feeling was mutual. "You and I will see each other again. If you choose to help, you will have helpers that will watch over you and teach you the things that you need to know to survive and help when the time comes—and I'll be there, too."

The tug on Peter's chest became stronger, almost too strong for him to resist, and his legs hurt so bad that he cried out.

"Time's up, my man," Michael told him as Peter's feet lifted off of the sand, and he felt himself being pulled backward, away from the angel. "Can we count on you?"

Peter thought about how cool it would be to help an angel… well, do whatever it was they had to do. Peter's 13-year-old brain already had him and his angel off saving the world from certain disaster. Peter smiled down at Michael and shouted over the suddenly-raucous blips and bleeps of hospital sounds.

"I'll do it. Michael, I'll help. Yes."

Michael gave a whoop. His fist shot up in the air, and he gave Peter the most glorious smile that he had ever seen.

Wow .thought Peter. *I've heard people talk about how people could light up a room with their smile, but Michael could power all of New Orleans with his.*

Ow. The pain in his legs was unbearable. Peter willed himself back to the beach one more time. There was something he had to know. He reached out for Michael's hand and screamed, "Pull me back."

Michael was startled, and grabbed Peter with both hands, planting him firmly on the ground in front of him and said, "Peter, I can't keep you here, and you can't fight the pull. It will only hurt more. What do you need?" Michael asked, slightly panicked.

"I need to know…" Peter trailed off as more pain hit him. He couldn't remember.

Michael grasped his shoulder once more, and took the boy in great hug, quelling the pain briefly. Peter felt calm. Michael spoke into his—ear? Well, yes, it was Peter's ear, but Peter felt his words on a visceral level, like he was speaking directly to Peter's spirit. And the voice was different. Commanding and confident, yet warm. It was, Peter imagined, very much like what being spoken to by an older, wiser brother would sound like.

"You'll remember one day, and we'll do great things, brother. Be well." Michael released Peter from his grasp, winked at him, and then, with one impossibly strong movement, flung Peter by his right shoulder directly into the chaos of St. Xavier's.

And with that Peter felt a pain in the shoulder that Michael had touched, in fact he felt pain all over. His body felt like a thousand hot brands had been taken to it. He had fallen into darkness and silence. No, not quite silence; there was a steady beeping coming from next to his head. He heard soft breathing coming from beside him and slowly opened his eyes. It was nighttime and nothing looked familiar to him. He became scared, and the beeping became a little faster. Peter turned his head to the side and saw his mother asleep in a chair next to the bed he was laying in. He saw that the machine emitting the beeping noises was recording his heartbeat. He looked down and saw his mother's hand resting on the bed next to his fingers. He reached out and tried to touch her fingers. In his mind, he could feel himself reaching out, but he couldn't summon the strength to bridge the distance between her hand and his. He breathed deeply and tried again. Still nothing. He racked his brain trying to remember what had put him here, and he had nothing. He was in a hospital for a reason, and he couldn't move at the moment, but he wasn't scared. Logically, he knew he should be concerned, but he was certain, for some reason that wasn't immediately apparent to him, that everything in his life was exactly how it should be. He let the expectation of movement leave him and just concentrated on reaching for his mom to give her comfort.

God, he thought, *my mom is really scared and I would really like for her not to be. Could you give me the strength to reach out and grab her hand?*

His progress was slow, and his body felt achy. His mother opened her eyes at his touch. She sat straight up from her slumped position and threw her arms around Peter.

"Peter, I thought I had lost you," she wept. Peter winced at the pain in his shoulder and his mother, sensing the movement, let him go. "I'm so sorry, Peter. That shoulder is probably very sore." She stood quickly and pushed the nurse's call button. Half a minute passed before a nurse walked through the door. "Look, Nell. He is awake," Peter's mother told the nurse with a big smile.

"Well. Praise the Lord," Nell exclaimed, and quickly raised her gaze in obvious reverence and joy. She approached Peter's side, bustling past Claire and hip-shoving the rolling tray that stood between her and her young charge. She positioned the stethoscope in her ears and held the metal disc to her mouth to breathe quickly and warm it before placing it to listen to Peter's up-until-recently faint heartbeat. *Strong,* she thought. *He's going to be fine, thank God.* She bent low to him and asked "How are you feeling?"

Peter looked at the nurse. She had a very friendly face, and he couldn't tell how old she was, but seemed like one of those very wise people that always knows what to do.

"I hurt," Peter rasped, placing a hand weakly on his neck, indicating his audibly scratchy throat, "and I'm thirsty."

Peter saw his mother reach for a pitcher and pour some water into a cup with a bendy straw sticking out of it. He knew the cup belonged to his mom because her lipstick was on the straw, but right now he didn't care. When the straw was placed in his mouth he took a long drink. The dryness in his throat eased. "What happened? How long have I been here?"

"That doesn't matter. You're going to be better now, sweetheart," his mother told him and hugged him again, and he winced again. She turned back to her chair and pulled it closer to her son's side. Claire Devereux couldn't remember ever feeling more relieved in her life. Peter had been through so much in the last 13 days—they all had. She was over the moon to have her baby conscious and responding, but knew he must be experiencing a lot of discomfort.

I just want to get him out of this place and home where he belongs, she thought. *Get him back to health and normality. I don't want to bother him with having to relive something awful that he doesn't even remember. There will be time for that later, if it comes up.*

Tears had started to gather in his mother's eyes as she thought about what had happened. *Too much*, she thought. *It's too much. If he doesn't remember now, thank heaven for small favors. I hope he never has to relive it.*

She dabbed at her eye and sat back down, telling Peter, "You have been in the hospital for over a week. The doctors had to put you into a medically induced coma so they could treat you. I stayed here waiting for them to wake you up."

Peter watched as a tear escaped and rolled silently down her face. The door to the hospital room opened, and in hurried a young doctor. He was shorter than average and reminded Peter of a TV show his parents used to watch; he couldn't recall much about it, other than it was about a kid doctor, which Peter thought was pretty great. Peter noticed the T-shirt peeking out of his green scrubs. Superman? Yes, the faded blue tee appeared to have the top of the iconic "S" in faded red and yellow. Not the letter S, he corrected himself mentally. Peter was a huge comic fan, and he knew that what appeared to be the Earth "S" was actually the Kryptonian symbol for *Hope.* He found himself hoping that this young doctor was as much a fan as him. The man's voice broke Peter's reverie.

"So," he said to Peter, "you woke up just in time for dinner?" He smiled at Peter as he visually scanned his chart and made a couple of notes. "How are you feeling? You look pretty great, considering."

Peter wondered what the doctor was "considering" when he motioned to Peter to make a scant bit of room for him to sit at the edge of his hospital bed. Peter edged over, and the young doctor carefully sat next to the boy.

"So, is it Peter, or do you prefer Pete? Petey?" the doctor asked. He smiled when he saw Peter blanch at the last suggestion and said, "Okay, Peter is it. Listen, my man, I have a couple of tests I need to administer. They won't hurt, and they'll be quick. Are we cool?"

The young man turned to reach for an instrument before Peter could respond, and Peter decided that he was pretty tired of people not listening to him when they asked him something before they did whatever *they* wanted. As if in answer, the doctor turned back to him and just smiled and waited. Peter was puzzled, until he realized that this doctor was waiting for his approval before he did anything. Peter nodded, and the doctor smiled again and proceeded to check Peter for his responses to outside stimuli by nearly blinding him and running a little spiked wheel over the instep of his foot. This last torture treatment caused Peter to squirm and emit a slight yelp. His response seemed to satisfy the doctor because he put away his little torture instrument and made a few more notes.

He then asked Peter to recite the alphabet, his name and address, and then asked him a couple of math questions. Peter thought this was all very weird and complained he was hungry. The doctor smiled, turned to the nurse and asked her to get Peter a light broth and some crackers to start, and then he asked Peter's mother to step out into the hall. They left the door open a little, and Peter found he could hear every word they spoke just like if they were in the room with him.

"So, is he going to be okay, doctor?"

"Please, call me Dr. Mike, Mrs. Devereaux. I believe that Peter is going to be just fine. Truly, it is an amazing recovery. Our concern was obviously great, but he is responding quite well. With the amount of time Peter was clinically dead, he should have sustained some impaired function. His motor skills appear normal, his wounds are healing with great speed, and I think there will be minimal scarring," he told her.

Peter noticed that he spoke to his mother in a much different manner than the way Dr. Mike spoke to him. He supposed that doctors must speak differently to kids than they did to parents. Still, he liked Dr. Mike.

"He was complaining about his shoulder being in pain." Claire told the young doctor.

"I could go back in and have another look, but that was not one of the places he was bitten, although when we used the defibrillator to bring him back, it could have caused some bruising. More than likely he is experiencing a bit of referral pain."

Peter winced and put a hand to his shoulder. That would explain why he felt so achy. His mother and the doctor came back into the room with the nurse, Nell, who brought Peter his soup. Peter ate his soup while Dr. Mike felt around on Peter's shoulder. There was only one area that seemed to be sore, and it was located on the front of his shoulder where his arm and body met.

The doctor explained to Peter's mother, "Couldn't be related to his accident, but judging from the redness and the shape, I would say this is a typical defibrillator paddle burn. Should go away in a couple of days. If any pain continues into next week, we can re-evaluate."

Peter noticed that Dr. Mike used the word "accident" and that put him one step closer to figuring out what put him here. *I have to find out more.* He was about to ask the doctor to expound on what happened to him, when he abruptly stood up and motioned to Peter's mother to join him on the other side of the room, out of earshot. Peter muttered to himself and sucked down the rest of his broth as they conferred.

Dr. Mike reappeared after a couple of minutes and approached Peter, holding up a hand to stay his questions as he was ready with answers.

"My name is Dr. Mike and yes, I like Superman, he reminds me that ordinary people can do extraordinary things. I didn't tell you my name because you didn't ask, and I assume you can read," pointing to the name tag affixed to his green scrubs. "I can't tell you anything about the events leading up to you being here. I'm sorry, but it's not my place," he said apologetically.

Peter evinced his disappointment, and the doctor came closer, laying a comforting hand on his aching shoulder.

"Remember, Peter—we can choose to be ordinary, or we can choose to do the extraordinary, like Superman did. Like you did. Just as heroic if you ask me," Dr. Mike said with a wink.

Peter blushed and thought about Dr. Mike's words. Strange, but to Peter it felt almost as if they had met before. As he stared quizzically at the doctor's back disappearing through the whooshy door, Peter realized two things: he had to find out for sure what happened from his father—because his mother was never going to tell him in a million years—and he didn't have any pain in his shoulder where Dr. Mike had touched it. Peter also realized he was pretty tired. He pushed away the broth on the rolling tray, settled onto his side and his now pain-free shoulder, and drifted off thinking about flying.

Chapter 6

Peter sat up in his bed, noticing that the furniture and décor was from his house now and not the hospital room at St. Xavier's, and he was relieved. He shook his head trying to dispel the last remnants of the dream, deciding he needed a glass of water. He got up and padded silently into his kitchen. He grabbed a glass out of the cabinet and poured himself some water from the pitcher in the fridge, and on a whim decided to grab one of the sandwiches Momma Rose made for him earlier. He went to the dining room table, sat down, took a bite of sandwich, and started replaying the dream.

Maybe it wasn't a dream, though, he thought. Peter did remember Michael in his hypnosis session with Dr. Jo. *Maybe this was a continuation of that memory.* The more he thought about it, the more that seemed to be the case. Peter grew excited and got up to find the journal he kept for Dr. Jo. She had insisted, as a condition of her continued assistance, that he keep a journal to immediately write down anything he remembered, or even thought he remembered. He hated to admit, but it had been super helpful, and had gotten them to where they were at present. He needed to write this down before he forgot anything.

Peter ran back to his bedroom and knelt down to retrieve the journal he stored under his bed. When he stood back up there was man sitting on the end of his bed. Three things happened in quick succession: he yelped, dropped the journal he was holding, and banged his heel on the nightstand as he jumped backward in his fright. He opened his mouth to use one of Momma Rose's wonderful swear words when the stranger, unexpectedly, spoke first.

"Yeah, don't say that."

Peter hobbled to his reading chair by the window and slumped, swallowing the word he was going to say, while he rubbed his bruised heel.

"Who are you?" He asked, angry and terrified that this stranger was sitting on his bed, in his house, telling him not to swear—and him helpless to escape should he find the need. "What the hell are you doing in my bedroom? What do you want?"

"Think, my man. You remember me—I know you do. Sorry to freak you out, though. Really, that was unintentional."

As Peter's pulse slowly returned to normal, he finally stopped to really look at the man sitting on his bed. Still bent over, rubbing his sore heel, Peter first noticed a pair of flip-flops, next came the frayed hems of a pair of jeans that looked like they had been worn on numerous occasions, a vintage t-shirt, this time though it was not Superman that the shirt displayed, it was an anime angel brandishing a comically large sword, with two sets of wings fanned out around it. Finally, Peter looked upon a face that was both familiar and unfamiliar to him.

"Michael?" Peter croaked.

"In the angelic flesh." He rose from his spot on the bed and embraced Peter warmly. "I heard that you had a breakthrough today in therapy and remembered me. Man, that's great, because things are heating up and we need you."

Michael searched Peter's face for a reaction and got—nothing. Peter was watching him with a dumb look on his face, obviously elsewhere in his thoughts. He waved a hand in front of Peter's face to gain his attention. "Hey. You in there?"

Peter narrowed his gaze, staring at the angel. "You are here, aren't you?" Thinking he may still be sleeping, Peter started to pinch his arm in an attempt to wake up, then remembered that he had just banged his heel on the nightstand, and the resulting pain could not be part of any dream.

Michael reached over and touched Peter on the foot he had just finished rubbing. The result was a warmth that spread to the offending heel, which stopped hurting immediately. The same as his shoulder in the dream.

"Dr. Mike? That was you, too, wasn't it, Michael? Of course it was—Superman."

In answer, Michael briefly morphed into the young doctor from Peter's recent dream, grinning.

Peter shook his head, wiggled his foot experimentally, and found that he felt no pain whatsoever. "That's a neat trick," said Peter, then he remembered what had upset him, at least in dream-time, recently. "I wanted you to tell me so badly what had happened to me. Why didn't you? I was looking for answers, and you had them."

There was hurt in Peter's voice, and he was surprised to hear it. He guessed it was a result of the revelation of the dream being so recent. He returned his attention to his now-pain-free foot and wondered again at the power of the angel. He hoped the work that lay ahead of him would afford him similar abilities. Peter had been thinking about this very thing since he awoke from his dream. He found his inner nerd excited at the prospect of saving the world with a host of angels and superpowers, and he smiled.

Michael raised an eyebrow at Peter and smiled in a way that led Peter to wonder if he could hear his thoughts.

"Yeah, I can—and you need to slow down, brother. I need to explain a few things to you and answer some questions, but don't worry—we'll get to your x-ray vision and super strength soon enough," Michael answered him with a wink.

It was true. Peter did have a ton of questions, but before he could ask the first question Michael held up a forestalling hand and said, "Before we get to your questions, let me explain a few things to you, okay?"

"Okay, shoot."

Peter appeared to Michael to really settle in for the conversation, shifting himself in the chair to be more comfortable, yet attentive. Michael chuckled at Peter's enthusiasm and began. "I need to give you some backstory before you can get a clear picture of the predicament that we're in," Michael began. "Eons ago, before the worlds were created, the Master chose to make a race that would glorify Himself in all that was created. They were designed to protect and defend another of the Master's creations, humans. You follow me so far?"

"Master being God. Yes, I've got it. Keep going."

Michael got up and started pacing, and Peter could tell that this was something Michael must do on a regular basis. It seemed a natural response for him, like someone who thought or carried a great burden. He suddenly looked to Peter to be wearing an appearance closer to his real age, which would be—older. *How old were angels? Thousands of years old? Millions?* Peter's mind reeled with the enormity of what was going on and the part he had to play.

Michael continued, "Humans were created to watch over the Earth, and we were meant to watch over the humans, but there were some within our ranks who were jealous of, not only the time the Master spent with the humans, but also the power the Master wielded. A plot was concocted, and a deal struck. Humans were brought down."

Peter interrupted him, "Wait. Are you talking about Adam and Eve?"

"Yes—and no." Michael answered.

Now Peter was confused, and it must have shown on his face, because Michael went on.

"Yes, it was Adam and Eve and, no, that is not all there is to this story." Michael stopped pacing and turned to face Peter with a look Peter could only describe as sorrowful. "Peter, this is about the beings behind the fall of humanity."

Peter did not remember a mention of any "beings" responsible for mankind's current Original Sin problem, other than a snake. He was confused.

Michael went on, "There was a plot behind the fall of the humans—only the start of what turned out to be an extremely bad idea. These beings wanted the power the Master held over life, death, creation, and annihilation. As protectors of the Master's other creations, they already had a lot of power. It wasn't enough for at least some of them. They started to work against the very creation they were sworn to protect. When the humans fell to the machinations of these beings—we'll call them *the Fallen*," Michael air-quoted and continued, "they were sent out onto the Earth to watch over and protect."

Michael suddenly sat on the edge of the bed and faced Peter, letting him know that what he was about to say next was very important, at least to the angel. "Man is amazing, Peter. They are made to learn. They are made to laugh in the sun, cry in the rain, love without limits, and build wondrous things. Create. Like the Creator who lovingly breathed into them His essence, they are special. You are special."

Michael bounced up off of the bed and returned to his pacing, continuing the recitation. "The first man was made to steward the Garden, to fellowship and learn from the Master. The three of them, the Man, the Woman, and the Master would walk and talk together all of the time, each growing in their love for the others." Michael noticed a look of puzzlement cross Peter's face, and he knew what he was thinking. "Peter, the Master loves all of you very much, otherwise He wouldn't have made the sacrifices he did. Never forget that."

Michael went on, "The woman was Man's helpmate, and learned to create clothes and tame creatures to help them and feed them. She was also to bear children. Believe it or not, childbirth wasn't originally intended to hurt. After the Original Sin, a lot of things changed, Peter."

Michael stopped walking and turned to face the window that looked down on the cobblestone street awash in the dim light and fog. He looked to Peter as if he was trying to recall an incredibly painful memory.

"Their betrayal hurt. It hurt all of us. Although the Master was wounded by their transgressions, He made sure to help them in other ways. In His great love, the Master gave the couple sunlight and rain, materials to make things, and the intelligence needed to create a home."

Peter could tell Michael was a thousand miles from Louisiana, and thousands of years from where they were. Peter thought in awe of just how old, regardless of how he looked, Michael really was. The archangel turned and smiled knowingly, and again Peter felt Michael knew what he was thinking.

Michael returned to his pacing past the dresser and continued, "After a few thousand years, the human population had grown, and the women of the Earth had become attractive to those sent to protect them. I believe you all call them guardian angels?"

Peter nodded, and Michael spoke again. "These *guardian* angels decided that they could take for themselves the daughters of men and have children. The offspring of these angel/human combinations are called—"

"Nephilim," Peter said with exuberance.

Michael smiled and nodded, "Yes, Nephilim. These are not what author's today and Hollywood would like you to believe. They were giants, abominations, and were not pleasant in nature. During this same time, humans were being corrupted to the point where the Master felt it necessary to intervene. He was so hurt and felt such betrayal and loneliness that He decided to wipe the Earth clean and start over. The Master loved all, but very few loved Him, and it hurt too much for Him to know that. Humans had lived very long, very prosperous, and very wicked lives for eons, so the Master decided to limit humankind's life on Earth to 120 years."

Peter gave a surprised look. "I don't know that I've ever heard of anyone living 120 years, Michael. I've never heard of anyone living much past 100."

Michael smiled, "Well, Pete, just know that if you took care of yourself religiously, you would still only get 120 years under the best of circumstances. May I continue?"

Peter shrugged and Michael returned to his telling of the tale.

"He found a human that was free from corruption and chose him and his family to carry on the human race, because the Master couldn't bring Himself to completely destroy it."

"Noah," Peter said, interrupting again. Michael smiled and nodded in agreement.

"Noah was the guy. The Master saw in Noah the same thing He would see in Abraham, and in David. He was an intercessor who convinced the Master that there was still part of humanity that was worth sparing. His love allowed Him to spare a man like Noah, who ultimately saved his family from death and assured that humans would populate the Earth once more, without interference this time. Noah was tasked with the building of the large ship and finding suitable wives for his three sons. This was no easy task considering the entire known world was corrupt, so Noah asked the Master for blessings upon the three women he found to become the wives of his sons. Noah did the best he could with the women that were available, but his time was short—he only had seven days to find wives for Shem, Ham, and Japheth. He picked the women that he felt the Master had pointed him to, and they were the sole inhabitants, or at least, they were supposed to be. All of the evil and wicked people who laughed and jeered at the family building the massive boat found themselves true believers in the cataclysm when it fell upon them, and there was a mad struggle to board the large boat with Noah and his sons having to fight off many who would thwart the Master's plan.

"And one did. A stowaway that was discovered only too late, spared the death due him by Noah's youngest son. He'll come up later—don't worry about him now."

Peter stood, mouth agape, not believing what he was hearing.

"The flood that rid the world of corruption also rid the world of Nephilim. Unlike the rest of the beings on the Earth, the product of humans and angels were not made by the Master and did not fit in his creation. He had planned and produced everything exactly how it should be in His time and in His way, but He never planned on the Nephilim, because they weren't supposed to exist at all. The Master's blueprint for you, for example, is exactly what you see when you look in the mirror, Peter. You were always meant to be exactly how you appear, as is every person on the Earth today, unless they have changed themselves in some fashion that is not of the Master. Upon the destruction of all living things except those on the ark, the souls of the Nephilim had nowhere to dwell, because no blueprint or plan existed for them in the physical world. They were adrift in the universe with nowhere to reside."

"I don't understand," Peter said. "What do you mean by adrift?"

Michael sighed and said, "Think of it this way, for every person and animal that was created by the Master there is a place for it to go after death. For Nephilim, no place like that existed, because they were not the Master's creation. Nowhere to go for them after they died—" Michael trailed off, as if lost in thought. He gathered himself and went on. "This presented a problem, since they never really died they could return by attaching themselves to the form of another, if there was any kind of tainted blood in them."

"Meaning..." Peter prompted.

"Meaning that of the three wives Noah found for his sons, there was only one free of corruption, the woman married to Shem. When Noah and his sons were tasked with repopulating the Earth after the flood, each son went his own way and fathered many children. Of those lines, Shem's was the only one without taint. So those Nephilim souls found purchase in the bodies of the descendants of Ham and Japheth. Out of these lines stem some of the greatest myths and legends, because the Nephilim could not reside inside a body that had a soul for long."

Michael stopped as if to judge Peter's reaction to what he had been told so far. "The Nephilim of this time used humans as guinea pigs, along with various other animals and creatures. They tried many different ways to extend the life of their host bodies and crossed them with other creatures. I trust you know the term, hybrid?"

Peter nodded, and Michael gave a grim smile and sat next to him on the arm of the chair. "This is where it got really strange—you'll see why in a minute. The abominations that came from breeding humans and animals were enough to sustain the Nephilim souls for longer, and this gave them hope and the idea of crossing different creatures with other creatures. Different cultures have alternate names for the products of those unions."

Michael searched Peter's expression as he named off the ones that he knew of from popular culture, myths, and folklore. "Giants, vampires, lycanthropes, satyrs, centaurs, griffins—pretty much anything that you have been told as a fairy tale or legend exists now, or existed at one point. What do you think of that?"

Peter stood as Michael named off the impossible list and started to do his own pacing, not believing what he was hearing. The implications were far too enormous and terrible to comprehend.

"What the hell..." Peter muttered and saw Michael wince. "Sorry," he said in response. "You're telling me that the things we read about as legends are totally true?" Peter asked still in disbelief.

"Yes," Michael answered, "and there are others in the world who know they exist as well and wish to preserve them—and make things worse than what you've already imagined while I was talking. Much worse. That's why we need your help, Peter."

Chapter 7

Peter's mind was in a state of turmoil. What Michael was talking about was something otherworldly, right out of one of the many new online role play games. Peter looked up to find Michael watching him expectantly.

"You're telling me that those things are real? Are they still around? The dinosaurs are extinct, so..." Peter stopped speaking as Michael again held up a hand for silence.

"Yes, they were real, and some lived a long time, some not as long as others, but most have been recorded through history as regional folklore, myths, or scary tales. Most people believe them to be legends or old wives' tales. The hybridization continues today, in a far more terrible way. We'll get to that. Do you have any questions? I know this is a lot to lay on you." Michael plopped down on the bed, as if weary from the telling.

Peter considered and then said, "This is really mind blowing, but what does this have to do with someone like me?" His mouth was dry and his head was humming. "I need a drink, Michael. Do you—"

Michael cut him off, raising a hand and smiling, "I don't typically eat or drink, Peter, but thanks all the same. Go get your drink and come back. We have more to discuss."

Peter rose from the armchair and walked to the kitchen, lost in thought. He grabbed a rocks glass from the open-faced cabinet and some ice from the dispenser. He poured himself a straight Crown and returned to the bedroom, where the angel was waiting to dive back in. Peter resumed his seat and waved to Michael as he sipped to continue.

"When the angels that were sent to the earth to protect humans corrupted the bloodline and created Nephilim, they cursed their own fate. The Master punished them to live deep in the Earth, what humans have called Tartarus or Hades. They haven't seen light for millennia, and won't until, or if, the Master decides to forgive them their transgressions. They have to want to be forgiven in order to even have redemption be a consideration. So far, none of them ever has." Michael gave Peter a piercing look, "That's where you come in."

Peter was overwhelmed and Michael could see it. It was a condition common with humans, and he was used to them needing the extra time to process massive amounts of serious information, so he waited. Peter understood the backstory and thought it amazing and frightening. While he was raised in a church, what Michael told him didn't quite match his memory of Bible stories. He sipped and let the warm whisky trickle down the back of his throat as he contemplated again.

How many bible stories started with the mighty T-rex mistakenly eating an absolution offering? Or all of those that accused Jesus of being a vampire after showing up three days after being killed? He started to think of some pretty far out thoughts. *Vampires fighting for the Amorites alongside of giants?* Fascinated by the scenario, Peter was unaware that Michael watched him as he processed this new information. Michael seemed fascinated by Peter and waited patiently for the man's creative process to catch up with logic.

Peter stopped and looked at Michael. "What exactly do I need to do? More to the point, what *can* I do? I'm no one—unless you need some very realistic looking armor or—"

Michael cut him off. "You're not no one, Peter. I thought I made that very clear to you 10 years ago when we met. You have a very important role to play. And no, I can't tell you what that will look like just yet, but to answer your question, this is what we need—the Master has set in motion plans that can only be fulfilled with the help of four of the fallen angels. The Heavy Hitters, I'll call them. You'll learn more about them as we go, but for any of them to be of service, we need them to be reconciled to the Master," said Michael.

"So, you need the four angels to make up and play nice?"

"Yes, in layman's terms," said Michael.

Peter asked what he thought was the obvious question, "How?"

"From the jump, we need the hybrid Nephilim kept secret. If these hybrids were made known to the world, panic would ensue, and the world would be thrown into turmoil." Michael looked at Peter longing for him to understand the unsaid.

"I get it," Peter said. "You want for the people to remain ignorant of the fact that there are werewolves, vampires, giants, and other monsters loose in the world." He nearly had a panic attack thinking about what might lurk outside his windows. Peter stood and semi-casually walked to his window, pretending to be glancing at the street below. He turned and smiled at Michael, turned back, closed his bedroom window and locked it for good measure. "I feel woefully unprepared."

"Then you are fit to be of use," Michael said with a grin. "How familiar are you with faith heroes, man? Abraham, Noah, David, Moses, Jonah? Any of them?"

"I think I know something about all of them. Why?"

"What did all of those guys have in common?"

"Beards?" Peter replied, semi-sarcastically. "I really don't know, Michael. They were great men—brave and strong and wise."

"Actually, you are wrong. On two counts." Michael crossed back to the window, and searched the night for—something. "It's amazing how arrogant and self-effacing you all can be, all at once. None of them, not one of the men that I named, was great. Abraham? He was a liar, and he wasn't very smart. Noah? He was a smart man and an upstanding citizen, but he was sort of a chauvinist. David? Please. Womanizer, adulterer, murderer. Moses? Not smart, not ambitious, and he had questionable hygiene. And I know you know about Jonah. By the way, David had a scar that prevented him from ever growing facial hair—just thought you might find that interesting. No, all of those guys had one thing in common and that was a love for the Master, a willingness to do what was asked, and a healthy dose of fear thrown in for good measure. That's all that you need, too. Be ready and willing to follow, and know why you need to do the right thing when it needs doing. As for help? You don't need to sweat that at all, brother. We have someone in mind that can help you. As a matter of fact, he is your assignment."

"Wait. What?" Peter shook his head as if to remove any unwanted thoughts.

"By helping Sam, you help humanity, just like you did your cousin's friend." Michael told him solemnly.

"Who is Sam?" asked Peter.

"Samael—the fallen angel that we need you to assist. Once a strong and loyal soldier of the Master, he was like a brother to me. He, like you, is capable of so much—if he can be redeemed and restored to his previous position. In other words, we need him. We need him to want to help our cause, otherwise he's..." Michael's face clouded over, and it was as close to what Peter imagined an angel would look like weeping as he would ever see. "He's—lost. Forever" Michael regained his composure, but his solemn expression didn't change. "We'll all be."

Peter understood. Michael and the other angels required the help of this Sam in order to proceed in an unhindered way. Peter wasn't sure he could help but was willing to try, if for no other reason than it would be a kick-ass thing to do. He realized that he had cursed in his thoughts and wondered if Michael knew, or was offended. In answer, Michael raised and eyebrow at him, giving him a cowing stare. Peter felt mortified, until Michael burst into laughter and a took Peter in a great bear hug.

"Oh, brother. You're hilarious. We have *so* many more important things to worry about, wouldn't you agree?"

Michael released Peter, and the young man turned, suddenly feeling overwhelmed. He let the enormity of the requests being made of him wash over him and pull him under emotionally. The mission that he was to perform had *eternal* importance, and

Michael believed in him. He didn't want to let anyone down, but this wasn't like forgetting to pick someone up a the airport, or not getting someone a proper birthday gift. This was a fate-of-the-world-hangs-in-the-balance type request, and at the moment, it was a bit too much for him.

"God. I want to help," whispered Peter, almost like a prayer. He turned to Michael, "But I'm not sure *how* to help. If the best of God's angels couldn't do it, what chance do I have?"

"No, Peter, it's not like that at all. This *must* be done by humans. I know you don't understand right now, and I just have to ask you to trust me and trust the Master. And I will tell you where to go and who you need to contact. There are others that will help you along the way, some willingly and others, unknowingly, but you will find that you have friends in the most unexpected areas. The important thing is, brother, you will at no time be on your own in this. I'm here with you until the end."

Michael made it seem like a great adventure, and that Peter should not be afraid in the least—that there would be friends all over the place to help him.

Peter, although excited about the prospect of helping his inner nerd become the savior of the world, was not naive enough to think that it would be easy. He smiled and said, "When do I start?"

Chapter 8

The sun baked the still bubbling blacktop, and the smell of the mid-afternoon Mississippi mingled with the odor of fresh tar greeted the pilot exiting the old Huey. As he slung his gear over his shoulder and grabbed his flight log, he paused to wrinkle his nose and note the fresh tarmac that was not present earlier at takeoff. Abe Sims had just returned from his second flight of the day, and he was feeling his age at the moment. He had shuttled a few disabled Korean vets to the newer memorial in Houston, as the current situation in Washington, D.C. prevented them from visiting West Potomac Park.

Abe always enjoyed talking with the old soldiers and hearing their stories, and this was no exception. The sergeant in the wheelchair that had talked his ear off for most of their journey had been in Pusan in 1950 and was not short of humor, detail, or profanity. Abe could easily relate to the man's tale, he himself being a veteran of Desert Storm in the early 91. All veterans and active duty had a special place in Abe's heart, and he could think of nothing better that he could be doing than giving these old timers a lift and listening to their war stories.

Abe had always wanted to be a soldier, but not a leader. He had grown up in Alabama, and after experiencing a lot of what black folks in the south had experienced in the 60s, he vowed not to carry resentment or hatred around with him. Luckily, as a young man, he had been taught the value of self-respect, respect for others even when they don't respect you, and most importantly, Christian love for his fellow man.

His father, an itinerant preacher who eventually settled himself and his family in a small Baptist community around Birmingham, had always told him, "You carry that around with you, you'll be no good for anybody. You've never been a slave or in chains, and if you find yourself in chains, dollars to donuts they are of your own making, son. Rise above and get your respect by respecting others. Remember what Jesus taught, listen to Dr. King, and you'll be alright."

That's how he had lived, and even after Memphis, after they shot and killed one of the greatest men who had ever walked the Earth, he didn't hate or riot or do any of the other stuff that those around him were advocating. His father's words were still there in his heart, and he lived them. He joined the army at 18 and did just what his father had instructed. He became an NCO in two years, gaining respect as he gave it. He became a warrant officer a year before the air war broke out, and a pretty damn good chopper pilot, too. He had lived as an Army officer for years, but he had found little respect when he returned from the Gulf War. He received no hero's welcome at the airports and bus station en route to his hometown of Gardendale, Alabama. He remembered not understanding why people at home were so upset with the returning soldiers.

We did what we were sent to do, nothing less, he thought to himself as he walked into the lower hangar and dropped his gear. He grabbed a bottle of water and unscrewed the cap as he sat on an old metal stool, looking back at his helicopter. *They wanted us to follow orders; we followed orders. It's not our fault that it escalated the way it did—and cost what it did*, he thought bitterly, absently glancing down at his left thigh. He had been loath to accept the derision of the folks at home, and even had gotten into a fight with his old gym teacher at a service station when he spat on him and called him a murderer. He rolled his eyes to himself and drove the memory down into the depths where it belonged. *Yeah, we probably deserved better, and, if not respect, at least appreciation*, he thought. *Those boys I flew today—the ones in Kabul and Tikrit and all of those other hellholes no one wants to find themselves in—they deserve honor and respect.* He wanted to make sure that the soldiers returning home to loved ones either whole and in person, missing limbs or in pieces, or even in a casket for burial, received the respect that they deserved. He felt that anyone who had served in the military understood why these soldiers did what they did, anyone else could only presume to know, and sadly, the majority didn't understand or didn't care. Abe was exhausted from his flight and the emotional toll it took on him. He was a humble man and did not expect praise for giving a soldier a lift home in his plane or in his chopper on the shorter hops. He looked out on the old UH-1 that he called Betty and smiled. She was in no way a replacement for the Chinook he flew in Riyadh that he had named Betty, but Abe loved her. He got the old chopper at an Army surplus sale a few years back. Abe stopped for a second and let the old twin prop helicopter occupy his thoughts.

God, I loved that bird, he thought. His job in the war was evac; get a medic crew or extraction team to the soldiers that needed it and get them out before hell found them. Abe had been in his share of it in the two tours he served, and they finally did get him in the summer of 1991—shot down along with his cargo—in this case two wounded and a forward observer he was taking to Bahrain. Abe carried the guilt around with him still that he was the only one to survive that incident. Abe had been able to ditch in the dusty foothills of the Zagros Mountains, but the damage had been done. No survivors and his cyclic control stick had tried to bury itself in his left hip, burning its way in.

He remembered feebly working the safety harness, but the rest was lost to the fog of his injuries. He was told later that the bodies of the two hurt soldiers and the FO were nowhere in sight at the ditch point. He also knew that, were it not for a passing artillery officer, he would be six feet under. He owed everything to him—Captain Michaels.

He had come to in an area away from the ditched bird and the searching Iraqi troops—armed to the teeth and determined to not come back from their patrol empty-handed. He started to panic, realizing where he was and what had transpired, but a hand on his shoulder steadied him and let him know he wasn't alone or without help. They both waited in silence for the patrol to pass, staying hidden in the brush, barely breathing.

Once the enemy soldiers were out of earshot, the young captain found a cave in which to lay low. He saw to Abe's wounded side and leg and gave him some water, letting him know that they may be unable to evac him for a little while. Abe was in and out over the next several hours, but when he was alert, he and the young artillery officer swapped stories and talked about their lives back home.

Captain Michaels was an excellent storyteller, and they became friends, often seeing each other in the convening years. Abe shook his reverie and gave himself a quick once-over; he needed to get a shower before his two o'clock meeting with Dr. Jo. He had been seeing her for more than a few years now and enjoyed their time together. She had helped him in so many ways, and on more than a few occasions seemed to have just the tonic for what was bothering him. Not to mention she was easy on the eyes.

He smiled as he made his way around the boxes and crates in the hangar for his next flight. He climbed the stairs to his loft apartment, built years ago by his much younger hands, and back, into the hangar itself. He loved planes, or anything that flew, really. He had never married or had kids of his own, and other than his niece, Abe considered his many aircraft his kids. He took care of them, and they took care of him. As Abe reached the top of the stairs leading to the loft, he heard singing coming from inside. Abe called it a loft but really it was an open-plan two bedroom, one bath apartment. He smiled as he opened the door and found his niece joyfully dancing and singing to an invisible audience as she mopped the floor. She did not see him step up behind her, and during her last pirouette opened her eyes to see her uncle grinning at her from the door.

She raised her hand to her heart and exclaimed, "You nearly scared me to death," rather loudly with the Michael Jackson tune still blaring in her headphones. She slipped them from her ears and said in a softer voice, "I wasn't expecting you back yet. You almost gave me a heart attack."

"Hey, not my fault, baby girl. You looked like you were having so much fun, I didn't want to mess with your groove."

She dance-stepped her way to the door and gave her uncle a brief hug. "How long have you been back?"

"Just landed. Man, I need a shower. It's stifling out there today," Abe told her as he blotted his moist forehead with a bandana. He stuffed it back into his pocket and said, "What brings you around? Surely it wasn't just to mop this old man's floor?"

He had raised Naomi after her mother had passed 10 years earlier. Naomi's father was a deadbeat and had not shown any interest in the girl, so he didn't put up much argument when Abe suggested Naomi live with him. She came to him at the ripe old age of 12, and now at 24 she was a beautiful young woman who unfortunately had decided that she liked planes and helicopters as much, if not more than Abe. He tried to pique her interest in other hobbies and activities for a while before he ultimately gave up. Naomi was who she was, and Abe figured that there were worse things she could be doing than flying, which in his opinion was the best thing man had ever figured out how to do in the first place. Naomi looked at the floor, decided that it was clean, and began to wring the mop in the bucket.

"New order into the office today." She used the term office lightly considering his office consisted of a table in the corner with a calendar, phone, and a decrepit computer that should have been replaced three generations ago.

"What and where to?" Abe asked her all business now.

"It's not that kind of order," Naomi giggled at the look of puzzlement from her uncle. "This order came from a Captain Michael Michaels—is that a joke, by the way?" she quizzed her uncle, raising one eyebrow at the unusual name. He shook his head no, but motioned for her to continue eagerly. She shrugged. "Anyway, said he was an old friend of yours. He asked if you would be free to talk with him." Naomi was surprised by the mix of emotions that flashed across her uncle's face, and she knew that whatever history her uncle had with the captain was significant. "I told him he could stop by to see you tonight. I hope that was okay?" She sounded nervous, and Abe smiled at her in reassurance.

"Yeah, yeah—that's fine. I would love to see him."

"Well, that's wonderful, because he will be here at 1400," she told him. She forestalled his next sentence by saying, "Oh, and Dr. Jo's office called to cancel your appointment today. You can call and reschedule for tomorrow, or they will just see you next week at the same time."

"Thanks," Abe said kissing her on the cheek on his way past her, "I'm gonna take a shower before Mike gets here."

"Okay, I gotta jet anyway. Will you be going out, or do you want me to throw a lasagna in the oven before I go?"

"Put the lasagna on if you will, Naomi. Where you headed?"

"I have to run some errands and get my nails done. Darius is taking me out tonight."

Abe scowled at her daffy expression. The girl didn't have many faults, but the ones she did have were doozies. She fell in love too easily, and it usually got her into all kinds of trouble. She also had a generous nature that made it exceedingly easy for her to be taken advantage of now and again.

"Aw, c'mon. Don't look at me like that. Darius is a good guy." She pouted a little at his scowl and was about to expound on Darius' finer qualities, but Abe spoke first.

"That's what you said about the last one. I swear, Naomi. I thought I was gonna have to put him through a wall before that was over. You let these boys walk all over you. You deserve respect, and you should expect to be treated like the strong, smart lady you are."

"That's how Darius is with me. If you would only meet him and talk to him, you would see." She reached out, and took Abe's hand in hers, and looked him in the eye. " I know you want to keep me your baby forever, but I'm out in the world now, and I get to choose who is in my life."

"I know, but as long as you are in *my* life," he said, shaking her hand for emphasis, "I will always want to protect you—at least until another man shows he's up to the task." Abe grasped her by her shoulders, demanding her full attention and fixed her with his kind, pleading gaze. "Please be careful. Your mother, God rest her, fell in love at the drop of a hat, and it caused her nothing but heartache until the day she passed. I don't want to see you end up like that. You need to exercise caution and discernment. You're going places. You're bound for great things, and you need a man who recognizes it." Abe looked determined, and Naomi was touched by his concern, although she thought it unnecessary *all* the time.

"I promise, I will be careful," she said. As she spoke, his expression softened into his typical easy half-smile, his eyes crinkling at the corners as if they were taking in too much light.

"That's my girl. Take the taser." Abe chuckled, then turned and disappeared into the bathroom as Naomi pulled the lasagna out of the freezer and popped it into the oven. She set the oven timer, and humming to herself, grabbed her purse and went out the door.

After a quick, refreshing, nearly ice-cold shower, as was his custom—he hadn't taken a hot shower since 1990 as he found them uncomfortable—he changed into fresh clothes and grabbed a Red Stripe from the refrigerator. He popped the cap and seated himself to gaze out the massive window into the afternoon sun, took a long pull from the frosty bottle, swallowed, and breathed deeply. Abe's thoughts turned to his old friend. He absently fingered the pendant he kept on a chain around his neck, a token from the young officer after a most unusual conversation that he for years thought he had concocted in the confines of his own warped memory. He wondered what Mike wanted to talk to him about. It had been almost 10 years since their last conversation at a memorial for another soldier. As it had been over the decades whenever they met, either by accident or intentionally, the young officer appeared much the same as he always had; tow-headed, slightly sunburnt, great teeth, smiling eyes, and a firm handshake.

The oven's buzzing timer snapped him out of his thoughts. He made his way into the kitchen, grabbed the pot holders off the counter, and pulled the lasagna out of the oven. He had just set it on the counter when he heard a knock. Abe made his way to the front door and eagerly pulled it open. A man dressed in boots, jeans, and a royal blue, yellow, and red striped polo stood on the grated landing, fanning himself. He stopped when Abe opened the door, and he flashed a brilliant smile.

"Mike," Abe exclaimed. "Get in here. How have you been? You look pretty good for an old war horse." Captain Michaels took Abe's proffered hand and shook it energetically, using his other to embrace the shorter man warmly.

"Abe, my friend. How are you holding up, chief?" he said, breezing past Abe from the stifling hangar into the air conditioning. Abe closed the door and turned to catch up to the taller man, crossing to the battered sofa.

Abe eased himself into the chair adjacent to the microfiber couch and gave a slight groan. Mike looked questioningly at him, and Abe waved away his concern. "Can't complain, cap. Well, I could, but it wouldn't make a difference." Abe chuckled, settling into a more comfortable position in the comfy chair. Almost as soon as he had lit on the closest cushion, the captain popped back up.

"Mind if I grab a beer? I'm dry as a bone."

"Absolutely, Mike—mi casa es su casa." He snatched open the door to the fridge, and Abe wondered to himself how the man always managed to move with such energy and vigor. They were very close in age, but the captain seemed just as spry as ever, and just as strong. The man was not small, and he was not short on muscle, having pulled Abe from the wreck along with his gear and his trashed communications equipment and medical supplies all by himself.

The man returned to the sofa, plopped down, snatched the cap off of the Red Stripe, and took a deep slug, finishing with a satisfied "Ahhh." Abe surveyed the man across from him, and figured he was on a mission—he always was. Mike wasn't a guy that dropped by; he moved through the world like a man whose time was valuable, and his itinerary reflected that. Last Abe had heard, Mike was in Sevastopol, and before that, Canberra.

"I'm always glad to see you, cap, but I know you. What brings you to my sweltering neck of the woods?" Mike grabbed a couple of coasters, placing one under each bottle on the table, and sat back, his fingers steepled under his chin, as if he were about to say something important and thought-provoking.

"Abe, we've known each other a long time, right?"

"Well on to 30 years now, I'd say," answered Abe, considering. He cocked an eyebrow, gave a questioning look to the officer, and said "Don't reach, cap—just say it. The suspense is killing me." Abe reached for his beer and took another drink, being careful to place it back on the coaster that Mike had placed under it. *Mike is like that,* Abe thought. *The utmost respect for his surroundings and the people he dealt with.* But at the same time, Abe couldn't recall ever seeing someone more at ease at making themselves at home than Mike. He liked that about him.

"Do you remember when we were pinned down in the Zagros? You were banged up pretty bad, in a lot of pain, and you had come upon my unit, but could only move a few out at a time." Michaels looked up at Abe and said, "You were the bravest man I had ever seen; fearless, and more concerned with getting all the men out of danger than for yourself." Abe took another swig of his beer, remembering, and a bitter smile came to his face.

"I was scared stupid. More afraid than I'd ever been, honestly. I had never had my wings clipped, and there hadn't been a time in my life where I ever thought I could walk away from getting shot down. I thought for sure that, even after I knew I had survived the crash, I figured that they would capture or kill me. They never forget a face, you know," Abe joked. "I think my picture was up inside a post office in Tehran." Abe laughed, hoping he seemed at ease with the memory, but he couldn't stop his hands from shaking.

Dammit, Abe thought. *Let it go. The damage is done. Your mind, your body. What you did. What you saw. Let it go.*

Mike reached out and placed a steadying hand on Abe's arm and continued his recollection.

"I remember, too, chief," he said softly. He removed his hand and grabbed again for his beer, took a drink, and set it on the coaster. "You went into that mess five times before they brought you down with that last round. We were incredibly fortunate that you crashed not too far from my remaining men and on the other side of the insurgents. We were able to get to you and set up a perimeter to hold a decent line, but it never would have happened without you. Your bravery inspired my men to fight and hold that zone. We were also able to call in another team to extract the rest of us. You had so much courage, and you were so selfless. I think you were looked after that day, for sure, but you inspired men, and the world is now better for it." Michaels looked at Abe, gauging his response to his most recent comments.

Abe looked right into Captain Michaels' eyes and said, "Just did my job the best way I knew how, Mike. I know that someone was looking out for me that day. I know it. I remember it all—everything about that day."

Abe affected a thousand-yard stare and turned to look wistfully out at his small fleet of aircraft. He was in his little apartment physically, but in his thoughts he was there once again, flying through the enemy's territory, death below and above him.

"I remember you being at my side as we waited for two days. Man. Longest two days of my life. I remember waiting for the second extraction team. They couldn't reach us right away, and the LZ had to be cleared. I remember the stories you told me to keep me calm. Mike, I remember this…" Abe reached down into the neck of his shirt and pulled out the medallion that he had worn on a silver chain ever since returning from the field hospital where the young captain had given it to him. It looked like a coin blank that someone had taken the time to carve a symbol into. It almost looked like an astrology sign. It had a small hook at the top that came into a long line into a triangle at the bottom flowing into another line rising from the triangle, then bending down to finish in a circle. Abe didn't know what the symbol stood for, and had, on many occasions, taken the token out to admire the workmanship of the etched design. "What is it, anyway? Did you make it?"

Abe smiled at his friend, and Mike laughed good-naturedly. "Nah, I'm not the Craftsman who made that, Abe. It's a symbol of our friendship, chief."

Abe looked up at Captain Michaels and said, "We've been good to each other, Mike. Helped each other out for over 30 years. I owe you my life, and you know I would do anything you asked. Anything, 'cause I wouldn't be here without you. I am pretty tired, so no heavy lifting, okay?" Mike raised one corner of his mouth in a half grin and let Abe continue, more seriously now. "I am still ready to fight. Just give me a mission."

Abe's eyes took on a glint that the angel recognized. Michael smiled, and knew he could count on Abe once again to get done what needed to be done for the Master. He clapped his old friend lightly on his still sinewy shoulder and said, "Okay Abe, but this will be the last one. One last mission. You're gonna be gone for a little while, though. Will Naomi be okay without you?"

"I will have to talk it over with her, but I'm sure she will be fine. She's like her mom, and Miriam was smart and stubborn. It served her well," Abe told him with a twinkle in his eyes.

"Then we are five by five, chief," said Mike.

Abe strode to the refrigerator, grabbed two more cold bottles, crossed back to the sofa with Mike in tow, and sat down. He handed the second beer to his friend, popped the top on his, took a long drink, and placed it on the table. He turned to Mike.

"OK, you've got me. What's the mission?"

"I need you to take someone to meet—someone." Michael paused as he took in Abe's puzzled expression.

"Someone to meet someone. I'm tracking, but that's awfully cryptic."

"I know," Michael sighed, "but this time you really just have to trust me." The man rose from the sofa and paced to the kitchen, thinking hard, obviously exasperated. "He's been too selfish for too long. We need him in a position to make choices—take action that will benefit someone other than himself." Michael was speaking as himself, and for a second or two Abe was confused. Michael continued wearing out the small patch of floor from the couch to the kitchen. "I think he is going to be able to make a great difference with something important—he just needs a little help. That is where you and Peter come in."

"Wait, who is Peter?" Abe asked.

The angel stopped his pacing and looked up at Abe. "Oh, yeah. Sorry about that. He is your mission. Peter Devereaux. That's who you are taking to meet—the other someone. Just need them to get together. That's where you come in."

Abe's mind flashed back to a sign-in sheet at Dr. Jo's office. Peter Devereaux is a name that he had seen on that list, and racking his brain a bit, he was able to conjure an image. It didn't impress him. Lean, small, bookish. Didn't look like he was good with his hands, didn't look fit to fight. Abe figured the kid was probably a nice enough person, but nice wasn't good for missions. Nice probably wouldn't even survive a mission.

"I've seen him. He's not what you want for this, trust me." Abe said indignantly. "I have always tried to help you with your missions, but this is..." Abe trailed off as Michael stared him down.

"Just like Turley wasn't what you wanted, right?" Michael referenced a young flight medic that Abe had rejected twice for his crew, until ultimately taking him under his wing. "You know he's a highly-decorated pilot in his own right, now, right? He was going to be a washout, and you almost made that happen. You remember what you told me back then?"

Abe put his head to his chest, thinking about the kid that had originally come to him, fresh from his mama apparently, and green as a stalk of spring grass. He chuckled to himself, and said, "He's too soft—trust me."

"And were you right?" Mike probed.

"Obviously not. It was the first time I was able to mentor a kid, and it was the best thing I've ever done, other than Naomi. Alright, you're right. Again. Does that ever get tiring for you?"

Mike grinned. "Never. You know that there is a reason for everything. Even if you can't see it. We need Peter to succeed. He may be the only one who can. I need you because you have the experience that he will need; you have the knowledge and capabilities that Peter does not. Abe, you are a shaper of men. Come on, chief. You are the best at getting blood out of a stone that I have ever seen. Peter needs you to make him fit and ready to face what's coming—and I need you to keep him safe."

"I only have one other question," Abe said.

"Just one?" Michael quipped.

Abe rolled his eyes. "Okay, two questions: How do I get in touch with Peter? I know he lives down in the Quarter. I've seen him walking to get to the doc's office. And—when do we need to go?"

Michael smiled. He picked up his beer from the coaster, drained it in two or three long gulps, and replaced it on the coaster. He started towards the door. Abe followed his lead, opening the door for the man.

Mike said over his shoulder as they exited the little loft and started down the metal catwalk to the stairs, "I'm starving. Feel like going to see Momma Rose?"

Chapter 9

Maggie put down her pen and rubbed her temples. The pilot of the Airbus A380 she was currently sitting in had announced they had arrived in Miami, and the temperature was a stifling 97 degrees with 87% humidity. She was sweating just thinking about it. She had just put down on paper her newest thoughts and theories on her latest piece, and longed for respite from the plane, her seat, and her thoughts, although she was flying first class on one of the largest and newest planes available—"*a unique experience that introduces you to new standards of in-flight comfort, from first class to economy*"—she remembered reading that in the brochure and smiled to herself at her ability to recall the phrase.

All her life, she had been told she was smart, she often heard the word clever used; Maggie herself had always thought that the various adults she had heard this from, from her parents, to teachers, to bosses, had always indicated, or at least inferred, that her intelligence came with a bent towards cunning, and even deviousness. She had also always been told she was pretty, but that never really mattered to her. She knew that she possessed many traits that men found appealing, and more importantly, she knew how to bring them to bear to get what she wanted from them. Most useful among her talents, though, was her eidetic memory—*a very handy skill for an investigative journalist,* she thought.

She had been thinking about Susanna. *I'll have to call her later. I haven't talked with her in a while.* She missed her a lot, and Maggie caught herself at the thought. She didn't normally miss much of anything, or anyone for that matter. She thought of a lot of things when she traveled, but home was not one of them. Maggie was not meant for domesticity, and she didn't miss her family much, or her place in Seattle near Green Lake, nor her colleagues. She had no pets, or boyfriends, or ties of any kind, other than a gym membership that she kept forgetting to cancel. No, nothing held her anywhere. The home she knew had wings and tiny bottles of booze.

Despite all of that, she found herself missing her best friend. *It's the damn story*, she told herself, willing her eyes to stay dry. As the pilot taxied, she thought about her assignment—human sex trafficking and its ties to the mafia. Susanna had been the victim of a sex trafficking ring, when they were younger, and although she escaped with her life, the experience had its way with Susanna.

She had been eight days shy of her 13th birthday when she was abducted. Maggie remembered vividly sitting at Suse's kitchen table, planning the festivities with her and her mother over Oreos, applesauce, and vanilla ice cream. When she was tracked down and rescued, the young woman that came back to Klamath Falls wasn't the girl that had been taken. Susanna today was still working through the negative effects that her time in captivity had created in her psyche, and had become an ultra-cautious, often frightened mouse of a woman. She went from rambunctious, all-American teenager to scared, suicidal victim.

Maggie was there for her when all her other friends treated her as damaged goods. Maggie was the one Susanna cried to, and she was also the one who found Susanna when she had attempted to end her suffering. She needed help. Maggie wrote to Susanna the whole time she was in the clinic. She would send Susanna stories she made up about non-consequential things, like the story about the mouse who stole a remote-control car and used it to torment the neighbor's cat, or the butterfly who dreamed of becoming a painter. Yes, it had been too long, and Maggie decided she would give Susanna a call after she checked into her hotel room.

Maggie was brought back to the present. She could hear the bustle and mild chaos in the coach cabin as everyone stood en-masse to debark, and she knew that she would be afforded the courtesy of leaving the aircraft before anyone from back there was able to part the curtain. She always travelled lightly, and had only her small attaché, her purse, and her notebook.

Having an unlimited expense account worldwide was liberating, and, at times, quite necessary. Maggie wasn't in a rush to get off the plane, so she watched as the other passengers pushed and crowded each other in an attempt to get off the plane first. She shook her head when the young man in front of her knocked into an elderly lady causing her to fall roughly into the arm of the seat she was trying to vacate and landed on the floor in front of her. Maggie stood and shouldered her way past a couple of people to get to the woman and helped her to her feet. This caused more than a few grumbles because Maggie purposefully stood in the aisle blocking anyone from leaving before the older woman. The woman looked at Maggie, a little dazed and rubbing what Maggie could only assume were very sore ribs.

"I'm sorry for getting in everyone's way," she said diminutively.

"You have nothing to be sorry for. That boy was careless." Maggie said with a scowl. "He wasn't concerned with anything or anyone but himself. Are you alright?" Maggie thought she was more upset about the incident than the older woman, who seemed to take it in stride, almost expectantly, as if this sort of thing happened to her all of the time.

How sad, Maggie thought. Maybe that would be her next piece-the way the youth of the world treated the elderly.

With a sigh, Maggie let the elderly woman in front of her and made sure she got off the plane without further incident. She helped the woman, whose name she learned was Ruth, up the ramp to the jetway. She walked next to Ruth inside the hollow, metal tube, and she could feel the temperature shift from the pleasant, albeit stuffy, circulated airplane air to the hammer of near-100 degree misery that was waiting for them once they left the air-conditioned terminal. She knew this sort of heat could be dangerous for people of advanced age or the infirm, and she hoped that Ruth would be taken care of and taken to some comfortable setting to relax.

As they reached the door to the terminal, Ruth's family was waiting for her, and welcomed her with open arms. Maggie trailed a pace or two behind the scene and stepped up to explain what happened on the plane. She was horrified when the man she initially approached, who turned out to be her son, scolded Ruth and admonished her to not be in such a rush, and that she should learn to be more careful. That earned the man Maggie's ire, but when she stepped forward to say something to him, she found Ruth had reached forward and gently laid her hand on Maggie's arm. Maggie looked down into the eyes of this very gentle woman and saw forgiveness and maybe a little sadness there.

Ruth just gave a small shake of her head, and with a melancholic smile said to Maggie, "Read Matthew 5:44." Turning back to her son and family, she announced that she was hungry and tired and asked them to take her home. Her son just shook his head and ushered them all out of the terminal.

"Thanks for your help, lady" the man called weakly over his shoulder. Maggie found herself standing inside the gate. She couldn't recall the last time anyone had mentioned a Bible verse in her presence, let alone asked her to read one. Maggie had actually written a compelling piece not 18 months ago about the death of the Bible and other religious texts as a source of guidance for society, with most people preferring to live according to their whims and societal norms, with some even fashioning their own moral code based on their own justifications and opinions.

Chaos and noise erupted on her senses like Krakatoa, breaking her reverie. Myriad conversations in several languages, shouts, children's crying and screaming, and terminal intercom announcements—*the music of doing business*—Maggie called them, greeted her. She wound her way through the throng to a small coffee vendor with a spare seat. She placed her attaché and purse on an empty chair a few steps from the order counter, and being late morning on a Tuesday, she didn't have much competition when it came to getting her coffee right away. She held her notebook in her hand, along with her smartphone, as she waited for her tall Americano. The phone, she paid with. The notebook never left her sight, or her grasp, if she could help it. She found herself frowning at the little notebook that wove continuously the tale of her life while on assignment.

My life as a reporter, as an agent, my diary, my story as a person... it is all there. Worth its weight in whatever passes for gold these days, she thought. She had considered, more than once, transferring its contents to some sort of digital storage, but that was a project for another day. She knew she would have to do it eventually, but there was comfort in being able to rub her hands over the old cover, open it, and impress upon its pages whatever she had to say to it. It was their secret, and it was worth keeping safe.

She amused herself with watching the activity passing her, and she sat sipping her coffee. Her hand went to the pendant around her neck without thinking about it, a habit she had picked up shortly after she started wearing the small device. Designed for her by her LACE tech team, it appeared to be a teardrop-shaped crystal of aquamarine, flat towards the bottom, but faceted and very sparkly. It was designed to look elegant, yet not flashy enough to steal, which was a good thing, because it contained the most sophisticated digital micro recorder ever conceived.

Maggie was never without it, and she never stopped recording—another habit. It had saved her more times than she could count, and she smiled thinking of what it had heard over the years. She patted the crystal, took the last sip of her coffee, to just about half-way—another idiosyncrasy she possessed, never finishing a beverage unless it's water—and deposited the paper cup into the nearest bin.

Maggie gathered her things and made her way to rent a car for the duration of her stay. She reached the outbuilding that served as the rental facility and decided she would languish in the air-conditioning a moment before approaching the counter.

She pressed a small button on her phone and spoke, "Call Max."

He answered on the second ring, which told Maggie he was not busy and not anywhere near his father.

"Max, I'm in Miami," Maggie squealed into the phone. She was only faking a little of her glee. While she was excited to be in Miami, she was also worried about her reception. She hadn't told Max she was coming and hoped that it would be okay with him. It was risky showing up unannounced, even if it was Max that would be receiving her. Lately she had pressed her luck a bit more with Max, and she knew it. Maggie had been able to parlay his feelings for her into increased access to the organization and their goings-on, which she had to hope would lead ultimately to Max's deviant father and his associates.

I cannot wait to nail that sick son of a bitch. Her thoughts were abruptly interrupted by a voice on the other end of her phone.

"Maggie, why are you in Miami?" Max asked her.

"I missed you. I thought it would be a nice surprise. You aren't mad, are you? Please say you're not angry. I couldn't bear it," she pouted prettily into the phone.

"I—I missed you as well, but I might not be in town very long. For how long are you here?"

"For how long are you?" Maggie teased. She could hear some muffled, hurried Russian on the other end of the phone.

"Where are you now?" he asked.

"I'm renting a car to take me to the hotel," she said with a smile.

"Do not. Boris and I will be there in 10 minutes. Go have a drink in the bar. I will meet you there." Max's voice took on an authoritative tone that Maggie disliked sometimes, but in this instance, she found it charming. It was endearing that he wanted to take care of her.

"Okay. I'll wait for 10minutes, but if you guys aren't here by then I'm renting a car," she told him. She had to let him know that, while she was allowing him to take care of her, it was an allowance she was extending, and she by no means needed him. Also, she wasn't going to wait forever.

"I'm already on my way, moye serdtse." He hung up before she could ask what he said, and she smiled at her phone. She spoke fluent Russian, in addition to the French, German, Spanish, Greek, and Farsi that she knew, but Max didn't need to know that, and his father definitely didn't need to know.

Can't know, she thought. *If he ever found out, it would be very bad, very quickly, for a lot of people. People she cared about.* She reluctantly exited the outbuilding into the heat, and made her way quickly back across the terminal, wending her way to the bar. As she threaded her way through the crowd, she bit her lip and thought she was getting way too attached to Max.

She could see the bar, but decided to make a small detour to the ladies' room to freshen up her makeup and change into the shorts and top she brought with her. She was smart enough to know that Florida was hot and humid first, beautiful second. She slipped on the cute wedges that showed off her legs and slid her flip flops into her Fendi bag. She fluffed her hair, applied some lip gloss, and slid on her oversized Chanel sunglasses before leaving the bathroom and making a beeline for the bar.

On her way, Maggie saw that the kid who had knocked Ruth down earlier was still in the airport. He looked frustrated and was making his way towards the bathrooms. Maggie smiled and turned on the charm, swiveled a bit as she walked, and that was pretty much all it took. The young man, who was watching her instead of where he was going, swiftly found himself sprawled out on the ground as he tripped over the luggage of an elderly man waiting for his wife outside the ladies' room. Maggie turned her face from the scene and thought it was only fitting.

Serves you right. Maggie sat down at the bar. She looked at the time on her Cartier, and finding that it was after noon, ordered herself a Dewar's neat and a cosmo. The Dewar's was for her, a love she and her dad shared, and the cosmo was for the *other* Maggie—the character she was playing to penetrate the Russian mafia. Maggie thought, as she downed half the scotch, about the various layers, carefully manufactured and applied, that went into the woman that Max thought she was. The clothes, the makeup, the food and drink preferences, the back story and fake occupation. He had been hard to warm up, and the persona acted as an effective ice breaker, once the research into Maxim Avatov's ideal woman had been done.

Painstakingly slow to gather, yet just like Max, reliable and consistent, the intel her field team had gathered allowed her to slip right into Max's circle like a sultry movie minx, and she had gained his confidence the old-fashioned way—with her looks and flattery. That was fine, until she realized that she had actually fallen for him, and in a big way. She found herself genuinely enthralled with his stories, engaged in emotional and meaningful conversations instead of letting her reporter's instincts lead her to finding answers. She cared about his standing with his father, and she knew that he lived a tenuous existence, not quite assured of his father's favor; the reluctant, dutiful scion of a disgusting and illicit legacy.

Max didn't belong in the world in which he found himself. He was good. He was honorable. Lev Avatov didn't deserve Max for a son—but did Max deserve the hurt and betrayal that Maggie would eventually bestow on him, once she got what she needed?

Is this story worth all of that? she thought. She shook her head as if to clear the cobwebs. *Of course it is,* she told herself. *Don't be a damn idiot. You know what's riding on this. You have to dig, and keep digging, until you can put Lev Avatov and his ilk away forever.*

Maggie spotted Max entering the bar and quickly stashed the rocks glass behind the counter, grabbed hold of the cosmo and took a large gulp. *Ugh,* she hated these foofy drinks.

He spotted her and made his way through the crowd at the front of the bar.

God, he is gorgeous .she thought.

He was wearing a navy blue suit with a crisp white shirt and no tie. The collar of his shirt was open to the third button, revealing just a hint of the tattoo that Maggie knew lay beneath. She sucked in a sharp breath when he smiled in her direction. His features going from granite to welcoming and sexy in the space of a heartbeat.

Oh man, thought Maggie, *I am in serious trouble.* She smiled at Max, and when he stopped in front of her she threw herself into his arms. "Max." She looked up at him and was pleased to see that he was actually glad to see her and wasn't angry that she was in Miami at all.

Max leaned down and kissed her on the cheek. "We do not have much time together, but I am glad you are here moye serdtse," he told her with a smile.

"What does that mean, Max?"

"It means *my heart*."

Maggie felt herself blushing and took Max's hand as he grabbed her bags in the other. Max led Maggie out of the bar and through the doors to a waiting limo. Maggie beamed at Max as the driver opened the door to the limo and bid them enter. "Boris, we need to go to…?"

"The Winfrey," she told Max.

"What? No, that will not do. You will stay where I am staying," he told her.

"But Max," she protested, "I don't have the money to stay somewhere else." She pouted and looked dolefully at her boyfriend.

Maggie hated pretending to be so flighty, but it was worth it when Max said, "My condo has more than enough rooms. You will stay there." In Max's mind it was settled. Maggie feigned gratitude at not having to pay for a hotel. This could be disastrous or a godsend. She let her mind dream of the dirt that she could uncover on Lev, but was nervous about staying with Max so close in his condo. She was already tempted by Max, so she wasn't sure what staying at his condo would do to her already-struggling heart.

She settled back against the seat and waited for Max to get into the vehicle. Max spoke quickly with the driver then climbed into the back of the limo with Maggie.

"We will be taking a quick detour. I have some business to take care of before we can go back to the condo," Max told her. The sleek black limo pulled away from the curb and had only traveled about a hundred yards before turning onto a side street that would take them to the cargo office.

"Ooh Max, are you getting ready to ship that dusty old stuff you bought in New Orleans?" Maggie asked him. Max scrutinized Maggie for a moment before he replied.

"Yes, there is the matter of payment which I need to discuss with my pilot. He will take the payment to Mr.—"

"McCreepy in New Orleans?" she asked with an innocent expression.

Max regarded Maggie for a moment before he answered. "I like that. It is appropriate." Max smiled and patted her leg. "My pilot will pay Mr. McCreepy. Then I will need to arrange for shipment."

"To Russia? To your father?" She knew she was pressing her luck again, and she tried to sound as innocently curious as possible; just his girlfriend wanting to be involved in his life, nothing more. *Might as well play it to the hilt*, she thought. "What does your father want with a load of old bones?" Maggie knew she had made a mistake as soon as she asked the question.

"How did you know about the skeletons, myshka?"

Damn. She thought lightning-quick. "I heard you and that geezer talking. I'm sorry, Max, but you were getting pretty loud. I heard that you wanted to buy some bones, and I thought it was weird, but hey who am I to judge what is important to other people?" Maggie finished in a rush hoping Max had bought the story. She was certain he knew she was eavesdropping but was relieved when he finished his silent assessment.

Maggie could tell he must have thought her story had merit because he told her, "They are very important to my father. Do not be concerned with them, though—they will be leaving in a couple of days. Unfortunately, I will be leaving with them." Maggie saw a look of immense dislike travel across Max's face before he could turn away. The driver stopped the car in front of a massive hangar. Maggie could see numerous large crates and two huge cargo planes being loaded for transport. There was a small group of people in front of the hanger and two of them, who looked like pilots to Maggie, had squared off against each other. A big bear of a man was yelling and pointing a meaty finger at the smaller man. The smaller man was trying in vain to placate the bigger pilot, gesticulating in a way that said he didn't know how to help the big man.

The limousine stopped next to the two men. Max stepped out and extended a hand to Maggie. Maggie alighted from the car and came face to face with the big pilot. Maggie blinked into the strangest eyes she had ever seen—very pale and green, with flecks of gold; they were quite striking, as was the man. Maggie made him at about six foot three or four, Latin, probably Hispanic, with very dark, very thick shoulder length hair that made him look like he belonged in a band, not in a cockpit. Broad shoulders, tanned skin, large hands and feet, but her intuition told her that he was more likely to talk himself out of a fight than start one.

She took a step back and bumped into the car. He didn't intimidate her exactly, but he was very attractive, and from the looks of it, very angry. He didn't spare a glance for Maggie as he brushed past and put his long index finger in Max's face.

"I don't like it when someone messes with my deliveries, Max," he growled. "I had the flight plan already laid out and submitted. All I required was a payload, and now you have me flying to New Orleans?" The big pilot almost spat the words at Max, who just stood there with a calm expression.

"Are you finished?" He took stock of the man's expression and continued, "It will be fine, Sam."

The pilot started in again. "Fine? You said it was important that we get the cargo to your father as soon as possible—something about a deadline, and now you have me flying to that stinking backwater four hours out of my way. It's going to cost, Max. Where *exactly* is the cargo, oso? Soon as possible does not mean *four hours* out of my way, or *five days* from now. I'm fairly certain Lev expects me there in two days. That means as soon as these crates are loaded,

I'm outta of here. Original plan, original cargo, no deviations. I *don't* like change, Max."

Max raised an eyebrow at the big pilot. "Remember, you do not work for my father," Max told him. "You work for me, and you will go where I tell you or not at all. Understood?" Max eyed the big pilot, "I like you, Samuel…"

"Sam," the big man butted in, grinding his teeth.

"Sam," Max corrected, "but you are replaceable. I do not want to replace you, frankly, so let us work past this. You just fly—leave my father and his plans to me, no?"

Maggie watched the exchange silently, reading the expressions of both men. She could tell the larger man was getting to Max by the small twitch at the corner of his mouth. Sam was an enigma, and Maggie felt somewhere in her gut that even had she known the large pilot before that day and that conversation, it would take many lifetimes to plumb his depths. No, she didn't know him, doubted anyone could, really, but she could tell by his bearing that he was not used to being told what to do. That struck Maggie as odd, considering the two men seemed to do a lot of business together.

"You know what the cargo is, and what needs to happen when you arrive in New Orleans," Max told him. "We have done business before, and I appreciate the way you work. There will be a bonus for you upon completion, provided you keep your decorum and my confidence. Please, consider this as a favor to me, repayable when you wish. I will take care of my father."

"Your cargo," Sam spat, with a look of disgust, "is precisely my problem. This is the *last* time I do this, you get me, oso?" Sam appeared to be weighing his options. He stalked away, a dark tiger pacing his concrete and tarmac cage. He alternately pounded on his thighs with his fist in agitation and swatted at an imaginary fly doing sorties around his temples. He turned around and walked back to Max, resigned. "Fine. But you owe me big this time, Max." The dark man sighed, and looked resigned. "We've been through a lot, oso. You know how much I hate this stuff."

Max smiled and took Maggie's hand. "No more than I, and, thank you, Sam. I will come and sign the orders for you, and we will discuss the terms of our arrangement." Max slapped Sam on the back and turned to Maggie. "Maggie, I would like to introduce you to the best pilot you will ever meet. This is Samuel Ramos."

"Sam," he said with exasperation. Forgetting Max, he turned to Maggie, fixing her with his incredible eyes. He extended a mammoth, and Maggie noticed, immaculately manicured hand, and smiled.

"Nice to meet you, Magdalene. Sam Ramos, at your *full* service."

Maggie twitched at the mention of her proper first name, but figured Max must have talked about her to his friend in conversations past. She finally got a good look at Sam. *He sure is pretty*, she thought. *Built like a power forward, hair as dark as the night sky, adobe-colored complexion that set off his angular features, and those eyes. What a striking man.*

The corners of Sam's lips turned up in a grin, like he could hear Maggie's thoughts. Disconcerted, she thrust out her hand and uttered a somewhat embarrassed, "Pleased to meet you," to Sam.

Sam's smile grew bigger as he took her hand and bent low to kiss her knuckles. A different kind of look suddenly crossed his face, and Maggie knew instantly, the way a good journalist does, that at least one of the Sams she was going to meet today was an imposter. She had worn that look early in her career, and it had signaled that a bit of acting was about to take place. Maggie had become quite expert at flipping her switch without giving anyone cause to doubt her, but what she saw from Sam was a fumbling, awkward reset of an entire three-act stage, with no manager helping with the curtain. Someone was getting fooled. Maggie had yet to determine who—but she had him, and she could probably use this revelation to her advantage at some point.

"What's a hot dish like you doing rolling around with a bowl of borscht like him?" he asked, jerking his thumb toward the now-perturbed Russian as his lips lingered over Maggie's hand. Maggie blushed prettily and was about to answer coyly when Max growled.

"Come, kiska," Max said, stealing her hand away before Sam's lips could make contact with Maggie's knuckles. "He has work to attend, and I have you to entertain." He took her arm and without looking back, exited the hangar.

While walking to the waiting limo, Maggie got the feeling she was being watched. She looked around, trying to spot the obvious lurker or badly-concealed henchman and got nothing for her efforts. The only person she saw looking in their direction was their driver and Max's cousin, Boris.

Nothing unusual there, she thought. He didn't look happy, but she assumed the look on his face was for the pilot, not Max. They kept walking past the crates being loaded into the cargo planes, and Maggie took in as much information as she could without giving away how interested she was with the crates and boxes.

Large crate, three men, two strapped with AKs and one seemingly unarmed. Why would a single crate need triple guarding? Maggie inadvertently tripped over some cords in her path, and Max pulled her up by the arms to keep her from tumbling over.

"Careful. This place is full of things that will ruin your shoes," he told her with concern.

Genuine concern, Maggie thought as she looked at him. He was acting out of kindness because of the exchange she had had with Peter coming out of The Royal, not knowing that she couldn't care less about the shoes at all. She was playing a part, and she was getting in deeper than she ever had. She gripped Max's arm tighter as they made it to the office. Maggie waited as the necessary documents were completed for Sam to travel, and Max took the clipboard from the attendant, ushering Maggie back toward the limo. Boris was waiting to open the door, a smile on his face, and nodded when they approached.

Yep, must have been for Sam, she thought. *Boris obviously has something against the big pilot.* She smiled at Boris as he opened the door, and she took her seat in the back of the black Mercedes.

"Wait here. I will return momentarily." Max brushed her cheek with the back of his hand, closed her door and said something to Boris. The driver gave a compliant nod and resumed his place in the front. Max walked swiftly to the hangar, exchanged a couple of words with Sam, pulled out a roll of bills, peeling off quite a few to attach to the clipboard along with the papers, and handed the bundle to the tall pilot. As Sam and Max shook hands again, Maggie watched for any other clues to the history between the two men. Her attention had been focused on the handshake, but her eyes drifted up to the faces of the men. Maggie was startled to see that Sam was looking directly at her with a half-smile and a single cocked eyebrow.

I know you. I know your secret. You will know mine when the time is right. Maggie shot back from the window, heart racing.

What the hell was that? She had imagined his words, spoken directly into her thoughts. She was very adept at reading people, and she felt for sure Sam was clueless to her and her real intentions. *Yeah, you're just closer to the edge on this one than you have been, and it's making you nervous. Relax, there's no way he could know anything about you*, she thought. The door opened next to her, giving her another start, but she quickly got it together again as Max entered the car.

"Now we can go home, Boris." This time Maggie was sure she had seen a flash of hatred pass over Boris's face after Max had turned away. Boris caught Maggie's stare and gave her a look so cold she shivered in response. Max looked at Maggie, and she managed a small smile for him in return.

Very interesting, Maggie thought. *Boris doesn't like Max, and Max doesn't know.* She made a note to ask Max more about Boris later. They were getting to the end game, and she had to turn up the heat. The girls were secure in that hangar and on their way to New Orleans. Each one of those kids wore Suse's face. She knew that she couldn't let anything happen to them. She doubted that she could disrupt things enough to keep them in Miami, so she sat back in the car and tried to think of a reason for Max to take her to Russia.

Chapter 10

Momma Rose was busily cleaning her already spotless countertop when the chime above the little door to her bistro announced the arrival of someone. She deposited the washrag that she had been scrubbing with into one of many pockets in her voluminous apron and turned to the door, brushing her gray hair back from her face. She exited the small offshoot dining area into the main one,and looked toward the door to see who was entering. The smile she wore was rare in the Quarter; a genuine smile for every person that entered her place. Where most proprietors there would give one pasted in place by years of under-tipping, drunk partygoers, Rose was grateful and humble when anyone visited her. When she saw who it was entering her establishment, the smile was joined by a hurried jog to embrace the patron.

"Michel," she said coming up and throwing her arms around him in genuine pleasure. "Ça fait trop longtemps. Où vous êtes-vous cache? (It has been too long. Where have you been hiding?)" Rose broke into easy French around Michael, and he hugged her back and chuckled.

"English, Rose. Otherwise, you're not playing fair."

She went on, hardly cowed, "Well, fine then. Where have you been?"

Michael released his embrace of the diminutive woman and said, "I have been working, Rose, as have we all. It's time to bring in some help." He stepped to the side and allowed his companion to enter. "I believe you know Abe Sims?" he said, one eyebrow cocked.

"Hello again, Abraham. So good to see you. Come, out of the street." Michael turned to Abe and excused himself to talk briefly with Rose at a table. Abe watched as the old officer and the small woman sat and quietly chatted, wondering what sort of situation he had gotten himself into.

"Michel, it really is so good to see you. But why now? I must know what you have been doing." Momma Rose grasped his hands and spoke excitedly, but something in Michael's countenance halted her questions and made her sit up, alert, and drop the angel's hands from hers.

"Rose, we are going to have help, and not just Abe. Please," he spoke, smiling, "call up to Peter and ask him to join us." Michael saw the reaction from the old woman that he was expecting. Rose's face fell at the announcement that Peter was to be involved. "Rose, this is a good thing. Peter so wants to be of use and to make a difference. He doesn't completely understand right now, but that understanding will come. You know better than any that his day was coming—why so glum?" Michael questioned her, patting her arm.

"Master's plan, Master's time, Master's choices," she said slowly as she worked toward calming her heart. "I only question it because I am his mother, as any good parent would when their child could be hurt—Michael, I *am* his mother," she said to Michael's raised, corrective hand. "I know that Claire bore him and raised him to adolescence, but I have kept him fed and safe and loved since he was 17, and I love him as if he were of my womb, right alongside my Jeanne. I will not fight this. God knows. He," she pointed to her tiled ceiling, but indicated well beyond it, "knows best, and I trust *you* to take care of Peter. Surround him with our best and make him the hero I know him to be, Michel. That is my ask." While she spoke, tears escaped the corners of her eyes, which had finally crinkled into a weak smile.

"I would not bear this lightly, Rose. What you give to the mission today is precious, and I love Peter. Do not forget that we have been well connected for these 13 years. I will not let anything befall him."

Rose stood, grasped the angel tightly, and then reached into her apron for the washrag she had deposited their earlier. She wiped the table where they had been sitting, brushed off her hands, smoothed back her hair, and dabbed at her eyes.

"Let us return to Abraham. Incidentally, what does he know?" she asked.

"Just what he knew years ago, and he's about to find out the rest, so we will need sugar and caffeine in copious amounts. Abe is going to be a very strong asset, as will Peter. This is exciting stuff."

Michael hugged her again, smiling, and she said, "Come, I will get you two seated and call for Peter."

She led the two men to a small room at the back of her bistro. The room held a small table and chairs for four. This was where Momma Rose and her daughter, Jeanne, took tea in the afternoons.

Strange, she thought, *that this room where so much light and airy conversation had taken place, most not the least bit serious, would be the setting for something eternally significant. There is eternal significance in everything,* she reminded herself. *Even in the mundane conversations between mother and daughter that happen over afternoon tea.*

The sunlit winter streamed through the small window directly to their right, and it cast the room in an otherworldly light, as if their meeting were being tended by the Master Himself, which, she knew, was true. Momma Rose liked the space and thought how appropriate that it should all start here for Peter. *Her* Peter. If Peter were to be used of the Master, to her there was no greater calling, and she was going to be supportive and proud, just as if it had been Jeanne that had been chosen.

Plus, she told herself, *she had Michael's assurances, and if you cannot trust an angel, who can you trust?*

She looked back at the two men who trailed her, and watched them as they entered; neither man walked timidly. Both Abe and the angel walked with confidence and strength, albeit a bit more slowly in Abraham's case, she thought. His years had caught up to him recently, but she knew him to be a wise tactician and a caring and patient mentor. Michael was right; he would be a valuable member of the team. Momma Rose gestured for them to have a seat and said, characteristically, "Michel, I know you do not eat, but," Rose turned to Abe, "you look like you could use something to eat, oui?"

She turned to let herself back into the kitchen when Michael called after her, "Whoa. Not so fast, Rose. You don't even know what he was after, do you?"

She turned back to the table, huffed slightly and smiled. "I have been feeding this wonderful man on and off for years—he will take a black coffee and two hot beignets, as always. Isn't that so, Abraham?"

Michael looked slightly dazed, and Abe burst into laughter, pointing at his friend. "Oh, man. You should see your face, Mike." Then, to the small woman, "Yes, Momma Rose, that is exactly right."

Michael just shrugged and said, "You know, she really doesn't miss a trick, does she? Glad she's on our side."

"Ok, cap—*our side*? Seriously, what is happening? What are we about to get into here?" Abe was visibly frustrated, still not exactly sure where he was or what was transpiring.

Ignoring him for the moment, Michael spoke again to the woman. "Rose, please call up to Peter and ask him to join us," he repeated, for Abe's benefit this time.

The smile on Rose's face faltered a bit but she nodded once and was out the door calling for her daughter to take over the shop.

"What's going on, Mike? What does she mean you don't eat, man? I've seen you take out an entire pizza before." Michael grinned, sat back in his chair and steepled his fingers under his chin, considering his answer. Abe went on, "Also, it doesn't look like she wants to bring Peter into whatever it is you want me to get involved in. I don't know how to feel about that." Abe looked at Michael with an arched eyebrow.

"This is a plan long in the making, and you and Rose are players in this great game," Michael told him, arms spread to encompass what Abe imagined was everything. "When I explain who we are and what the mission is, you will have a choice to make. If you decide it is not for you, then no harm, no foul. Life goes on. But I know you, chief. You are one of the most selfless humans I have ever met. Over the thousands of years you all have been around, anyway. Abe, before you ask—here it is, again, just like I told you in that field hospital in Bahrain thirty years ago—I'm an angel, well, actually *the* angel, His First. I'm Michael, and you've known that in your heart for a while. That," he gestured to the symbol hanging around Abe's neck, "is my sigil, and you've been under my protection since 1990. You have been chosen for the greatest mission, which," he motioned to the back stairs and the noise of Rose descending, "you are about to find out all about."

Abe sat agog, but only briefly. "You're right, and that's weird. I *did* know it, somehow. This is heavy, though." He sat, contemplating, and the angel almost laughed at what he knew was coming next. "You *really* don't eat?"

Michael laughed and shook his head no. He reached over to grab his friend's hand and said, "I know this is a lot to take in, chief, believe me. You *can* say no," Michael said with the confidence of someone who didn't think a rejection was going to be coming.

"You would tell me this and then let me go back to my normal routine, knowing the information you told me?" Abe asked him.

"I guess you will have to take my word for it." Michael said. "We don't force people to help us, we ask—nicely. I will say this, Abe," Michael shrouded his face in seriousness, and Abe paid closer attention, if that were possible. "I have known you half your life, and I know the man—the *soul* you are. You will accept, because you have *always* been meant for this. You are a man of honor, and love and sacrifice is in your blood—just like someone else I knew, a long time ago. You remind me of him."

Michael smiled and started humming under his breath. Abe couldn't make out the words, but the greatest sense of peace and warmth spread throughout his body. He relaxed back into his chair, a smile on his face, and waited for the other parties to gather. A few moments passed and Momma Rose came back into the little room carrying a tray with four cups, a pot of steaming coffee, a basket of delicious beignets, and a plate of sliced, fresh strawberries.

Abe watched as Momma Rose set a beignet in front of him. "Bless you, Momma Rose," Abe said as he picked up his beignet and tucked in.

Momma Rose smiled and said, "It is my greatest pleasure. I love when people enjoy my food so much." She turned to Michael and said, "Peter will be down in a moment, and Jeanne will watch the bistro while we talk. Michel, tell me about my Peter. What is his role? I worry…" she said, trailing off.

"I know, Rose, but this is the chance we have been waiting for. I feel that now is the right time to have this conversation. As you are aware, Peter has recently remembered the events that have led him here, and we have already discussed the things that are harder to believe. He *believes* them. He is ready. I think if Peter has accepted the outlandish truth, now he just needs to accept his role and our mission."

Abe sat listening, wide-eyed, wondering what was coming. Peter backed through the door at that moment, a beignet clenched between his teeth, another in his hand, along with a mountain of napkins, and a cup of coffee. He turned to the table and came to a complete stop. He saw that Michael was sitting next to Momma Rose, and his mind started to work, furiously. Michael and Momma Rose obviously knew each other, but did she *know* Michael? He was dressed in a polo and jeans, and he looked a bit different than the last time he had seen him—a bit older, maybe? And he seemed more clean-cut, like a soldier, but there was no doubt it was Michael.

He also noted that the man from Dr. Jo's office, Abe, was also among them at the table, and he looked sort of confused. What was going on? He was pretty sure that introductions would be made and was proven correct when Michael jumped up, came around the table, and clapped Peter on the back.

"Peter, it is good to see you again," said Michael, grabbing the napkins and his coffee. Michael pulled a chair out and set the coffee and napkins down, taking the other beignet out of Peter's hand, placing it on the plate in the middle of the table. "Peter, I think you two have crossed paths if we have done our job right, but let me introduce you anyway: Abe Sims, he is an old and dear friend, as well as a talented pilot. Master willing, you two will be working together soon."

Peter finished off the beignet in his mouth, swallowed, brushed the powdered sugar from his hands, and reached out to shake the old man's extended hand.

"A pleasure to meet you formally, Abe," Peter said. He turned and spoke to the small woman wringing her hands with worry. "Momma Rose, *ce qui donne? Tu le connais? (What gives? You know him?)*" Peter asked her in confusion.

Michael rolled his eyes skyward, smiling, and reiterated for Peter's benefit, "English, folks. We aren't going to get anything done with French today."

Momma Rose looked at Michael and then at Peter and said, "Michael and I are old friends, Peter, much as you two are." Rose gave Peter a knowing look, and Peter's sense of confusion grew until Michael, who still had his arm around Peter's shoulder, pushed him into the nearest seat and said, "All in due time, Peter. All in due time."

Peter sat back against the chair he had been pushed into and noticed the food and drink on the table. He looked sheepishly at Momma Rose, and she just shook her head and laughed.

"Always you think with your stomach, mon chou. Today, I think, you eat all you want. And listen." He helped himself to another beignet and some coffee and waited to hear what needed to be said.

"Peter, we already had a discussion regarding the things that go bump in the night, but do you mind if I bring Abe up to speed?" Michael asked him. "I promise that I will get to why you are here in a moment."

Peter looked at Abe, who shrugged, so Peter did the same to Michael. Michael smiled and turned to Abe.

"Do you remember the stories that I used to tell you in the cave? While you recovered from your injuries so long ago?"

A look of confusion wormed across Abe's features, and he muttered, "Sure do, those stories were some doozies," Abe said with a grin, glad to be back in familiar territory.

"Everything I told you was the truth." Michael looked Abe straight in the eye as he said those words, and Abe got the feeling he was being judged on his reaction.

"Everything? None of what you talked about was believable, Mike, and some of those stories were pretty scary. Of course, what you just told me a few minutes ago is right up there, so..." Abe said. He stopped and shrugged and repeated, incredulously, "Everything?"

Michael nodded to Abe and said, an eyebrow raised, "Everything."

Abe swallowed and thought of all the stories of creatures that preyed on humans, and the angelic forces that fought against them. He had enjoyed listening to the stories in the Zagros, anything to take his mind off what was happening around him and how much pain he was in. He had thought at the time that his young officer friend was an excellent storyteller; that he may go on to be a great author or screenwriter someday, and he appreciated the man giving him something to think about other than his impending death at the hands of the insurgents. Abe looked up into the blue eyes of his longtime friend and could see the truth behind his statement.

"Okay. Wow, but okay. What does that have to do with me?" Abe asked him. "I'm too old to go out fighting monsters. I'm not some damn Terminator."

Michael chuckled and said, "I wouldn't want you to fight in that way, we have—people for that." Peter and Abe looked at Michael with the same confused look.

"You have ninjas? Oh, please, tell me you have ninjas. When can I meet them?" asked Peter with awe in his voice.

Michael chuckled again, "Yes, and yes, but not right now. Now we are having a different conversation. I want to tell you about the organization. It's old, it's vast, and it was put together to fight the creatures you were told about—and some you weren't. Needless to say," said Michael, rising from his seat to do his usual pacing, "you are being thrown into a diverse mix with a lot of resources, skill, and firepower. Let me tell you how you guys can be heroes." Michael, turning toward the light-effused window, smiled and raised his hand in a small salute. Turning back to the table, he continued, "As I've said many times to both of you, we need your help." Michael pointed first to himself and then at Momma Rose. Peter looked from Michael to Momma Rose, aghast.

"We? You know about this? *Knew* about this?" Peter asked Momma Rose, rising from the table roughly. Rose winced a little at the hurt in Peter's voice, but answered him with an affirmative shake of her head.

She spoke softly, "Mon chou, it was going to come. I was going to tell you—how could I not? I just did not know that day would be today, in this place."

"Do not be angry with her, Peter," Michael said, coming to Momma Rose's defense. "She has been with me—with *us,* a long time and came here to watch over and protect you. Everything she has done, she has done out of love and duty. Remember when I told you that there would be others put in your path to help you? Momma Rose was sent when the enemy first recognized your family, Peter. She was there when you were bitten by the snakes, and she was watching you the night the enemy took your parents." Michael's voice took on a hard edge and Peter was stunned by the implication of the words that Michael just uttered.

"What do you mean, *took*? They weren't taken—they died in an accident. Are you telling me that my Mom and Dad were killed? By monsters?" Peter asked Michael, overwhelmed and angry. Stammering, he continued, "So, so, so—if we were under *your* protection, why did they die, huh? Whose purpose did *that* serve?" Peter asked the question that he had been thinking, not sure if he really wanted to hear the answer, as Rose started to softly cry.

"I'm sorry, Peter," Michael said, reaching out to steady Rose and put a calming hand on her shoulder. "We were there the night they died, but the grunch were there as well..." Michael's voice trailed off and Peter spoke into the silence.

"Grunch? No. No. They don't exist," he said, shaking his head. The grunch were terrifying when you were six or so, but became a sort of joke to the rest of the bayou adults. Grunch were little bloodsucking troll things that mommas scared their unruly babies with. An old wives' tale. *An old wives' tale that had murdered my parents*, he thought sadly. He shook his head again and said, as if willing it to be true, that somehow the words could undo what had been done, "The grunch do not exist. They don't exist."

Still, he thought about everything Michael told him about vampires and werewolves. *If they exist, then logically the grunch exist, too.* Everything he ever feared exists, apparently.

"Yes, they exist, and a group of them ambushed your father and mother as they were driving back to your home that night. We had one of our agents following their car because our intel had told us the Collective was moving, and your parents had been made, but the sheer number of them that night was astounding. Your father tried to evade them, but the grunch are related to the vampire and possess the same unearthly speed. Even after our contingent thinned their numbers, they were still too many. Your father lost control of the car trying to get away, and it crashed—off the bridge into the water. The grunch had our people tied up and they couldn't get to your parents in time." Michael crossed to stand behind Peter and conveyed with his face the sympathy that he felt for the young man. "They never made it out of the car."

Peter wasn't aware he was crying until he felt a drop on his hand. It had been years since his parents' death, but he still missed them. Peter returned to the table and wiped his eyes on his sleeve, sitting, almost missing the chair.

This is so much for him to take in, thought Rose. *Not a boy, no—not anymore, but still so naïve in many ways.* She wished that she could spare him—continue sparing him, from what he was learning now.

She *tsked* and handed him a napkin, stroking his hair. Peter smiled sheepishly at her and with a *thank you* blew his nose in the napkin.

"So, that's it. Monsters are real, the world is doomed, and we're supposed to somehow save it?" Peter was processing, speaking out loud, and suddenly seemed to remember that he was not alone in the room. He turned to the angel. "Thank you for telling me about what really happened to my parents. I knew they had drowned that night, but the sheriff's department could not find a reason for the accident. It wasn't raining, my parents weren't drinking, and I remember that my father had just put tires on the car before the accident. It never made sense to me," Peter said.

"Buckle up, kid," came Abe's voice from the opposite side of the table, "because I have a strong suspicion that a lot more stuff won't make sense before *this* day is over."

Chapter 11

The afternoon outside the little bistro wasn't aware of what was taking place inside La Cuisine Ouverte. The tourists still came and went, the sun traced its way across the sky, and the Mississippi continued to roll and roil. Life went on. Inside, at Rose's tea table, Abe couldn't have been more stunned by the conversation than if he had been hit by a bus. Vampires, werewolves, and the grunch, real? Amazing, and scary all at the same time.

Abe was never much of a movie-goer, but he had enjoyed the occasional Creature Feature on TV. That wasn't this. What he knew of the creatures that were suddenly very much real, had learned from Hollywood and popular culture, was definitely highly romanticized, inaccurate, and outdated hogwash. His mind suddenly flashed back to his time awaiting evac with Mike, and as he examined what he thought were fevered dreams of a wounded soldier in shock, he realized that he was not dreaming. He shuddered, and was suddenly very glad that he had given Naomi a can of mace and the self-defense lessons. Abe wasn't going to lie to himself—he did remember seeing things out in the desert. Some of the images he remembered seemed to come straight out of horror movies. Now, hearing that creatures like vampires and werewolves exist, he could totally imagine the horrors in the desert were real, and he could distinctly remember Michael, not Mike, making an appearance. A fierce angel warrior, wielding a gigantic gleaming sword, fighting—something away from Abe. Abe looked up into a pair of golden eyes and found the truth in their endless depths.

Michael turned back to Peter and said, "Are you ready to hear the rest, brother?"

Abe could hear the audible gulp that came from Peter before he said, "Yes. I think so."

Man, Abe thought, *the kid really did have guts. If all of this heavy stuff had been laid on me when I was in my 20s, I would lose my mind.* He wouldn't have thought it at first glance, but Peter was tough, and he had Abe's respect.

"Okay. Peter, I know we discussed this briefly, but I need to get Abe on the same page as us." Michael turned to include Abe in the rest of the story. "There is balance in all life," Michael started. "The Master created everything to have a place in this world, just like the tool outlines on your workbench," he smiled at Abe, "and the assigned places for your creations in your shop, Peter. Some of the angelic forces were sent to keep a watchful eye on the Master's creations." Michael stood and started to pace the small room. "As humans progressed through the ages, the Watchers were moved and developed feelings for the humans. They wanted to show them things to make their lives easier and were looked upon as gods themselves. They forged bonds with the daughters of Earth and created children with them. These children, *beings*," Michael corrected, "were formidable. Larger, stronger, faster, smarter, but they were savage in actions and beliefs; corrupt and lacking in compassion." Michael paused in his telling and turned to the others. "They were the cause of wars and suffering for many thousands of the Master's creations, both human and animal. Age upon age went by before the Master had had enough. He tried to reach the masses but in the end they were too far gone—given over to their wickedness and corrupted by the power of the Watcher children, the Nephilim—giants and abominations in the land of men, who caused destruction and chaos wherever they went. They were never happy with what they had, and were always in search of war and lands to conquer."

Abe thought that Michael was looking a little sickly with the retelling of this particular story, almost as if it physically hurt him to recount it.

"The Master had seen enough in the world to know it was not the same world He had originally created. Although it hurt to do so, the Master decided that the only recourse was a complete white out—cleansing the world completely with holiness and a fresh start."

Michael swallowed hard and Abe thought he could see a glisten in the angel's eyes. He sat up as a thought hit him.

"The flood was holy?" he asked Michael.

Michael turned to Abe, and with a sad smile he said, "Yes, the Great Deluge was consecrated and sent with the holiest of purposes. Since everything in the world was created by the Master, it had a place to go when the Master chose to send the flood to kill it. He had chosen to spare Noah as an incorruptible man, but he had also chosen to include Noah's wife and three sons. So, ideally, Noah would have closed the ark with his family and two of every land and air creature onboard."

Abe watched Peter nodding his head at the retelling, like he was listening in Sunday school class. Abe shook his head and looked to Michael, "I really hope you aren't going to tell us that Noah was a vampire or something—are you?" he asked concerned.

"No, Abe. I'm not. Point of fact, Noah and his family were the last pure humans on the Earth. When the Master flooded the earth, everything died except for what was in the sea or on the craft," Michael told his rapt audience. "Unfortunately, that did not get rid of the Nephilim taint on the Earth. You see, Noah petitioned the Master shortly before the flood to allow Shem, Ham, and Japheth to take wives. This was not in the Master's original plan, and the Master forbade it. Noah was so disheartened for his sons, that the Master, moved by the love he had for his sons, relented, and instructed Noah to find them wives. Noah did not have a lot to work with when choosing brides for his sons. He chose the best of what was available to him, choosing among the humble and devout, but even there, he could not escape the corrupted flesh. In two of the women, the taint was diluted but present," Michael said, and Rose began to softly weep and pray. Abe and Peter looked at her, and then each other, surprised, knowing the implications of what came next.

"After the flood water receded from the Earth and the doors to the ark were opened. Noah and his sons went in separate directions, charged by the Master to repopulate the Earth," Michael said looking at his audience in turn. "In the years following the flood, the population of the Earth began to grow, and creatures and humans of the Earth thrived. With each new generation the corruption grew a little more in the lines of Ham and Japheth. Their children received the taint through their wives, and their children passed it on to their children, and so on down the line. It was through these lines that they still work today," Michael said through gritted teeth.

Abe could tell that Michael was at a point in his retelling that he really didn't like. "Wait, how could the Nephilim use the tainted lines if they were all killed in the flood?" Peter asked, clearly confused about something.

"Now we are getting somewhere." Michael said excitedly. "When the Master created the world, every living thing in it had a place and a purpose. They were all part of the greater plan. Everything at that point that was supposed to exist, did. The Nephilim were not created by the Master, but by the Watchers. They did not have a place in the world, so when the Earth was flooded, their Earthly bodies perished, but because they were not created by the Master, there was no place for their souls to go. Do you understand, Peter?" Michael watched Peter for any sign that he was following what was going on.

Abe thought he understood, but checked his theory by asking, "So, because they weren't created by the Master, they couldn't go to heaven?"

Michael smiled broadly at Abe and said, "Or hell. They have no place except Earth in which they can dwell."

"But if they died, there shouldn't be any of them around to worry about," said Peter, still trying to comprehend this new information.

"Right," said Michael, "however, the spirit of the Nephilim, since they did not go to heaven or hell, had to find another way to survive. They found that they could attach themselves to any of the survivors that had the taint." Michael waited a few seconds for the others to process that information before adding, "Each time a new generation was born, another Nephilim would attach to the helpless newborn, and the taint would grow stronger in that line."

"That doesn't explain the vampires and werewolves and such, though," Peter pointed out. "They would have been attached to a human and been vulnerable to disease, famine, and many other things that could cause an infant back then to die, right?" Abe nodded in agreement.

Michael said, "The Nephilim didn't want to spend the rest of their lives waiting for new infants to be born into the world so they could inhabit them. A grown group of them that had already been born onto the Earth got together and started to experiment with the strongest creatures they could find to create bodies which they hoped to inhabit. They started with creature to creature experiments; hybrids, if you will. You've seen them, in your mythologies and histories. Things like the griffins, dragons, centaurs, dinosaurs…" Michael went down a list of what he hoped were recognizable creatures to the two men.

Peter interrupted, "Hold up," Peter said in awe, "are you telling me that the T-Rex was a science experiment, created by a bunch of power-hungry ghosts?"

"Well, in a manner of speaking, yes," Michael told him, pointedly. "The Master never made a tyrannosaurus. Any of the great beasts He made would have been herbivores."

"How did the T-Rex come into being then?" Peter folded his arms waiting for Michael to give his a credible answer.

"Please remember that the Nephilim are a product of humans and angels, they would have powers that a human would not; speed, stamina, long life, and extra intelligence to name a few, but when they mixed their tainted essence to the souls of the creatures that the Master created, it warped them and made them into creatures that should not have existed," Michael told them. "A little bit of Nephilim goes a long way—it can devastate the stoutest animal or human. For example, a bit of the Nephilim taint mixed with a peaceful herbivore and it twists into a hungry killing machine." Peter looked astonished at this news.

"How did the Nephilim corrupt them if they were all killed in the flood?"

"Well," Michael said, "remember I said that when their earthly bodies died in the flood their essence was left in limbo because it was not created by the Master and had no place to dwell?" Abe watched as Peter nodded his head emphatically. "Their essence looked for, and attached itself to, new hosts. They basically stole new bodies for themselves from those left. Once they attached themselves to new hosts, the host was warped and twisted into something different. They have tried all kinds of hosts throughout the years, but the host always dies within a very short time of habitation and the Nephilim has to search for someone, or something, new."

"What is being done about it? It seems to me that God could have stopped this from happening a long time ago," Peter said indignantly.

Michael turned to Peter and said in a gentle voice, "The Master has a plan, Peter. We don't always see what it is, but do not ever doubt that it'll work out to His purpose." Michael turned back to the others and finished his story. "Now, you know what is out there and you know why. The new questions are, why are you here, and what is your purpose in all of this? The Nephilim have reached the point where they grow stronger, and they are recruiting others to find ways to prolong their host bodies in order to stay on the Earth for longer periods of time. When Nephilim die they have to go through a period of regeneration before they are strong enough to inhabit a new host. Usually, it is a period of years. However, in recent months, they have been quietly gathering new hosts together and experimenting to see if they can transfer before the host dies to spare themselves from that transition cycle."

"So what you are telling us is that these Nephilim are bypassing the regeneration cycle and just jumping from host to host?" Abe said, scratching his beard stubble. "What do they do when they transfer? Do they have to seek permission, or can they just jump from one person to another by touch?" Abe couldn't get the implications of this through his head.

They could be anyone or anything—it was like Invasion of the Body Snatchers. Abe shivered a little at the thought. "What are we supposed to do if we don't know what they look like?"

Michael put his hand on Abe's shoulder, and Abe felt a peace flow through his body and the tension drain away.

"Peace, Abe. You aren't alone. We have a network of people who have been recruited to help, and they are working as we speak."

The angel crossed to the window and peered out at the horizon above the opposite rooftops, orange and dark blue with the waning daylight. "It's time we lift our eyes to the hills, people."

Chapter 12

Orange and pink streaked the sky at Lakefront Airport as Sam touched down nimbly in New Orleans. He was glad to have a smooth landing, and more importantly, an uneventful trip. The cargo on this particular plane ride would definitely appreciate being on the ground, although their lot would not improve appreciably once freed from their current situation.

Sam unlatched his seatbelt and walked through the door from the cockpit to the back of the plane. He thought about the important meeting that he had later with Abe. The two men had successfully waylaid or reacquired the cargo of several of Max's father's planes. Not all at once, but a few here and there over a period of years. Max had recruited the pair about eight years earlier and, together they had managed to pull off numerous jobs in the last few months.

The usual jobs consisted of stolen information or merchandise, occasionally a drug or weapons shipment. Drugs or weapons were always riskier than, say, their present cargo, because Lev Avatov cared about anything he could convert into money. Money equaled power and influence for Max's father, and when he had to give up either he tended to be put out. Lev didn't care about the girls. No. To him, they were a means to a nefarious end. Truth be told, men like Olivier were a more detestable sort than even the cutthroats and criminals of Lev's organization would care to associate with, and Lev found the whole business vile and annoying.

Of course, Sam wasn't supposed to know about any of it. The manifests that he carried were doctored and all the right people were paid well to keep their mouths shut and see nothing. Sam opened the door to the cargo hold and walked through to the back of the plane. The crates that were set into the back of the craft took up all the available space. Sam had to squeeze through to make it into the center of the plane where the crate he was looking for was stowed. It wasn't a large crate. That concerned him a little, considering how many girls were locked in there. He knew that he wasn't supposed to know about them either, but Sam always made sure to know exactly what went on his plane. He knocked on the wall of the container and heard a couple of stifled squeaks.

Earlier when he was looking at the container he found a well-concealed hole that allowed him to see inside and talk with the girls. He learned that they were all around the same age—between 12 and 14—and that they were all taken from various places and sold. And that they were all really frightened. Sam knelt down to where he knew the hole was in the container. The stench hit him right in the face—sweat and urine. These girls were hot and scared, and they were currently penned and shackled like prisoners in a box with no toilet or air. Sam didn't believe there was such a thing as a special place in hell, but he sure wished in this particular instance there were.

He bent down and whispered, "Everyone okay in there?" He heard a scuffling and saw a small finger appear in the hole. It disappeared, and he heard someone crying softly, then another trying to comfort the girl crying.

He waited another minute and was rewarded with a wary, "Who are you?" The voice sounded defensive and protective—*The de facto leader of this small band*, Sam thought, and he was happy to know she sounded like she had some fight in her. Oddly, he could tell from her voice that she couldn't have been one of the older girls.

"My name is Sam," he told her. "Is everyone all right in there?"

A few seconds passed before he heard the answer. "Yes, everyone is alive, but a couple of us had to pee and there is no toilet, so it smells gross in here. And somebody threw up. Are you going to get us out of here?"

Steady, he thought. *She sounds more determined than scared.* Sam could tell she was still distrustful, and he didn't blame her, given the things that had transpired.

"What's your name, honey?" He tried to sound authoritative, yet caring. He could tell she was weighing in her head whether or not to disclose her name, and after deciding that things really couldn't get much worse for her and all she wanted at that particular moment was to get the hell out of the box and get some air, she relented.

"My name is Sarah. I'm 12." Sam could tell that she was feeling a little better, so he pressed her.

"Sarah, what happened? How did they get you? How many of you are there?" Right away her voice came back through the hole.

"There are 13 of us in here. It's really cramped. My friend Madison and I are from Van Nuys, and we…" she broke off.

Sam was floored. There were 13 girls in a small cargo container with no water, lights, food, or restroom. Sam could feel his blood start to boil and what little calm he could find was on the verge of escaping him. Even though it was nearly night fall, it was still a humid 88 degrees in New Orleans, and there was no air conditioning in the cargo hold. He knew those girls were going to roast before too much longer.

He took a couple of deep breaths and when he finally got calmed down he said, "Listen, we are going to help you as soon as we can. I want you guys to be ready to move when we come to get you, okay?"

Sam saw the small finger poke through the hole again and heard a muffled, "You mean it?" His heart broke at the thought that these young girls had to endure this torture.

"I promise," he said and touched her little finger. "Just be ready to go. My friend Abe and I will get you before anything else can happen, okay?" He saw the little finger disappear into the container and heard her talking with the other girls. He could tell that her message was well received, and he was glad he could bring them that small comfort. "We will be back to get you later." He stood and knocked lightly on the side of the container. He heard an answering thump and squeezed his way past the cargo once more.

He and Abe would have to give this some serious thought and planning. The crate was in the middle surrounded by bulk cargo. Sam knew they would be unloading later in the dead of night after Max contacted that creeper Olivier. Sam also knew there was time right after the handoff of the payload when it was left for a short period while the drivers get the necessary documentation to take the cargo from the airport. Hopefully that would be the time when they could work their magic and get the girls off the truck and onto another truck without incident.

There were a lot of variables to consider before attempting this kind of maneuver, and he knew that he had to get with Abe quickly in order to plan this out. Sam grabbed his gear from the cockpit, rifled through and rearranged his paperwork, and set out to check in at the office with his new manifest and departure times. He was impatient to get over and see Abe before these girls disappeared into the seedy New Orleans night forever. NOLA was greedy and she didn't give up her vices or her secrets, and these girls, if allowed to reach their final destination, would be simply unrecoverable.

If they failed to rescue those girls tonight—well, Sam didn't want to think about that. The drugs they would be forced to take, the men who would be forced upon them—it was almost too much for his heart to bare. Sam may look dangerous and not at all friendly, but he had a soft spot for children in need. Sam gave nearly all his money to organizations that helped children: orphanages, non-profits that taught self-defense, arts programs for children, and especially organizations that helped those children fighting cancer or other childhood diseases. Sam shook his head.

Save those girls first, he thought. *Worry about the rest later.*

After getting all his manifests signed and posted, he shouldered his bag and took off at a lope to the other side of the airport and Abe's hangar. This was going to be a long night, and he needed help. He shot a look skyward and thought, *If you're ever gonna help me, now would be the right time*. Sam didn't *not* believe in God, exactly—he had done enough flying to know that there was something that lived in the clouds, protecting them all. But he didn't really let it keep him up at night, either. *If there is a real God, I'm sure He's got His hands full with way more than the likes of me*, he thought.

Sam stopped and looked fully skyward, taking off his aviators, squinting and silently praying. *I'm not asking for me, you know. I am asking for those little girls, and if You don't feel like it or can't get to it, we are all going to be in very big trouble down here. Do me solid, will you?*

He considered the sun, felt it on his face, replaced his sunglasses, and walked to the other side of the tarmac, planning as he went.

Chapter 13

Michael looked up for a moment and then turned to Abe. A smile lit his face. "You have to go home now," he told him.

"Uh, no way, cap. You owe me some answers. We haven't finished our conversation, and I still have questions, Mike. I would like to know about this support program you have."

Michael forestalled him with a raised hand. "Abe, relax. Take it easy—we are going with you. The person that we need Peter to help is on his way to your place."

Abe raised a quizzical eyebrow. "The other someone? At least tell me this: do I know him?"

"Not only do you know him," Michael told him with a smile, "you have done some of your best work with him." That got Abe's full attention. "Rose, you are more than welcome to come along."

Momma Rose made a tsking sound and waved her hands at Michael. "No, you have spent too much time here already, and I have work to do. You boys go along, and do whatever boys do." She winked at Peter as she passed him causing him to smile in return. "I will pack you something to take with you."

"If I eat any more I may explode," Peter told her.

"Good thing it is not just for you then," Momma Rose told him as she walked into the kitchen. Peter shook his head in confusion but figured she knew what she was talking about.

Michael smiled and slapped Peter on the back. "Rose is always prepared Peter; she has been gifted with foresight. She also really makes me wish that angels needed to eat."

Peter mulled that over as Michael and Abe spoke quietly. He decided that it made perfect sense to him. Momma Rose always seemed to know what Peter needed before he did. He shrugged his shoulders at himself and caught the small smile that played across Michael's face. He figured that the smile was for him, and Michael seemed to confirm it when he turned slightly to wink at Peter. Momma Rose came bustling back into the room with a large hamper and a jug of sweet tea.

"Wow, Momma Rose, you planning on feeding an army?" he asked in astonishment.

She put the basket down and turned to him with a smile, "You never know who will need to eat, and besides, who doesn't like Momma Rose's cooking?" she said in a mock challenge. All three men held up their hands in surrender.

Michael said, "I'm sure that whatever you have packed will be just enough." He kissed her cheek as he grabbed the handle of the basket. Abe grabbed the jug of tea, and Peter followed the two men out the door after giving Momma Rose a fierce hug. The three men walked out of the café into the dusk. They hailed a pedicab to take them out of the quarter where Abe had parked his truck. Peter let himself be distracted by the noise and activity of the quarter at sundown.

The revelers were out in full force, and Peter could see a few patrons that had already imbibed dizzily making their way to the next bar. The innumerable styles of music blasting out of the innumerable bars they passed met his ears in a raucous cacophony. The noise, in his opinion, was not the best thing about living in New Orleans. He really did like the people, though. He enjoyed people of all walks; he liked listening to their stories, where they came from and where they were going. He just wasn't particularly good with people, which is probably why he had been so successful in activities where he was sequestered away from them. It's why he created and invented alone, with the exception of the occasional intrusion by Travis or Tammy.

Peter was awkward when it came to talking to new people. He was never really sure what to say, so he tended to not say anything at all. That made people think of him as introverted or stand-offish when he was young and anonymous, but now that he had money and influence, especially at his young age, they thought of him as eccentric.

"Peter," Michael said, pulling his attention away from the streets and back to his current situation. "I know this may seem a bit overwhelming to you, but you are in a unique situation that will help save countless people. You are more prepared for this than you think, and you don't give yourself enough credit."

The pedi-cab stopped at the end of the street, and the three men filed out of the cab. Michael and Peter followed Abe around the corner to the parking garage and his old pick-up. They got into the F-150, and Abe started it up. He pulled out of the parking space and made his way to the front of the garage.

"Alright, Mike—we're here. Now, will you please tell us who we will be meeting, and who this help is that we are supposed to get?" Abe asked Michael.

"Sam Ramos."

"I didn't know you knew Sam," Abe exclaimed. "He is, uh—not the friendliest dude I've ever met. He's roped into some shady dealings sometimes, but he always tries to make it right. We've *misplaced* some pretty bad cargo over the years." Abe laughed. "He loves to push his envelope further than I push mine, but he's good people. He's just a bit rough if you don't know him. How does he figure into this?"

"I'm glad you feel that way, Abe. He's in a bit of trouble, and Peter is going to guide him." Michael sent a thumb in Peter's direction, all the while grinning at Abe.

Abe's brows furrowed, and he was instantly concerned for his friend. "What is going on with Sam? I thought you said he is on his way to see me?"

"He is on his way to see you, Abe. He is also a very special person—or not. I mean, yes, he is a person as all people are people, but not a *person* person, really. Look, remember when I was talking to you about the Watcher angels and how they married and produced children with humans?"

"Yeah, I do. Do you mean Sam is one of them? A Nephilim?" Abe replied.

"Well, no. It's complicated, but..." Michael continued, breathing a heavy sigh. "Sam Ramos is Samael. He's an angel, Abe. More specifically, he's a Watcher," Michael said like that would clear up any questions.

"Man, nothing surprises me anymore," said Abe. He pulled off his cap and flipped his hand around to wipe at his forehead, then replaced the hat back on his head. "So fine. Sam is an angel. So—?" Abe prompted, causing Michael to sigh again.

"So, Abe, all of the Watchers were cast into a great pit after the war of the heavens, except Sam."

"Interesting. Why was Sam excluded?" Peter asked, piping up from the passenger seat. "Did he escape or something?"

"No, Peter, he didn't escape—well, figuratively I guess he sort of did. I went to the Master to ask for leniency on his behalf. I interceded, which is why he is now my responsibility."

"Why?" Peter asked him.

Michael waved him off and quickly said, "That part isn't important right now. What is important is that Sam needs to be restored to his former self, and there is only one way to do that."

Abe turned onto the off-ramp to the airport and decelerated the Ford. Michael was running out of time and started telling his story in earnest.

"Sam has been forgiven, but he still has a lot of anger. His heart must change. Sam needs to *want* to be forgiven his past indiscretions and *want* to be restored. Right now, he blames himself—and me—for a lot."

"What does he blame you for?" Peter asked, his curiosity piqued.

"I promise, you will find out later, but now it's not important, other than to say the thing that he blames me for was done by someone much closer and unexpected. He needs to forgive himself and want to be forgiven in return. That task is yours, Abe. I know he's not the most open person, but since you already know Sam, maybe he would be willing to talk to you about this."

Abe shook his head. "I don't think I'm qualified to help Sam, who is an angel of all things, sort out his feelings. I am an old soldier, and he is—do angels even have feelings?" Abe turned to Michael. Michael gave him a wry smile, and he continued. "Look, I'm not the guy. I could see if he would talk to Dr. Jo?" he said and turned the corner to where the hangars were.

"Dr. Jo would not be able to help him, Abe," Michael said. "She is special, but she cannot help Sam in this instance."

"Why? Wouldn't Sam be open to seeing a psychiatrist?" Peter asked, causing Michael to belly laugh.

"No, let's just say that Sam would not benefit from a visit to Dr. Jo. This task must fall to Abe. You however, have a different task," Michael said, ending the debate. "Sam is in over his head in this new venture he has undertaken. The men he is dealing with now are as devious as they are ruthless, and they are meddling in things that are better left buried." Michael, searching the evening out the windshield suddenly pointed and said, "Hey, pull over here, Abe."

Abe pulled off to the side of the road, his hangar clearly in sight. Michael looked at both of them.

"I have warned you that the Nephilim have tried and failed to produce a body that will sustain them. They move from host to host like a virus. They are currently trying to reproduce some of the old ways and magic from before the flood. In order to get that information, they are digging up the past. Literally." Michael turned very serious, and Peter wasn't sure he liked it at all. "The order of the Nephilim are into some of the worst things imaginable—trafficking, slavery, drugs, weapons of mass destruction, you name it and they are behind it. Sam is getting mixed up in their world. If he goes too far he will be lost. But if you can help him, then you could save countless lives. There are a lot of innocents mixed up in this mess."

"What do I need to do?" Peter asked.

"First, you need to meet Sam and get him to take you to Russia on his next flight," Michael told him.

"Russia?" exclaimed Peter. "Why would he want to take me to Russia with him?"

"There must be a way, Peter. You will think of something," Michael said in a rush, opening the door with a creak. "I gotta go now, but I will catch up with you again soon. Have faith, boys—the way forward always presents itself." With that pronouncement he was gone. Not with a *poof* like in a magic act, he just wasn't there anymore. Peter shook his head and smiled at Abe.

"I've got to learn that trick."

Abe smiled back, then asked Peter, "So, how are you gonna get Sam to let you fly with him? He is awful particular about his plane."

"Well, I thought that I would just do what I normally do when I would like for someone to do something—appeal to their better nature and flatter them," said Peter.

"What do you do when that doesn't work?" Abe asked.

"Offer him a lot of money."

Abe looked a little stunned.

"There is an Ichiharu convention coming up in a week. It's not really large enough for Guardian normally, but I have plenty of things that could go over to be sold, including a large piece that I just finished. An item that would require accompanied shipment on a cargo plane," Peter told Abe. "Those, along with some money to grease the skids, should get me to Russia." He finished his statement with a thoughtful glance at Abe. "What do you think, Abe? Would it work?"

Abe scratched his whiskered chin and answered, "Well, Sam really likes flying, and he really likes money, so yes, I believe it would. Now, let's go meet Sam."

Abe restarted his old truck and they drove around the last corner to the hangar. As they got out of the truck, Abe noticed the shadow before Peter and sprang into action, he pushed Peter to the side and drew a hidden baton from his pocket. With a *click* it extended as Abe swung it up in front of him.

"Whoa, easy Abe," came a disembodied voice from the shadow. "It's just me."

Abe shook his head and swore. "Sam. Damn you, man. You nearly scared me to death." Abe collapsed his stick and put it back in his pocket. He wipes his brow with his bandana and shook Sam's outstretched hand. "How you been? It's been a while." Sam smiled and looked beyond Abe to Peter who still looked as if he was going to wet himself.

"Who's your friend, Abe?" Sam asked him suspiciously.

"Yeah, this is Peter Devereaux. Peter, Sam Ramos. He's the pilot I told you about earlier. Peter here needs a pilot to fly him and some stuff to Russia for some big comic nerd thing."

Peter laughed and said, "It's Comic-*Con*, Abe, but that isn't until October. I really need someone who can get my newest project to Russia for Ichiharu next week. Nice to meet you, Sam," Peter said, holding out his hand for Sam to shake.

Sam looked at the outstretched hand like it was a snake bent to strike without notice. He gave the hand a quick shake and turned back to Abe. "Why me?" Sam asked.

"Well, I seemed to remember that you do a lot of flying back and forth to there, and I was going to give you a call to ask you when your next trip is. That's what Peter and I were coming to get, and low and behold, here you are. Talk about great timing, huh, Peter?" Abe winked at Peter and smiled at Sam.

"Yeah, it is great timing if you are going that way and have some empty space. I have some cargo that needs to get to Russia." Peter said excitedly. "This newest piece is sure to bring some big bucks." He looked at Sam with a hopeful expression.

"Yeah? Tell me," Sam asked, dubiously, "what do big bucks look like in your world, kid?" He doubted very seriously that this kid had even close to the amount of money required to make this trip worth it, or even possible. *Damn millennials*, he thought, *have no idea what things cost and think the world owes them.*

Peter was a bit perturbed and was about to give the older man the blasting that he deserved, when Abe spoke up.

"Hey, man. This *kid* has made a name for himself in many circles worldwide and has created a company that he runs with limited help that strictly relies on his imagination. He's *loaded* and *well-connected*."

Sam looked as stunned as Peter. Neither said anything but continued to stare at Abe.

"What?" Abe said, "I can read, can't I?"

Peter looked at Abe and grinned. "Thank you, Abe. It did take me awhile to build my business, but with the sci-fi genre gaining in popularity, we do a lot of private collection acquisition and movie and TV pieces. I'll probably have to either expand and bring on other artists or become a strictly commissioned creator. All that to say this, Sam: I can pay you very well to assist me. Do we have a deal?" the younger man said, holding out his hand to seal their agreement with Sam's handshake.

Sam stayed his hand momentarily, then spoke. "Give me a minute, Peter. I'm more than certain money won't be an issue here, but there are some logistics to work out. Can I speak with Abe a sec?"

"Sure, take your time," said Peter, pleased at his newly-acquired cred within their conversation.

Sam turned to Abe and spoke, shifting his weight from one foot to the other, clearly agitated. Abe got that all was not well.

"What's up, man? You don't look good."

"I am offloading some cargo this evening," he started, giving Abe a look loaded with double meaning. "It will be offloaded late tonight, and I could use your help—like in Tacoma," he finished.

Oh, God. Abe knew immediately what Sam intended, and felt sick. *More girls*. He caught himself and feigned nonchalance. "Oh well, maybe I could help. I remember that job." Abe suddenly got an idea, "Shouldn't take too long for three people."

"Yeah, I'd be happy to help, Sam." Peter said, oblivious to the underlying meaning.

"I don't think there will be a need for that, Peter," Sam said through his teeth, boring a hole into Abe with his eyes. "There are only a handful of pieces. Abe and I can cover it. You know, it can be dangerous getting cargo off a plane. Things shift in flight, and sometimes people can get hurt." Sam stood with a stony expression, the only show of impatience being the tapping of his aviator glasses against his leg.

Peter spoke, dismissing Sam's statement with a wave, "Not worried about it. What are we going to do about the cargo tonight?" he asked.

"Wait, wait, wait." Abe held up his hand, shaking his head and pacing. *What's more important,* he asked himself, *the mission that an angel charged me with, or getting these abducted girls to safety?* He prayed quickly for guidance and trusted what he heard. "Okay," Abe said, and turned to Peter. "What size payload are we looking at here, Peter? For your show?" Peter hesitated, and Abe got irritated. "Come on, Peter. You know. You do this all the time. What size?" Abe asked.

"Uh, about 8 x 8 foot crate would do?" Peter answered, surprised, then more sure of himself. "Yeah, four 8x8s should work."

Sam looked over at him. "Excuse me? That is a lot of room. What can you possibly be shipping to Russia that needs that much space?"

Peter smiled widely and with pride in his voice said, "I have designed and fabricated full mechatronic, armored suits. They easily stand about seven feet tall and are about five and a half feet wide with an extra foot and a half for a weapon." Now Peter had Sam's full attention.

"That sounds like something that I would love to see. Tell me, are these suits wearable, or are they strictly to look at?" Sam asked with a speculative glance.

"They are made to be worn by people. Fully functional. I have scared quite a few people testing those suits. Each one has been personally tested by me, so I know that they work correctly." Peter said. "They weigh about as much as a small car, and are fully air conditioned."

Abe saw Sam's wheels turning, and he crossed his arms and asked, "You look like you have an idea?"

"Yeah, I do, actually." Sam said to Abe, excitedly. He mouthed the word *Tacoma* to Abe, turned to Peter and made an offer. "If I gave you a discount to get you there, would you be willing to loan me one? Tonight?" Abe suddenly got what Sam wanted it for.

Peter looked pensive. "What are you going to use them for? I mean, you break it you bought it. As long as that's understood, and I accompany it, we have no problems." Peter was through negotiating, and crossed his arms in finality. "Oh, wait," Peter said, smacking his head like he had forgotten something. "All of the suits are crated for shipment in my shop. We'd never get them unpacked in time. But," he said, thinking and tapping his chin while he paced, "I do have the original prototype. I mean, it spends most of the time in a corner collecting dust now. I usually only refer back to it to get new ideas for the current builds. It doesn't have any great flourishes to it, and it is completely black primer. Will that work?"

Sam considered, "Yeah, that works—well, everything but the you coming with part. That's a no-go. I fly a machine that's probably more complicated than your prop suit, so we'll do what we need to do and get it back to you, good as new." Peter laughed, but it wasn't because Sam had said something funny.

"Nu-uh. I don't believe you heard me earlier, Sam. This isn't negotiable. You have to take me along, considering I'm the only one who knows how to work it." Peter grinned then. "And, if you think that your plane is something to see, you are in for a big surprise."

Sam looked at Abe for some help, but Abe just shrugged and said, "Kid's got a point, Sam. What if you jump in that thing and can't control it or blow yourself up?"

Sam sighed. "Peter, you win. Ten grand and the loan of you suit—with you *in it*," Sam said, as Peter held up a finger to object, "for the job tonight." The pilot sighed, holding out his hand for a shake. "You're a slick negotiator, son, but I don't think you know what you're getting into. This could end up being very dangerous. I want you to know that up front, but from the sounds of your mech units, I don't think we will have as many problems as we would have."

Peter took the proffered hand and shook it eagerly looking back and forth between Abe and Sam. "This sounds like it's going to be a blast."

Sam looked at Abe and grinned, the three of them reached the door to Abe's hangar, and as they walked inside Sam clapped his hands together and said, "Alright, gentlemen. We have a lot of planning to do and only about four hours to make it all happen."

Abe immediately went to the kitchen and started the coffee. "Peter, why don't you break out those beignets we brought from Momma Rose's?" Abe told him. Peter set the bag he was carrying on the counter and took the plate from Abe's outstretched hand.

Sam sniffed appreciatively, but held up a hand, "Thanks, but not hungry at the moment. Let's get to work." He sat at the table and took out his phone, a pen, and a pad of paper.

"That's cool—more for me." Peter smiled and grabbed a pastry. In a matter of minutes, they were all sitting, planning, drinking, and talking.

Abe said, "Peter, I need you to give me a full load out and capability run down on your suit. Sam, I need any intel on the movement schedule and whatever you have on Olivier's men. I already know the gaps in the security movements, so we're fine there."

Abe was looking at a printed plan of the service road, and Peter turned to him. "Look, I already get that this isn't offloading cargo. What are we trying to sneak out of here? Don't get me wrong," he said quickly, "I'm down, but I want to know the details. I hate being out of the loop."

Abe turned to Sam, and Sam shrugged.

"Might as well—he'll know shortly after we start, anyway." Sam swore, a muttered *Dammit,* to himself, glared once more at Abe, and finally relented.

"Ok, Peter, here's what's actually going down," Abe began, setting down the beignet and standing up to pace. "We are, that is, Sam and me—we're going to correct a mistake. Sam and I, along with others, have had the opportunity in the past to waylay some ill-gotten goods from some very bad dudes, and that is what we are going to do tonight."

"Like, something that was stolen?"

"Abe, for God's sake, just tell him," Sam said, equaling Peter's impatience. Abe held his hands up empty. He couldn't find the words, so Sam turned to Peter and laid it out. "Look, Peter. There are girls, 13 of them, ranging in ages from 12 to 14, and they are being shipped to a very bad man. We are going to rescue them and get them home. That is what you are assisting with here."

Peter looked stunned. "Why are there girls in your cargo hold, Sam? Who the hell do you work for?" Peter couldn't believe what he was hearing, and he stood up suddenly. "Show me," he said.

Abe turned to Sam, "Did you really have to say that? Now he's just going to worry." Abe snatched at a beignet and chomped angrily.

"His skin is as much in this game as ours now, chief. He needs to know why, and what happens if we fail."

Human trafficking, Peter thought. *Sex slavery.* He'd heard of it, but never come across it, and definitely wasn't expecting it. These girls would not come to any harm if he had any say in it, and apparently he did. He sat down next to Abe and Sam, determined, and said to the pair of them, "Okay, here's what we are going to do."

Chapter 14

Maggie looked at herself in the bathroom mirror. She had spent the last 48 hours in a flurry of activity and had just made it to Miami in time to catch Max before he had to fly back to Russia to meet up with his father. She needed to convince Max to take her with him to Russia, because the only way she was going to learn more about this mysterious organization his father controlled was to become immersed in it;

And the only way that was going to happen, she reasoned with herself, *was to get Max to take mer along*.

She picked up her brush and began to brush her fiery red hair. She had always liked her hair, although the pale skin that went with it was a bummer. Max enjoyed her hair when she left it down, and it curled gently around her shoulders.

Maggie put the brush down when a knock came from the bedroom door. She left the bathroom, reached up to her pendant to activate it, slipped her newest pair of Jimmy Choo's on her feet, and answered the knock. Max was waiting on the other side of the door, looking way too handsome and far too awake for Maggie's coffee-deprived mind. She smiled and rose on her tiptoes to give Max a lingering, sweet kiss.

"Good morning, Max." she said, hugging him and breathing him in. *Wow, he always smells so good* .she thought. *Sandalwood, leather and gun oil. These are a few of my favorite things...* "What an amazing place you have—and thank you. Thank you for letting me stay in your beautiful home. It is so stunning."

Maggie never was a morning person and had to really try hard for a bubbly personality.

Max raised an eyebrow and grinned at Maggie. "I see that Miami, just like New Orleans, New York, Seattle, and Los Angeles, agrees with you. You look very beautiful this morning, kiska," he told her, and she blushed. "You also look like you need some coffee. Let us go, and I will give you the big tour." He grabbed her hand and pulled her from the room.

"Grand tour?" Maggie asked.

"Okay, then, the grand tour," Max said jubilantly over his shoulder. She followed him down the massive hallway into the large living area.

This room would fit my entire place inside it, thought Maggie. They continued on to a massive dining room, dark and classic, paneled with walnut. It should've been darker, but it was lightened by creamy cabinets and completed with a classically elegant, long dining table and great crystal chandeliers on the ceiling. She was bowled over by the enormity of this place in which only one single man lived. Max was saying something about the interior and its furnishings reminding him of the Gatchina that Catherine the Great had built for Count Orlov for helping with the plot to murder Peter the Great. Meanwhile, Maggie's mind was building a complete fantasy sequence around this room that featured a talking candelabra and floating dishes. *I really am in desperate need of coffee.*

Max continued to pull her along until they came to a gourmet kitchen attached by a hallway to the dining room. The kitchen was the stuff of any chef's dream; industrial-sized everything, enough counter space to run a restaurant, and a small army of people to do it. Maggie also noticed that there was a small alcove at the back of the kitchen that housed an unassuming set of petite doors that looked like they led to a patio. Max pulled her along until they reached the alcove.

She found it was a delightful little sunroom that was positioned off the back of the kitchen. Maggie smiled and looked out over the ocean. This really was her favorite of all the rooms she had seen in the gigantic mansion. It was small and cozy, had views of not only the ocean on one side, but a beautiful garden on the other side. Maggie sucked in a breath and turned to find Max staring at her,

"Oh Max," she said breathlessly, "this is just—wow."

Max grinned at her and swept his arm toward a little table in the corner. It was laid out with a variety of breakfast foods and a big pot of what Maggie hoped was coffee.

"This was my mother's favorite room when we visited here. Most of the winters in Russia were long and brutal," he told her with a sad smile. "I do not get here as often anymore, but I am glad to be here today, and I am glad that it has made you smile. My mother would have liked you, Maggie." He came to stand beside her and partake in her joy as she took in the expanse of the shore and the jade green and turquoise water.

She reached up to grab the hand that he had gently placed on her shoulder. "I wish I could have met her. Thank you for showing this to me."

They stood this way in silence for a long minute, both taking in the beauty in front of them—Maggie staring out at the endless ocean, and Max staring at the girl he loved. It was Max who stirred first, and he broke away to pour Maggie a cup of steaming coffee.

"Come." He motioned her over to the gilded tea table. "My mother always said, 'my favorite room is where there is tea, there are chairs, and there is room for conversation.'"

She sat lightly in one of the white and gold wrought iron chairs, took the cup that Max proffered, and sat unspeaking, looking alternately at him and the expanse of water just to her right.

The intimacy and quiet made Max uncomfortable. He longed for Maggie to be light-hearted and chatty this morning. She sniffed appreciatively before allowing herself that first sip of caffeinated heaven.

"Mmmm," she said. "This is turning out to be the best day ever. I will be so sad to see you go tomorrow." She looked over at him demurely and smiled a sad smile. "How long will you be gone for, again?" she asked him.

He frowned at her and said, "I am not sure. It could be a couple of weeks or a couple of months before I can escape. I have some things I must attend to with my father and his associates."

Maggie was looking down at her cup, which gave her the opportunity to process and strategize without Max watching her face work. *I'm running out of time to get inside,* she thought. *I have to get to Russia, and he's going to be tough to convince.* He could not leave without her this time.

She set her coffee down, turned on the tears, and abruptly leapt from her seat to move to the opposite side of the patio with the garden view. Maggie knew that men didn't know what to do with that type of display, and would typically be more agreeable to any forthcoming suggestions.

On cue, and startled, Max followed her and said, "What is wrong? Did I say something?" He stood behind her, brushing the red curls aside from her shoulders to place his hands comfortingly on her—and she liked it.

Nope, not the time, she thought. But it *did* feel good. She said between her affected sobbing, "Oh, Max. We were just starting to get to know each other really well. I will really miss you while you're gone. I always do." Fresh sobs, and sniffing.

"I miss you as well, kiska. I wish I did not have to be gone all of the time." Max said it, and Maggie knew it was sincere.

Keep going, she thought, *you almost have him.* She turned to him, looking up dolefully, fluttering her eyelashes, mostly to see through the real tears, but also so he could see her sorrowful expression. "I wish there was a way that you could stay longer, or I could stay with you. I want you close to me, Max." She brushed a tear from her eye.

He reached over and ran his thumb down her cheek, "I, too, wish I could stay, kiska. It is a pity you could not come with me."

Bingo, she thought.

She immediately brightened at the prospect, and flinging her arms around him, she beamed, shouting "That's a great idea, darling." She could see the rejection spring to his face, but before he could utter the words, she pressed on. "I have some time off, and Charley won't miss me for absolutely eons. I'll call her and tell her now."

Maggie had concocted her backstory early on: designer at up- and-coming Milan house, Michelangelo, Charley was her eccentric, never-reachable boss—*thank you, 70s detective drama.* The fib allowed for Maggie's lifestyle, cash flow, and ticked all of the right boxes to allay suspicions from any of Avatov's men. She was beginning to feel the sting of lying to him, and every time she revisited an untruth on Max, it stuck in her gut. But she continued, "It's only a couple of weeks, but It would allow us to spend some more time together."

Maggie leaned into Max, gave him a slow, lingering kiss, and let her gaze meet his, sultry and earnest. "Don't you want to see, really, where this could go?"

Max was not given to impractical flights of fancy or romance, but Maggie knew him well enough by now to know she had gotten to him. He seemed to mull over the idea for a moment. Maggie smiled inwardly, knowing she had won and would, very shortly, be taking the next crucial step in her mission. But Max surprised her.

"No. I am sorry, kiska, but no. It is not a good idea. I will have to see my father while I am in Russia, and he is not a person to whom I care to introduce you."

Maggie had to double down. "I don't have to meet your father while I'm there. Truthfully, I don't have to meet anyone, really. I want to be there for *you*—no one else. I can just stay at your place until your business is concluded. Then I will allow you to show me your city," she told him with a wink.

He raised an eyebrow and smiled at her.

She pushed a little, adding, "I want to know all there is to know about you. Show me the wonderful place you love so much, Max."

Maggie swallowed hard. While she was playing a part, she truly did have feelings for the large man sitting in front of her. She did not wish to cause him any problems or place him in harm's way just because she wanted to get closer. Closer to Max, definitely, but that was a want; a desire. She *needed* to get closer to the evil his father dealt on a daily basis. She had a promise to keep.

Max frowned and agonized over her words. Maggie could tell that he, too, wanted to spend more time together, but it was against his better judgment.

Maggie took his hand and looked him in the eyes beseechingly. She made an absent stroking motion with her thumb over the palm of his hand.

Max looked at their entwined hands and then at Maggie's face He sighed loudly and said, "You win."

Maggie felt relieved and instantly sorry she had asked this of Max. She knew the trouble this could put him in, and although she couldn't tell him now, she vowed that one day she would make sure he knew just how grateful she was. She needed this story and Max, although she hated to use him, was the key.

"We leave tomorrow morning. Do you have your passport?" Max asked her. Maggie, while downing her coffee, held up a finger to forestall him.

She replaced the cup on its saucer, swallowed again, and said, "Never leave home without it. I brought it on the off-chance that you would let me accompany you after I threw myself at you." She threw her arms around Max's neck. "Thank you, darling. This will be good for us, and I can't wait to see the city you were raised in."

Max smiled absently, and Maggie could tell that he was really torn at the idea of bringing her along—that he wanted her there, but she could also tell that it worried him to no end that she would be there within reach of his father. Maggie fell a little harder at the realization that Max was trying incredibly hard to give her what she wanted and to also protect her from the evil he knew could get at them both. She knew Max's father dabbled in just about all aspects of the illegal and immoral. *Sex slaves, guns, drugs, you name it and Lev Avatov had his hand in it, like a surgeon rummaging around in someone's entrails*, she thought disgustedly.\

Like most organized crime around the world, he ran these illicit deals under the guises of several well-run businesses. Lev had money, connections, respect from others for what he could do or have done, and a small army of people who were utterly loyal to him that would carry out the unpleasant. He wasn't afraid of anyone talking about his organization because he controlled them with fear. Fear of reprisal against them or their families.

Maggie was used to looking after herself. After the incident with her best friend, Maggie's parents had insisted that she learn how to protect herself. She prided herself on her black belt in jiu jitsu, and she took her training a step further and learned kendo and aikido. She never thought she would ever use Japanese sword fighting, but a girl couldn't be too careful.

Besides, she thought, *it's a great way to relieve stress.*

Maggie took a bite of her bagel and sipped her coffee appreciatively. She looked up to find Max staring at her. She smiled and cocked her head to the side. "What?"

Max gave a little chuckle and shook his head ruefully, "What am I to do with you?"

She looked at him questioningly, and he answered the unspoken question. "You have me so wrapped up inside. I cannot deny you anything," he told her. He lost the smile and a look of concern came back to his face. "My home is not a safe place. Since you insist on going with me, I want you to make me a promise." He gave her a minute to nod in acceptance.

"Okay?" she asked him, expectantly.

"You cannot leave my side. I need to know that you are safe, and the only way for me to do that is to keep you with me," he said. "If I have to leave you at the house, you are not to go out. If I cannot be next to you, then it will be Boris next to you."

Maggie shuddered a little at the thought of even going near Boris. That man seriously gave Maggie the willies.

Max mistook her shudder for nervousness and sought to console her. "It will be okay, Maggie. I will not let anything happen to you.

We will have a good time, I can show you things that most tourists will never see." He was warming to the idea, and Maggie smiled at his exuberance.

"I have such a love for old churches. They help inspire our designs." Maggie leaned over and told him in a whisper, "They are always so—holy," she finished lamely.

Max chuckled and told her in a conspiratorial whisper, "We have many—*holy* churches," he teased, earning himself a slap on the arm from a slightly embarrassed Maggie. "Really," he said laughing openly at her now. "There are many great churches just in St. Petersburg. You will love it."

"Ooh," Maggie squealed, "this is going to be so much fun Max, you'll see." She reached over the table and threw her arms around Max's neck and kissed his cheek. Maggie thought how utterly cliché and girly the next thing she was going to say would be, and she literally laughed out loud.

"What? What is so humorous?" Max inquired.

"I have nothing to wear." Maggie again laughed heartily at the absurd statement. "But, seriously, I don't, Max. All of the clothes I brought were for Miami, not St Petersburg. I have nothing that would be appropriate for Russian weather."

"I thought you would say that. It is my last day in Miami for a while, so let us go shopping."

He called out to a passing servant and asked them to tell Boris to have the car ready to go in 20 minutes.

As they finished eating their breakfast, Maggie skimmed the articles in the newspaper, sipping another cup of coffee. She stopped at a local piece and started to read. She found herself so wrapped up in the article that she started when Max asked her, "Is there a problem?"

She looked at his concerned expression and told him, "A little girl went missing last night from the beach. Her family was here on vacation and had rented a condo. She was building a sand castle. The next thing her family knew, she was gone," Maggie finished.

As Maggie was recounting the story she had just read, she was watching Max's face for any changes. She was rewarded with a tightening of his lips and eyes, the only indicators that he was upset.

"I am sorry about the little girl. Do they have any leads?" Max asked, his voice taking on an almost imperceptible edge.

"I don't think so," she said as she continued to scan. "Wait, there's this: Authorities did say, however, that there was a balloon vendor that the little girl had wanted to visit, but her father told her no. She might have slipped away to find him." Maggie felt tears at the corner of her eyes. These types of stories always brought up bad feelings for her, mostly guilt.

"Are you okay, Maggie?" Max asked. She was visibly shaken, and he wondered if it was owing to her generous and kind nature, or if she was touched by the episode personally somehow. His eyes had softened, and his voice carried the concern she saw when she looked at him.

She smiled at him and said, as if reading his mind, "I am a soft touch, and this kind of stuff does get to me, but it's more personal than that." *Am I really going to do this?* she thought. *Am I going to tell him?* She weighed the implications against her feelings. Her feelings won, but she knew it may be something she would rue later. She breathed deeply. *Here goes nothing.*

"My best friend was abducted when we were 12, Max. She spent the better part of a year as a sex slave. She had to endure being sold to one person or another before she was found and released back to her parents. This hits home."

Max reached across the table and took her small hand in his massive, strong one.

"Oh, my God. I am so sorry. Are you still close? How did it affect her?" Max winced a bit at the latter question, and Maggie could see that he dreaded the answer, but had to know.

"She was not the same afterward, and really, I don't know who she would have become if this had never happened. She went through a long battle with depression and shame, and she is a much harder woman than she probably would have been. When we were kids, she was always the dreamer, the one who helped me stretch my imagination. She thought that we could do and be anything, could have anything, go anywhere. These days, she rarely leaves her bedroom."

"I will never let anything happen to you, Maggie," he told her. Maggie shivered as she looked into Max's eyes and saw the glint of his true heart in the tears. She felt as though she could fall right into their depths.

"Thank you. It means a lot to hear you say that. I wish someone had said that to her when we were young and meant it." Maggie shouldered the guilt like a pro, having carried it around for so long.

Max caught the hook of the guilt barb that had buried itself into his girlfriend and said, "Listen to me, Maggie. I have known you long enough to know that you would never leave a friend in a predicament if you could help it. Weak hands and strong hearts are not compatible, and no one should ask a child to bear such a burden. You are strong and kind and resilient. You are resourceful and gracious and beautiful. You are loyal. You are what anyone would want. What I want—"

They sat, staring, studying each other intently, their faces inching closer as if to gain a deeper insight of the depths of character and soul they'd yet to plumb in each other. A raspy voice clearing its throat made itself known behind them. They both turned in unison to see Boris standing with a smirk on his face.

"The car is ready. You are coming or not?"

Max frowned at him, and any warmth Maggie had seen earlier disappeared in a blink.

"We are coming now," he said.

He stood and offered his hand and a warm grin to Maggie.

"Shall we?"

They walked around Boris, and both missed the look of hatred that flashed across his face.

Chapter 15

Sam crouched low next to one of the many old cypress trees that lined the secondary access road out of the airport. Since the remodel of the airport, the contractors decided it was too difficult to get their heavy equipment in and out using this road, so they built a larger, paved road to service Lakeside Airport. This one sat forgotten, wearing its age and antiquated utility like a badge of shame. A few locals still traveled the road, but it was also popular with smugglers. Sam smiled to himself when he heard, for what seemed like the hundredth time since they arrived out here, a smack, followed by a lot of mumbling from Abe.

"Why don't these damn things eat you like they do me?" Abe complained in a whisper to Sam.

"I guess they only like dark meat," he said with a chuckle.

"Funny. What do you do for an encore?"

"Hey, guys," came a squawk over the radio. "There's a truck coming up the road. Is this them?" Peter was stationed a little up the road from them and had obviously been paying more attention than Sam and Abe.

Sam looked around. He couldn't shake the feeling of being watched, and it annoyed him. He wasn't a paranoid person and rarely if ever worried about something he couldn't handle or take down, but with Abe and Peter to look after, he had his head on a swivel.

He said into the radio, "That should be them. Are you ready?"

"Absolutely," came the reply. "It will be nice to know exactly what these suits can do. I'm recording everything onboard for any improvements my team can make to the armor's performance."

"Whatever you need to do, homes," Sam answered. "Just make sure you're where you need to be when I need you, copy?"

"Yeah, I got it." Peter was excited at the prospect of using the high-tech armor he had created in a real situation. He had run many field trials so he knew that the suits would function the way they were intended, but to have a battle, or at least situational-proven unit—that was beyond his hopes for these machines.

The thought had occurred to him, more than once, that his creations would be very easy to mass-produce as adjuncts to the current military armament available, but he was no arms dealer or warmonger. *No*, he thought, *these are just for play—and for me to help my friends right now.*

While Peter was thinking, he failed to notice the wisp of golden, smokey ozone appearing behind him. Michael had heard, as he was very nearby, Peter's plan to record their encounter, and as much as he hated to do it, he was about to put the kibosh on that plan.

Sorry, Peter, thought Michael. *Can't have the possibility of any footage being hacked from your machine, even if it could help us.*

While Peter observed from his perch in his metal and carbon fiber creation, he heard a slightly audible, *Zap,* and then smelled ozone. He looked up to his left inside the structure and noticed a fizzle and sparks.

"Sam. Something's happened to the OCU. I need to see if I can fix it." OCU was onboard chronicling unit, just a fancy way of saying Go-Pro with an expanded chip and enhanced capabilities. Peter loved acronyms, and he used them whenever he could in his inventions.

"No time—stick to the plan," came the reply. "Sorry, kid. No footage this time."

Michael felt a little guilty about overloading Peter's video system, but he couldn't risk any video of this operation getting out. He knew that, with what they would be dealing with, proof floating around, readily available, would be very bad, indeed.

"Here they come. Hold up the gun like you mean to use it," Sam told him. "This will only work if it's completely believable."

"Got it." Peter said, still annoyed at his camera's untimely demise. "You guys just be ready to move because you won't have a lot of time to act when they figure out the gun doesn't actually shoot. As soon as I draw them out you need to get the girls and get out."

They could all hear the truck getting closer and instinctively crouched lower to avoid being seen. Sam watched as Peter stepped into the road in his mech suit and had to give props to the kid again for his ingenuity. It definitely looked the part. The suit Peter had created really did look as if it had stepped out of a video game.

Peter had said it was a prototype, but to Sam it looked real enough. It was seven feet of metal that allowed for anyone between 5' 7" and 6' 5" to control it. It was fitted with a sword which, at the present, was ensheathed at the back of the unit, and what appeared to be a mini-gun, which Peter was currently holding in order to get the truck to stop.

The old access road was buffeted on either side by cypress trees, mangroves and brackish, mucky water, so it didn't allow for a truck to turn around, only to go in and out. *Perfect ambush spot.* The truck driver must have known this because the truck had come to a stop and Sam was expecting men to come flooding out of the back. When no one emerged, Sam nudged Abe and the two snuck around the cypresses and made their way, Sam sprinting and Abe sort of speed-walking quickly behind him, as quietly as possible to the back of the truck.

The two worked silently as only well-trained soldiers could. Sam snuck a quick look into the back of the truck, searching for any support troops for the traffickers, but found no one. *Strange*, he thought. He knew that he would never move any cargo out in the open without backup, but maybe these guys weren't that smart.

He motioned for Abe to wait while he jumped up into the back of the truck and made a beeline for the door to the crate. The lock was still on the door and Sam motioned for Abe to come and pick the lock. Abe worked deftly and quickly. Sam wasn't really sure where Abe had picked up this particular gift, but he had assumed it was a parting gift from his childhood. The lock clicked easily. As quietly as possible, Sam opened the door to the girls in the back of the truck. He motioned for them to be quiet and beckoned them out of the back of the truck. Abe had jumped down out of the back of the truck, ready to assist the children that Sam started to hand down to the road one by one.

Sam was simultaneously trying to keep an eye on the girls' progress and on Peter who had not given ground or moved in the last five minutes. He kept repeating the phrase, "*You are trespassing on airport property. The authorities have been notified. You will remain in your vehicle.*"

Sam kept thinking it all seemed too easy when, from out of the cab of the truck, he heard a shrill whistle. *Backup?*, he thought. From the trees, including the one from which he and Abe had just come, came an abundance of what looked like small men on furry little goat legs, with red eyes and rather pasty complexions.

"What the hell? No!" Sam heard Abe say. He looked at the terror on Abe's face and knew without asking that Abe was familiar with these creatures. The goat-men-dwarves made their way towards Peter's mechanical suit.

Not good. They will tear that thing apart, and then they will do the same to the kid, Sam thought.

He noticed a machete laying near the tailgate of the truck and picked it up. "This may come in handy," he said, watching as Abe lowered the last of the girls to the ground. The rest of the girls were crouching in a ditch on the other side of the street waiting anxiously for Sam and Abe. Sam was just getting ready to signal Peter they were finished when the last little girl looked over at the creatures that had exited the swamp on the other side of the street and screamed.

The creatures turned and looked at the girl. Sam grabbed her up quickly, jumped the ditch in one colossal bound, and ran into the swamp away from the truck.

Peter took stock of the situation. He had not moved at all since he had stepped into the road. With the lights on his helmet, he could make out shapes of men in the cab. One man with a beak-shaped nose and very dark eyes leaned out the window and whistled.

Who is he calling to? thought Peter. He knew there had been no one in the rear of the truck, and the recon that Sam had done prior to staging the suit had made certain that the surrounding swamp contained no soldiers or backup.

Then he saw them. *Men—no, not men. Things. Oh my God—the grunch.*

Peter grew up in New Orleans and knew what the grunch were. These beings answering the whistle were right out of the stories that his father used to tell him when he was a kid. Standing about four feet high, some were walking upright like a man and others were running on all fours like a goat. They were spectre pale and had the eeriest red eyes.

Peter shivered and took a quick look at Sam who was standing at the back of the truck watching the creatures approach. He shifted his stance and decided that he may better off with the sword. Peter reached back with the gun and hooked it into position and quickly unhooked the sword and swung it free. He locked the hand in the closed position and brought the sword before him in a defensive gesture just as he heard a scream from one of the little girls. Peter looked over and saw her.

She was a grubby-looking, dark-haired girl with big brown eyes, maybe 12 years old, standing at the edge of the truck staring at the grunch and Peter with a look of pure terror. He imagined the sight of a seven foot robot with a sword and small demonic-looking hairy goat-men would be enough to traumatize any child. *I know a great shrink*, thought Peter, sardonically. He watched as the grunch turned to look back at the girl and saw Sam swoop in and snatch the girl up into his arms and disappear with her into the woods.

The grunch looked back at the truck as if for instruction, and with a flick of his wrist, the mystery man sent half chasing after the girls. Peter took a step to go after them when the rest of the pack of grunch fell on him en masse. Peter swung the great sword with all his might at the first of the creatures and heard the metal clang off its skull. It went sprawling to the ground about 20 feet away, and the rest stopped to watch the downed member. It struggled for a moment before it fell back to the ground. Peter couldn't tell if it was unconscious or dead, but the others let out an ungodly screech and advanced on him in earnest.

Peter cried out for Michael as he flailed with his sword, over and over. He managed to knock away another of the beasts and saw three more coming in fast. Another set of lights came out of the darkness behind him. He didn't know who was there, but before he could turn around, he saw four of the creatures go down and heard the rest howl in response. A great boom caused the remaining contingent to scatter, giving the truck a long last look before fleeing back into the swamp from where they had emerged.

Peter looked to the truck and saw the occupants vacating the cab and running for the back. The one with the nose was leading the others and Peter saw him stop at the back of the truck briefly and watch as Peter was surrounded by a group of people with guns drawn and swarming toward the truck. Peter took a step towards the back of the truck as if to pursue, but the leader decided to cut bait and run. He disappeared in the time it took Peter to blink.

What? Where the hell did he go? Peter swiveled around to look for him, but his attention was quickly occupied by the cavalry he didn't remember calling. The largest of the group broke off from the others and came up to Peter.

He knocked gingerly on the exterior of the suit and said in a loud voice, "These come in red?"

Peter pushed the control that raised the helmeted portion of the suit and said, "Yeah. Yellow, blue, and black as well. This was just a prototype so it resides in primer. Who are you? Thanks, by the way."

The man smiled at Peter and said "My name is Joshua. Special Agent Joshua Sargent. I'm with the FBI. Our bureau chief sent me—you may know him. Michaels? He sent us to help an operative in the field," he told Peter stressing the *Michaels* name. Peter caught on quickly.

"Thanks again for your assistance."

"Where's the rest of your team?" Sargent asked, looking around.

"My team? The rest of my *team* took the payload from the truck into the swamp heading in that direction." Peter pointed in the direction Sam and Abe took the girls, using the hand that still held the big sword.

Joshua ducked quickly and said, "Whoa, there big fella. Maybe you want to put that thing away now?"

Peter, slightly embarrasted, returned the sword to the mech's back and exited the cockpit. Jumping down, Peter could see that agent Sargent was, indeed, a large man.

"I don't think you're going to fit in one of these, agent. What are you, 6' 6"?"

"Yeah, about that. And call me Joshua." He quickly turned to bark some orders, rapid-fire, to a couple of lingering agents, then turned back to address Peter, more authoritative now.

"Your team should be meeting up with the team we have coming in from the other side. Right about—now." Joshua reached inside his coat pocket as the radio went off, and the agent on the other end told him that they had Abe and the children about a mile and a half up the road and had watched as a glowing pilot with a machete dealt with a large number of wild goat-dog-men before they ran off, then the glowing pilot just disappeared.

"Jokes, Smith? Inappropriate right now, don't you think? Glowing pilot?" Joshua said with a wink in Peter's direction. "Ten-four; meet you back at the hangar." He smiled over at Peter, "See? No worries. Let's go meet your friends. Bring your toy," Joshua said, slapping the side of the mech unit like it was Peter's shoulder. Peter nodded to Joshua.

He clambered back into the cockpit and said in a loud voice, "Try to keep up." He closed the suit's canopy again and, after making a few adjustments, turned back towards the direction of the hangar.

Leaving a very impressed agent behind, Peter engaged the mech and took off at a run. Peter did not build this feature into the units he was releasing to the public, but this one was his, designed to specifically flex its muscle and test future capabilities. He had added a few perks for himself, as well. This unit would top out at thirty-eight miles an hour, but to Peter it was no different than running in the park. The agents had to back the truck down the road because, on the small access road, there wasn't a way to turn around.

Peter thought the suit could cover more ground quicker if he counterbalanced the servo motors, when the rear end of the truck entered his peripheral vision, startling him. Soon the cab of the truck drew even with the mech's position, and Peter turned to see the agent. Joshua was in the truck and caught up to Peter going backwards. Peter was impressed by Joshua's driving skills, and thought if anyone could handle Peter's armor suits it would be this guy. He would have to see about making a model better-suited to someone as tall as Joshua.

They made quick work of the mile and a half of access road, and in no time they were stopping in front of Abe's hangar. Peter walked the unit into the building and back to the specialized storage container that housed it. The box would be moved back to his warehouse on the other side of the city later. He hopped down out of the suit and made his way back to the group waiting for him at the entrance. He could hear them discussing the mission as he walked up.

"Abe, did you meet Agent Joshua Sargent?" Peter asked Abe, questioning him silently about the absence of Sam. Abe shook his head, and Peter could tell it was in answer to both questions. Peter wondered why Sam had decided to disappear from this meeting.

"*special* Agent Sargent." Joshua gave Peter a sidelong glance, and then winked. "It's Joshua. Pleased to meet you, Abe." Abe grinned at the cowed look on Peter's face, and turned back to the large man.

"Pleasure to meet you. Thanks for having our six out there," Abe said stretching out his hand. He gestured with his free hand and said, "Welcome to my place, such as it is."

"No worries," he said. "You live here, Abe? In the hangar?" Joshua asked with raised brows.

"Yeah, I have a small place upstairs," he told them. "You are welcome to come up for some coffee, unless you would rather talk here. I personally could use some Advil, a beer, and a change of shorts." Peter and Joshua laughed at the joke—Peter nervously, but Joshua a little more heartily.

"That would be great. Let me just make sure that the others have their marching orders." The tall man turned and walked up to a female Hispanic agent. They spoke briefly, and she looked over at Peter and Abe, then back at her boss. She nodded her head, and Joshua, apparently satisfied that she understood, dismissed her, walking back to the men. "Agent Sanchez is setting up accommodations for the girls for tonight and—"

He was interrupted by a loud, "*You better get your hands off of me unless you want to lose them. This is my hangar!*" Abe's attention swung instantly to an agent trying to keep a very indignant Naomi from gaining access to their group.

"You may want to tell your people to let that one through. I can't guarantee their safety if they don't." Abe chuckled and Joshua smiled. "My niece is—spirited," he told them with a grin.

"O'Brien." Joshua yelled and O'Brien swung his body, still fending off Naomi, in the direction of Joshua and he continued, "let her through." Relieved, O'Brien released Naomi and stepped back quickly. Naomi stuck her tongue out at him and bolted past, sprinting the last of the distance, and threw her arms around her uncle.

"Uncle Abe, are you alright? What the hell is going on?" she asked him in a rush, glaring first at Peter and then at the large, older FBI agent.

Abe patted her on the back and told her, "I'm fine, but you have to calm down. I will tell you, but you keep yapping and nobody will be able to tell you anything."

Joshua jumped in and said, "My name is Special Agent Joshua Sargent, but please call me Joshua. Your uncle, and his friend Peter here, are heroes. They helped us stop some bad guys tonight."

Naomi's eyes had gone really wide, and she looked back and forth from Abe to Peter. She turned on Peter and started to yell, "What did you get my uncle into? He just doesn't—who are you?"

Abe barked sharply, "Naomi."

She stopped yelling and looked at her uncle.

"Apologize to Peter. This was *my* idea, not his, and you will apologize to me for being disrespectful," he finished in a no-nonsense tone, and a glare to match.

Naomi looked to Peter like a fiery angel. She was dressed for a night on the town, clad in a well-fitting black and gold dress and high heels, but she looked ready to battle anyone on behalf of her uncle.

Peter spoke to Abe quickly. "She was just concerned for you, Abe. It's understandable." He smiled at Naomi who was glaring at him in response to his chivalry. Lessening the intensity of the glare somewhat, she softened slightly.

"No, no, he's right. I apologize for the assumption, Peter. Obviously, my uncle thinks that he is invincible and has decided to try to give me a heart attack, but let *me* just apologize for not getting all the facts before showing concern," she finished, rolling her eyes at the absurdity of it.

Peter was impressed at her spunk and awed by her beauty. "In your situation, I think I would do the same thing. Very glad to meet you, Naomi."

Her ire cooled at his sincerity, and she smiled tentatively, saying, "Likewise. Now, what *is* all of this about?"

Abe frowned at her and said, "I'm sorry you were worried. I'm also sorry that you felt that I could not handle myself. I'm *also* sorry that you couldn't take a minute to assess the situation before losing your damn mind. If you would take a minute to look around you, you would see a bunch of very frightened children, and your bellowing probably frightened them even further."

Naomi looked around and noticed for the first time the little girls that were huddled together, crying, and holding each other. They looked at her with fear, and her countenance changed from annoyance to maternal concern.

She is possibly the most beautiful thing I've ever seen. How come I can talk to her? Peter searched his brain wildly for an answer to his thought, but had nothing. *Adrenaline? Don't know...*

She turned back to her uncle and said, "Again, I'm sorry—really this time. I should trust you know what you're doing, but all of this was sudden, and it scared me." She gave her uncle a quick hug, and turning to the very tall agent, looked up at him while removing her shoes.

She definitely means business—good, he thought. *We can use her help.*

"Give me something to do," she told Joshua.

Abe smiled and patted her on the shoulder, "That's my girl," he said with obvious pride.

Peter thought, *You should be proud, Abe. Not only is she beautiful and fiery, but compassionate and caring.* Peter didn't care for most people his age. At the very least, he didn't care for their self-centeredness. While Peter had only known Naomi for the last few minutes, he knew that he would be fine with her. In the same way that Abe had skewered his view of him when he stuck up for Peter with Sam, Peter knew that Naomi was very much her uncle's niece when she displayed such concern on the heels of her tirade. *This could get very interesting,* he thought.

Joshua said, "These girls will need a place to stay tonight while we begin the process of getting them back to their families. Some of the parents have already been contacted, and they will be flying into the airport, so someplace close would be ideal."

"You can put them up here," offered Abe. "I'm sorry it isn't bigger than it is, but I have two bedrooms, and the sofa makes into a bed as well. There are plenty of pillows, and I think in one of these shipping containers there are emergency supplies like cots and blankets. We could set them up in the living room or even here in the hangar. Naomi, could you stay and help the agents with the girls? I'm sure after all they have been through, a woman's presence would be preferable to a man's." Abe turned to Peter and asked, "Do you have an extra room for me?"

"Sure, no problem. You're welcome as well," he turned to Joshua. "Matter of fact, I only live about 20 minutes from here in the quarter—your agents are welcome to stay as well," Peter offered.

"We have accommodations in the city, but you are right about the female agents. We will post a few guards on the doors, and the rest will go back to their assigned quarters," Joshua told him. "If you don't mind, I will accompany you and Abe. There's a few things we should discuss."

Naomi had been following the conversation and piped up, "I still want to know what is going on. What it is you are keeping from me?" Peter could tell that she knew there was more to the story than they were letting on.

Abe changed the subject by turning to Sargent and saying, "If any of these girls needs transportation to their home states, Naomi is a pilot and she can use one of my planes to take them home. Just say the word, no charge."

"Thanks, Abe. We will gladly use your planes, but the government will pay to take the girls home."

"Naomi, would you please go see about getting the hangar loft ready for the girls, and see if there is anything you can throw together for them to eat? The boys and I will see about those cots." Naomi looked as if she was going to argue, but at that moment one of the little girls came up to Abe and yanked on his arm.

"Mister Abe?" she questioned, "I'm Sarah. This afternoon, Sam came to tell us you all were going to set us free. Where did he go? Where is Sam?"

Naomi looked at the girl, who she figured was around 11 or 12, then over at her uncle. She saw him wince a little. Joshua bent to address her, "Who is Sam, Sarah? What can you tell us about him?" She looked at all of the adults in turn, and she appeared to be taken with Naomi, so she addressed the lady directly instead of the huge agent.

"Sam's my guardian angel. He rescued us from the truck tonight, and then again from those things."

She shivered and Namoi knelt down and grabbed her in a hug. Peter saw that the girl had started to cry and held on tight to Naomi. Abe looked over at Peter and shrugged. Joshua watched the exchange and Peter figured he thought they didn't know who Sam was.

"Can you describe Sam to us?" Joshua asked her in a soft voice. She looked at him over Naomi's shoulder and let her go enough to be heard by all of them.

She nodded her head and said, "He was with me out in the swamp, I screamed when I saw the things with the red eyes." Peter could see the strength in her and noticed that she wasn't flinching.

This girl is something, he thought. *She's not afraid.*

"I was surprised at how fast they were, because they were shorter than me, and didn't look like they could run. They got on us pretty quickly," she continued, matter-of-factly.

The agent kept up the softer tone. "Then what happened?"

She looked at Joshua and said, "Sam grabbed my hand and started running through the swamp. We ran and those things started to chase us. He let my hand go and told me to run after the other girls, that he would keep the things busy. Then he turned around and swung his big knife at the creatures. He started to glow and the things were afraid of him. They circled around him and I ran..." she trailed off, staring at Peter and Joshua, not at all phased by her description of a glowing person with a knife. "I haven't seen him since, but I think he is probably fine. He looked like he was handling the things. The policeman found us then and I told him about Sam. He ran off to find him, but I don't think he did because Sam isn't here. I have a feeling he got away, though."

Sarah looked exhausted. Naomi put her arm around the girl, and they went up into the apartment. Peter watched her ascend the metal stairs, the young girl close to her side.

What a person she must be, Peter thought. *I hope I can spend more time with her.* Abe watched as Peter stared after his niece and knew what he must be thinking.

You better watch yourself, Peter. She's as likely to break your legs and your heart, he thought.

"I'm going to run upstairs and grab my gear. Don't leave without me," Abe said as he trotted after his niece.

While he was gone, Peter took the opportunity to step away, get some fresh air, and think. He excused himself to the agent and walked to the front of the hangar to catch the faint breeze. Peter figured that Sam didn't want any attention, and that is why he chose to disappear. He also figured that when he was ready he would reappear. At least Peter hoped he would reappear. He needed Sam to get him to Russia. He turned to stroll back to where the agents set about finding cots for the girls. He joined in pulling stuff out of the supply crates, and when they had them all settled for the night, Abe, Joshua, and Peter left together in Abe's old truck for the city.

Peter let the night wind whip at his face, surveying the hangar behind him in the side view mirror when he noticed two things: a pale, ghostlike figure melt into the woods outside the hangar, and Sam smiling at him from right behind him from under a tarp in the bed of the truck.

Chapter 16

Peter was relieved to know where Sam had disappeared to, but he was also concerned about the figure he saw melting into the shadows. Could that have been one of the grunch at Abe's hangar, or was it his imagination playing tricks on him? Peter wasn't sure if he really saw anything. It had been a very trying day after all, and he just wanted to go home.

As it was, he wasn't sure he would ever sleep again. Those things they had encountered, although real enough, were straight out of his worst childhood nightmares. *Well, the ones that didn't involve snakes, anyway,* he thought.

Peter was sweating, but it wasn't because of the New Orleans heat. October nights in the bayou were typically mild if not cold, so the temperature wasn't the issue tonight. He figured the shock of their recent escapade was finally catching up with him, and his overactive imagination was beating up his poor, defenseless psyche.

Of course, Peter reasoned, *if I tell anyone other than Dr. Jo about tonight, they will think I'm a lunatic.* He thought back to a man that he had met as a child, Jera Piquane, who used to troll up and down Royal Street and talk to himself, and on occasion yell at passersby. One particular day stuck out to him: he had been with his nanny, and it was a brutally hot day in late August. She had offered to buy him a Nehi before they caught the cab for home. She had rushed out to buy a book for her required reading before school got back in, and he had to tag along. On these trips that were on the down low and not sanctioned by his parents, he always received a treat for not snitching. They had stopped at Royal Pharmacy and gotten their drinks. Peter hadn't remembered seeing the man on the way in, but he sure remembered him on their way out. Jera had a reputation as a *couyon*, a Creole fool, and mostly he was just ignored by the people in the Quarter. His preferred subject for his tirades was always the government or some conspiracy, and like most crazy people, he was loud and intense. Peter had just inserted the straw into his grape soda and pushed the door open when he was greeted by Jera and his rantings.

"*Dey come, cher. Dat gronch one mean sumbitch. Eyes like blood and dey skin like a ghost. Listen your momma, cher.*"

The man had looked frantic and ecstatic all at once, which is to say quite insane. Peter remembered the wild-eyed man had scared him both with his erratic behavior and his words. Peter had never been one for superstition, and he knew better than to fear the boogeyman, but Jera had certainly believed what he spoke, and that sort of sincerity is unsettling.

He brought himself back to the present and peered out the window. *Nothing out there now,* he thought. He turned back toward the front of the truck, and found both Joshua and Abe staring at him from across the seat.

"What?" he asked.

Abe just shook his head and looked at Joshua. "You said that you had questions for us? Now's as good a time as any to ask them."

Joshua cleared his throat and said, "We aren't getting any younger, and the events of tonight deserve some explanation. I'll make you both a deal; you tell me what you know, and I'll return the favor."

"Fair enough," said Abe, and Peter nodded his head in agreement.

Joshua reached into his sport jacket, pulled out a pack of Camels, plucked one from the gold foiled box, lit it, took a hefty drag, and blew the smoke long and slow out of the passenger window.

"Mind if I smoke, Abe?"

Abe glanced at the man sidelong and just replied, "Aren't you already? Yeah, that's fine. Keep the window down."

Joshua chuckled, flicked his ash out the window, and began, "Maybe I should start by explaining who I am and who I'm with."

"I thought you were with the FBI?" Abe said warily, surprised that what he assumed may not be the case. He panicked. "You'd better start explaining, man. I left my niece with your people." Abe was now glaring at Joshua. Peter sat, content to wait on the large agent's explanation.

"Okay Abe, settle down. Your niece is perfectly fine and in very capable FBI hands," he told them. "I'm talking about another organization entirely. This one is led by a mutual friend of ours.".

"Michael," Peter said.

Abe's gaze went from Joshua to Peter and back to the road in front of them.

"That's right, only he's Chief Special Agent Michaels at the bureau. Longtime commander, exemplary agent, squeaky clean record—allows him, and us, to do a lot and get a lot of help. The other organization that I am with is the one that Michael told you about earlier. He left you guys in the truck at the hangar and dispatched us right away. It was a hasty mobilization, and we didn't have all the X's and O's worked out. Michael wasn't expecting the grunch out there, or he would have sent the Guardians along with us, I'm sure of that."

Peter sat up and asked in an excited voice, "Guardians?"

Joshua looked at Peter and with a tired smile said, "Yeah, sorry. Guardians as in guardian angels. I don't see them except on very special, very specific missions—mostly when we are fighting something otherworldly, like vampires, the occasional werewolf, those sorts of creatures. Did you know that vampires love candy? And that werewolves can't stand on two legs in lycine form?" Joshua and Peter looked at each other in a shared geek-out moment, and Joshua continued, "Then sometimes, like tonight, we get the obscure regional creatures that most people have never heard about. Or worse, have heard about and dismiss completely." Joshua continued to watch Peter's face, and Peter could feel his inner geek bouncing up and down in the seat with the thought that the creatures he had only read about and built in his workshop were actually real.

"So, these guardians—what exactly do they look like?" Abe asked, just as curious as Peter. The two of them looked at Joshua who stared at the traffic zipping by them on the highway.

"They are indescribable, really, and just between you and me, if they weren't on my side, I'd rather see a thousand vampires or werewolves or grunch. They are truly terrible," Joshua said to Peter's disappointment, "but I will give it a shot. "The reason I said they are indescribable is because, like humans, they vary in appearance. They can be short or tall depending on the situation. They can be menacing, terrifying, protective, attractive, innocuous, even invisible. Every single one that I have met has a wicked sense of humor. I truly think that they have fun at their jobs, and sometimes when faced with large numbers, they hold contests among themselves to see who can destroy the most enemy combatants."

Peter was watching Joshua as he spoke of the Guardians. *He's totally got angel envy.* he thought.

"I think that one of my men experienced something similar tonight," Joshua finished.

"How so?" asked Abe.

"Your guy, Sam—we know who he is, obviously, and I believe he went angel tonight on those grunch. He's probably still pretty pissed off, but he won't remember," Joshua told him. "Sam has only shown his angel a handful of times that I've heard of, mostly when he is really angry, and he never remembers it. He doesn't know who he is—part of the curse, I guess."

Peter couldn't resist a peek in the back of the truck. Sam was still there under the tarp.

Hell of a curse, Peter thought. *Poor guy.*

Again, Peter found himself wondering about Sam—if he didn't remember who he was, or more importantly *what* he was, what had his life been like for all of the years he had been on the Earth? Why had Sam disappeared back at the hangar?

"When he *angels out* as you call it, what happens afterwards? If it's holy amnesia, how has he been on the Earth so long and not figured it out?" Peter was perplexed and looking for answers.

"Question for Michael, I'm afraid, Peter. I just don't know the answer."

Peter tried to reason it out, and he supposed that maybe there was some sort of reset that Sam went through. He didn't strike Peter as a man that got attached to anyone, so there would be no family or friends that would be around to tell him, and he was outliving anyone he may know besides. It was something he would definitely ask Michael.

"Hey," Abe said, checking his phone, "we are supposed to fly to Russia in a few hours."

Peter was pulled out of his thoughts by Abe's announcement to Joshua and found that they had made it back to the Quarter.

"We really need some sleep, Peter, but we also need to talk about next steps. Do you think Momma Rose is awake? I'm kind of hungry."

Joshua got a funny look on his face at the mention of Rose, and Peter had noticed.

"Something wrong, Joshua?" Peter asked.

"Nah, just thinking about what I'm going to tell O'Brien later."

Peter turned back to Abe, who had brought the truck to a stop in the same parking garage, blocks from the bistro. "Momma Rose has always been awake when I come home late, it doesn't really matter what time it is. She always waits up. We really don't have a lot of time, so let's go."

Peter opened the door to the old truck, and he and Joshua piled out one side as Abe got out on the other side. He ushered Abe and Joshua forward while he tapped lightly on the bed of the truck to signal Sam to slink out of the back and into the shadows. Peter than turned and jogged forward to catch up with the other two, both questioning him with a look.

He patted his pocket when he reached them and said, "I thought I dropped my wallet in your truck. Turns out I just moved it to a different pocket. Let's get going." He grinned and they both shook their heads and continued to walk to where coffee, beignets, and friendly faces awaited. The bistro was lit, and the little wrought iron tables that had been painted a pristine white shone from the light that poured out of the spotless windows. Momma Rose was a stickler for a clean place and always had either a broom or a cleaning cloth of some kind in her hand. Tonight was no exception. She was busily wiping down her already immaculate counter as the trio walked in. She looked up as the bell over the door announced their presence.

"Peter," she exclaimed. "Thank the Master you are okay." Peter was stunned when Momma Rose dropped her cleaning cloth in a heap on the counter and rushed to give him a hug. It was then that she finally noticed the stranger in their midst. Peter turned to introduce their friend but was preempted by the tall agent.

"Rose," was all Joshua said.

Momma Rose was strangely silent and very still. He saw her expression change briefly, and thought she looked a little sad. As quickly as it had appeared, she marshalled control over her features and managed to draw herself a smile again.

"Joshua, nice to see you. How have you been? Where have you been keeping yourself?" she said carefully.

"Here and there, hither and yon, Rose. You know me."

Joshua opened and closed his mouth a few times like he was going to say something further, but in the end he turned to Peter and asked, "So, where do you want to talk? We need to discuss what happened this evening. And plan."

Momma Rose take a deep breath as she said, "I will go get some coffee and food from the kitchen. If you wish to speak in private you can follow me to the kitchen." She turned and left without checking to see if they followed.

Peter turned to Joshua and said, "I don't know the story between you two, but I have to think she meant that for you."

"Given our history, you're probably right. If you will excuse me." Joshua eyed Peter and looked at Abe to judge his reaction. Abe just shook his head and flicked his eyes back to Peter.

"What did happen between you two? Are you friends?" Joshua gave Peter a negative expression. "*More* than friends?" Peter asked, not wanting to know the answer.

"Peter, don't wear me out on this. I know you are family, so let's get that out of the way. It's complicated, and it's between us. Between. Us." Joshua emphasized the two words, and Peter responded with an understanding look. Joshua waited another moment for Peter to process this. "Now, how about we go talk about the bad guys?"

Peter hesitated a moment and looked over at Abe who had been silent throughout the whole exchange. Abe once again made no comment other than a slight shake of his head. Peter figured he was indicating to pick your battles, and this one was not pressing.

Peter strode off in the direction of the kitchen, leaving the other two to follow. He walked into the back room and was hit with a sense of déjà vu. He shook off the feeling, knowing that just hours earlier he, Momma Rose, Abe, and Michael were all huddled around the same table.

Joshua commandeered a seat across from Peter and Abe. Peter thought this was an ingrained habit on the part of an officer, and he got the distinct impression this was going to be more interrogation and less friendly chat. It would be his second debrief today, and he was tired.

Momma Rose came in the room and handed out cups of coffee. She placed a plate of cheese, fresh fruit, and bread on the table between them, then handed Abe and Peter a plate and placed the third on the table without looking in Joshua's direction. She turned abruptly and left the room.

Peter raised an eyebrow at Abe as Joshua heaved a heavy sigh and picked up the plate from the edge of the table. The three men helped themselves to the food, and as they sipped their coffee Joshua turned to Peter and said, "So why don't you tell me what happened tonight?"

Peter gulped a bit of coffee, swallowed, and said, "I was just tagging along, honestly. Abe?" He deferred to the old officer.

"It was like this," Abe said sipping on his coffee. "Sam landed with a questionable shipment, again—I think you know what I mean."

Abe looked meaningfully at Joshua, and he nodded, "Yeah, I get it. This for Avatov again?"

"Bingo. Anyway, Peter has business with Sam and me moving some of his cargo, so we meet up. He was there when Sam told me about the kids. Peter offered to let us borrow his gear, but only he knows how to control it, so he became part of the op. Sam and I should have been alone, but the plans changed." Abe grumped.

"Hey," Peter countered. "You know that if you hadn't taken me along you would have gotten your ass handed to you, courtesy of those little white freaks." Besides, there wouldn't have been enough time to teach you all the controls." He turned back to the agent, "We only found out about the kids a couple hours before—not enough time to uncrate and prepare the suits that were shipping, so we used my prototype." Peter picked his sandwich up and took a big bite.

"I'm not saying you weren't welcome, Peter. You did a great job." Abe said, and he meant it. "I just didn't want to have to involve anyone else in those kinds of dealings. Those men are ruthless. They won't hesitate to put a bullet in anyone who gets in their way."

Peter seemed mollified, and Joshua took the opportunity to jump into the conversation.

"He's right, Peter," the agent said. "Listen, you two. We were able to identify at least two of the suspects in the truck. Unfortunately, the third was too much in the shadows to see who he was."

Peter earnestly offered, "I'm sure I got everyone that was there. Want me to see?"

"You're joking. Really? I thought your video fizzled out?" The agent seemed genuinely stunned.

Peter sat back in his seat, spread his arms in a wide shrug and said, "The unit is designed to record every moment from power up until you deactivate it. The OUC malfunctioned, sure, but the visor should have recorded some stills. I know that I looked at the cab of the truck a few times and remember seeing our mystery man as he leaned out the window. Guarantee you I've got him," Peter told him confidently.

"Even with no light? It was very dark, and the lights from the truck were on the suit. I doubt that the suit would have been able to get a clear image," Joshua told him.

"The suit is auto-aware, Joshua." Peter paused for effect. "The cameras will adjust based on light or lack of it. What I mean is, the suit will modify the light in order to see what it is focused on. I should have a clear picture of whoever was in that truck regardless of whether or not there was light shining on the suit."

"Wow, kid. I'm impressed. When do you think we could get a copy of that?" Joshua asked him.

"How about now? I have the SD card in my pocket. When we go upstairs we can plug it into my computer, and I'll send it to you," Peter said, leaning forward in his seat. He rested his elbows on his knees, folded his fingers into steeple and used his paired index fingers to prop up his chin as he spoke. "As far as what else happened tonight, the creepiest part was the mystery guy seemed to have a connection with the grunch. They responded to his whistle. I mean, how does something like that even happen?" Peter sat back in the chair, rubbed his weary eyes, and muttered. "Dude must have made a deal with the devil."

Joshua lost the grin from his face and said, "You aren't entirely wrong. The grunch are not human. They are also not known to be in the company of humans—ever. They are solitary with one exception." Joshua stood to address the two men gravely, leaning his hands on the back of the wrought iron chair. "The grunch have been known to become thralls for vampires—something about a vampire being able to communicate telepathically with them and make them understand. Maybe our mystery man is a vampire," Joshua opined.

Abe looked concerned. "All those children are at my hangar. Do you think they will be okay? I mean, can't vampires turn into bats and stuff?"

"No, that's just something that Hollywood made up. They don't glitter, either. That's just stupid." Joshua sat back in his seat, the hours catching up with him. He was tired as well, but they had to press on. He continued, "They do have a thirst for blood and are unbelievably strong, though. They also move incredibly fast, which is why we typically leave them to the Guardians. I will report this back to Michael. I'm sure that he will send the others to watch out for everyone at your place. I will handle all the paperwork, and the local authorities, so don't worry about that. What's your next move?" The agent leaned back, addressing Abe and Peter. "Russia?"

"Yeah, catching a plane in the morning. Well, in a few hours," Peter said, looking at his watch. "I need to get some sleep." He yawned and stood up to leave. "I need to let Momma Rose know that I will be leaving, well—today. Here are the keys to my house, just go out the door and you will see a set of stairs that leads to my door. I'll be up in a few minutes."

Peter handed the keys to Abe and shouted for Momma Rose. Abe and Joshua went out the side door toward the stairs Peter had indicated and ascended to his house. Peter watched from one of the side windows as they opened the door and walked inside. He started when the front door chimed a new arrival. Sam walked through the door as Momma Rose came out of the kitchen.

She smiled at Sam, who sat at a nearby table, and said to Peter, "Why are you shouting for me? You knew I was in the kitchen." she admonished.

"Yes, I knew. Sorry." He bent and kissed her cheek. "I wanted the others to leave and needed an excuse to stay behind." He cocked his head in Sam's direction, and Momma Rose nodded in response. "Oh, by the way, I will be flying to Russia in the morning—I mean, in a couple of hours. Do you think I could take some food with me, please?" he asked her, giving her puppy dog eyes.

"Mon chou, you constantly are prevailing on my *bonne nateur (better nature)*, but yes, I will make certain you have something for the trip. You know I will do anything for you. You must sleep while the pilots fly, or you will be no good to anyone, no?" she said with concern.

Peter ignored her. "I should only be gone a couple of days. If it's longer, I'll call you. I'll bring my keys by when I leave." He gave her another kiss on the cheek and turned to Sam.

"Where'd you get to tonight? You kind of had us worried when you disappeared." He sat down across from the larger man and asked, "Do you need a place to put up for the night?"

"I can't have my face known to the feds." Sam said, "That kind of thing could get you killed by the people I work for."

"Who do you work for, Sam?" Peter asked.

"Nobody you need to ever be concerned with, kid," Sam said. "And as far as your previous question is concerned, do you think I could stay with Momma Rose? I mean, do you think she will let me crash in the restaurant tonight?" he hurried on after he caught Peter's look.

Peter grinned and said, "Momma Rose is used to taking in strays of all kinds. She has a cot in the back room for the ones she thinks are too drunk to get home at night. I didn't see anyone in the back room, so I guess you could use it," Peter told him. "You need to get some rest, though. I'm trusting you to get me to Russia in one piece, and I don't know how to fly."

Sam grinned at Peter and said, "It's a good thing I don't require much sleep then, isn't it?"

Peter led the way to the back room where Momma Rose let the occasional inebriated patron crash for the night. Usually they woke up and didn't know where they were or how they ended up there, but Momma Rose always made them feel at home and never had a bad word to say about any of them.

"Feel free to make yourself at home, but I should warn you, don't go into the kitchen. Momma Rose is very protective of her kitchen."

"Duly noted. Don't go into the kitchen."

"I'll meet you here in the morning. I'll try to sneak out without the others waking. With any luck, we will be in the air before they notice I'm gone. By the way, Joshua said that one of his agents saw a golden warrior with a giant sword in the woods tonight. Can you believe that?" Peter laughed slightly, shaking his head. "Did you see anything like that while you were out there?"

He watched Sam for a hint of recognition or even acknowledgment that such a thing could have occurred, and that he knew how and why. Nothing. Sam was not giving anything away, and Peter was almost certain that he really believed he didn't know about it.

"No, I don't remember seeing a glowing warrior with wings and a giant sword tonight."

Peter studied him closely. "No worries, it was a silly thing anyway. Hope you can rest for a few hours. I'll be back here at five to get you."

Peter left Sam in the little back room and made his way to the side door. Sam watched Peter leave and thought about the question that had been burning through his brain all evening.

What had happened out in the woods earlier? He had tried to work through the details on the ride over in the back of the truck. *I remember I was running with—Sarah—The grunch came at me from out of the shadows of a cypress hammock. I got knocked down by one of them. Sarah peeled off from me—I looked up and saw one of the grunch tailing her and gaining. I remember a burning anger welling up inside, consuming me. And then, just—images—feelings. Sensations. Strength and brightness and heat. Overwhelming wrath. Wind, fast and biting. The sounds of the forest whirling. The anguished cries of so many unholy beasts. The beating of great wings.*

He didn't know why, but he felt that this had happened to him before. He *knew* it had. It was exciting and frustrating all at the same time. It was like having a memory that you can't quite remember, you know you have done or tried something before, but you just can't remember all the details. The only thing that Sam knew for certain was that this had happened to him before and—*It felt right*.

Peter walked up the stairs, turned the knob, flicked on the switch for the outside light and closed his door. Closing the door on Governor Nicholls Street. Closing the door on this weird and exhausting and frightening day. He walked through his darkened house and thought about the conversation minutes earlier, recalling all the details of their exchange.

I don't remember seeing a glowing warrior with wings and a giant sword tonight. Those were Sam's exact words, and they gave him hope. Peter had never mentioned anything about the warrior having wings.

Chapter 17

After a not so restful couple of hours, Peter decided he needed to get moving before the other two woke up. He padded into the bathroom and splashed some water on his face, then crept quietly down the hall with his bags in tow. Out of the kitchen strolled Abe, holding a cup of coffee. He raised an eyebrow, and Peter could swear he heard him questioning why he was trying to sneak out of his own house. Peter pulled him back into the kitchen and spoke in a hushed voice, "I was trying to get ready without waking you up—or Joshua. Clearly, that didn't work out. How's the coffee?"

Peter jutted his chin in the direction of Abe's cup as he struggled with fastening a carabiner ring to his overloaded backpack.

"On either count," came a voice from behind him.

Peter gave a yelp and spun around. "This is why I live alone, you know."

Joshua chuckled, helped himself to a cup of coffee, and asked, "Why didn't you want us awake?"

"Sam doesn't know you know about him, and I stashed him at Momma Rose's place last night. I told him I would meet him this morning to get back to the airport for the flight to Moscow."

Abe said quietly, "How were you planning on getting back to the airport? You don't have a car."

"Oh, I was going to call a cab or one of those new ride share companies. Now that you're up, though, would you mind taking us back? Sam knows about you."

"What about Joshua?" Abe turned to the man in question.

"Don't worry about me—I'm covered. I'll call one of my agents to come pick me up. One of the perks of being the old timer."

Peter smiled. "All settled. We need to get moving, though. Come on, Abe. Joshua, stay as long as you need to. I downloaded those files to a flash drive for you and put it on the desk in the office. Please lock the door when you leave. I'm leaving Momma Rose my keys. I'll stay in touch and let you know where I'm staying when I land in case you have any more questions. Thanks for everything, by the way."

Peter pushed Abe out the front door. The last thing he saw as the front door closed was Joshua calmly sipping his coffee and shaking his head. Peter and Abe made their way downstairs in the chilled early morning to find Sam. As they went in through the little side door that Peter thought of fondly as *his* entrance, they heard voices coming from the kitchen. The aroma of fresh bread and sausage wafted enticingly through the air.

Peter and Abe looked at each other and rushed to the kitchen in time to hear Momma Rose say, "You eat as much as my Peter. Mon dieu, I thought he could polish off a plate fast, but I believe you may have him beat."

"Give me another chance, Momma. I'll make you proud," Peter joked from just inside the doorway.

Momma Rose spun around clutching her heart. "Mon chou, don't sneak up on me like that, unless you are trying to kill me. Then who would make your meals?" she teased.

Peter grabbed her up in a hug and swung her around. "I would never hurt my girl."

Momma Rose giggled and swatted him with her trusty cleaning towel. Peter put her down and grabbed a beignet from the nearest plate, which earned him an additional swat.

"Leave those. These," she said, holding up a large bag, "are for you."

Peter took the outstretched bag from Momma Rose and pulled her in for another hug. "I'm gonna miss you while I'm gone," he told her.

She smiled and patted his cheek. "You be careful, and call me as soon as you land."

He handed her the keys to the house and told her that Joshua was still upstairs. Could she please check that he locked the door when he left?

"Of course."

She had lost a little bit of her spark when he mentioned Joshua, so he asked her, "Are you okay?"

Once again she smiled, but it didn't reach her eyes. "I'm fine." For a second, she seemed far away to Peter, but just as quickly, she was back. "Peter, really. I'm wonderful, and you are not going to be so wonderful as you will be late, mon chou. Get. *Get.*"

"Okay kid, time to go. Rose, it was a pleasure, and thank you for letting me stay last night," Sam told her. "Abe we're catching a lift back with you, I assume?"

"Yep. Rose, can I have just one more for the road?" Abe asked her beseechingly.

Rose reached behind her and brought a second large bag forward. "There are plenty in here for you and the girls at the airport. Now you boys make sure that they make it to them, you hear?"

"Rose, you really are an angel you know that?" Abe said with a big smile.

This time the smile that Rose gave the trio was genuine, and Peter could tell that she liked the compliment very much by the tinge of pink he saw on her cheeks. Momma Rose waved to them through the glass window as the trio marched out of the little café.

"I must say, you are a lucky man, Peter," Sam told him.

"You sure are," seconded Abe. "I think my waistline would take a severe beating if I lived near that woman, though."

"Momma Rose has been very generous around you two. Maybe I should have you by more often. Most nights she fends me off the beignets and hands me a plate with vegetables and some sort of pasta or meat with it," Peter told them.

Sam was having a hard time deciding if Peter was being serious or not and said, "Oh, you poor thing, to have someone who looks out for you and cooks for you. The horror—the absolute horror. She should be horsewhipped."

Peter's caught Sam's feigned look of horror and busted out laughing. "I guess you're right. She is the best, but then so is her food."

Peter looked at the bag he held longingly but was determined to make the provisions last as long as possible. The trio made their way to Abe's truck and climbed inside.

Sam made a couple of phone calls to the airport to check that his plane was loaded and ready for takeoff. He had registered the additional cargo and one passenger for his flight to Russia and wanted to be sure that they were listed and all the paperwork was in order.

Abe turned on the radio and was humming along with "*What a Wonderful World.*" Peter had always loved the song, and today he wanted to believe that it *was* a wonderful world. Some of the seedier things that he had recently experienced aside, the world as a whole was a great place. He would love to be one of the people responsible for making it better, but he knew the responsibility for that rested on everyone. If everyone in the world took time to stop and be nice to one or two people in a day, and they did the same, the ripple would widen to reach everyone in the world. He knew that there were people who didn't or couldn't return a kindness shown them with kindness. They were the people that needed the most help.

Sam looked at Peter and said, "Can't reach them all, kid."

Peter stared for a moment. "How did you know I was thinking about helping people?"

"You had that look like you were trying to solve the world's problems," Sam told him. "Look, we can't always be there to offer protection like we were last night. We can only watch and help as much as possible. We did what we did last night because those kids needed help. There wasn't anyone around who could do what we did. We keep doing it until we die or get caught—that's it. There are units and agencies that work in the big cities to take these monsters down. But out here? We're it."

"I've been thinking about that, myself," Abe piped up, "and I'm going with you. You're not going to be any good trying to do this haul by yourself, Sam, and someone needs to watch out for Peter while you watch everything else."

"I'm not going to argue with you, buddy boy. I'll take the help of a damn good pilot any day and any time it's offered," Sam agreed, and immediately called the airport to amend his earlier manifest request.

"Abe, are you sure? What about Naomi and the girls?" Peter asked.

"They'll be fine with Joshua and his agents, Peter. As you have no doubt already seen, Naomi is quite capable of taking care of herself. We," he added in a slightly quieter voice so Sam could not hear, "have a mission of our own, don't we?" Abe gave Peter a pointed look with his eyebrows raised, and Peter got the point. The girl's horror that they had discovered and helped to mitigate last night did not cancel out *his* mission, and Peter felt glad for the help.

"Yeah, I hear you," Peter agreed. "You know, I would like to find out more about the people in New Orleans that help kids the way Sam was describing. I think I could do some good there."

"Son, you're going to do a lot of good for a lot of people before this is all said and done. I'm certain of that. We're here. I'll just be a minute," Abe said, bringing the old truck to a halt in front of his hangar.

Peter got out of Abe's rusty old truck and stretched his back. He knew there would be a long flight ahead, and even though he wasn't the one flying, Peter had never been able to sleep in a moving vehicle of any type. Plane, train, car, or bus, it didn't matter. He just couldn't let himself relax enough to fall asleep.

They strode purposefully across the tarmac. The cool air brushed past them, and a breeze whisked Sam's dark hair around his head, in too big of a hurry to be polite as it rushed to join a zephyr somewhere far away. The two men stopped in front of a cargo plane. Although Peter had caught a glimpse of it the previous night, he didn't remember it being so imposing. He climbed the stairs to board and noticed that although the plane itself was massive, most of the available space was taken up by cargo, and the seating choices were limited.

I guess on a cargo plane, you are part of the cargo, Peter thought wryly.

Abe passed him by, concentrating on some interior checkpoints, giving the plane a good once-over and ignoring him completely. Sam brushed by him and went to the wall of the plane. He unlatched and unfolded an additional seat.

"Seat's yours. Sorry it isn't larger, but if you want to lay down and sleep—" he gestured to the stowed cot at the far wall. "It folds out the same way the seat did. Make sure that you lock them well when you aren't using them. Last thing I want is a body out the back on this trip." Sam turned and went back into the cockpit and sat down.

"He's not serious, is he, Abe?"

Abe laughed and chucked Peter on the shoulder, then turned and joined Sam who was busily making preparations to leave.

Peter glanced back at the wall and made sure that the latches on the bed were secure. He sat down in his little jump seat and strapped in. Peter was not fond of flying, which is to say he hated it. It didn't scare him, but he found it boring and exceedingly uncomfortable, due to both limited space and pressure.

Peter knew enough about cargo aircraft like Sam's to know that they come with environmental control systems for any passengers that may find themselves in the cabin of a cargo plane, and he knew that the ECS of Sam's plane should keep him comfortable and warm for most of the trip. Still, he preferred being on the ground as much as possible. He had people who usually did the big shows for him, and he rarely had to travel out of Louisiana, so when he had told Travis, his operations VP that he was going to work the big show in Russia, he about laughed himself silly.

"You know where Russia is, right?" was Travis's response. He knew this flight would be around 22 hours, and it would be over the ocean and freezing cold at altitude if the ECS didn't do its part.

Abe and Sam made the final adjustments. They had already walked around the plane and checked the storage areas to make sure that everything was in place and secure. Peter noticed that they made a good team and worked in tandem to get things done fast. He supposed that this was because they were both experienced pilots. He felt anxious, but knew that these two wouldn't let anything happen to him. It helped settle some of his worries.

Before long the plane wound up, making an ungodly racket, and lurched forward. The violent start-and-stop reminded him of taking his driver's test the first time and not being able to quite master the brake pedal in his dad's Jaguar. His BPM's went up a tick or two when the plane started to pick up speed for the ascent into the azure expanse of morning.

He grabbed the handle next to the jump seat like it was a long-lost friend until he noticed the words, *EMERGENCY EXIT,* written on the handle. Peter jerked away quickly, as if the handle had burned him, and decided instead to clasp his hands together in his lap. He cursed and swallowed hard, trying to get his ears to pop to relieve the pressure he felt build up behind his eyeballs. After a half a minute of increased pressure, he reached for the pack of gum in his parka, unwrapped two sticks of Juicy Fruit, popped them into his mouth, and chewed vigorously. *Ah, that did it*, he thought.

When they reached cruising altitude, Abe came back to check on him. "You okay, Peter?"

Peter nodded, and Abe sighed and rubbed at the sides of his head, massaging his temples. The last two days had taken a bit out of Abe as well, and he was wearing his fatigue on his weathered face. Abe smiled a half-smile and said, matter of factly, "We're 5,760 miles from Moscow, so to say we have time on our hands would be the understatement of the damn century. Why don't you break out that bag?"

Peter grabbed it and unrolled the top, letting the smells escape into the plane, immediately making them feel better. " I think she also sent some coffee," Peter said, grabbing the thermos. He wasn't going to let a little thing like flying come between him and Momma's cooking.

Peter filled both of their cups and asked, "Sam need some?"

"He got his already." He pointed to Sam who raised his tumbler without turning around. Peter grinned as he took a sandwich from the bag, then held the bag up to Abe who took one for him and for Sam. Abe turned and walked back to Sam, who held out a hand for his, then sat down next to him.

"Feel free to unlatch the cot and get comfortable. It's going to be a long flight," Abe said to Peter as he munched.

Feeling much better about this flight and the next few days, he sighed and decided to make the most out of this trip. Peter stood up and stowed the jump seat. He carefully unfolded the cot and settled the coffee thermos and the bag on the cot before settling himself in. He decided to catch up on his reading and leaned back against the wall. Peter could feel the fatigue of the last day finally catching up to him. He figured that he had been awake for around 30 hours. Although he went to bed the night before, sleep had eluded him in those final hours leading up to this flight. He wasn't really sure what to expect.

For that matter, he thought, *I'm not really sure of much anymore.* His thoughts refused to be corralled. *The girls. The grunch. Michael, Sam, Russia, Dr. Jo.* It was overwhelming, and too hard for Peter to compartmentalize and make sense of at the moment, so it just served to make him anxious.

He started when he heard a voice, if not audibly (although he couldn't swear it wasn't) then at least in his head, say, *Peace.*

Peter thought, *If I could manage peace with all that's happened, I would have been able to sleep last night. No peace for me, it seems. Not now at least, and maybe not anytime soon.*

He closed his eyes and worked through the relaxation exercises Dr. Jo had given him so long ago. He focused on his breathing first—*slow and even, in and out.* When he reached the point that his breathing was level and even, he focused on relaxing the muscles in his body—*feel the tension leaving the muscles*—and slowly, finally, he focused on turning off his brain—*relax… relax… blank slate, blank canvas.* It seemed to Peter that this was the hardest part, ever since his parent's accident he'd had problems sleeping, and as part of his therapy, it was suggested that he do these relaxation exercises. He focused his thoughts internally, and just when he thought sleep would never come, he heard a voice in his ear that sounded strangely like Michael.

Sleep.

Chapter 18

Max held the door open for Maggie as she made her way into the foyer, side stepping a gilt pillar festooned with fresh flowers, and smelling of spring—odd in the late Russian fall. Since their arrival, she had not much time in Max's palatial home. They had been in St. Petersburg for a couple of days, and they had been all over the place.

Their first stop was Peterhof, just outside of the city. Maggie had been impressed by the grand castle and grounds, and found Max's father's lab there of even more interest. She had met no less than 20 men and women in direct employ of Max's father, but had yet to meet the man himself. Max seemed not to mind his father's absence, and knowing what she knew of the mysterious and cruel Lev Avatov, she didn't suppose that it was a great surprise that Max preferred to eschew his father's company.

She and Max were, all things considered, having a wonderful time. They dined and explored all over the area. He had taken her through Alexandria Park and Oranienbaum, and they had even made a trip to Gatchina. She was treated to the best of Russian architecture, cuisine, and culture, and all the while Max kept her entertained with local lore and history, engaging in deep and fervent discussions about their respective pasts, interests, and dreams. She found him engaging, charming, intelligent, and passionate.

They enjoyed being with each other, laughing, exploring, and being affectionate. Just like a couple. They discussed the antiquities that Max had purchased in Louisiana and Florida. Max explained that part of the purchases would go to the Hermitage museum and part to the Russian museum. There were a few special pieces that would stay in his family's collection. They were to be tested and verified as authentic, then moved to the Avatov compound. When pressed, Max refused to elaborate and would change the subject.

Since the laboratory and museums were their first stop, Max showed Maggie the Peterhof grand palace and explained that it was built by Peter the Great and was situated 50 feet above sea level. Maggie knew that Peterhof was usually mobbed in the summer, but she felt as if they were the only visitors in the late fall snow and ice, and she could easily imagine them as the sole inhabitants of the vast compound.

Her job didn't leave her latitude for romance or romanticism, and she had always had a practical bent that was so rigid it almost hurt, but she could really roam free in this place, and she let her fancy take flight. Max showed her around the gardens, and they talked about their lives. She talked about her life in the states. Some things she even let be factual. Max added a few snippets from his life in Russia, but for the most part he just asked Maggie questions about herself.

Last night he had taken her to the Marrinsky Theatre. Once Maggie was inside the theater, she was awed. She spun around trying to look everywhere at once. The ballet performed Swan Lake, and Maggie thought it one of the highlights of her life. As she was ushered into a waiting car from the chilly steps of the theatre, Max protectively shielding her from the snow until she could get fully situated in the seat.

It occurred to her that the quality that she loved and admired most in Max Avatov was his utter lack of guile. Maggie lived a false life. Deception was her stock in trade, and it was refreshing to spend time with a man who, although a bit naïve and serious, wanted nothing from her except her presence and happiness.

She sighed inaudibly at her complete contentment, and even allowed herself to find Max's strong chest with the side of her head as she rested on this incredible man, closed her eyes, and re-lived in her mind the happiest four days of her life.

Maggie wasn't a woman that allowed herself much. She wasn't given to indulgences of emotion or self. She lived her life on a perpetual mission, with every conversation, every destination, every person that she crossed paths serving as a means to an end. Not to say she was dismissive or a user, but she was a seeker in every relationship, always looking for—

What? she wondered briefly. *Justice, mostly.*

Justice for Suse had been a driving force in her life since she was 17 years old. It was the reason she originally became a cop and eventually an investigative journalist. She found out early on that what she did as a journalist was far more exciting and effective. In law enforcement, her adversaries would be turned over to the court of law and a plodding, corrupt system for judgement. Because of what she did, the bad guys were turned over to a more severe and unforgiving jury. The court of public opinion could be far more damaging, and its verdict always lasted longer than a prison sentence.

Every day of her life from the time of Susanna's return to a week ago, she began her day thinking of her best friend and returning the smile to her face. *Every day but the last four. Here I am*, she thought. *I always promised myself that I would find time for—whatever this is, after. After justice. After restoration. After I did my duty and completed my mission. Oh, God. Has it already taken me nearly five years to get to where I am? To put me in position to take down the very slime that had preyed on, not only my best friend, but on countless others, some just little girls?*

She had no right to be in this place with this person and be this much in love. But here she was, and fully aware that she was in way too deep with Max. She thought this assignment was supposed to be easy. She wasn't supposed to like Max, let alone fall in love with him. *No complications. No strings.* It had to be that way so that exposing his father would be easier on everyone involved.

"We are here." Max's baritone reverberating, joining his heartbeat in her ear, snapped her back to the present and her current situation.

Avatov. He was here, and the moment of their introduction was upon her. *Here we go,* she thought, as the door opened to her left, and Boris' hand extended into sight. She took the proffered fingers and was ushered from the back seat of the long black car, where Max, who had exited quickly and was arriving to take her arm, appeared.

In any other place and in any other time, if I were any other girl, this would be perfect, she thought. *This would be everything I could want. If. Just two little letters makes such a big word. I don't live in a world of ifs. I live in reality, and my reality is a lonely one—at least for now. Maybe someday, but not today.*

Max strode confidently through the open doorway, and after a brief exchange with a butler, he turned and walked back to her. The little man smiled at her as he rushed past to tend to other duties, and Max returned to her, somewhat regaining his composure.

"My father is in the library. We have been instructed to present ourselves to him. Now." He said this through clenched teeth, and Maggie now understood why Max was glowering so ferociously. He had been summoned to his own house like a lackey, like one of his father's goons, and this was by design. Lev wanted to drive home to his only son that he was still in control, no matter where in the world Max found himself or what he was up to. Lev called all of the shots, even in this place that was so special and safe.

"Do I have time to freshen up a bit?" she asked.

He smiled briefly and said, "Yes. Do not be too long. Boris and I will go in first." He kissed her on the cheek, and she scurried up the stairs to the guest room she had been given. Maggie went to the closet and opened it to change the outfit that she had worn for sightseeing. She pulled out one of the dresses that Max had purchased for her yesterday and put it on. Heels next, and a gold bangle. She went into the bathroom and made sure her hair and make-up were flawless and spritzed herself with Chanel No. 5.

It was not odd that she had everything that she would need for the meeting laid out in almost a militarily-precise fashion. She had drilled for this time since they had arrived and was well prepared.

As she looked down into the drawer at the display, all of the tools of her trade, she couldn't help but wonder what Max would think once the piece was done and published.

She had many things at her disposal to take down the bad guys, wherever she was, but the most important weapon in her arsenal was always with her. She removed the pretty, large pendant from her neck, an undetectably porous crystal surrounded by an intricate golden wire cage of leaves, and opened the concealed clasp to remove the microrecorder that had been running since her day with Max started. Once the small pearl recorder had been curated and the fresh one placed and concealed, she refastened the necklace in place, put on a matching bracelet, and left her room.

She made her way down the hallway and descended the ornate staircase. She thought as she walked steadily and deliberately toward the library, at how different the house looked to her now. When she and Max had arrived at the start of the week, the grand home seemed welcoming and stately, just the sort of place that she preferred. She loved the history and attention to detail, and Max had taken great pride in showing her all of the things that made it such a special and beloved place for him, including many pictures of his mother and sister, and treasured mementos from his childhood.

Max had a cultured upbringing, and his mother was very nurturing, according to him. He thought of her fondly, and she could tell that Max loved her and missed her very much. She was touched at his sentimentality.

She reached the last step and stopped to look at the house's interior. It was evening, and light from the Russian countryside trickled through the snowy windows. She did not see a warm, inviting country estate tonight. Tonight she saw a shadowed, massive hall, hauntingly stark and hollow, not reflective at all of the kind and caring man that she had come to know so well over the last year of her life.

Tonight, this house is all about Lev Avatov and his evil. And she was about to do everything in her power to put a stop to whatever he was planning. She had a promise to keep.

Chapter 19

As she neared the library, she heard raised voices.

"I am sure I do not know what you are talking about?" Max said from beyond the heavy oaken door. "The packages were delivered as requested and on time. I cannot help it if the man is a fool who cannot keep better track of his possessions."

Maggie thought she could detect a bit of disgust at the mention of Olivier again. Maggie paused to listen.

"I hear that you have brought a whore back with you from America," someone said. Maggie felt sure it was Lev Avatov.

She was highly offended at being called a whore and was about to announce herself to the library when she felt a hand on her shoulder. Maggie looked up to find Leclerc, the diminutive butler standing behind her. He quickly put a finger to his mouth in a plea for silence, and she nodded her head to let him know that she understood. She sidled out of the way as he knocked at the library door.

Lev ordered the man to enter, but instead of stepping forward, the man looked purposefully to Maggie, holding her gaze. Max, quietly and kindly, bid him enter, and Maggie gained all assurance that he was indeed the younger Avatov's man. She believed, as he strode past her, that she could count the butler Leclerc among her allies in this place. The man was asking about refreshments when Maggie, after bolstering her courage and plastering a smile on her face, strode into the library.

Max's granite face softened as she entered, and he beckoned her to his side. Maggie did her best to sweep gracefully through the comparatively large distance and arrived to take Max's arm.

"Maggie Preston, Lev Avatov."

Lev reached forward and trapped Maggie's outstretched hand in a firm grip. Maggie instantly felt queasy, but fought it back.

"Indeed the lion, Mr. Avatov, as your namesake suggests. That's quite the grip. Do you break that out on all women that you meet, or am I special?" Maggie had been in similar situations and it was time for her to decide to demur or press. Both had their drawbacks—something about this man, this evil, pompous man, made her definitely want to press.

She had once had to stick her hand into a clogged garbage disposal, and could remember the sensation almost making her physically ill. The slimy mess against her skin and the stench that invaded her nostrils was almost unbearable. *This is worse.*

She felt as if she had been violated and even a thousand showers would not get her clean again. She looked fully for the first time at Lev Avatov, and the cognitive dissonance hit her like a sandbag. The man was beautiful by all worldly standards—tall and built well, with a handsome face, striking dark Russian features, and an olive, well-tanned complexion. Geometrically and geographically, the older gentleman was perfect. Perfectly straight teeth, perfectly coiffed, and perfectly dressed.

But he was far more than the sum of his terrible parts. The evil in the pale blue of his eyes strained and clawed like a caged beast, longing to burst from its captivity, to wreak as much havoc as time and the laws of physics would allow.

The feeling disconcerted her so much that her carefully placed smile slipped a notch, and she pulled her hand from his grip in reaction. She tried to cover it up by touching his sleeve and saying, "I've certainly been looking forward to this. Glad to meet you, Mr. Avatov. Max has told me very little about his father. You, sir, are a complete mystery."

She forced her smile back up to a thousand watts and watched Lev's eyes for reaction to her words.

"I have only recently found out about you, and I was unaware that Maxim had brought you to Russia. How are you enjoying your time here?" the gangster asked politely, although his eyes said that he wished she were anywhere else.

"Oh, Max has shown me the beauty of the Motherland. So grand! The palaces and the museums are awe-inspiring. I was truly impressed by the Avatov collection both in the Russian museum and the Hermitage. So many interesting and varied pieces. I was surprised at the eclectic nature of the exhibit. Tell me, Lev; was it your idea to group them that way? It must have taken a long time to gather that many different pieces together. Most curators would display them according to their historical era, thereby accentuating their historical significance, but the Avatov collection is separate from all others. A daring choice."

Maggie had been to every great art and antiquities museum, from the Guggenheim to Getty Villa, from the Egyptian Museum in Cairo to the Museo Egizio in Turin. He did not have a well-curated or well-displayed collection, but what he did have were a great many rare pieces, and she was interested in how he obtained so many that others could not.

"It has taken me many years to amass the pieces that you saw at the Russian Museum. It is not nearly all of my historic pieces, and I am afraid that the curator of the museum and I do not see eye to eye on how best to display them."

He wrinkled his nose in obvious distaste for the job that the curator in question was doing, but he let it be known with a dismissive wave of his hand that he knew better, and his puffery continued.

"He does want to split the pieces up and put them in their corresponding era areas. I disagree. Do you not think, Magdalene, that a collection of such treasures should stand alone?" He looked pointedly at her, and it was not lost on anyone in the room that the man had used her given name.

A name he shouldn't know. She swallowed hard, but Lev continued as if unaware that he had said anything unusual, and he was just seeking to ascertain her honest opinion.

"I want my pieces placed together in one big display so that everyone will know that I am the *collector* of history. What I draw to myself is always rare, always valuable, always useful, and always unique."

He had worked himself up into a bit of a lather. Maggie knew his type, but never had she known his type on this scale. Lev collected, alright, but it should be noted by anyone who would cross the man and his organization that he always took from someone else to add to his collection. His wife had belonged to a powerful enemy, his estate had belonged to a descendant of Orlov himself, and his antiquities all had the same thing in common—*they were taken from someone else. His type has an insatiable libido for power and displaying that power is what they get off on.*

Max had warned her about his father, and she felt it was best to play into his power trip. "I couldn't agree more. The exhibit was grand and just as it should be. All of the artifacts were prominently displayed within the era they were created and all together made for an impressive arrangement," Maggie told him.

He watched her closely as if judging the sincerity of her words. Satisfied, he turned to Max and said, "See, Maxim? Even one such as your Maggie agrees that the pieces should be kept together."

Maggie winced imperceptibly at the endorsement and continued trying to butter up Lev.

"You said that there were better pieces; surely they deserve a place of honor in your collection? Why are they not being displayed?" she asked innocently.

Lev took her hand from his arm, placed it in the crook of his elbow, and led her to the settee. His touch made Maggie's skin crawl once more. She couldn't remember a time in which she had a reaction to someone this violently. *Keep it together, idiot,* she thought as she fought the revulsion threatening her.

"The better pieces are going through rigorous testing and cleaning processes. Some of the pieces are being restored and dated by the best minds in Russia. Some will go to the museums in the future, and some will go into my private collection."

Maggie couldn't help herself, and she smiled an anticipatory grin at the thought of having access to one of the pre-eminent and secret collections of antiquities in the modern world. Lev didn't much care for the American, but he was not the type to miss an opportunity to show off what he owned.

"Would you like to see the collection?" Lev asked her.

Maggie knew that refusing the offer, especially in their current circumstances, would definitely irritate the man, and she was okay with that. She glanced sidelong at Max, who gave an almost imperceptible nod of assent.

"Not right now, Lev, but thanks for the offer. Maybe later, if we have the time, but I know that Max has planned many exciting things for us to do before I leave." Max relaxed his stance a little upon hearing Maggie's words, and she knew that what she said was okay.

"It will be a shame if you do not get the chance to see it." Lev was not showing the irritation that Maggie expected, but he was speaking through teeth that, although smiling, were slightly clenched.

Good, she thought, *let's see what trips your trigger, you scumbag.*

"Is that not right, Maxim?" he asked, turning in Max's direction.

"I will do my best to bring her by before she has to leave," Max said dutifully.

Lev got up from the settee and turned to Max, his face going to granite, much like Max's did when he was trying to hide something from others. "Maxim, I will expect to see you tomorrow with an update on your trip to New Orleans."

Max, whose face was already like granite, hardened even more and he nodded his head to his father. "I will be by tomorrow at 9:00," he said.

"Make it 8:30. I have another meeting at 10:00," Lev demanded. He turned to Maggie and offered his hand, which she declined to take, instead choosing to pretend to struggle with her gloves. "It was a pleasure, Ms. Preston. Please make sure that Maxim brings you by the house before you leave Russia, or you will have missed the greatest private collection that you will likely ever see." With those words he turned and left the library. The whole conversation lasted only a few minutes.

Not even enough time for Leclerc to return with the refreshments. Maggie had just finished that thought when the servant appeared at the door. He was only holding enough refreshments for Max and herself, so he obviously knew that Lev would not stay long. Leclerc put the tray of finger sandwiches and two herbal teas on the table in front of where Maggie stood and looked at her with a wink. She smiled at him, and he glanced at Max who frowned at the display.

"She did well with your father, sir," Leclerc told him.

"Yes." Max was frowning intently at the spot near the door that his father's back had occupied moments ago, and it seemed to Maggie he was trying to recall something far away. Max returned to himself and centered his gaze on Leclerc. "Yes, tovarisch. Indeed, she did."

Maggie could tell that Max was upset by his father's visit because he had slipped into an exaggerated Russian dialect. He only did that when he was really upset or he was trying to hide behind his Russian heritage. Leclerc nodded his head and left the room. Maggie looked at Max as he studied her.

"What is it, Max? Did I make a mistake?" Maggie was unsure of the look she was receiving from him. Max went to her and pulled her into a hug.

"No, Maggie," Max told her, "I was very concerned when my father came by, he is not known to be so…" He stopped, searching for the correct word. "Magnanimous," he finished.

"Is it a credit to you to say that you are not like him at all?" she said, taking his hand and steering his gaze to her eyes.

"How do you mean, kiska?"

"Well," she said, smiling at him, "you are kind and loyal and funny and warm, and your father gives me the creeps. He's smug, dismissive, and indifferent, and he uses people the way I use Kleenex. I'm sorry if that offends you," Maggie told him, hugging herself and rubbing her arms. She was still weirded out over the feelings that Lev evoked in her at his touch. Max smiled at her anxious expression.

"I told you that you would not like him. He is not a nice man, Maggie. He has done bad things in his life. He did not always come by his *collection* ethically or even legally. The people that he employs are as bad—nothing but thugs that he has trained like pet monkeys to come at his command and do what he tells them."

"Why are you telling me this, Max? Are you trying to frighten me?" she asked him, slightly frantic. She was in full-on ingenue mode, and right now he needed to see her scared. "Because if you are, it is working and I do *not* appreciate it."

"I only tell you this to make sure you know to watch yourself around him or any of his employees. They are loyal to *him*, Maggie. They will not hesitate to tell Lev anything they learn about you that will help him," Max said. "If you think that he will go easy on a woman, or that he will not use you against me or vice versa, you would be wrong. That is exactly the type of person he is," Max finished bluntly. "I need you to stay with me at all times, especially now that Lev knows you are here. I wonder how he found out?"

Maggie had asked herself the same question, and she was sure she knew the answer. She had decided since they were in Miami to keep a close eye on Boris. *I don't trust him, and I know that he doesn't like me or Max.*

She had not seen Boris since they landed. He had separated from them at the airport, and at the time she assumed he was going home, but she bet her best Montblanc that he went directly to Lev. Max needed to be made aware that Boris may be disloyal.

"Maybe Boris told him?" she questioned innocently.

"Boris knows better than to tell my father anything. He has been at the receiving end of his anger a few times. No, Boris does not volunteer to be in Lev's presence any more than I do," Max told her shaking his head.

Maggie wasn't so sure, she had seen the looks that Boris threw

Max's way when he wasn't looking. She wouldn't put it past him to tell Lev anything just to get Max in trouble.

"Am I going with you tomorrow when you meet your father?"

"No. I want you to stay here with Leclerc. I will try to find a time when I know that my father will need to be someplace else, and we will visit right before it is time for him to leave. If we show up unexpectedly, he will not be able to cancel, and you will have kept your word to visit," Max said smiling. Maggie put her arms around Max.

"You navigate your father well. You have obviously learned all the tricks, Max."

Max hugged Maggie and bent to kiss her forehead.

"I have only learned one thing of usefulness from Lev," he said, putting his forehead on hers and looking her in the eyes, "and that is how to survive. Survive above all else."

As Maggie gazed into Max's crystalline blue eyes, she felt the tears gather for the little boy who never had a real father or a real childhood, but grew up to be a fine man. It was clear to her that Maxim Avatov was almost entirely a product of his mother.

Kind and generous. Loyal and upright; well, as much as he could be working for someone like his father. Disciplined, with a controlled maelstrom of power that he could marshal against anything that threatens me.

Maggie was afraid that it was too late for her, she had lost her heart to the man standing in front of her. *I'm in real trouble.*

Chapter 20

Dark elf fire mage pyroblast. I will defeat you, Archimonde.

Peter was wrested from his battle with the sorcerer by a persistent poking in is side. He rolled over and promptly fell out of the cot he had been laying on. He heard a laugh from above him and opened his eyes to see a grinning Abe smiling down at him.

"Have a nice trip?" Abe chuckled again at his own humor and offered a hand up to Peter who grumbled.

"Very funny Abe. Where is Sam? I'd hate for him to miss an opportunity to share in a laugh at my expense."

"His boss called him just as we were landing the plane. It seems he is on his way to the airport as we speak to pick up the stuff his father purchased."

Abe motioned Peter back to the cot, and Peter stowed it and took his place in the jump seat. Abe gave him a serious look, conveying the gravity of what he was about to tell him.

"Sam has been telling me about the men that are associated with his boss. These are not the type of dudes you want to get caught up with, Peter. These are some really bad guys. Sam wants me to make sure that you do not get in the way while he is talking with his boss, so you and I are going to get your paperwork in order and speak with the people in charge about moving your cargo to the Igromir Expo. Let's go."

Abe motioned him towards the back of the plane where they were offloading cargo. As they were walking to the main building, a procession of cars and one big moving truck flowed through an open gate and wound their way to the cargo plane. Just before Peter and Abe disappeared into the building, Sam came down the ramp at the back of the cargo section and greeted a large man at the front, then the large door closed.

Sam could tell that this was not going to be easy when he saw the scowl on Max Avatov's face. He looked over and found Boris watching him as well.

Ah, so that's his play, he thought. *This is going to be for the benefit of Lev's nephew stooge.* Sam expected a good dressing down in the presence of the driver, so he mentally prepared himself to take it. Max had such a look of intense displeasure that Sam knew it was being affected for Boris' benefit. *Max never lets too much get to him, and he would never have that look on his face naturally. I'll play it up,* he thought. *This is always fun.* He approached Max, hand out, and shook with the large man.

"Max," he said gruffly. "What's happening?"

"My father," Max ground out with his teeth clenched, "has requested that I come find out how the cargo from his last shipment went missing, and how he had not heard of this loss the day it happened. Why," he continued, huffily, "in fact, he had to find out from the person to whom the goods were to be delivered." Max's piercing blue eyes bored into Sam. Sam lost the smile from his face.

Here we go—gotta make this good. "I delivered your cargo just as you directed. I cannot help what happens to it after that. I didn't know about it until just before I left, and I thought it prudent to leave as soon as possible without causing a scene. I would have hated to have to welcome the authorities aboard my plane before we left Lakeside," Sam said hotly. "I delivered that cargo just as I am about to deliver this stuff." Max waited a moment before turning to Boris.

"Have the men retrieve the cargo, Boris. Be careful. We want no further incidents." Max turned away, and Sam saw such a menacing look of complete hatred engulf Boris' features that he was sure Max could feel it even if he didn't see it. Boris turned and caught Sam looking at him. With a look of pure distaste and an evil grin, he turned on his heel and barked orders at the remaining men. Max and Sam watched them march to the back of the plane and disappear through the opening. Max turned to Sam with a grin. "Sorry about that. A job well done, Sam. I take it they all got away safely?"

Sam was used to the charade the two of them put on for others and grinned back at him.

"It was epic. We had it all—action, fantasy, robots," Sam told him. "It wasn't easy, and without help would have been doomed to failure."

Max raised an eyebrow. "A robot? Care to explain?"

Sam laughed. "I will but not until they leave."

He bobbed his head towards the men exiting the plane. The six men continued to unload the rest of the smaller crates until only the largest remained, which needed to be removed by forklift.

Boris appeared shortly and said to his cousin, "It is done. Are you coming?"

Max stood with an unreadable expression on his face. "No, I need to—*review* with the pilot what happens when a shipment is lost and how, in the future, there will not be any more lost shipments." Sam threw up his hands and looked at Max nervously, while Boris grinned at the possibility of violence.

"I told you I dropped off the package to that geezer. It's not my fault he lost it."

Max feigned ignoring Sam irritatedly, and instead said to Boris, "Give me the keys. You can hitch a ride in the truck."

"I think that I should remain with you, Maxim. *In case*," Boris said.

Sam could tell that Max was seething inwardly at the implication from his cousin that he needed to be checked up on, and with a voice of frozen steel said, "You will go with the men and deliver these things to the lab for testing. Report back to my father. Never call me Maxim, only my father uses that name."

Boris didn't try to hide the dislike on his face for the reprimand or the order. He was seriously pissed. Without another word, Boris reached into his pocket and pulled out the keys to the Mercedes parked a few feet away. When Max reached for them, his cousin dropped them on the ground. He then turned and walked to the Range Rover, and pulling the driver out of the front seat, took his place. The driver hurried to the truck and jumped in just as the Range Rover peeled away from the plane.

Sam turned to Max, "You sure know how to piss him off. He hates you, you know that?" Max grinned at him.

"Boris is bark only, and a foolish dog at that. I have had many years to practice on him, my friend. Come," Max said, slapping the pilot on the back and smiling. "Tell me of the adventure that you have had this time. What about this robot?"

Sam grinned and pointed over Max's shoulder at the two men walking out of the terminal building. Max turned and spotted the men as Sam said, "I will explain it all and introduce you to the two men who helped me relieve our greasy friend of his cargo."

Sam waited with Max until the two men reached them and said, "Max, I would like to introduce my good friend, Abe Sims—ex-Army, all around great pilot, and pain in my ass."

The two men shook hands, and Sam motioned to the younger man coming up behind Abe. "And this is my new friend, and the maker of some of the best robotics I have ever seen, Peter. Guys, this is Max Avatov. He is the one who gave me permission to liberate the girls after I had delivered them."

Max studied the two men. *So unalike, but likable*, he thought.

Abe, the older man, smiled when he shook his hand but the other just stood there looking at him.

"I know you," he finally said.

Max looked at him, confused. "You may not remember me, though I am sure you remember Momma Rose—she just about maimed you with her broom when you broke her favorite tea pot." Peter laughed. "You were with that pretty redhead, right? Maggie? How are her feet?"

Max scowled. He didn't remember much about that night. Tequila was never his friend. He did remember the little French woman that grabbed his ear when he tripped over his own feet and smashed her teapot. Maggie had laughed at him, and there was a man that laughed along with her and got the old banshee to let him go. This must be his savior, since Maggie was laughing too hard to help him.

"Ah, I believe I owe you my life," Max said with a grin. "I do not remember too many things from that night, but I remember the she-devil. She held me in a deathgrip by the ear until you told her to let me go. Peter intervened in what was surely a battle I could not win. Maggie made me pay her what was in my wallet as restitution. She did not realize that it was $500"

Peter was stunned. Momma Rose had not said how much she had received from Max, but come to think of it, she did have a big smile on her face the next day.

"If I know her, and I do," Peter said, "she still has every penny of your money stashed away in a spice jar in her kitchen. I can get it back to you anytime. I take care of everything she needs, anyway."

"Nonsense, tovarisch," Max said, laughing. "We are both men of means, obviously, and that encounter with that charming woman was delightful at any price."

Max smiled, shook Peter's hand, and turned back to Sam while also including the others. "Anyway, I am dying to hear the story of your adventure."

Sam gestured to the cargo hold. "I suggest that we move this party somewhere a little more private."

The four men walked into the now almost empty hold. The rest of the cargo with the exception of the three large crates holding Peter's tech suits had been offloaded. Sam unfastened two folding chairs from the wall and lowered a cot similar to the one Peter had slept on during the flight over. They all sat facing each other, and Sam started in sharing details about their liberation operation. When he got to the part about Peter's tech suits, Max's curiosity got the better of him, and he derailed the recitation with question after question. Peter and Max agreed to revisit the creations, after which the story went on to the grunch.

"As I said before, Max, Olivier was the oddball in this mess. I think he is a vampire, and the grunch are under his control," he finished.

Abe and Peter agreed with quiet nods of support, and Peter added, "These were not normal men. They moved faster than I have ever seen. And those grunch things…" Peter paused to contemplate his next words, "they are pure evil. Red-eyed, quick, darting out of the shadows—they didn't verbalize that I could hear. They seem to communicate with each other telepathically. If one of them was hurt the others knew it and reacted. I've only ever read about such things in sci-fi books."

Max wasn't sure about what the others were telling him. He found it hard to believe in the supernatural, but with the relics that his father had collected over the years, the strange and obscure things in his private collection, and some of his nocturnal associates, he shouldn't be surprised by the account of what happened that night.

"Gentlemen, I have not seen what you have seen, but I will tell you that there have been many strange items added to the Avatov collection in recent years. The more obscure or unbelievable, the more Lev wants it, usually by any means necessary."

Max looked at Peter. "May I see one of your creations?"

Peter beamed, and together they all stood and opened one of the crates still on board. Max caught his breath as the gleaming blue, mechanized armor suit appeared. It looked very much like he imagined. He had made a point to be present when his father spoke with Mr. Olivier, causing him to hear the retelling and description of the contraption. The metal was polished and sleek and, inside the crate, there was a sword as tall as the suit. The blade was etched and filled with a blue resin-type material.

Peter explained that he designed the sword so that at a command from the device's interior the sword would light up.

The other item in the crate was smaller, but that did not diminish its menace. Max whistled and grabbed what he assumed was the gun that Peter used during the heist. It was smaller than the sword but had to measure five feet long. It was solid black metal and looked to contain a rifled barrel and what looked to be a grenade launcher. Max assumed that the style was taken from the A1 grenade launcher the US military uses, although this unit had not one launcher, but three of varying sizes.

"This gun is not practical," Max said to Peter, "It is too big. I think that the suit could not handle both the sword and the gun at one time. It is impractical to have to put one away in order to use the other. Would there be a way to incorporate the blade and gun into one wieldable weapon? Also, I think that the color is not right for things that the mech would be utilized for. Black or carbon fibre would make much more sense, and cloaking is very practical, if," he paused, looking at Peter meaningfully, "someone wished to make use of them for their intended purpose."

Remembering how he almost fumbled getting his gun put away and his sword out in the grunch attack left Peter wondering the same thing.

"A hard-learned lesson involving the weaponry makes me agree with you, but since these will be going to die-hard fans and private collectors, I don't think they will mind," he told Max.

"So you have them all sold, then?" Max asked him.

Peter could see his wheels turning. He considered the practical application of having a fully weaponized and optimized piece of armor that they could keep at their disposal for any other liberation missions that pop up.

"All except this one. This one will be on display this weekend and hopefully sold before the end of the expo." Peter considered the weaponry and the other suggestions that Max had put forth.

"What do you call them?" Max asked.

Peter shrugged and said, "Well, I've been calling them BMS's."

"BMS's?" Abe questioned.

"Uh… Big Metal Suits."

The other three groaned and Sam said, "With all those brains, the only thing you could come up with is Big Metal Suits?"

Peter looked sheepish and said, "Hey. Isn't it enough that I conceive and build them? I shouldn't have to name them. I have people for that."

"I think it might be time to upgrade the people," Sam chuckled. "Why don't you call them SAMS?" he told him. "Stealth Armed Mobility Suits."

Peter smiled, "Ooh, that is so much better. Can I use that?" he asked Sam, bouncing on the balls of his feet.

Max grinned at the display, as Sam said, "Sure, kid. Just pay me my 35 percent."

They closed the crate, and Max sobered a little as he thought of the sensation these suits would bring here in St. Petersburg, *Which means my father will find out.*

"Is there any way I could persuade you not to show your remaining suit at this expo, Peter?" Max asked him.

"Why would I want to do that?" Peter asked.

"Lev knows that his cargo was stolen by a very large robot. What do you think he will do if he finds out that there is a man who lives in New Orleans that is here in St Petersburg showing off his very large metal suits that happen to fit Olivier's description?" Max looked at each of them and finally made his way back to Peter. "If I know my father, he would want to make an example of someone. These types of slights are not to be taken lightly, but crushed viciously and swiftly."

Peter swallowed and said, "Well, two of the suits will leave from here, so they don't have to leave the airport. The third one I was hoping to sell at the expo. I have a lot of capital tied up in these, and I need that money to get a jump on further orders," Peter told him. "I'm sorry, Max, but I have to sell this last suit."

"What if I bought it from you?" Max asked.

"If you bought it there would be no need to go to the expo at all," Peter said to Max.

"Fine, then," Max said, "I will buy the suit, and Sam will take it back to Florida for storage away from St. Petersburg. You can attend the expo as a visitor instead of a vendor, and Lev will not need to know," Max finished. He turned and started for the exit to the cargo hold.

"No can do, Max. I appreciate the assist, but my booth and my team are already there. I'll tell you what I will do, though," Peter said, scratching his whiskery chin. *How long has it been since I shaved?* "I have other products that I can feature, and the promo materials featuring the armor didn't make the trip, anyway. Your dad will never know anything about those mechs."

Max thought for a moment, then relented. "That is agreeable. I will wire you the funds—just give your information to Sam."

"No need," Peter said, handing him his business card. "But, Max," he said, "I didn't even tell you how much they are."

"Whatever it is, I am good for it," Max said with a backwards wave to Peter and Abe. "It was a pleasure meeting you both." With those final words he and Sam disappeared from the cargo hold.

"Well, that was interesting." Abe said to Peter.

"Tell me about it," said Peter, "I don't even have to get off the plane if I don't want to."

"Are you gonna tell me you are not going to go to the expo at all?"

"Not a chance. I'm the CEO, and I can't miss this opportunity." Peter said with a grin. "Wanna come with?"

Chapter 21

After the successful delivery of the first of the tech suits the previous day, Peter, Sam, and Abe were in high spirits, talking and laughing. As the bitter cold and remnants of a snowy night sought to do battle with the rays of the bright autumn sun, the three men sat precariously in the tram that sped them through the streets of St Petersburg. They were discussing the city and the sights and comparing notes, when all three had to grab for handholds as the tram skittered to a wavering, icy stop. The travelers disembarked from the small vehicle to stand in front of the Church of Our Lady of Smolensk, and Peter, in particular, was caught up for a moment in the stark white walls that finished themselves off in spectacular parapets of icy blue.

Once off the tram, and one block adjacent to the Expoforum complex, no one in the party had to ask which way to proceed. As they walked north from the church, they heard it before they saw it. From their right, they could see a mass of people that Abe could only assume were circus performers.

This is absolute chaos, he thought. The riot of color and sound and spectacle that greeted them was a lot to behold at once, and Sam and Abe in their turn felt positively assaulted by it. Peter, who was used to what they were witnessing—men and women in elaborate costumes carrying fantastic weapons and props—wanted to get them moving before they succumbed to the sheer weirdness of it all.

"Come on, you guys. I have to get to the vendor's control area and sign us in," Peter said, hopping a low plastic yellow chain and alighting on a path that took them to the front entrance of the Expoforum.

The complex itself was made up of three exhibition halls, two hotels, and numerous areas for restaurant vendors and drink sellers. They made their way to registration encountering less of the hullabaloo from earlier, and Sam supposed that not many of the con-goers came this way. They reached a box office counter, and Peter removed the messenger bag he had been toting at his side to produce some paperwork which he handed to the person on the other side of the glass.

"Peter Devereaux, Guardian Craftworks, 118."

After the young woman behind the counter took his name and booth information, she handed Peter the three vendor passes on lanyards, a map to the grounds, and a list of the vendors and speakers for the day.

"Mr. Devereaux, would you mind waiting here for a moment? Mr. Hawsey would like to have a quick word before you enter the complex."

"Yes, that's fine. Please let him know that I'll be happy to talk to him."

Peter placed his lanyard around his neck, as the other two men gave him a quizzical look.

"Dunno," Peter shrugged.

A door opened to their right and a rather outlandish looking man in a black suit approached Peter. It wasn't the black suit, but the bright pink and blue paisley tie and pocket square with glasses to match that pushed the outfit over the top. As he approached in a flurry, whisking back and forth as he did, Peter noticed that the silk lining of his jacket bore the same crazy colors and pattern. The man rushed Peter with his hand extended.

"Mr. Devereaux, darling. Thanks for waiting. Such a pleasure to meet you at last and in person."

Peter shook the extended hand.

The man squeaked a little as he spoke, "Such. A. Pleasure."

The little man shook with one hand and fanned himself like a fainting Southern belle with the other. The exchange would have made Peter uncomfortable if he weren't used to meeting people like this on a pretty regular basis.

"Not at all, Mr. Hawsey. The pleasure is mine. What can I do for you?"

The man withdrew his hand, still smiling broadly at the young inventor, absently plucked the pocket square from his suit jacket, and gave his right hand a quick wipe before replacing the handkerchief. Peter's raised eyebrow told Hawsey of a slight offense.

"No offense at all, darling. I simply cannot abide germs, you understand?" he explained with a dismissive gesture and a sincere countenance. "I never shake, darling. Never. The reason I extend the honor to you, sir, should be evident. I want to thank you. Your generous contribution, not only with your inimitable and fantastic creations, but also your timely and um, sizable contribution, has allowed us to continue to host the convention, once again, in the heart of St. Petersburg. The organization thanks you, and I thank you. We are at your service while you are here. Please do not hesitate to let us know if you need anything. Well, not *me*, of course." The little prim man called over his left shoulder with his hand raised, "I will be a busy little beaver, for certain, but, well, *someone* will tend to your every whim. *Every* whim."

And... he was gone, disappearing through the large door.

"That was..." Abe started. "Um..." he tried to come up with a description and stopped. "Yeah, I got nothin', Peter. He was a weird cat. Just how much did you give them?"

Peter glared a bit at Abe, obviously embarrassed at the exchange. "Can we go, please? I have a ton to do."

"By all means, *darling*." Sam couldn't resist the jab, lighthearted as it was.

They all laughed and went through the door on the left leading to the huge entrance of the convention floor. Peter was supposed to have debuted his SAMs at the show, but had to pull out after Max warned him about Lev. The Expoforum personnel were not happy at the last-minute cancellation of the debut of such a highly-anticipated piece of cosplay tech, but had a replacement ready for just such an emergency. As they walked down the long wide hallway, Peter handed out the other two lanyards.

"I have to go check in at my booth, but then we are free to get out and see all of the action."

They turned a corner and were met with a throng of con-goers in full regalia.

"I think the action has beat us to it," said Sam.

Two women dressed as elves, although *dressed* was an overstatement, sauntered up the hallway, looking the men over as they went. They seemed to take particular interest in Sam. Sam was, by most women's standards, very attractive, and this was not the first group of women to take notice while they were all together.

Peter silently wished that a group of women would look at him like that someday. He shook his head as Sam brushed past the women without looking at them, and they continued on through the throng.

"It's going to take me a while to go over product placement and displays, but you guys can wander around. Just don't go too far. Lev can easily get to us here, but we have strength in numbers."

"I didn't think you had anything else except the SAMS," Sam noted.

"I sent everything else over a week ago along with one of my associates. You guys will meet her. She's perfect for this kind of thing—Tammy enjoys the travel and loves people. She has a heart for the crazies, and is a con favorite. She is one of my main agents."

Peter watched Abe out of the corner of his eye, he was ogling everything around him, so much so that he had tried three times to put his lanyard around his neck, but it kept getting caught. Peter finally took pity on him and freed the lanyard so that it fit neatly around Abe's ballcap.

He looked at Peter and said in an awed voice, "I have never seen anything like this, and I've seen a lot."

Peter laughed and took the big man by the arm.

"Gentlemen, we're here. Welcome to the freakshow."

The three of them walked to the double doors that led into the cavernous expo center. When they finally opened the doors, Abe and Sam felt positively assaulted. The noise level rose a few decibels as a wash of voices, audio from displays and games, and music battered their ears. Lights and color were everywhere, and their senses were challenged to take it all in. Abe literally was so overwhelmed he didn't know where to look. Peter corralled them,.

"This way—we're near the con entrance."

Peter explained to them his idea to always ask for a booth nearest the entrance, that way people would see your products on the way in and the way out. Abe had been impressed with Peter since the box office. He was seeing Peter in a different light; he wasn't just a 30-something shy kid. Abe was seeing Peter the entrepreneur, Peter the tech head, Peter the marketer, Peter the diplomat, Peter the expert. He was truly impressed, and Abe made a vow to not be so quick to judge a youngster by appearances in the future.

Peter looked over the items and tech they had set out to sell and set about arranging and tweaking busily. The products that GC had displayed were flanked on either side by impressively lit and flashing LED models of some of Peter's creations, along with the catalogue of items available for custom jobs. His business cards and pamphlets littered the table. At the front of the booth stood a ladder, and on that ladder stood the diminutive woman Peter had spoken of to his companions earlier.

"Guys, this is Tamara Kent—Tammy."

He gestured up the ladder to the figure atop it. She was a pretty woman in her late 20s, with purple hair that fell past the middle of her back and kind, excited eyes. She was dressed similarly to many of the folks that were milling around the forum, sporting white and red boots, a red skirt, a white armored bustier that looked like a sailor's tunic, and a gold and purple diadem.

She looked down from where she was dressing a mannequin in a costume that was little more than a bikini, a belt with a gun holster, a pair of thigh high boots, and a small red cape, and gave a small wave and held up a finger to let them know she would be right down.

Abe looked at the dummy and nudged Peter.

"What's that supposed to be?"

Peter grinned and said, "Red Riding Hood, Wolf Hunter. Paramount, 2017. We made a mint on that movie."

Abe whistled in response. Having finished the mannequin to her satisfaction, Tammy carefully made her way down to the last two rungs of the ladder, then bounded down in one leap, almost landing on top of Peter.

"You finally made it, boss." She flung her arms around his neck, reaching up a bit to do so. "I thought you would never get here. Where is the suit? You didn't have trouble getting it in did you? Marquez is here, by the way. Did you see the orders?" she asked, seemingly all in one breath, and she gestured to a small stack of paper on the edge of the nearest table.

Abe was tired just watching her move and listening to her speak. She was what his grandfather would have referred to as *spunky*. She flitted about with excited energy, and her smile was lovely and infectious. When she had finally worn herself out, Peter answered.

"Got in yesterday, the suits are all sold, and we will not be able to debut them here. I thought Marquez had decided to pass on this one? The mannequin is perfect. What did we sell? Oh, by the way, this is Sam and Abe, they are the pilots that flew the SAMS over from New Orleans. Guys, this is Tammy Kent."

Tammy looked over at the two guys, lingered a second over Sam, and said, "Nice to meet you guys. Wait, SAMS?" she turned back to Peter, "What are SAMS?"

"Oh yeah, I forgot to tell you that I renamed the suits. They are now called SAMS, Stealth Armed Mobility Suits," Peter said.

Tammy grinned at his enthusiasm.

"I'm glad you finally got rid of BMs." She turned to Sam who was grinning, and she matched him, saying, "I know, right? I always thought of the bathroom when he said that."

Sam barked a laugh and Abe hid his grin by looking the other direction.

Peter's face turned red and he said, "If you hated it so much, why didn't you say anything?"

"I didn't want to hurt your feelings, honey. I know how long it took for you to come up with the name in the first place." She laid a hand on his arm in a placating gesture. "The suits are your genius, but names are not your forte. Anyway, Todd Marquez wanted me to let you know he would like for you to stop by their display. He has a piece he wants your opinion on. Also, did you know there were some people looking for you earlier? Yeah, a really beautiful woman and her two associates. They kind of looked like they were Takame Rereta Seishin, but I couldn't pinpoint them. The guys that were with her were suits. Not normies, but not cosplayers, either. And she's definitely a she—not a trap."

"Oh, how beautiful was she, and why would she want to see me?" he asked her, but all of his attention was now focused on the answer.

"Oh. She was stunning, with long silver hair and the most vibrant lavender eyes, and her voice was smooth and warm... like the caress of a lover... in the dark." Suddenly she stopped and shook her head as if to clear it and blushed prettily at the three confused men. "You are the great Peter Devereaux. Boy Wonder and hero of cosplayers and replicators *everywhere*. She probably wants you to know that you changed her life by creating the Pascal Pack—I dunno why she wanted to see you, honey," she shrugged, referencing a highly-detailed jet propulsion device that Peter had fabricated for Pink Star Arc, a movie series that had been huge in Russia. "Anyway, she made the best vila I have ever seen, and you know I've seen it all."

Peter looked at the other two and then back to Tammy, "I'm sorry I missed her then. Sounds interesting."

"Oh, that's not all," Tammy said, "she had two really big guys with her, maybe they were her bodyguards, the Good Lord knows she needs protection. The weird thing is they were just as striking as her. They were a matched set, twins by my guess, they didn't say anything and watched her like they couldn't wait to do anything she asked. I should have someone look at me the way they were looking at her."

She became sullen and looked as if she may cry, almost like she couldn't help herself. Peter knew that Tammy had a hard time finding dates, but this sort of despondency was far out of character for her. Her diminutive size and charismatic personality were at odds with each other on a daily basis. She was not a shrinking violet and definitely had opinions. She also had an overpowering love for life and excitement. Most of her dates came from a dating site, and when they met her in person they can't help but feel intimidated by the small woman with the larger than life personality. Tammy also figured that anyone who couldn't take her the way she was wasn't going to be worth her time, and it was their loss.

Peter agreed. Her confidence and exuberance was one of the many things that made her attractive. This was not Tammy—this was—something else, and Peter was worried.

"Hey, Starburst, what gives?"

He took her by the shoulders to look him full in the face and used the nickname he had given her due to her ever-changing hair color.

"You okay?"

He looked encouragingly at his friend, but she just shook her head vehemently, as if trying to jar something loose and turned to Abe and Sam.

"Peter said you are pilots, right?"

Abe and Sam shook their heads in the affirmative. "Well, there is a new exhibit down that way," she pointed in the direction of a large group of people at the end of the aisle, "that has been giving everyone fits."

Peter looked questioningly at her.

She offered as an aside to him, "Yep, it's MJV's piece. Those bastards."

She turned back to the two pilots. "It is a flying simulator built into a new RPG game called *Kill Zone*. I have heard bits and pieces from the people who have tried it—the reviews are rave. Supposed to be extremely challenging, even for seasoned pilots. The thing splashed an F-35 ace and two Blue Angels just last month."

Abe looked at Sam with excitement.

"I have never met a simulator I couldn't master," he said proudly. "Everyone knows what kind of scrubs the Angels' pilots are."

Sam sarcastically scoffed and rolled his eyes.

"I haven't met a plane I couldn't handle, either."

Sam raised his eyebrows and looked excited at the prospect of giving the machine a go. "I was born to fly, you know."

Peter thought, *Yeah, you were definitely born to fly, Samael. Question is, how do I get you to agree to what Michael is asking? I need to find out what you care about.* He zoned back in on the exchange.

"It's not just planes," Tammy told them. "From what I hear the game has everything from an Apache helicopter to a Stealth fighter, and even some top secret spacecraft. *And* it is customizable for the skill level of the person. They were looking for people here with flying experience to test some of the harder levels earlier—maybe you two should go beat it up."

Peter watched as Sam and Abe grinned at each other in anticipation, then both turned to him.

"Nope, not me. I've got a business to run. You guys go ahead, and I'll catch up with you. I'm going to help Tammy for a little while."

He watched as Abe and Sam made their way down the aisle and disappear into the throng of people. He turned back to Tammy who was still looking a little down and said, "You okay? What was all that a minute ago?"

She shook her head again and smiled. "I don't know what the hell that was, Peter. That's not me. Sorry—I guess it's jetlag or something. The air in here is weird, too. You don't have to worry about me, honey. I'm tip top. But thanks."

Tammy looked at Peter with her characteristic big smile and did her best to reassure him that the thing that wasn't quite right with her at the moment was really fine.

He gave her a hug and said to the air in a loving mock, "Girls."

She rolled her eyes and shooed him away, laughing.

"Speaking of girls, you could do way worse than that vila bombshell that blew in like smoke. It's a shame you missed…" She was looking past Peter when her eyes locked on someone. "You speak of them and they appear, and it looks like she has gathered some more admirers."

Peter turned in the direction that Tammy was looking and saw a strikingly beautiful woman walking towards his booth. She was covered from head to toe in a material that floated and swayed with every movement, diaphanous and sort of not-there. Peter took a closer look and saw that it was feathers that floated and moved with the woman. The feathers were all white except the tips—they were a burnt orange color, roughly akin to the colors in a russet sunset. She moved with grace, and following in her wake were two very large men. They were identical from the dark sunglasses they wore to their matching suits. They looked every inch the body guards Peter assumed they were. Behind them, Peter noticed a large group of men who were following the woman, but keeping their distance from the Wonder Twins.

The woman caught sight of Peter and smiled. She was a picture of grace and femininity. The closer she got, the more rapid Peter's heart beat. His chest tightened, and he found it increasingly harder to breathe. The old feeling of insecurity he had tried so hard to rid himself of was trying to make a spectacular comeback.

Man, he thought, *I come all the way across the world and I can't escape it. Super not-helpful at this particular moment.*

He closed his eyes and breathed deeply. Before he could open them again he heard a sultry voice.

"Hello. You must be Peter?"

Peter opened his eyes to the most vibrant purple eyes he had ever seen. He thought she must have paid a fortune for the lenses he was sure she was wearing. Normally, Peter would not be able to speak with a woman like this. He would freeze up and get tongue tied.

Tammy tried to help by saying, "I was just telling Peter about you, Miss…?"

She held her hand out in question and waited for the woman to make herself known.

"Serena."

She said her name without taking her eyes off Peter, peering at him strangely. The longer she stared at Peter, the more he came to dislike her.

That's new, he thought.

He was usually a very friendly person, and he couldn't pin down what made him feel so negatively towards her, but it was there, definitely. He found himself experiencing a sudden, strange annoyance. He didn't know why, but it was plain he couldn't stand her.

"Hello… Serena, was it? What do you want?"

The question took Tammy by surprise, not only because he asked it, but because of the brusque manner in which he asked. She turned to the woman apologetically.

"I'm sorry. He just got off a plane and is still a little jet-lagged." She shot Peter a *what-the-hell-are-you-doing* look and offered, "What he meant to ask is, how can we help you today? I'm not sure what we can do though, your costume is the best I have seen."

Tammy was trying to placate the frowning vila, but Peter was not in the mood to placate. He heard two growls come from the statues standing behind Serena. He looked over to them and smiled. He wasn't sure where this newfound courage was coming from, but he was glad to have it.

Serena looked past Tammy dismissively, not even acknowledging that she had spoken. It was clear the woman was only there to address Peter, and he noticed Tammy looking dejected and sullen again. He was beginning to think the strange girl had something to with her countenance, and that made him even angrier.

"Miss, I am quite busy. What can I do for you?"

"I heard that you were showing off some robotic suits today and had to come and see for myself. Your talent as a fabricator and designer are very well-known, Peter. Show me what you have created."

It wasn't a request, and it wasn't a fan asking. It was clear that the woman expected him to supply what she required without any blowback from him or hesitation.

Who does she think she is? I don't like the affect she seems to be having on Tammy—I need to get her away from her.

Peter didn't feel like playing along, and he started to shake his head, smiling at the woman's gall. This was about to get interesting. Peter looked over to Tammy and caught her eye as she looked solemnly at the woman.

"Tammy, can you go and see if Sam and Abe can help me with a few things? Just tell them that they can spend their time goofing off later. I'm going to talk with Serena here about the suits. Thanks."

Tammy watched Peter closely and then gave a slight nod to her head. She took off down the aisle and pushed her way past the growing crowd where the simulator was located. Peter could hear the shouts from the bystanders cheering on whoever was in the simulator at the moment. He turned back to Serena.

"No. I don't think I will. Have a nice day."

Quite a few things happened all at once. Peter turned back to the table to re-re-arrange the stuff there at the exact moment that the woman let out a slight, otherworldly shriek as if she had been struck. At the exact moment as he showed his back to her, he felt a clap on his shoulder, and he suddenly found himself facing the woman and her two bodyguards again, but there was precisely zero indication that anyone had touched him, and he didn't know who to glare at.

She wasn't pleased, and it showed. Peter noticed a creepiness to her exotic look, and where Tammy saw beauty, he saw cruelty and capriciousness.

Dear God, could she actually be *a vila? A real live vila?*

If he hadn't experienced the events of his recent life, he would have had a different answer. She was probably the real deal, and that would explain why she was so surprised when he didn't fall under her spell.

Why didn't *I fall under her spell? Got to ask Michael when I see him... if I see him agian.*

Vilas were dangerous and cunning, and who knew what her henchmen were capable of. One thing was for sure, the people in the forum were in real danger. He had to play this the right way because he had done something that she wasn't used to. It pleased him to know that he refused to comply when he was sure countless others had not, but this was not the time. He had to get her to leave, and so far, boldness had been working in his favor. He decided to keep riding that horse until it bucked him.

"*Excuse me*? What do you mean, *no*? Perhaps I didn't articulate my desire clearly enough—*show me the suit. Now.*"

Peter smirked, and he knew he was all in on whatever gambit this was.

"Serena, you made yourself perfectly clear, and I am telling you again—No. I am the owner and chief designer at Guardian, and I have chosen not to debut them here. Not that it's your business, but there was an issue that made them unfit for unveiling here. Maybe we can do business some other time. Thanks for stopping by."

Serena pursed her lips at the obvious dismissal.

"You are playing a very dangerous game, Mr. Devereaux."

"Oh? How so?" Peter asked flippantly.

The twins growled dangerously, and Peter saw one of them reach inside his jacket. He swallowed hard but stood his ground. He had never hoped so hard for interruption from an angel in his life.

Michael, if you can hear me, I could really use some help right about now.

Serena laid a hand on the guard's arm and smiled at him. Peter saw him visibly relax, and his hand drop to his side. She turned back to Peter.

"You have angered some very dangerous people. *Who* is not important, but *what*... that is of utmost importance. Can you think of the *what* that I am referring to, Peter? Thirteen little sluts in a box, perhaps?"

The vila threw her head back as if to laugh, and Peter could see the exposed vocal cords and innards of her throat and thought he may vomit.

The vila is working with Olivier.

That vile man had reach across the world, and Peter realized he had severely underestimated the scope of what they were dealing with. Serena returned her gaze to him, and Peter definitely did *not* see any beauty in the creature, unlike the followers around her. She would kill him. Here. Now. He had no doubt about that. He also had no doubt the girls were going to be in terrible danger if anyone found out where they were holed up.

She continued. "They feel that you owe them something of value, something that will take the place of the items that were stolen from them."

She's not guessing—she knows.

Peter was certain that Olivier had briefed his people thoroughly and told them of the mech's involvement in springing the girls and destroying the grunch. Still, he decided to play dumb and hope it worked.

"What are you talking about, Serena? When could I have done what you are suggesting, considering I've been traveling for the last couple of days?" Peter said.

"Just know that reparations must be made or your worst nightmare will become reality."

"Look around you, Serena. My business is nightmares. You don't scare me."

Peter clenched his fists and swallowing hard. The two goons with her instantly stepped in between Serena and Peter, and the larger of the two placed a meaty palm on Peter's chest. Peter was sure this could get out of hand quickly.

"Peter, everything alright over there?" came the familiar voice of Sam.

Peter breathed a sigh and said, "No, I believe that our business is finished here."

"I do not believe it is, Mr. Devereaux." Serena had stepped out from behind her two henchmen and directed her gaze towards Sam and Abe. "You must be Mr. Deveraux's friends? Pilots, if I am not mistaken?" she asked arching one beautifully sculpted eyebrow in question.

Abe quickly stepped up and held out his hand to the woman.

"Guilty as charged. Abraham Sims at your service. You are stunningly beautiful. Like an angel from heaven."

It seemed to Peter that Abe was just as smitten with Serena as the rest of the lovesick bystanders. It made his blood boil and just as he was about to step forward and say something, Sam laid a hand on his arm. As he looked over at his friend he received a small shake of the head indicating that he shouldn't move. The protective streak in Peter was strong, but he trusted Sam's instinct and stood firm.

"Such a flatterer."

Serena's silken voice oozed over Abe. She turned to Sam and said, "And who are you?"

"Not important. What you may be more interested in is who my boss is, but I have a sneaky suspicion you already know. He isn't someone you want to piss off, so you may want to take your weebles and skeedaddle."

Peter turned and gaped at Sam, joining in on the expressions of the vila and her henchmen. Peter thought he noticed her eyes turn a darker purple, and for a moment they seemed to glow while she vacillated between fury and fear. Serena quickly returned the sweetness to her gaze and honey to her voice.

"Sir, whatever do you mean?"

This time, Peter was certain he saw the hue of her irises change, and he felt like he wanted to reach out and touch her, just for a second.

He began to bring his arm up, but Sam grabbed it firmly and shook his head.

"What do you want, sweetheart? We're all sort of busy here, as you can see. Spill it."

Peter had never heard the flippant and sarcastic Sam be so forceful, and it made him immensely proud to be his friend.

"Oh, don't be like that," she said with a mock pout. "We were just getting to know one another, right, Abe?"

She placed a familiar hand on Abe's sleeve, and Peter saw her eyes flash again. Abe turned around to face him, and Peter noticed Abe's glassy eyes and vacant expression. Abe was not himself, but his voice came out clear and loud.

"You guys are being rude. Serena just wants to talk to you. To *warn* you."

Sam faced the vila.

"We know who sent you. We have no intention of heeding your warning, witch."

Her smile remained dazzling, but her eyes clouded over and became a dark and violent storm of violet and black. She looked over their shoulders and smiled. Peter turned and looked where Serena had been gazing. It took him a minute, but then he saw her. Tammy, glumly walking up the stairs to the second story leading to the food courts, taking measured, deliberate steps. She walked as if in a trance, and Peter could tell by the look on her face that she had been crying. She looked over the balcony towards where Peter, Sam and Abe were standing. He saw her shoulders shake as she cried, and she turned and fled further into the building.

Peter swung back to the vila and reached out to grab her, but he was forestalled by the full girth of one of the twins holding him back.

"What did you do to Tammy? I swear, if anything happens to her—" His anger was bile in his mouth, and he spit at the woman. He had never felt rage that was so palpable.

"I am answering your question about what will happen if you ignore my warning. We are strong, little man, and we are not alone."

Serena turned on her heel and started to walk away, one twin in tow while the other still had a grip on Peter.

She called absently back over her shoulder, "Oh, you will want to go find your friend. We wouldn't want anything *bad* to happen to her."

Without waiting, she walked through the sea of men. They parted before her and followed in her wake. Sam grabbed Abe's arm as he went to follow Serena.

"Let go, Sam. What the hell?" He moved as if to confront the angel, but Sam spoke in a calming tone while holding his arm in a very formidable grip.

"Trust me, my friend. You want to let that one go."

Abe tried to shake him off, but Peter said, "Abe. Abe. Hey. We have to find Tammy. Stop thinking about yourself. That thing did something to Tammy, and she ran off. We have to find her, or I think something bad could happen to her."

They were able to keep Abe still long enough for the vila to disappear from his sight.

Abe slumped. "She got away. Some friends you are."

Peter pulled Abe in the opposite direction.

"Come on. You go to the second floor. Sam will go up to the top floor, and I will go to the food courts. That was the direction I last saw her go. Please, guys, we have to find her."

Sam and Abe went in the directions that Peter indicated, as Peter went off to the second floor with a horrible dread in the bottom of his gut. He hated feeling helpless, and he hated seeing innocents harmed. Right now, all he could do was hurry and pray.

So, he prayed quickly and silently as he ran to the last place he saw Tammy. He was worried that he would be too late, but for what he was not sure. He knew that Serena was serious in her warning, and that she had done something to both Abe and Tammy that made them act strangely.

He walked with a purpose searching for any sign of his friend. Her size did not help him in the least. He was searching for her purple hair, but at a con, so many people were dressed outrageously and had purple hair that it was like trying to find a needle in a stack of needles. Purple was a popular color—not as popular as bright red or electric blue—but still it seemed everywhere he turned he saw someone with purple hair.

He made his way to the stairs and saw Sam ascend to the next level. The open concept of the building allowed for those people on the second and third floors to see down into the lobby. Peter moved over to the rail and looked down into the lobby. He spotted the vila there with her entourage. She looked at him and smiled, then looked farther up. He didn't see anything in the direction that the woman was looking, but he heard a scream a little further down the landing.

Most of the patrons stopped moving, and people were looking up and pointing. With a sinking feeling Peter followed there gazes to the third floor. There standing on a railing was Tammy. Peter felt his heart seize in his chest.

"No. Tammy, stop," Peter cried.

He ran, torn between sprinting with his eyes straight ahead and not wanting to take his eyes off of Tammy. He felt as long as he could see her and kept her in his line of sight, nothing bad would happen to her.

There were people, mostly girls, pleading with Tammy to get down, but she was crying and shaking her head. Peter pushed his way through the masses. He reached a spot that he could clearly see Tammy. She looked hysterical and dazed, reminding Peter of a man he had seen on a bridge once on the news… *right before he jumped to his death.*

She was shaking her head and wringing her hands. Peter could tell she was speaking, but he couldn't make out the words. He saw Sam step out of the crowd behind Tammy and calmly start talking with her.

She looked back at Sam and said something that Peter couldn't hear. As she talked to Sam, she inched closer to the edge of the rail. Peter could only watch in terror as Tammy crept closer to oblivion, nothing but air below her. A drop from that height would be fatal...

and messy. He looked over the railing from the second story and noticed that Serena and her mob had not moved from the spot he had last seen them.

The men with Serena had started a chant. It had begun low but was now building in intensity and volume, and Peter was disgusted and terrified. They were chanting, "*Jump.*" He was certain that Serena was pulling the strings, controlling the innocent Tammy, but she seemed helpless to stop what was happening to her. He did the only thing he could think of—he prayed for all he was worth that help would come to them before it was too late.

He cared deeply for Tammy. She was a person that knew the real Peter and still liked him, even with his paranoia and unreasonable fears. Peter watched horrified as a group of men made a semi-circle around his friend, blocking him from getting any closer. They were all looking at him with the same zombie expression, chanting in his face, "*Jump. Jump.*"

Peter could see from his vantage point that the closer Tammy got to the edge, the greater the joy on Serena's face. Peter felt a great wave of anger swell up in him and he yelled.

"*Serena, stop!* She has nothing to do with this."

Peter flinched as the man in the mob closest to him suddenly stopped chanting, turned to face him with glowing purple eyes and spoke in Serena's voice.

"You will not be the hero this time, Peter. You caused this slut's death. She will not be the last."

The eyes flashed, and Serena's wicked laughter erupted from the bearded face. Peter silenced the man with a quick elbow to his jaw. The man dropped and the eyes closed.

Peter watched as everyone turned from him to her. Serena pursed her lips in annoyance and with a flick of her wrist, dismissed the whole situation, turned and walked through the parting crowd.

Peter looked from Serena to Tammy. She stepped one step too far and tumbled over the side of the balcony. Peter watched it, helpless where he stood to reach her, but having an excellent view of the ground floor, he watched it all happen in slow motion. Tammy tumbled forward and screamed, turning to face the crowd and him with a look of shock, sorrow, and realization.

He started forward to catch her, even as he watched her body fall down towards the lobby floor. From the corner of his eye, Peter saw a blinding light and felt a whooshing of air that moved him from the place where he, moments before, had been watching his friend fall to her death. He heard a rush of—*something*—and caught the corner of a wing in his very blurry vision.

When his eyesight cleared, he saw a figure standing on the lobby floor with a very surprised and unabashedly sobbing Tammy in his arms. The figure—so substantial was he that the crying and spent woman all but disappeared into his embrace as he cradled her like a beloved child. He stood well over nine feet tall and wore...

The dark, Peter thought. *He just looked like—night.*

Peter fought to find a word in his mind to describe the garb, but he had never seen anything so black, so utterly void of light. The robes weren't just black, they were as fiercely dark as being a mile under the ocean on a starless and moonless night. Everything seemed to disappear into the folds of the suffocating black of his robes.

Peter tore his eyes away from the body of the figure and noticed it had the face of a man, with six wings that spread out behind him, black as pitch and magnificent to behold. Peter heard before he saw a truly terrifying detail that had escaped him in his assessment of the being—it had the face of a man, and that's what faced him, but on either side of the creature's head were additional faces, both of men, one shouting praise and the other pity.

"Mourn. Mourn all who hear. For Death is among you and in you, about you and above you. The Maker and Master of all sends his best to his worst. Crawl and repent, the least of you. Mourn, for Death comes to take and devour and bring grief."

The voice was unlike anything he had ever heard. The other sound was a hushed and steady hymn of peace that touched him so far into his inner being that he felt calm on a spiritual level he had never experienced before. The song was so beautiful and sad, with no language that he recognized or could describe, but it made Peter feel like a great event was taking place. He found himself caught up and drawn to the haunting music. He took a step towards the spot where Tammy had been standing only seconds before.

"No," The face facing him said, and Peter felt real fear.

When the gaze of the being swept over him, it left him thinking upon his own death and what good he had done in his lifetime. Upon it's back was a fearsome sword, and he watched as the creature lowered Tammy gently to the floor. The creature was smiling and weeping what Peter assumed were tears of joy over her. The creature said something and laid a tender hand on the girl's head, and then looked up directly at Peter.

Peter found the face recognizable, but didn't have time to think about how. Peter locked eyes with the creature and heard a voice say, "Look not upon me."

Peter felt compelled, strongly, to bow his head. He was afraid, and he knew the voice speaking to him was Death, the *real* Death.

He also knew, without question, that the voice was Sam's.

Chapter 22

Maggie slumped lazily in a chair looking out at the early morning washing over the garden. She imagined what it would look like in the summer, ablaze with color and warming sunlight, and she was a little sad that she would most likely never see it in its verdant glory. She had determined that there was not any chance on God's green Earth that she would return until Lev was taken care of, either by incarceration or… other means. She watched as kestrels gamboled and dove among the icicled trees and drank a steamy cup of tea fresh from the samovar next to her. She absently fingering the pendant around her neck.

She grabbed for her tablet and clicked open her news feed. She was scrolling through the latest when she stumbled on some footage from a local convention. The item was not from a news source, at least neither of the big two, anyway. It was instead done by one of the participants. It showed a winged creature saving a woman from taking a header off a third floor balcony.

Maggie watched the attached video four times in hopes of discovering some sort of elaborate set up for the convention. After all—a crazy-looking, angelic creature helping a damsel in distress at a comic book convention? It was every con-goer's dream.

She giggled to herself and took another sip. *What will they try next*, she thought. *Sensationalism, girl—it's your line.* Well, really *her* line was truth: unapologetic, unadulterated, and unrestricted.

She studied the article and the video, trying to pick out where the obvious signs of theatrics being at play lay, although she had to admit that it looked incredibly real. She downloaded a copy for Mikey. Maybe she could think of something to do with it after her current piece was finished. Maggie had texted him earlier that morning, and debriefed him with what she had found on Lev Avatov. She had been left at the Avatov compound—*sort of like hiring DB Cooper to guard Fort Knox overnight*, she thought. *If they only knew.*

She perused the paintings she had seen earlier on her tour, but, in actuality she was noting anything and everything she could to use during her *quiet time* later, when the guards had settled down. The house had multiple corridors she had not explored, and where there were corridors, there were definitely rooms to sleuth through.

She had to wait for Max and Boris to return from the airport, and since they were not too far away from the mansion, and Lev was not going to be around, Maggie talked Max into letting her stay while he and Boris were away. It had taken quite a bit of encouragement to get Max to relent, as he felt she wouldn't be safe.

"Darling, you worry too much. Trust me, I'll be careful. Your father won't even be here, but even if he does show up, he seemed to like me."

She reached up, threw her arms about his neck, kissed him quickly, gave him a wink and said, "Now that that's settled, what are you going to pick up for me while you are out? I hear St Petersburg is absolutely loaded with places for a strong, handsome man to pick up a pretty bauble for a deserving girl."

Max had smiled reluctantly and gone into a bit of detail about some of the local shops, but Maggie had quit listening and was instead planning her moves to make certain she covered as much ground as she could, as quickly and quietly as she could. There were more than a few moments while Max was gone that Maggie had wished that she had left with him.

Lev Avatov has a few people, Maggie thought, *that even I would not want to meet in a dark alley.* Petrov Abramkin was one of the men that was stationed at the Avatov compound. While he wasn't forthcoming with information, or really talkative at all, he was told by his boss to allow Maggie to see the artwork around the compound. Maggie was shown the antiquities in the Avatov vault as promised, but she couldn't shake the feeling of being watched.

Of course not, she thought to herself wryly. *You are most definitely being watched. A man like Avatov takes zero chances and leaves nothing unattended, so watch your step.*

She reached up to the pendant and toggled the imperceptible microswitch. *Look up first, always. Every room, every hallway. Find the camera—find the eyes.*

Petrov took Maggie all over the compound and was the perfect host, but he gave Maggie a bad feeling. He stared at her a little too much, and she caught him sniffing her hair when she stopped to look at a painting that caught her eye.

This guy has probably not been on a date in a very long time.

Maggie found herself wondering if mobsters actually *went* out on dates? Did they just order hookers? Did they marry? Have kids? Go to church? She had watched enough gangster movies to know that the picture that was painted of the traditional Sicilian mob family was not even close to reality, and she had to assume that it was much the same here in the Motherland. In her research, she had discovered a very businesslike approach to organized crime in the major cities here. Many syndicates were comprised of now-grown members of orphanages and gyms.

She couldn't picture Max being in league with them. That was not the man she knew... *the man she knew, as she herself was known? Touche, brain,* Maggie thought. *Knock that off.*

She had resolved to tell him as soon as she could when they were safe. *Safety first*, she thought, *truth later.*

Maggie spent the morning meandering up and down the aisles of Avatov's various galleries and display areas. She had a friend who was an art history major in college, and she would have given anything for him to be here as she gazed upon the painting *No. 6* by Mark Rothko. Her art history friend Mel had told her all about the Russian billionaire that had purchased the painting in 2014. Maggie wasn't an art history major herself, but she would have bet her last nickel that the portrait that hung on the wall in the Avatov compound was the same painting that sold for $186 million at auction. She would also bet that for every painting or work of art displayed here that Lev had paid good money for, there were five that were ill-gotten. The thought made Maggie shudder. She did not put it past Lev Avatov to kill for a painting.

Or a sculpture, or a rare bottle of wine. Lev got what he wanted, damn the dirty work.

After he had shown her everything he could think of in the Avatov compound, droning incessantly on with vanilla talking points that PBS would be proud of on each piece, Petrov led Maggie back to the library and ordered her to stay put. He had other obligations, and they didn't include chaperoning her the rest of the afternoon. She had agreed to wait for Boris and Max in the library, so Petrov had left her to her own devices with specific instructions to not wander.

"Maxim should return soon, so please to stay here and wait. No walking freely around, yes?" Petrov had said, trying to seem nice.

"Oh, absolutely." she had said, clasping her hands in front of her and flashing him a fantastic grin, the very picture of innocence and trustworthiness.

Petrov exited the far side of the library with a satisfied grunt, and Maggie waited for the sound of the big man's footsteps to recede out of earshot. Seeing her chance, she decided to go exploring on her own. She gingerly opened the door on the opposite end of the library and glanced around the corridor. She was, of course, looking for any of Lev Avatov's goony henchmen, but she also wanted to gage the general activity level on the second floor of the house; servants working in the areas she was hoping to snoop in would not be a good thing.

She scanned with her eyes and ears. Not seeing anyone around, she snuck out of the library and down the hallway. It was dark and empty. The thick carpet muffled her footfalls, and she found that she was able to fast-walk without much noise at all—*All the better.*

The quicker she found what she was looking for, the less likely she would be missed from the library. She looked in room after room until she found the one that had caught her attention upon her initial visit. The chamber wasn't out of the ordinary, but she had noticed a door partially hidden behind a large tapestry when she and Leclerc had visited the room the first time. She had cocked an eyebrow in his direction upon seeing it partially revealed, and he had returned the gesture without speaking.

Come to think of it, thought Maggie, *hadn't it been Leclerc who brushed the tapestry aside while he was showing me the Cezanne? Did he mean for me to see it?*

She thought on this as she quickly and quietly strode over to the door and tried the handle. She had half-expected it to be locked, or at the very least, if unlocked, a massive, eerie groaning when she tried to open it. Maggie was shocked to find that the door opened easily and silently. She couldn't believe her luck.

No. Way.

Maggie took advantage by pulling the door open and slipping through. She found a stairway leading up. This surprised her a little because she thought if anything untowards were going on surely it would be beneath the ground. She climbed the staircase. She knew it must be hidden inside the walls because there was no evidence of a staircase on the outside of the house. The outside of the house was only two stories, and she was coming to the end of the staircase, so she assumed this must lead to the attic area. What she found at the top of the stairs intrigued her, and also set the hairs on the back of her neck to tingling.

The landing was not dusty, ancient, or abandoned. It was clean, the wooden floor polished, and it was well-lit.

On your toes, girl—this is not the forgotten, ancient room you were thinking. What is *it?*

The door was especially surprising; too new and too high tech to be part of the original house plans. Maggie figured this was added much more recently. The door reminded her of the one that she had seen at the UN building a few years ago. There was a retinal scanner along with a fingerprint reader on the wall. Biometrics were all the rage when it came to physical security; she had been searched enough to know there was something valuable behind this particular door.

But was it valuable to Lev Avatov, or to someone who opposed him? She had to see what was behind it. *Dead end for now,* she thought. She possessed neither the requisite hand or eye to get into this room.

She stood looking at the door, wondering what it protected, when she heard a soft voice say, "Who's there? Mon dieu, Petrov is that you? You worm-man. Come to torture me some more?"

Maggie was at a loss, the voice on the other side of the door was clearly female and had said something about being tortured by the super-creepy Petrov.

"Hello? Hello?" Maggie asked quietly through the door.

"Who are you? Are you a servant? No, not a servant. You are American, no?" The voice became more agitated and fervent, speaking faster. "You cannot help me, and you cannot stay, whoever you are. My husband will harm a woman just as readily as he will a man. Leave, now."

Maggie heard the person on the other side of the door approach the door.

"I need to get you out of there. Have you been harmed? Your husband?? Are you married to Lev Avatov?"

Maggie was unaware that Lev had been remarried after Max's mother's death, but she was much more concerned at the moment that there was a woman on the other side of the door who had been regularly tortured. What she heard next almost knocked her out.

"I am Margueritte Manette Avatov. Who are you, and why are you here?"

Maggie was dumbfounded. Max had told her that his mother was dead, so either he was a really good actor, or he didn't know his mother was alive.

"Max's mother?" she asked, incredulously. The woman's voice went from frail to frantic.

"You have seen my son? How is he? It has been a long time since I have seen anyone but Petrov. How did you come to be here? You must leave before you are found." Margueritte said in a flurry. She sounded distressed to Maggie.

"I can't leave you here. How long have you been here?"

"You must leave, if they find you here you will not live long enough to tell anyone that I am here. You must tell Maxim that I am here. Tell him that I am here and that—I love my little Phillipe. Tell him that. Go. Tell him."

Maggie was confused. "Who's Phillipe?"

The woman had come to sit on the floor just on the other side of the door and spoke softly, with melancholy. "Maxim Ygevny Phillipe Avatov, I did not choose his name but I added Phillipe to the birth certificate without Lev's knowledge. It was not the worst beating I ever had. I was nursing at the time." Maggie heard the door open down the stairs.

"Is there another way out of here? Damn. Someone's coming."

She heard something crash into the door downstairs and some soft cursing as if someone had dropped something.

"I'm sorry, but I do not know. I haven't been out of this room in years. I do remember seeing a window, but I'm not exactly sure where it is. Go now before you are caught."

Maggie raced down the stairs until she saw the window in question. Frantically, she pulled on the window latch to get it to release. She could hear the steps drawing closer to where she was. Finally the latch gave way and the window opened. The ledge outside the window was not large enough to stand on, but as she leaned out the window Maggie caught sight of a trellis that ended just under the window. She scanned below to see if anyone would notice her should she step out of the building. The backside of the house appeared to be unguarded for now, so she crawled out the window and stepped carefully onto the top of the trellis. She very quickly and quietly closed the window until she was satisfied that whoever was coming up the stairs would not see it was open.

Just as she started to duck outside the window, she saw a person coming up the steps holding a tray toward the lone door at the top. She heard the keypad beep as the combination was punched into the keypad. The man told Margueritte to move back, and he opened the door to her prison. As the door closed behind him, Maggie took a chance and climbed back in through the window and made her way down the stairs. She rushed through the hall on her way to the library when someone stepped out of a doorway in front of her.

"Where are you going, miss?"

Maggie stopped with a little squeak, she put her hand on her chest and said, "You startled me. I was trying to find the bathroom, but all the doors look alike, and I can't remember where that man said it was. Can you help me, please?" she smiled sweetly.

"I will take care of her, Andrei. Go back to your duties."

Maggie winced when she heard Petrov's voice, but she was prepared and quickly regained herself. In her line of work, it was not uncommon to get caught in places she wasn't supposed to be, and she had become quite adept at wriggling out of trouble when the need arose.

Lord, she pleaded silently, *get me out of this. I need to be able to tell Max about his mother.*

She spun around and smiled at him, looking grateful and reaching out a hand to grasp his arm, slumping over as if to catch her breath. She appeared to be very flustered and genuinely upset. *So far, so good*, she thought.

"Thank God." she exclaimed, which she was literally now doing. "Petrov was it? Petrov, I thought I could remember the way, but I was mistaken. Could you show me where the bathroom is?" He rolled his eyes derisively and frowned.

Tupaya korova (Stupid cow), she heard him mutter under his breath. "Miss, if you had paid attention earlier you would have known it was across the hall from the Library. Now, if you will follow me, I will see you to the bathroom and then back to the library. Mr. Avatov does not allow unaccompanied visitors in his home, and I wouldn't want anything to befall you. After all, you are a guest."

His tone was very condescending and it made Maggie want to punch him in the nose. She felt relieved that she seemed to be in the clear, once again. She silently congratulated herself for her quick thinking and superb acting. The clearing of a throat made both Maggie and Petrov turn to see Max standing in the hallway. He gave Maggie a nod

"I am glad you are so concerned with Maggie's welfare, Petrov. I would have not been pleased at all to find out that any harm had come to her in my absence," Max said with a voice of steel.

Maggie noticed Petrov pall a little at the veiled threat, but he did not back down. Instead he said, "Then I will let you show yourselves out. Good day, tovarisch."

He gave Maggie another sneer before he turned and made his way down the hall.

"Max. Thank God you came back when you did. I have something that I need to share with you." Max laid a finger over her lips to quiet her and leaned in to whisper in her ear.

"Not here, the walls have ears here."

He kissed her lightly on the forehead and escorted her back through the hall, past the library, and out the door to his waiting car. Once they were safely inside his car and on their way back to Max's mansion, he turned to Maggie and said, "Now what is it that you needed to tell me so desperately?"

It always amazed Maggie at the transformation that came over Max's countenance once he was away from his father or any of his father's henchmen. He became almost carefree, as if a great weight is lifted from him whenever he is away from them. It made her more determined to get him away from this life. Maggie looked at the man that sat across from her, and she knew without even needing a mirror to see it, that he was seeing love in her eyes. That is what she felt. She loved Max, and it was that love that made her realize she didn't know what to say or how to say it, so she did the next best thing; she bought herself some time to think while she stalled.

"I went on the tour at Lev's place. He really does have some valuable pieces. Was that really Rothko's *No. 6*?" Maggie asked him.

"Yes, it was, but I doubt that the painting and your admiration of it is what you could not wait to discuss, is it, kiska?"

He lifted his left eyebrow and gave her a smirk as he drove. The look said, *spill it already.*

She cleared her throat and said in a rush, "Your mother is still alive. She's alive, Max." He looked fiercely at her and swung the large black sedan into a parking lot.

The announcement stole the boyishness from his face as he said in a quiet voice, "That cannot be."

This is too important for him not to believe me, She thought. *Should I play him the recording?* Maggie motionlessly shook her head, removing the idea from her obviously addled brain. *No, you dope. You cannot reveal everything now. Think, Mags, think. Use your words, he'll believe you, eventually.*

Maggie swallowed audibly before saying, "Your mother, Margueritte, is alive Max. I spoke to her today. Through a door, but she talked to me."

He grabbed her hand and held it to his chest, looking at her with pleading eyes and said, "My mother died a long time ago. I do not know who you think you spoke with, but it was not her."

His voice told her that he didn't believe, but his face told another story. She could see the boy he must have once been—devoted to his mother and beauty and culture and kindness and life. She watched as he went from disbelief to anger and finally to hope. Even as his head was telling him that it was impossible, his heart was telling him that maybe she was, in fact, alive.

"Look Max, I know you don't really believe it."

Max stopped her and brought her hand to his mouth and kissed it. "That is where you are wrong. I believe you. You would not lie to me. I do not have the luxury of companions or friends that tell me the truth. I do not even have a family that will not lie to me to suit their purposes. Maggie, I may doubt who you spoke with on the other side of a door, but I truly believe that *you* believe she is who she says, because, you do not lie to those you love."

Oof. Maggie felt the gut punch as distinctly as she would have the real thing. *You do not lie to those you love.* His words ricocheted around her brain like a wayward, frenzied bullet, ripping her to shreds and flooding her with guilt. What had she done but lie to him, since the day they met?

Now isn't the time for this, she thought. She willed herself to push the feeling aside and pulled her hand back gently.

"Max, she asked me to tell you—" she paused and pushed on through her embarrassment, "she loves her little Phillipe."

After she said the words she watched the most astonishing thing happen—the man of steel melted into a puddle of tears. He wept openly and unashamedly in front of her. He shook with the force and strength of his emotions, and Maggie reached out and held him, stroking his umber hair and rocking slowly, silently reaching up to turn off her pendant. This was a private moment.

Max must be feeling so many things, she thought. *Joy, surely—he must be over the moon that his mom is still alive. What about the time lost? The regret of missing time with his mother? What about the anger?*

As she held Max, she felt like she could feel a fury welling up within the mammoth man, and it scared her. For him.

With this knowledge, what will he do? Will he confront Lev?

Certainly, it would be in Max's character to demand justice for his mother and his sister, being lied to and left for years without their dear mother. Lev Avatov was ruthless, heartless, without remorse, and utterly indifferent to anything that he didn't want or deem valuable. That included his family. While these thoughts toyed with her, Max's sobs subsided and the shaking was no longer coming from him being wracked with emotions of joy. Now the shaking was coming from a very different, very serious place. Max was enraged. She could see it in his red eyes—eyes filled with blood and vengeance.

With tears coursing down his face he looked at Maggie and said, "Where is she? Where is my mother? Where in that vile place is she?"

The plea came from a place of knowing and disbelief. He knew where—she had only been in his father's home. He knew who, but he still couldn't believe it. She confirmed his suspicions with her words.

"There is a room, a secret upstairs room."

"How did you get upstairs? Petrov would never allow it, nor would my father."

Damn, she thought. *He's right.* She continued quickly.

"I went to find the bathroom and instead found a door behind a tapestry that led up a staircase to a door at the very end. Your mother was there. She sounded so relieved. She said she had been held captive there for a long time. She also told me to leave because she couldn't get out, and I couldn't be found."

Max was livid. His face had turned crimson, and he was clenching his jaw so hard she thought his teeth would crack. Without a word, Max put the car into gear and spun out of the parking lot. Maggie knew they were headed back to the Avatov compound; back to a showdown. She knew that a reckoning at the compound was inevitable, and she was afraid. Not only was she afraid for herself, but also for Max. This revelation would have dire consequences for someone.

"Max, I have to tell you that your mother told me, inadvertently, that they torture her on a regular basis. I'm not sure in what way because she never said, but even being locked away against your will is torture."

Max didn't say a word, he just kept steadily weaving his way through traffic. They pulled into the Avatov compound in record time. Boris met them in the driveway and placed a hand on Max's chest. Max pushed him away and told him to watch Maggie. Boris sneered in Maggie's direction, before following Max inside. Maggie quickly got out of the car, switched on her recorder, and followed Max into the house. He came to the room in which Maggie knew the hidden door resided. He threw open the door and nearly ran over Petrov in the process.

"Maxim, did you forget something?" Petrov asked with a smile. Max growled in response and pushed past him looking for the hidden door. Maggie saw him yank the tapestry that was hiding the door off the wall and pull the door open so hard that it banged against the newly bared spot behind it.

Petrov tried to stop Max from going through the door by grabbing him from behind, but Max in his fury was an unstoppable force. He grabbed Petrov by the neck and shook him like a ragdoll before tossing him into a table in the corner. He didn't get up, but Maggie let out a breath when she heard him groan—he wouldn't be out long.

Maggie followed Max up the stairs while Boris stayed below. Maggie didn't trust Boris, but at the moment, her need to help Max was greater that staying below and watching Boris. Max came upon the door at the top of the stairs. He took in the lock and pushed past Maggie as he flew back downstairs.

Maggie went to the door and said, "Margueritte?" She waited a moment or two before calling out again. There was no answer from inside the room. Maggie heard Max coming back up the stairs with a sickly looking Petrov in tow.

"Open it. Give me the passcode or I will kill you where you stand," he said in a deadly voice.

"Max," Maggie gasped.

"Stay out of this. I told you to wait in the car." Maggie took in his steely expression and decided silence was the best option at the moment.

"You can kill me if you want, but if I let her out of there I will be a dead man anyway."

Max growled again, grabbed Petrov's right hand and broke the smallest finger. Petrov screamed in pain.

Max leaned over to whisper, "I learned from Lev many things. You will tell me the combination to this door or your finger is not the only thing I will break today."

Petrov swallowed hard before he said in a weak voice, "It is your birthday."

Max stumbled back against the wall before catching himself. He turned and tried the code and the door unlocked with a click. He pushed open the door and stepped through to see small room with no windows. The inside of the room was kept neat. There were no comforts to the room itself except a table and single chair, a small bathroom with a toilet and sink only, and a small bed in the corner.

On the bed was a skeletal figure, small with dark hair and a ragged gown that looked to be two sizes too small. It rode up her skeletal thighs almost exposing her most private parts. Max only took two steps, and he was at her side smoothing the hair away from her thin face.

He looked up at Maggie and with an almost helpless expression and said, "What is wrong with her, Maggie?"

Maggie looked at Max helplessly and started searching around the room looking for anything that would explain why the woman she spoke with earlier lay so still and lifeless on the bed. She went over to the small table next to the washroom and noticed the edge of a bottle sticking out from underneath a washcloth. As she bent over to retrieve the bottle, she heard Max swear and a thud followed by a yelp from Petrov.

"What is wrong with her? What have you done to my mother?"

Max was holding Petrov so tightly up against the door frame that the other man was turning blue, his lips opening and closing but no words were forthcoming.

"Max. He has to be able to breathe to speak, but I may have found your answer." She showed him the bottle that she had found.

"Scopolamine?" Max sounded confused.

"They call it Devil's Breath. It makes a person unable to fight or assert their will in any way." Maggie said, sounding disgusted. "It is used by perverts to drug a woman. A date rape drug, mostly."

She heard Max growl and watched as he picked Petrov up and tossed him down the staircase. Maggie decided if he wasn't dead, he was going to wish he were when he woke up.

Max went back to the bed on which his mother was resting. Maggie could see that she had not eaten enough and was emaciated. Seeing Margueritte in her current state made Max sorrowful; his once vibrant, funny, and beautiful mother so severely neglected. Her hair, though neat and clean, was not the shimmering mass of curls he remembered so well from his youth. Now, the hair atop her head was a dull and lifeless black with no discernable curl or wave.

Dead, Max thought. *Like my mother was.*

How much had been stolen from them? His eyes stung and he wiped away bitter, acidic tears. How many birthdays, holidays, outings, quiet talks? How many moments when he needed his mother and instead had to run to her captor, his father, the villain of his nightmare? He looked lovingly at his mother. Her eyes were dark-rimmed and sunken. Her once perfectly-rouged cheekbones were gaunt. Her skin appeared papery and ashen, and anyone looking at her from across a room would think her a corpse.

"Max. *Max.* We have to get her somewhere safe before Lev returns."

Maggie snapped him from his bout of nostalgia and pity. Max grunted in response and scooped up the frail frame into his arms, so carefully. Maggie watched for a moment. The way Max held his mother as if she were the most precious thing in his world made her almost cry. The tenderness Max displayed could only come from a place of indomitable strength and courage. Whatever was going to transpire with Max and Lev, Maggie was certain that Max would not back down until he felt that he had exacted all of the justice due his family.

Maggie quickly grabbed the threadbare blanket from atop the bed and laid it over Max's mother, trying to be as gentle with her as her son. They made their way carefully down the staircase to the room that held the hidden door, both gingerly stepping and constantly checking on the frail woman.

As they reached the tapestry door, Max heard a voice say, "Maxim, I am disappointed. Margueritte, did you not teach the boy not to touch things that do not belong to him?"

Chapter 23

Max froze as he focused on the area where the voice had come from, and Maggie quickly reached up to her pendant. Lev sat quietly in the highback chair across from the door and took in the trio with an irritated look. Boris stood off to his side, ever the loyal lapdog, and sneered openly at Maggie and Max.

"I have come to collect my mother. She was never yours," Max said.

"Yes, yes—you are quite right, Maxim. She was never mine. That has ever been my problem." Lev said.

Max was confused. Ordinarily Lev would have been hurting someone by now, but in this instance, he was calmly taking in the whole scene. Max didn't trust him at all.

"Maggie, get behind me. Now," Max whispered.

Maggie edged her way behind Max and was regretting not staying in the car at this moment. She was a highly-accomplished fighter, but there were way too many variables in play for her to assert herself at this moment, so she demurred. She said a small prayer instead for assistance in getting them out of this mess.

"You have gall, father. She gave you everything, and then you lied about her dying? Why?"

Max could mask most of what he felt from Lev with anger, but Maggie knew that he was hiding the hurt in a cloud of rage. That cloud threatened the storm of the century, right there in that opulent library.

Max is either going to liberate his mother or get them all killed in the process.

"Max," she whispered from behind him while tugging on his sleeve, "let's just go."

She knew in her gut that Lev would never let them leave alive. She inched towards the door pulling him along after her. Max shrugged out of her grasp and faced Lev again, matching calm for calm, both men marshalling a maelstrom that could be unleashed at any second. Maggie wasn't sure if Max had heard her until he took a step backwards towards the door. She knew then that while he was trying to get answers, he was also trying to make it out of the house alive, for all of their sakes. As it turned out, Lev would be the first to break.

The man shook his head and spat, "That cheating shlyukha. Lying pizda. Maxim, your mother was not the faithful wife you thought she was. She cheated on me. On us, son."

Maggie recognized the tactic, and hoped against hope that in his vulnerable and emotional state Max wouldn't fall for it.

Max stopped moving.

"What do you mean?"

"She was seeing another man, and as much as it pains me to tell you this, she had his baby."

Maggie could tell that Lev was looking for sympathy as the victim of adultery. She couldn't see Max's face but she could tell by the way he stood that he was waiting for the other shoe to drop.

"If she was cheating on you, why not divorce her? Divorce, not fake her death and torture her for 14 years. You imprisoned her in *our home*."

The thunder in Max's voice clapped directly in his father's unflinching face, and Maggie could see the indifference and annoyance that Lev really felt, not the act he was using with his son. She never hated anyone more than she did Lev Avatov at that precise moment.

Burn in hell, you heartless bastard, she thought.

Lev threw his hands in the air in a gesture of exasperation.

"I loved your mother and didn't want her to be with anyone but me. I was jealous, son. I wanted her to myself, to us. You needed your mother as I needed my wife. As punishment for cheating, she was sentenced to a life without everything she loved, and when her bastard daughter was born, she stayed with her until she was of an age to be shipped off to boarding school."

Max was stunned. If what he was hearing was correct, his sister, Ilyana, was not a full sister but a half sister. A baby by another father. Max looked down at the frail woman in his arms and then back at the man who had never been a true father to him.

"If she had a baby by a different man, maybe it was because you were not man enough to keep her."

Max heard a growl coming from Boris. Lev just smiled a small, cold smile. He walked up to Max as he held his mother in his arms and smacked him across the face. Lev stepped back from Max and wagged a scolding finger, as if disciplining a small child.

He's toying with him now, thought Maggie.

"Respect, Maxim. You will show respect. I am not only your father, I am also your employer."

Max spit onto the oriental carpet. He smiled an icy smile at his father.

"I was finished showing you respect the moment Maggie told me my mother was alive."

Lev turned his cold stare on Maggie, and she knew that from that moment she was a marked woman. She wasn't sure how, but she knew that Lev had a special kind of hell in mind for her.

"How kind of you to ruin everything for me. You have successfully taken not only my property, but my son as well."

"I would do it all over again if given the chance. *No one*," Maggie emphasized, "deserves to be treated as you have treated Margueritte. You are a monster, to not only your son but to the woman you love."

She was surprised by the sharp laughter that burst forth from Lev.

"I never loved Margueritte," Lev said nonchalantly, "A means to an end, nothing more. I treated her well until the stupid cow betrayed me."

There's 'stupid cow' again, thought Maggie. *Do they teach them that insult in gangster school?*

Lev's face took on a tinge of crimson, the only indication that this altercation was taxing his patience. He smiled and brushed a speck of lint from his sleeve, pulled slightly at his meticulous French cuff, smoothed the front of his jacket.

"I took Margueritte as a trophy, from a rival. I will not be denied or bested."

"You are a sick man, to not only use this woman, but to steal her away from someone who could give her everything you wouldn't." Maggie said.

Lev laughed. "I am an uncomplicated person, Ms. Preston. Simple to get along with and appease. If one does things the way I want and sees them as I see them, we will get along. If not..."

He let the question hang in the air like a smoke ring. He quickly crossed the four steps to get directly in her face, which frightened her for a second, and caused Max to flinch, torn between protecting his frail mother and the woman he loved.

With Lev's unctuous smile, inches from her face, she could only stand and receive whatever was coming. He spoke through perfectly white teeth.

"I get what I want, young lady..." He let the sentence drop.

Maggie was not under any delusions about the sentiment of the statement. Lev was an extremely dangerous person. With your average gangster or mob-type, enemies disappeared. Police and intel agencies were still a greater enemy to be feared by most criminals. When Lev Avatov marked you, you didn't disappear. You could be cut down in broad daylight. Lev and his people did not fear anyone, including the authorities. They were as close to untouchable as existed, and there were frequent reminders the world over for any who might have forgotten. The implication was clear, Maggie had made Lev angry. She was actually quite surprised that they all hadn't already died in a hail of bullets.

He must need us for—something.

Max pushed in front of Maggie who had inched her way around him to confront his father. He wanted to make sure that the focus was on him and not Maggie.

"What were you going to do with her? When would you have let her out?" Max asked him, bringing the attention back to the conversation at hand.

"I would not have released her." Lev said with a shrug, "The bitch would have died there, and we would have had her disposed of. Like one of my horses."

His nonchalance about the subject of death made Maggie squirm. No sane person could speak of death and not show some kind of respect, or fear, at its utterance. Before anything further could be said, one of Lev's henchmen came in and whispered into his ear. Whatever the goon had said had made the blood drain from Lev's face.

He said to Boris, "I must leave. The Chairman is here. Take Margueritte back to her cell and lock those two in the dungeon until I am able to deal with them."

Without another word, he walked out of the room. Boris turned on Max with an evil grin, spreading his arms wide and laughing to the sky at his good fortune.

"How the mighty have fallen. The golden child has finally fallen out of favor over a couple of stupid sluts."

Maggie could tell Max wanted to punch Boris by the clenching of his jaw. He had walked over to the settee in the corner and was careful in laying Margueritte down onto its velvety surface. Maggie walked over to stand by the settee and watch over the unconscious woman. Max looked briefly at Maggie before turning to face Boris.

"This has been a long time coming, Maxim—you know it as well as I. We were never brothers as we once swore to each other. We are rivals. One that is close to power, one that is close to Lev."

Boris and Max circled each other. Maggie thought it rather strange that Lev had not called anyone else to help Boris with Max, but then again, maybe this was another of Lev's sick and twisted games.

"I am uncertain what I did to make you hate me so, Boris. At this point, I no longer care. I will tell you that with Lev there is no acceptance, no love, and certainly no power. The only thing that Lev will give you is orders. I tried for years to be let into his confidence, and I am his son. What would you offer to him other than your loyalty? He had mine, and it did no good."

Max was yelling, and Maggie could tell that part of his tirade was that of the hurt little boy who could not gain his father's affection. The other part was worry over how he was going to get Maggie and his mother out of the house.

Margueritte was moving around a bit like she was trying to wake from a deep sleep. Maggie knelt down, and while Max was busy yelling at Boris, she worked on rousing her enough that the older woman slowly opened her eyes. Maggie grabbed her hand and with a quick check on what was happening in the room, focused her attention on Max's mom.

"Margueritte, we are here to rescue you, but Lev found out and has sent Boris to stop us from leaving. Is there another way out of the house other than the front door?"

Margueritte's eyes wandered for a moment and then focused on Maggie's voice.

"Way... out?" she asked in a small voice.

Maggie could tell that she was still having trouble processing information but pressed on with her questions.

"Margueritte, Margueritte listen…" she snapped her fingers at Margueritte to gain her attention once again. "Max is in trouble, and we need another way out of Lev's mansion. Is there another way to escape the house?"

Margueritte placed a small hand to her head as if steadying it and said, "There is a back way; under the house through the tunnels," Margueritte said. "Lev showed it to me when I was pregnant with Maxim. I was only told so I could guard his progeny," she spat.

The short burst of energy seemed to be leaving Margueritte, so Maggie pushed on.

"Where do we find the entrance?"

Margueritte seemed to have fallen back asleep so Maggie slapped her lightly on the cheeks.

"Margueritte, wake up and tell me how to get to the tunnels."

Maggie was a little louder than she had wanted to be and stole a glance at Max and Boris, who had stopped pacing and stood facing each other, both ready for the confrontation they knew was destined to take place. Maggie shook her once again and her eyes fluttered open briefly.

"Through the wine cellar in the service kitchen."

She seemed to fade out, as if that sentence took the last mite of energy she had in her. She lost consciousness, but immediately jolted with a wild look in her eyes, staring at Maggie.

"The tunnels. Sn— p—pl—"

Maggie didn't catch the last thing she said. She was out again, but Maggie knew where they needed to go.

Not a moment too soon, for Boris let out a great bellow and rushed Max. Max was ready for him, and being the more nimble of the two was able to sidestep, pivot, and grab Boris by the legs. The look of surprise on the man's face was priceless, and Maggie would have loved to savor it, but it disappeared from her view, along with him. Max had flung Boris backwards over his shoulder and onto the great desk in the center of the library, the crack resounding off the walls.

Boris hauled himself up, and they started to circle each other again.

To Maggie, they resembled two great bears fighting for territory in the woods, pawing and swiping at each other. She had watched enough to know that they were evenly matched and decided that a little help was in order. She grabbed the fireplace poker from where it sat in the elegant, brass set against the wall, and brandishing it like a sword, moved forward and swung it against the back of Boris's great head with a sickening thump.

Boris stopped circling and instead fell, spasming and seizing in a great heap at Max's feet.

Max looked at Maggie in shock.

She shrugged and said, "So that's that, then. I know where we have to go, Max. Grab your mom and follow me."

Max, mouth still agape at her audacity, bent over and carefully lifted Margueritte into his arms. He turned back to Maggie as if awaiting an order.

"Got her? Let's go."

He needed no further prompting as she turned and headed out the door. Max followed Maggie as she made her way towards the kitchens. Petrov had shown the wine cellar to Maggie on her earlier tour as it was one of Lev's favorite places, and yet another thing that he could not resist bragging about. He had not taken her all the way to the back of the cellar, but Maggie had seen enough to know that Lev's cellar was worth a mint, and that there was a secondary door that had no explanation. This had to be the way out that Margueritte had mentioned. Maggie led Max through the kitchen to the door in the cellar.

"The wine cellar?" Max asked, perplexed.

"Yes, your mother woke long enough to tell me that there is a secondary exit through the wine cellar. She also said to be aware of something, but it was so garbled I couldn't make it out. I can't imagine that it would be any worse than what we were facing in there."

Max leaned over and kissed her gently on the head.

"We will find the way out, myschka. Incidentally, you are quite the—something. I hope you continue to amaze me."

He flashed her a dazzling grin that made her brain go soupy and turned her legs to Jell-O. Max strode past with Margueritte into the darkened cellar. The only lighting was in eight-foot intervals along the walls. The cellar extended back about to what Maggie figured was the size of a football field. The cellar was massive as well as being grandiose and gaudy. About halfway through there was a door for which there was no evident lock. It looked to be older but well maintained.

Maggie figured this had to be the way out, so she pulled the door open with little resistance. The smell that hit her as she pulled open the door was one that she had only experienced at the reptile exhibit in the local zoo. It was a musky, earthy smell slightly reminiscent of rotting cucumber that did not help her anxiety level. Screwing up her courage, she stepped through the door into the inky darkness.

She felt around the wall, which was damp and slimy, just inside the door and found a switch. The heavy duty switch let out a cacophonous *clack*. The corridor was around 20 feet long and narrow, all natural stone cut from a solid piece of rock. Maggie wondered how long Lev must have had someone work to build this tunnel under his compound, and who he had do it in the first place. From what she knew of gangsters and their ilk, the builders and laborers were most likely still here, inside the walls.

The thought made her shudder. *Or is it the cold? It's really chilly in here.*

Not enough that she could see her breath, but being underground in the Russian fall brought with it a noticeable drop in the ambient temperature. The hallway ended with another door. This one had a deadbolt attached to it, and Maggie knew that the door would be locked before she ever tried to open it. Frustrated, Max growled in the background.

"Now what do we do. I do not have a key to this door. I did not even know this door existed."

Maggie held up a hand to forestall any further lamentations from her companion. She reached behind her head and removed the lovely amber comb and placed it in her pocket.

"You have got to be kidding me," Max offered wryly. "This is literally a trope from every old movie. I hope you do not expect me to be able to pick a lock."

As her tresses started to unravel, she produced two bobby pins, causing the riot of red curls to fall in waves to her shoulders. She bent the pin so that she could stick it into the lock and after fiddling with it for a moment they heard a click as the lock disengaged. Maggie smiled at Max

"You and I need to have a little chat later, do we not?" Max said.

Maggie's smile faltered briefly. "I suppose we do."

Maggie pushed the inner door open and allowed Max to enter, carrying Margueritte. Closing the door behind her after following him inside, she searched the walls for a light switch. Upon finding one, she switched on the yellowing incandescent lights, again with a very audible *clack*.

The lights in this room were so old that the light itself did not reach all the way to the corners, and Maggie thought she saw something move in her periphery. A soft rustling was heard throughout the room and then went silent. Maggie's frantic, peering gaze swept around the room as she waited for her eyes to adjust. She was finally able to take in their surroundings, and that left her utterly speechless. She covered her mouth to keep from crying out at the horror that was in the room around her.

We have stumbled upon an honest-to-God mad scientist's lab.

Chapter 24

There were shelves lined with containers and large vials and jars. Inside those were the carcasses of creatures. Nothing that Maggie had seen before, but a few that she thought she had recognized from stories in children's fairy tales. A gigantic, bloody, and raw bone took up the center of the room. Maggie had been inside plenty of museums, and also to a few crime scenes in her day, and bones as a rule didn't bother her.

Where the hell did this come from?

This bone had a section of it cut out to reveal the meaty core, bloody and grisly, not like a museum-display bone at all, but a fresh bone that had once been part of a living creature—probably recently. As if in answer to her silent query, she spied a forgotten saw sitting forlornly off to the side of the bone on a cement block.

Next to the bone sat a table with a large jar on it. In the jar was a small human-like figure, it was completely green with webbed feet and hands. On its back was a shell-like carapace, like that of a turtle. She tapped the side of the jar and followed it down to the neatly scrawled tag—*Kappa, found in in Japan ca. 1838.*

Maggie wasn't sure what a *kappa* was exactly, but she was finding the lab more and more intriguing. That was the type of person she was, horror gave way to curiosity and intrigue more often than not. It's what made her one of the best at what she did.

She surreptitiously reached up to her pendant to ensure it was switched on. Max had moved over to the small couch settled by a wall in the corner and arranged a place to settle his mom. He walked over to Maggie and flicked the glass jar with his finger.

"Have you ever seen this before, Max?" Maggie asked him.

"I have. Some of them are recent purchases, but some of them I have not seen before," Max told her.

"What does he do with them?" she asked him.

"I am not sure. He keeps the information to himself. It looks as though he has someone running tests and experiments down here, though. Look."

Max pointed in a direction, and Maggie's gaze automatically followed to a stainless steel surgical table with the body of a small child upon it. Maggie recoiled until she realized it was not a child at all but a small humanoid creature. *A dwarf, maybe?* It was covered in hair with a beard that was half the length of its body. Two small horns projected from it's head, and it was covered in bruises and had small patches of hair removed along with the skin.

Maggie shivered and moved closer to Max. He placed a protective arm around her and pulled her to him.

"The poor creature. Do you know what it is, Max?"

Max looked around and spotted some notes on a clipboard by the corpse. He let go of Maggie and scanned the notes.

"It says it is a *domovoi*." Max said with wonderment. He shook his head, "It cannot be. They do not exist except in children's tales."

Maggie had never heard of the domovoi and said as much to Max.

"I forget that you did not grow up here. The domovoi is like a helper or house elf. It can be mischievous and sometimes harmful." He thought for a second and brightened. "I believe you may call it a *brownie*?"

"Ah, ok. I've heard of those. But, Max, this doesn't seem—logical."

Maggie thought maybe Max was having some kind of meltdown. House elves sounded very magicky to her. They turned to look around some of the other tables before Max could see her smile. She made her way to a very promising desk in the corner. The papers that were scattered around the desk showed tables and graphs on various tests completed on numerous subjects, all stamped in large red letters, UNVIABLE. All of them.

Maggie wondered what experiment or test could they all have

been subject to, but none would pass? It seemed that no matter the subject or data entered the result was still the same. All of the test subjects tested were deemed failures.

Maggie was not sure what or who the subjects are or where they are currently, but if the domovoi on the table back there was one of the subjects, then she could guess the rest.

Max had moved back to his mother's side. She had once again gained consciousness, and Max was stroking her hair away from her face. The look that passed between them was heartbreakingly sweet. Maggie watched for a moment longer before turning her attention to the filing cabinet beside the desk. She quickly scanned the various contents stopping briefly on the file marked *dragon* and another marked *elf.* It seemed that each file held a brief summary of the creature and if a specimen had been found and tested. Maggie shook her head at this nonsense.

Dragons and elves weren't real. Domovoi weren't real, either.

She stole a quick glance at the small creature on the table.

Real enough to be dead and dismembered on Lev Avatov's table.

She heard that slithery sound again off to the right of where she stood. It was a lot closer than it was the last time she heard it. Maggie was just getting ready to shut the cabinet again when another folder caught her eye. Magueritte's name was listed on one of the files in the drawer of oddities:

SUBJECT:

MARGUERRITTE CHARLOTTE-LAVAL MANETTE AVATOV

She pulled the folder from the drawer and shoved it in a garbage bag she pulled from the front of the cabinet. She noticed a few other files in the drawer:

UNNAMED VAMPIRE

UNNAMED VILA

UNNAMED WEREWOLF

Maggie wasn't sure what they meant, but she took those files too. A hissing sound came from behind her. Maggie spun around and let out a scream. Standing behind her was a great snake, standing on two feet. Maggie threw the first thing that came to her hand, a coffee mug, at the thing behind her. She spun around and ran back towards Max and Margueritte clutching tightly to the bag in her hands.

Max had stood and was halfway to the frightened Maggie when they heard another yell, although this yell was weaker but recognizable as Margueritte. Max spun around quickly and retraced his steps, but was only quick enough to see the door closing on a frightened Margueritte being held by one of the snake people.

"Mother," he yelled as he made it to the door just in time to hear the locks click into place. "Maggie, help me," Max screamed as he pounded on the door with his fists. He quickly abandoned this tactic and retreated a couple of steps, only to rush as fast as he could, ramming the door with his massive shoulder.

"Max, stand back," Maggie said, grabbing his arm to keep him from ramming the door once again.

Using the same hairpin, she worked her magic once again. *Alohamora,* she thought.

They heard the sweet sound of the door lock clicking free, and Maggie barely had time to get out of the way before Max wrenched it open and flew through. He ran down the passageway to another entry at the end. This door was unlocked and opened easily. Max burst through before she could shout for him to be cautious. It wouldn't have mattered; nothing would keep him from rescuing his mother now.

With no regard for his own safety, he bulled through to whatever lie in wait on the other side, and Maggie followed, clutching the file bag in one hand and a metal pry bar she found laying next to an open crate in the previous room in the other.

This new room was cavernous. Maggie could tell this really was a cave Lev had dug into when creating his wine cellar. The existence of the cave either came as a wonderful surprise to Lev, or he already knew of it. He had lights put in place but only in the middle of the room, leaving the periphery dark.

Maggie could hear the hissing and slithering sounds again, but this time it was all around them. Max had stopped moving and was watching and listening as well. From the shadows a figure appeared. Max was able to get a better look at the thing, and in better light than when they were in the dark lab.

"Come into the light," he spoke. He wasn't even certain he would be understood.

What sort of language do snake people speak, anyway?

It didn't matter; he wasn't leaving here without his mother, period.

The creature half-walked/half-undulated into view, and Max was greeted with the strangest sight he had ever seen: a serpent's head covered in pale gray and brown scales peered at him with human-like eyes. The head moved constantly, twitching slightly left or right or up or down, hovering sort of the way a helicopter would, and a black tongue darted from between slightly parted jaws. Below the hooded head, the creature had a mostly human form, with lanky yet powerful limbs that terminated into web-fingered hands and feet. It was like something out of a comic book or movie, and he half expected a creature like this to be sporting some brightly-colored costume or armor and have a great weapon at his disposal—but this monster did not look formidable. It looked tired, desperate, and frightened.

Desperation makes anything dangerous.

He reminded himself of his training. Despite not knowing the first thing about it or its type, Max got the impression that this creature was a youth. Max brought both of his hands up slowly, empty, with palms out and exposed to the creature; the universal symbol for being unarmed and coming in peace.

Maggie watched this exchange and hoped desperately the snake-thing understood. The creature's head stopped twitching long enough to nod slightly in acknowledgement of the gesture, tongue still flicking away frantically as if tasting the air.

"Exsssschange."

The creature suddenly spoke, high and wispy, and gestured to two figures flanking it. Maggie could see that they were all nearly identical, although the one on to his left seemed slightly smaller of build and seemed to have...*breasts? A female?*

"What are you? Exchange for what?" Max asked, hands still raised.

He appeared to be relieved at the speech from the creature. The creature did not respond audibly, but pulled its hood in to its body, and its companions on either side did likewise, revealing Margueritte standing dumbfounded behind the one that appeared to be female. She looked pale and had silent tears running down her cheeks.

Maggie's heart went out to the older woman—to be rescued from one monster only to end up with another. The hoods extended from the snake heads once again, and she disappeared from view.

"Give her back," Max demanded.

The creature tilted its head to the side and said in a hiss, "Return yourssss. Return ourssss."

Max looked confused until he noticed the snake man point to the bag that Maggie clutched in her hand.

"Maggie, give me the bag," he told her, holding out his hand.

"Max, there is information in here that you need to read..."

Max shook his head and held his hand steady.

Maggie sighed and put the bag into his hand. Max took the bag and walked toward the snake man.

"I give you this, you give me her."

Again, the snake man tilted his head in that odd way some animals do and flicked a forked tongue out of his mouth.

"Yessss."

Max held out his right hand to Margueritte, and the other hand with the bag he held out to the snake man.

The snake turned to the female and nodded slightly. The female retracted her hood and gestured for Margueritte to come forward. As she walked towards Max, the snake man reached out to snatch the bag that Max had let go of in order to use both of his hands to catch his collapsing mother. Max pulled his mom to him and backed quickly into the light beside Maggie. The snake man pulled the bag toward him and faded into the darkness.

Maggie, Margueritte, and Max stood and listened to the slithering recede until they could no longer hear anything. Margueritte, who had been clutching Max's arm for support, crumpled to the ground.

"I told you about the snake people," she said.

Max lifted her into his arms.

"Which way should we go?" he asked, looking at Maggie.

Maggie looked at Margueritte who pointed weakly and said, "One hundred paces from this point then turn to your left. Another passage will lead you out of here to the river. The *naga* will not bother us now that their possessions have been returned. They are very territorial, but they keep their word."

"Naga? Is that what they were?" asked Maggie.

"Yes. They are an old race. Lev struck a bargain with them when he dug his wine cellar into their nesting area. I was told of their existence only when he showed me the way out. He said he told them to protect his 'pet' if she should come down into the cellar to get away. I reminded them of their duty."

She smiled and closed her eyes as if resting.

Maggie used her phone's flashlight to light the way into the darkness. She kept count as they walked, and when she reached 100 they turned to the left. The promised passage was there in front of them. They followed the new passageway, every once in a while hearing a slither or a hiss from nearby, but it seemed the naga were only following to make sure that the *pets* reached safety as they promised.

After what seemed hours, but in reality was only 15 minutes, they reached the entrance to the cave. It dumped out near the palace grounds. Max sat Margueritte on a boulder near the entrance and pulled his phone from his pocket.

"Who are you calling, Max?" Maggie asked.

"Leclerc," Max told her. "I am going to have him get our bags and meet us here. Then I am going to call some friends to get us out of Russia and away from my father."

Max ground out the word *father* like it left a bitter taste in his mouth. As Max talked to Leclerc on the phone, Maggie sat by Margueritte's side.

"Are you okay?" she asked.

Margueritte said on a sigh, "I am better now that I am back with my son."

She had great, dark circles under her eyes and looked like she needed a good meal, but all in all, Maggie thought the older woman looked determined. She had the same look in her eyes that Susanna had after she had been rescued from her own personal hell.

"I had a friend that went through a similar experience. You're going to be fine. Max won't let anything hurt you again. He really is extraordinary."

Margueritte smiled at her and said, "You are correct. My little Philippe has grown so—I'm afraid I have a lot of catching up to do. There were so many things that I missed—like shopping. I think that will be the first, no, second thing I will do."

"Oh, what is the first?" Maggie asked.

"The first will be to get my hair and nails done. It has been too long since my hair was cut last," she told her and then laughed.

It was the first genuine laugh Maggie had heard from her, and it sounded wonderful. Max returned and smiled at the sight of his mom laughing with Maggie.

"Leclerc is on his way. The pilots will have the plane gassed and ready for takeoff when we get there," Max told them.

Maggie was eager to get somewhere safe.

"What about your father? How do we know he won't pursue us?"

"He is with the Chairman, which means he is not to be disturbed. He will not know of our escape until the conclusion of that meeting. Besides," Max said, thoughtfully, "he either is not concerned with where we go and what we do, or he needs us alive. Otherwise, he would have ordered his men to kill us already."

"Where are we going, Max?" Maggie asked.

"Back to New Orleans, to see a friend who I hear can help us."

She cocked a questioning eyebrow at him, but said nothing. He didn't offer any explanation, so she shrugged and lightly kissed him, then turned toward the river. She walked a few paces, rubbing her temples and looking skyward, wondering how she had gotten through everything, and how so much could transpire in less than 24 hours. They had confronted Lev, Max's mother was alive, they had found some sort of secret laboratory, and to top it off she was pretty sure they were the only people besides Lev and his select lieutenants who knew of the existence of, and had met, the fabled naga.

What a day, she thought. *And it's not over for you, girl. Not by a long shot. You* have *to tell him. You were on the receiving end of one of the most sincere and heartfelt declarations of love in the history of history, and you are* still *lying to him.*

A tear slipped from her eye and rolled as a silent, guilty witness of her shame and dishonesty down her cheek.

He deserves better than me, she thought. *I am what I do and my crusade is my love, right? Hasn't it been, since… well, since Suse? Isn't she why I do what I do? Human trafficking, and murder, and conspiracy, and sedition, and corruption… that's my husband, my love. This is bigger than me. It's even bigger than Max Avatov.*

She pondered this and thought about how, in her heart of hearts, she never felt like she deserved to be happy. Not really. She always figured that she was destined for a life of sneaking and deception and sensationalism, and if she were honest with herself, that's what would probably get her killed. *Young.*

She laughed to herself chidingly. The thought of settling down or even having someone think she was important enough to protect, to love, was laughable to her. She was a bad person. If she needed any further evidence, she had seen it in those cloudy blue eyes. Those honest eyes—the ones that looked on her in love and admiration, while she could only manage self-loathing and self-pity. She angrily wiped her face and knelt to splash water onto her hot cheeks.

Look at you, she thought, seeing her reflection in the crystalline and cold water. After all of that—after everything that had happened she still looked runway ready, other than her hair being down around her shoulders, and even then, she noted it still had just the right amount of body.

You're a flouncer and a fake, lady. You couldn't tell the truth if someone held a gun to your head, and you don't deserve him. Go on being Ms. Perfect and leave the poor man alone. He's been hurt enough by his father, by fate, by circumstance, and, yes, like it or not, by you. How much more will you make him suffer? You come clean… then what? All is magically forgiven? Happily ever after? I don't think so. Think about this: who would ever trust you? You don't just deceive people for a living, it's your passion. You get off on it. Someone like you should not be with someone like him. Period.

Max's beckoning snapped her out of her thoughts. She splashed once more, took one last look at the rippled, perfect face in the water, and turned to meet Max, all the while trying to think of how best to let him go.

Chapter 25

Sam and Abe were just finishing loading the plane with the last of Peter's gear. Peter was trying to make Tammy as comfortable as possible in the small area Peter sat in on the way to Russia. Sam's phone jingled a snappy tune alerting him to a new call.

"Yo," said Sam into the receiver. He listened for a moment before saying, "We can be up in 30. The flight plan is already set and submitted—St Petersburg to Sevastopol, then Helsinki, then Reykjavik, then PEI, then Boston, etc, etc, etc." He listened a moment more before exclaiming, "What? Snake—what? What do you mean, *snake* people?"

Abe turned at Sam's exclamation, and Sam, seeing his interest, waved him over and put the call on speaker. Max Avatov's voice came through the speaker loud and clear.

"We ran into a little trouble with my father It is a lengthy story. Right now, we need passage for three out of Russia as soon as possible. Where are you bound?" Max asked.

"I'm taking this lot back to New Orleans. Peter has finished his business here and is returning home. Abe will help me fly the bird back to the states. I'm sure we can find room for you and the others. It might be tight, though. This ain't Delta." Sam told him. "I'm still interested in these snake people you say you ran in to. It sounds like a great time." Sam told him. "Later."

A higher, recognizable voice came over the line.

"Ask him about the crazy angel thing that rescued the girl that showed up at the Igromir. I know they were there."

"Did you hear that, Sam? Maggie wants to know about—"

"Yeah, I heard, Max."

Sam turned to stone, his fingers gripped his cellphone so hard Abe reached over and rescued it before Sam broke it.

"Sam," Max said, "are you still there?"

"He was called away, Max. This is Abe. How soon do you need the plane ready?"

"We should be there in an hour. Please have Sam standing by with the engines running. I cannot be sure we will not be followed. This could be a potentially dangerous situation. I have a person that was declared dead 14 years ago and a father that is responsible."

Abe whistled, "Whoo—I thought my life was messed up. I think I might know someone who can help you, Max. Just get here and we will talk about it more on the ride to the states."

"Thanks, Abe. Tell Sam we will arrive soon."

Max hung up and Abe turned to Sam. He snapped his fingers in front of Sam's face.

"Hey, man. Snap out if it. We have things to do." Sam shook his head as if coming out of a hypnotic state.

"Sorry, Abe. I keep seeing things."

The last part was mumbled and Abe almost missed what he said.

"Seeing what?"

"It's not important," Sam said, blowing off the incident. "So, when are we leaving?"

"We leave in an hour."

"Okay, let's get this bird ready. You take the front, and I'll take the back. You know what to do."

Sam grabbed his phone from Abe, turned, and walked away leaving Abe standing alone. Abe shrugged and figured that Sam needed a little time to work through whatever was going on with him. He made his way to the front of the plane to start his pre-flight check.

Sam walked under the plane to inspect the landing gear. As he walked he thought about what happened at the convention center. He skirted the back of the wing, running his hands over the trim flaps, but his mind was elsewhere. He stopped, turned out towards the Russian afternoon that waited just beyond the hangar, ran his calloused hands through his dark hair, and tried to remember. The problem was there wasn't a whole lot he *could* remember about it.

He remembered looking for Tammy. He remembered beeps and whirs and shouts and even the sound of the loud air conditioner that serviced the expo center. He remembered spotting the purple-haired girl, and seeing her perched precariously on the balcony. She was sobbing and mumbling something about never finding Mr. Right and how she was too small, too outgoing, and too ugly to ever find someone special.

That was odd, because he shouldn't have been able to hear her speaking over the din and everything else going on, but he heard every word as clearly as if she had whispered it right into his ear.

The crowd around Tammy was split—half the people were yelling at her to jump, and the other half was telling her not to do it. Sam was confused until he saw the vila in the lobby.

The vila. He remembered her as well. He remembered her trying to bore into his head like she had many of the other men there. He remembered being angry at her. She smiled up at Sam and in the next instant the crowd pushed forward, Tammy was jostled and screamed. Sam saw her fall. Everything after that was blank.

He was not sure what happened or how he ended up outside staring at his plane. He remembered answering the phone and talking briefly with Abe who was at the local hospital with Peter and Tammy. The doctors had released her, with a prescription for a mild sedative, to Peter's care to return to the states.

Sam continued to walk and search his brain for any information regarding the missing time from his life. This was not the first time that it had happened; he had a similar episode in New Orleans right before they came to Russia. He had been running through the bayou with Sarah. He noticed that she had the sweetest smile, it lit up her whole face. When he had helped her down from the truck she had looked at him and smiled sweetly and thanked him. She reminded him vaguely of someone—*Another child, maybe?* The memory, as all the others, was lost to him. He pulled out his wallet.

He went searching through the various slots searching for the card that Peter had handed to him that night in New Orleans. He had told him that he had a friend named Jo, and that she could help him recover some of his memories if he would let her. He found the card he was looking for—a basic white card with gold embellishments. In the middle of the card were two lines: Her name and her phone number. Sam had a few minutes to himself, so he took out his phone and dialed the number on the card.

"Hello?" A velvety voice said from the other end of the line.

"Dr. Jo, my name's Sam."

"Is there a last name, Sam?" Dr. Jo asked him.

"You first," he said.

"Phillips. And you?"

"Ramos," he said, then paused and rubbed his hand across the back of his neck to ease the tension that had accumulated there. "My friend Peter gave me your card and said that you might be able to help me remember some things."

"Peter?" she questioned, "Peter who?"

"Peter Devereaux" Sam supplied.

"Oh, that Peter. I see lots of people, so it is often hard to differentiate names. Why do you say you are having problems remembering, Sam?"

"Well, there have been periods of time where I will blackout, and—and I wake up. I wake up somewhere else with no knowledge of how I came to be there," he sounded frustrated, even to himself.

"Yes, I can see how that would be pretty scary. Do you think something bad happened during those events?" she sounded interested.

"No, I don't think I did anything bad, but I have a feeling that I am missing something important—like there is part of me missing."

"Well, I would certainly like to try and help you. Where are you now? Can you come to my office this afternoon?"

He laughed. "Today would be tough. I'm currently in St Petersburg."

"Florida?"

"No," he laughed. "Someplace a bit chillier and a lot further away.

Russia—sitting on the tarmac waiting to take my plane, cargo, and passengers back to the states. We won't be back until late tomorrow."

Her laugh over the phone was light and carefree.

"I can see how that would be a problem—and why you called me at four o'clock in the morning."

"Oh, man. I forgot about the time change. I just really need to have some answers, and Peter says you're the gal to give them to me. Sorry about the early hour, though," he finished lamely.

"It's no problem Sam. I am used to getting calls at all hours. Please, think nothing of it," she told him graciously. "Can you come to my office the day after tomorrow, then?"

"Yeah, that's fine. Do you think you will be able to help me?"

"I can almost guarantee it."

She sounded so sure it helped calm the last of Sam's nerves.

"I'll see you at ten in the morning on Thursday, okay?"

"It's a date. Thanks."

Sam ended the call and let out a breath. He turned and finished his portion of the preflight check just in time to see two vehicles pull up to the plane. Sam walked up to the first car as a small man appeared and ran around to the back, opening first one door, then making his way around to the other side and doing the same. Max popped out of one side followed by a small redhead. He walked rapidly around the car to help a frail looking woman out of the other side. The small man had moved to the second vehicle where he, along with the second driver, pulled luggage out of the back. Max, helping the older woman along, approached Sam. Sam was astounded as a smile lit the face of the stoic, younger Avatov.

"Thank you for doing this, my friend. I want you to meet my mother, Margueritte." Max told him and he laughed at Sam as he tried to find the right question to ask.

"What? How?" Sam finally said.

"It is a long story. By the way, we need to leave. Now." Max emphasized the *now,* and Sam nodded in acceptance.

"Well, it isn't like this ride is going to be short. There will be plenty of time for discussion. Welcome aboard." he said with a mock bow and a flourish of his imaginary cap.

He followed the others into the belly of the transport plane. They had finished bringing in the last of the luggage, and Abe was making sure it was stowed properly. Sam brought the others forward into the plane itself.

"Sorry, but just like Peter and Tammy, you guys will have to strap into the jump seats until we are airborne, then you can unfold the cots. Peter can show you how. He's a pro."

Sam grinned at Peter, who had stopped moving when he saw Max and the two women appear in the doorway.

"Hey," Peter said, "Maggie, the girl with the Jimmy Choos." He smiled as he saw her remember him. "How did you make out with the shoes?"

"Hi, Mr. Devereaux. Well, you were right—they did kill my feet," she told him, then added in a mock whisper, "but I still wouldn't have worn anything else."

Max scowled in response to their banter, and his mother slapped his arm affectionately.

"Here, let me show you how these seats work, and you all can get strapped in."

Peter showed the others how to fold down the jump seats and strap in, then he resumed his seat next to Tammy and smiled at her as she watched him.

"I noticed that there was no stuttering when you were speaking with *her*," Tammy whispered as she leaned toward Peter.

Peter smiled and bumped shoulders with her.

"I think I'm cured," he told her with a wink.

"So are you gonna ask her out?" Tammy whispered again.

"What? No! Not if I value my neck. See, the big guy with her is her boyfriend, and I'm pretty sure he would beat me to a pulp."

She laughed at the face he made and leaned into his shoulder with a big yawn.

"That's too bad. She's really pretty."

Peter smiled and gave her a peck on the head as he heard the engines whine and felt the plane start to roll. When he looked back down at Tammy, she was already asleep. He would make sure that she had a place to lay down after they were in the air.

Abe came through the cargo hold door and secured the latch. He smiled and gave Peter the thumbs up on his way through to the cockpit. Once he sat in the co-pilot seat and strapped in, the pair made their final calls, and the plane taxied onto the runway. In no time it was airborne. Peter was glad to be going home. Once he was sure Tammy was settled, he'd talk to Maggie. He wanted to find out how she had ended up in Russia and on this plane. It seemed they had all had an eventful trip.

Chapter 26

The plane had been in the air for about an hour, and all the while Maggie had been contemplating her next steps. She had moved over to the end of the seat after Max and Peter had folded down a couple of the stowed cots. There, she carefully removed the crumpled notes that she had managed to yank from Margueritte's file down in the underground lab before she followed Max into that cavern where they had met the naga.

This adventure had taken such a turn in the last 24 hours—she was still trying to wrap her head around it. She reached into her bag and pulled out a black scrunchie and quickly put her hair up. She rubbed her tired eyes. She felt like she could sleep for a year, and she desperately wanted a Dewar's.

She pulled out the pages that interested her in particular; Margueritte's file was the largest and Maggie figured that a few pages torn from the inside of the file wouldn't be missed right away, if at all.

The pages were dated at the top, and the first one she had ripped out was the very last page. She had sporadically taken pages from different sections of the folder before closing it and shoving the folder back into the bag. Her instincts told her that pulling pages in that way would tell her enough of the story. She was glad she had thought to take her own samples from the folders she had grabbed before the bag had been taken from her. She had learned, doing what she did for a living, that you have to back up your work and, whenever possible, provide proof of what you have seen or experienced.

This one is going to be hard enough to believe. I'm not taking any chances.

She only wished that she would have been able to take pictures of the creatures that they had encountered under Lev's estate. How she was ever going to be able to share that story, she didn't know. She knew that her recorder had captured the exchange, but video was what was needed, not audio.

Mikey let her get away with a lot, and he trusted her implicitly, but she didn't think even he would believe this story without visual proof. Maggie skimmed over the page with the latest date. It looked like the group responsible for the atrocities in the lab did a bunch of testing on Margueritte: blood, urine, and a pregnancy test for starters. The panels had revealed that she had A negative blood. *Rare*, Maggie thought. She wasn't pregnant and she didn't have any infections. Then she found what looked like DNA results at the bottom of the page.

The categories that they had put the results into were not typical of DNA testing, though. Nothing denoting ethnicity. Instead of the usual information, the categories were: *Human, Angel, Vampire, Werewolf, Vila, Naga*—In Margueritte's case the line under *Human* was 100 percent. Although Maggie was glad Max's mom was totally human, she was confused as to why that was even a consideration.

Wasn't all humanity, well... human? There is more to this, she decided.

She rubbed her eyes and continued reading. The comments under the findings for this report jumped out at her.

Subject of this testing all human... viable for future tests... mustn't let ARC find out about this current subject... could be the mother of new breeds and mustn't be separated from the project... harvesting is an alternative to human conception, and the offspring can be raised in the lab... subject must never be allowed to know and will not be awake when the harvest is taking place.

Maggie was astounded. *Harvesting? Harvesting what?* Her answer came from a small note in the margin of the same page, near the top, scribbled seemingly as an afterthought.

100% human ova source—rare... will not be released. They had taken Margueritte's eggs and used them for God only knows what. *The worst part is that the poor woman doesn't even know that she had been used like this.* A tear slipped down Maggie's cheek and she looked over to where Max and Margueritte were sitting quietly together talking.

Max looked up at her and smiled, then cocked his head slightly when he noticed the tear tracks down her face. She quickly wiped them away and shook her head, and she smiled at Max.

She realized that something as little as smiling at him made her feel better. She always used her real smile, seemingly only reserved for him these days. Max had become such a big part of her life and was set to hopefully become more than what he had been so far. Maggie's face sagged and she turned away from the pages as she kept confidence with the wall of the plane. She was keeping from him, and she suspected that maybe even he knew. Not the content, but the fact that she was unsettled around him and needed to unburden her heart to him. How could he not know?

He knew surely by now that she was in love with him, and she was certain that Max knew by now that she was not a fashion designer. This couldn't go on if they were going to have any kind of a chance at a future. She was torn between the fear that she felt at the thought of letting him in—*really* in, and the guilt that she felt for lying to him. Her heart warred with her common sense and cynicism.

Logically, he will be upset and feel betrayed and this will go down like all of those scenes on TV and in the movies where one person is not what they seem, she thought. *He will not be okay with this—he may not be like his dad, but he definitely will not understand why you lied to him, repeatedly, when you could have come clean and found an ally. Honestly.*

Her heart allowed only the slightest hope that he may understand enough after hearing her story that he could overcome her deception; that Max could see past her behavior to her true feelings. She smirked to herself at the thought, knowing her Preston Luck and what usually happens in these situations.

The heart won the war, and she came to a decision: it was not going to be easy for her, or him, but she had to tell him about the things she knew about Lev. She had to tell him about herself, all of it—about how she purposely went out of her way to meet him so that she could learn more about, and ultimately condemn, his father. She needed to tell him about Susanna and the ordeal that led her to do what she does.

A hand on her shoulder startled her back to reality, and she immediately felt slightly nauseous. *This is it*, she thought. She noticed that Margueritte was laying down and had drifted back to sleep. Maggie scooted over and let Max sit on the cot next to her. She also noticed that Peter had his friend Tammy's head in his lap and he was snoozing sitting up, his head leaning against the bulkhead. That was another story that Maggie would like to hear.

She shifted her mind to her present situation and the handsome man that had stolen her heart over the past months. She smiled at him and leaned in to kiss his cheek.

"How is your mom holding up?"

Max looked from her to the sleeping woman and then back to Maggie. He smiled another beautiful smile, and Maggie thought how much more handsome he was when he wasn't scowling. She could glimpse and felt bad for the little boy who was cheated out of his mother in his eyes.

"She is a miracle, Maggie. I never dared to hope to ever see her again. All those years, being told—I thought she had died…"

Maggie noticed a play of emotions pass over his face before his ever-present scowl returned. She could tell that now he was really thinking about what had happened to them and to his mom over the past day. He had processed only part of the information, but she could tell he was good and pissed now.

"I could kill Lev for what he has done."

The venom in his voice was a scary thing.

Before he could get himself too worked up, Maggie said, "Max, you have been through so much."

She reached out and grabbed his substantial hand and held it with both of hers, looking into his bottomless, stormy-blue eyes. *Stop,* she warned herself. *Now—do it now. Rip off the Band-Aid, or you will be too far gone.* She replaced his hand gently in his lap, took a deep breath.

"Max, I need to tell you some things—things about me, about what we've been through together. But first, I want you to know what you have come to mean to me. I know you know that I am in love with you. I see in you, not your father, but your mother. She has a gentleness and kindness to her that I see in you. Oh, there are aspects of Lev, but they seem to be forced rather than natural."

Max looked down at his hands.

"I love you too, Maggie. I am the luckiest I could have ever hoped to be, but I fear I am not worthy of your love. There are things about me that I wish I could change. My father was only one of those things."

He looked to be castigating himself wordlessly, and her heart went out to him again. He carried his father with him, and he would never leave him. Maggie knew that, and she hated Lev all the more for it. He had taken a beautiful, loyal, and gentle boy and turned him into a walking paradox. His heart always belied his actions, and she knew he hated all of the things that he had to do in service to his father's organization.

"And, you are not wrong. Anything that I have had to do for Lev is almost always evil in nature and is always forced on me. I have tried on my own to keep his crimes minimal, thwart his efforts as much as possible, or to go about things in a way that is less—well, let us just say that I do not do things as Boris or Lev does. It is not nearly enough, but know that I always tried to do things the best way I could stomach. Lev stole everything from me, like he does everyone else. I hate him. I hate him, Maggie, and I will kill him."

"I know this Max, but what if I told you that there is a way to get back at your father, without resorting to killing him?" Maggie asked him.

He looked at her sideways.

"What are you talking about?"

"Just remember that I love you and that will not change, but just like you there are things that I wish I could do differently."

Max looked concerned and Maggie took his hand.

"Max, I'm trying to tell you that I think I can help you bring down your father."

Now it was his turn to look confused.

"How can you do that? I am sure that you have contacts and people that would help you, but your business is fashion, Maggie. Lev is a very dangerous man with no soul. Just knowing that you were in his home makes me sick." He shook his head at her. "Maggie, I do not want you any more involved than you are at present. Even now Lev knows you were instrumental in our escape with my mother. He will be looking for payback."

"That is why I want your help to take him down before he can do any further harm."

She found herself getting excited and agitated being so close to making a breakthrough with him, and the rest just came rushing out. She hoped he could see the love in her eyes and not damn her too much for her confession.

"Max, I'm an investigative journalist. I have been gathering information on your father for years." She hung her head at his look of disbelief. "I wasn't at the club that night with friends. I was there with my agents, pretending we were all having a girls' night out. I was there to meet you, Max. Just to meet you. You seemed like the best way to get to him, and I had been following you for months. I knew you would be there that night. I purposely bumped into you and acted as if I had lost the girls I came with. I don't even have friends."

She rolled her eyes, now filled with tears, and went on, huffing between sobs.

"I really was there alone. My goal was to get to your father through you. Only along the way I fell in love with you. I fell in love, and I just couldn't let you go on thinking that I was ignorant of the deeds your father has committed. I can tell you every move your father has made since the beginning of last year, and I probably know more disturbing things about him than you do. But, Max, this is where we can get him back. We can pay him back for you, for me, for your mother, for all of the girls he's ruined, everyone he has wronged. I have plenty of evidence to put him away, but Max, I just can't do it unless you tell me it's okay. I'm so, so sorry. I've never felt this way, and even if you walk away—and believe me, you have every right—just know that I love you."

She looked at him again with tears streaming down her face, her perfect makeup now a dumpster fire of black, purple, and wet. Maggie knew that telling Max this information could backfire on her, and he could ultimately want nothing to do with her. She wouldn't blame him. She wasn't sure that she could handle him rejecting her, rejecting her feelings for him because of her need for justice and her methods of getting it. She waited a moment longer before continuing.

"Max, there is something else you need to know."

She slowly slid him the crumpled papers that she had been reading. He looked at her, shell-shocked and still trying to absorb what had just been said.

Maggie muttered, "I took them out of the folders before they were given back to the naga. You aren't going to like what they say."

Max started reading, and before long he sat up straight, and his concentrating scowl deepened into a visage of an anger of such conviction and permanence that it shook Maggie.

In a voice of metered ferocity, he asked her, "Why. Did. He. Do. This?"

Maggie shook her head and reached out for his hand.

"I don't know, baby. I don't know. I've been wracking my brain. Do you know why Lev would want her eggs or anything about the underground lab?"

"Maggie, Lev is a monster. I have told you that much before. I did not know anything about his secret lab or any experiments, and

I certainly would not have condoned his treatment of my mother." Max said vehemently.

She laid a placating hand on his arm.

"I know that you didn't have anything to do with what was done to your mom. You would not do anything like that. What Lev does, not only to your mom, but to girls in general, is atrocious. He needs to be stopped." Her vehemence turned quickly to solemnity. "I didn't tell you the reason I started looking into your father in the first place. Your father's organization is known throughout the world, but it's known to me as one of the most vile and cruel human trafficking operations going."

He had clenched his hands together and was rubbing vigorously on the heels of his hands as if trying to rub out any blemish or spots. Shakespeare ran briefly through her head, and she shook it to get back on track.

"When I was 12, my best friend, Susanna, and I were walking home from the bus stop. A big black van passed us by. We didn't think anything of it. It turned around, and when it reached us two men jumped out of the side door and grabbed us from behind. There wasn't anyone around and they were so quick—"

She had gotten over her own attempted kidnapping years ago, but even so, she shivered a bit reliving the moment of her abduction.

"We were stuffed into the back of the van and taken to a warehouse. Susanna had a plan to get away when they went to take us out of the van again. They didn't bind anything but our hands and those were loose enough that Susanna was able to get mine undone. I was working on hers when the van stopped. The two men opened the doors before I had enough time to get Susanna free."

She pulled her legs up on the cot and wrapped her arms around them. Max had not moved throughout the whole tale. Maggie started rocking back and forth as she went on.

"Susanna was always the braver of us. Her parents called her reckless, even. She would always stand up for people and do crazy things like jump her bike over the ramps that the boys in the neighborhood had made. Suse was calm and I was scared. She kicked out at the first guy to stick his head into the van."

She smiled slightly, recalling her friend's actions.

"She caught him in the head, and he fell back into the second man. It was the opportunity we needed to run. I heard Susanna tell me to run, and I sprinted out of the van and kept running."

She stopped and turned her face to look at Max. The anger on his face was present, but Maggie couldn't tell if it was for her or at her. She took a deep breath and said in a small voice.

"I thought she was behind me, Max. Right behind me."

She started sobbing and he wrapped his arm around her shoulder.

"I couldn't get her bindings undone. By the time I noticed she wasn't with me, they were driving away with her."

Max started to stroke her hair in a soothing way.

"I ran until I found a 7-11. There was a lady filling up her car, and she took one look at me and asked if I needed help. She was so sweet and compassionate. I broke down and told her what had just happened and was told, at a later date, that I got out enough information for her to get a hold of my parents before I fainted."

She looked up at Max, and he brushed the hair that had fallen to cover her cheeks with his hand.

"What happened to your friend, Maggie?"

His expression told her that he wasn't sure that he wanted to hear the answer to his question, but he asked anyway, needing to know.

"The police were called and met my parents at the hospital. They asked me what felt like a hundred questions. What did the men look like? Did we know them from the neighborhood? What color was the van? What was Susanna wearing? What else did I see in the van? What did the warehouse look like? Did I see any other girls? I kind of shut down after they left, but I did hear them telling my parents that there were smugglers that looked for girls around our age to sell to other people. Susanna's parents were there, and they seemed happy that one of us got away, but I could tell that they were disappointed that it wasn't their daughter."

"I do not think that true, Maggie," Max said to her. "They were probably very happy that you made it, otherwise they would not have any information about what happened."

Maggie gave him a small smile and said, "Thanks, Max. It took some time before we finally found her. She was not the same girl, Max. She wouldn't look anyone in the eye, she jumped at everything, she didn't want to be touched. I spent every day with her that I could. For the first couple of months, she wouldn't talk to me. She sat in the corner and stared at nothing for weeks, barely eating or sleeping. One day, I just started talking about what had happened to her. I told her how sorry I was that I didn't help her, and how it was all my fault—what a lousy friend I was, and that I was going to get even with those men. She seemed to snap back into herself at that moment, she had been going to see a therapist for months, but I mentioned revenge, and she seemed to come alive. She looked me in the eye, Max. She grabbed my face and she pulled it close to hers and she made me promise that I would find out who was responsible. I had to find him and take him down.

"We had just turned 15. Fifteen, and here I was making a dangerous oath. Now I was the reckless one. Anyway, I promised her that I would put an end to them."

She turned to Max and she saw it click with him.

"I followed the trail for years, Max. I went to college for criminal justice, originally, but after working for years with local law enforcement, I discovered that I would get further, faster, a different way. I needed answers. I needed to be let in. I knew that it would take too long to move up the ladder in that world, so I changed to journalism. Susanna continued to see a therapist and went on to help run a center for those previously trafficked and battered women. I left the police force, determined to become someone that could make a difference. And I did. I became—" she paused to see his reaction.

"You became a fashion editor at LACE. Everyone knows that, and you do make a difference. LACE is the top fashion house in the world, thanks to you. Are you able to do something behind the scenes for your friend with that? I do not understand…"

She held up her hand to shut him up, and smiled at his naivete.

"No, Max, you don't get it. Yes, I'm Maggie Preston, contributing editor at LACE, but that's not where my difference is made. Max, I'm also Delilah Mourning."

Max sat back suddenly, mouth agape, and stared.

"You are Delilah Mourning? Maggie, there is no one that does not know you. Internet, television, print. How? You are everywhere."

"Not so fast—Delilah Mourning is everywhere. I don't even exist in that world, so I am safe. This is by design. I have exposed some of the most dangerous people ever, Max. Your father fits into that category, don't you think?"

Max gathered himself and resumed his stance at the end of the cot.

"Yes, I believe he does. So, what happened? How did you get from there to here?"

Max seemed genuinely interested, and it was almost as if their world wasn't crumbling around them for a moment. They were just two people getting to know each other. Truth be told, she was very eager to let Max know about the real Maggie. She retraced her steps back through her history.

"We still keep in touch once or twice a month and I try to visit with her whenever I am able. I was a junior officer during college, but police work wasn't going to help me find Suse's attackers. Once I graduated, I moved quickly and while working for a magazine doing fashion articles, spent every other moment searching for missing children, learning the names and faces of people in organized crime families that specialized in human trafficking.

"I found men who would talk to a beautiful woman that stroked their egos and plied them with drink. I worked with police. I worked with the FBI. I worked with the CIA and Interpol, MI5, and even rival criminal organizations. I started helping these agencies close cases, learning what I could, absorbing everything about design and international crime. Not to brag, but I am very good at what I do, and nothing will doom a person faster or more completely than the court of public opinion and the power of the poison pen.

"I would research, the agencies would arrest, the court would convict. When the magazine I was working for went under, I was approached by LACE with a unique proposition—they would fully fund my continued investigative reports anywhere, anytime, no questions asked, plus pay me a tidy sum on top of it as salary. I was worried because there is no way that they should have known about my, um, other endeavors, but I got the feeling that it was okay. I think they wanted me to succeed as much as I did. In return, I was to take a specialized role, not only as editor, but also as an agent on their team, which had nothing to do with fashion. Mikey told me I was peculiarly qualified for, and that no one else could do for him, what he needed. He wanted me to teach his models what I knew; how to operate and do what I do in that world. So, now, I do that, and I'm glad for the help. That's LACE—fashion house, magazine, femme fatale central, hotbed of espionage and investigative journalism.

"I've been on this mission, working until I could find out the information that led me to the one person that was responsible for what happened to Susanna and me. I'm so close, Max. Your father may even be the last piece of this, but as much as this means to me and the reasons behind it, I want you to know that you mean more. I won't do anything unless you tell me it's okay."

She had grabbed his arm again and squeezed as if she could hold on to him and keep him with her. Max put his hand on hers and patted it gently. It seemed that he had made up his mind somewhere in the middle of her story.

"I want you to know that I do not blame you, Maggie. I have done many things for which I am not proud. I try to help. I do, where I can, but living with my father started to change me as a person. I am not using that as an excuse for the things that I have been an accomplice to over the years, but I also could not condone what my father has done, either. I am sorry that the seedier side of life touched you in such a profound way, and I do not wish for you to not get your story or your revenge after all these years. I will ask one thing of you, though. Please wait to do anything with this story until I have a chance to find a place to hide my mother, out of his reach. Never again will he touch her."

His voice had changed with his declaration.

"I, too, want my revenge on Lev Avatov, probably more so than you do. Today was a day of revelations. While I was talking with my mother, she told me the story of how she came to be with Lev in the first place. You see, she has an older sister, and they lived in Paris. Her sister married a military man who was in Paris on leave. He was a very handsome man with a twin brother. Theirs was a whirlwind romance, and although he was stationed in Paris-Orly during the last part of the Cold War, he was to be shipped back to the states and she couldn't bear to be parted from him. So my mother helped her sister elope with the handsome pilot and they moved to the states.

"My mother was left in Paris where she had met the young Lev and his friend Rene. They were students at university in Paris. According to her, she fell hard for Rene and accompanied them all over Paris. Rene loved the theater and museums and anything cultural, and when Lev was a younger version of himself, he enjoyed those things, too."

Max had taken Maggie's hand and was absently stroking the back.

"Lev had made it known to Rene that he was going to ask Margueritte out on a date, and the two men got into an argument about who should date her. It was decided by the two men that they would let her decide who she wanted, and vowed that whomever she picked, that the other would step aside. They both asked her on a date the same day, each in his turn without the other."

"She decided to go out with Lev?" Maggie asked, astonished.

He smiled at her and said, "It turned out that she had turned down Lev's offer and told him that she was in love with Rene. It angered Lev so much that he went out and got drunk at the nearest bar." Max laughed a little at the thought of his mother turning down Lev's attention.

"I'm confused as to how she ended up with Lev, then?"

"She and Rene decided to marry after a year together. She had not seen my father in those months and figured that he had moved on." Max's countenance clouded over. "It was a dark day when he showed up on her doorstep. My mother, being who she is, was naturally happy to see him. She noticed right away that he had changed. His demeanor was not the same, he seemed cruel and although pleasant, he was not the same person she had met the summer before. He told her about his new association with an important organization, and how they had moved him up so he was a man of some importance. She was happy with his success and told him so, but when she mentioned Rene and her upcoming wedding, he seemed to become agitated and told her that it should have been him she was marrying.

"Lev asked her if she had thought about what would have happened if Rene was not around. She answered that she had, on many occasions, wondered what would have happened if she had not found the love of her life. She, in fact, told him 'I thank God that this came to be'. That seemed to anger Lev, and he said that choices would have to be made. If she wanted to see Rene live to an old age, that she would have to let him go. When she asked him what he meant, he replied that a choice would have to be made, and if she chose to be a foolish, love-addled girl, he would make Rene disappear forever. She was to break it off, tell Rene that she had made a mistake, and she was meant to be with Lev. That was all."

Max took a deep breath and looked over at his sleeping mother, then he turned back to Maggie looking her in the eye.

"His eyes told her, and she believed, he could do the things that he had threatened. He had become a dangerous man. She would not let him hurt Rene. She told Lev that she would break things off with Rene and meet up with him later that night, then she went to meet Rene. When she told him that she could not marry him, that she had made a mistake, he went a little crazy. He asked her why and she told him that she had finally figured out that she loved Lev and that she could not be without him. He, of course, did not believe her. My mother would not be able to hide her love for anyone."

Max turned to look at Maggie and smirked.

"Or, her contempt. Rene wanted to confront Lev to get the truth. She begged him not to go but he would not believe that she loved Lev like she claimed. It was the last time she saw Rene."

He looked down at her hand that still rested lightly on his arm.

"She told me that she was pregnant at the time. Rene was the father, and she never got the chance to tell him. The baby was me, Maggie. I was Rene's son. Lev was never my father, but they got married so fast after Rene disappeared that it was never suspected that I was not Lev's child."

Maggie was stunned by the implications. Max was free of Lev's taint. He was his own person.

"So, does this mean that you forgive the fact that I have been keeping a secret from you?" Maggie said tentatively. "I really didn't think I would fall for you, Max, but you are so different from Lev. Funny and smart, serious—but you can be silly, hard, and protective, yet soft on the inside. I love all those things. I love that you want to shield me. I wanted to tell you that I would help you take him down, but you seemed to try so hard to please him that I couldn't trust that you wouldn't have handed me over without a second thought."

Maggie looked at him as she stroked their interlocking fingers.

"I think you are so much more than how you see yourself, and that your mother would be so very proud to know that her son has saved so many girls from Lev's clutches. I still am not sure what he does with them, but if it is anything like what happened to your mother, I am glad you saved them from that fate or worse."

Max looked over at Maggie and smiled.

"I am not mad at you Maggie. I am glad that there are women in the world that are willing to stand up for not only themselves, but for others around them. There are so many monsters in the world, both human and not so human, we need to make sure that the human side wins over the monster."

He patted her hand and said, "Please keep looking over the papers you have taken. There is probably some clue as to why Lev is doing what he is doing. Let us just hope that you swiped the right ones."

He turned serious for a moment and said, "Maggie, we must be vigilant from now on. Lev will want revenge on you. Not only did you steal his son, but also his prize and all in one day. He will be out for blood—yours. If I am correct, he has been able to ferret out all that you hide, and you will not be safe alone."

With that cryptic statement he stood.

"I must go find Sam. Please study those papers some more; anything that can be learned from them must be found, verified, and used against Lev."

Maggie nodded and looked at the mass of loose papers she had managed to pull from the files before racing after Max into the snake people cavern. She shivered when she recalled seeing the naga for the first time. She wondered how they came to be locked up in the facility. She saw Peter staring at her and decided she had best get back to work, she wasn't interested in playing 20 questions, and she wasn't sure how much he had heard or knew. She looked down at the sheets in her hand and decided to pick up where she had left off. She had work to do and, as she thought about the man who had stolen her heart and looked at his sleeping mother, she decided she had more reason than ever to want to take down Lev Avatov. She needed to find out what A.R.C. was. She had her fair share of experience with secretive organizations, and if Lev didn't want Margueritte found by them, then that is exactly where she should be.

Chapter 27

The plane streaked, figuratively, toward America, and it wasn't lost on those aboard that it almost took a full day to go through the endless three-hours-then-fuel routine. From Russia to Ukraine, to Denmark, to Norway, to Greenland, to Boston, to Nashville, and finally to New Orleans. They landed shortly after five o'clock in the morning. They had just taxied up the runway and were heading towards Abe's hangar when his phone rang.

He answered on the second ring.

"Hey, sugar," he said then his tone changed abruptly. "Wait, what? Slow down, Naomi. What about Sarah?"

His unease was evident, causing Sam to take notice of the conversation as he awaited clearance to approach the far side of the airfield. His demeanor changed. The color drained from Abe's face.

"We're here now, Naomi. We will see what we can find out. Call Joshua. We'll be there as soon as we can get this bird put to bed."

He disconnected his cell and looked at Sam.

"Sarah is missing. Naomi said that she put her to bed last night and when she got up this morning—gone. She said that she has torn the hangar apart. Maybe she just decided to mess around or snoop and got lost, but she found one of the windows had been broken and a piece of Sarah's hoodie was hanging from a broken piece of glass. There was blood on the window sill. She thinks that she may have been hurt when she was taken," he finished.

Abe watched as Sam processed the information, his face awash with surprise and anguish at the girl's disappearance. Abe knew that she had wormed her way into Sam's heart. He couldn't help but think that maybe she reminded him of someone.

"You go. I'll handle this. I'll get the plane settled—your mission is to find her."

"Sam, we need to follow protocol and secure the plane—it will be much faster with both of us. I want to find her, too, but this is no time to lose your head."

Abe put a hand on the big man's shoulder, grabbed his logs and flight bag, and headed out to the cargo area. Sam called after him, willing the plane to taxi faster.

"Do you think that the grunch came for her? Or do you think that Olivier has her?"

"Either way, I think that creep has her again, and if those things were working for him then he still ended up with what he wanted," Abe said. "She won't survive what they plan for her. I can't stand to think of that little girl going through something like that."

Abe slammed his fist into the open palm of his other hand.

"Naomi is blaming herself, Sam. She could have been hurt and there is nothing I could have done. I hate feeling helpless."

Peter poked his head into the cockpit and noticed the charge in the air and dark looks the other two had on their faces.

"What is it?" he asked.

Sam pulled up to the hangar and was powering down the plane by the time Abe had finished telling him about Sarah. He saw Naomi step out of the hangar with Joshua in tow. Peter could tell that she had been crying. They quickly made their way to the door of the plane, the two men following a frantic and fatherly Abe who scooped Naomi into his arms as soon as he reached her.

Max and Maggie were helping Tammy and Margueritte down out of the plane when Joshua gasped.

"It can't be. Margueritte?"

He took off across the tarmac to the plane, running. Peter turned to the others, offering a thumb over his left shoulder to follow Joshua's run to meet up with the rest of the deplaning group.

"Does he know *everybody*?"

They watched as Joshua reached the others and saw Max step

in front of his mother. Joshua stopped and he saw Margueritte place a frail hand on Max's shoulder. The big man looked down at his mother and stepped aside. He was close enough to protect her if needed and looked like he wanted to pounce on Joshua, but he allowed the two to face each other. They were not close enough to hear the exchange but saw Max relax as Margueritte hugged the agent.

"We need to get after Olivier. I don't like that so much time has passed, and that creep has Sarah," Sam said. "It doesn't look like we will have a hard time enlisting help in this. It looks like that just worked itself out. Now, if only we can find Sarah as easy."

They heard a stifled sob and turned to see Naomi bury her head in Abe's shoulder once again. Abe scowled at Sam and stroked Naomi's hair. He whispered softly what sounded like a prayer as he rested his bowed head on top of hers, their hands interlocked.

When they finished and Abe offered her an encouraging smile, saying, "We're going to find her, baby girl. Don't you doubt that for a second," Peter thought it may be okay to approach.

He walked gingerly up to the two, knowing that they were sharing a meaningful moment together, and offered, "Naomi, please don't blame yourself. We will get her back. Have faith."

Naomi gave him a small smile in return for his kindness. *She is breathtaking*, he thought. *For that smile, for any smile from her, I would charge hell with a SuperSoaker.*

Peter found himself taken in by the young woman; it wasn't so much that she was the untouchable type of beautiful that gave him that unsettled feeling in his stomach. No, she was the type of beautiful that had substance, the kind that Peter had always valued in women, especially his mom and Rose and Tammy. The aura of confidence that glowed around them was like a beacon to him. The smile that told the world of a generosity of spirit and kindness and care that lived within. He knew that he could grasp and hold the hand of a woman like that and see the gentle elegance and fierce strength together.

Naomi felt like a weight had been lifted from her, but her uncle had always been able to make her feel better. Uncle Abe had always been able to help her pull her worth back to herself when it seemed to have left her, and she had just had the distinct displeasure of being about as low as she can ever remember.

Sarah was my responsibility and I let her get taken.

Joshua and the rest walked up as Peter finished speaking, and he said, "Naomi, it wasn't your fault that Sarah was taken. If I had to guess, I would say that Olivier has known where to find her, and for that matter you, all along. These creatures." The agent temporarily lost his cool, slamming his hand on his thigh in frustration. "They are smart, and they don't lack for resources. They also don't fear getting caught. They sold their souls a long time ago, and that makes them more dangerous than you can imagine."

Max and Margueritte stopped next to Joshua, and Max told her, "It is true. They will do anything to fulfill a contract, but I do not think this is just about selling girls to the highest bidder anymore. Maggie found some documents that prove that there is a connection between the stolen children and Lev Avatov."

Max turned to look at Naomi squarely and let the weight of his next words wash over both of them.

"My father."

Naomi bristled and let the anger flood from the place where guilt pooled just moments earlier.

"Your *father*? Are you telling me that you had something to do with this—"

She lurched towards Max, and Abe caught her quickly and spun her to face him.

"Hey. Get a hold of yourself, girl. Max is here to help. He wants nothing more than to take his father down and see that he pays for his crimes, right, Max?"

Abe turned to see Max nodding his ascent and Max added, "Naomi, my father has made a mistake this day. Let us go somewhere we can all discuss what Maggie and I have found." He turned to Joshua and said, "I will help you take down Lev if you can find someone to help my mother and Maggie. Lev will be after them both. Maggie, for what she did, and mother, for what she means to his organization and what she knows. Does your agency have anywhere we can take them?"

"I know just the person who can help, but it may be bit of a shock," he said only to Margueritte and Max.

"Good." Max said, "We go—the sooner we get there, the sooner we can plan."

Joshua turned to the others and said, "You guys go. I will meet you there, but I need to look at that window and see if I can find any other clues that might be helpful. I will get my people scouring this place like a bunch of dirty dishes." He fished keys out of his pocket and tossed them to Peter. "You can take my Suburban and I will meet you later with Abe's truck."

Peter looked down at the keys in his hand and out across the sea of faces, all anxious and determined. Then a thought occurred to him,

"Uh, Joshua? Where am I going, exactly?" Joshua smiled, sort of an impish grin Peter recognized by now as the man's way of keeping a juicy secret that only he knows.

"I thought you would have guessed by now, kid. Home, Peter. You're going home."

The weary travelers turned to trudge across the tarmac, making their way into the large hangar and out the other side to reach Joshua's Suburban. The large vehicle had enough room for all the travelers to pile inside. Peter was chosen to drive since this was his hometown, and he was able to sleep on the plane ride over. Peter grinned as he thought of home.

Of course, I should have known. He grinned at the thought. It was starting to make sense now, and he knew for sure that he and Momma would have a long conversation at some point in the near future.

"And Peter," Joshua shouted, "save some of the beignets for me."

Peter laughed and started the big truck. The drive didn't take as long as Peter remembered, and he figured that was because he missed being home so badly. He parked the truck in a lot down the street, and the troupe walked the remaining distance into the Quarter. He had missed it, but couldn't recall when he had ever missed the smell and the din before. Tonight, the noise and the bustle was like air to him.

At this time of the morning, however, shopkeepers were busily cleaning up from the night before. The nightlife of the Quarter was boisterous, but left a big mess that had to be addressed on a daily basis. Shopkeepers actually used fire hoses to blast away the mess from the sidewalks in front of their shops and clean up the broken glass and pick up the trash that was strewn about by the drunk revelers of the previous night. In some instances, the owners of the shops and bars had to wake up a patron that was found sleeping it off in a doorway.

Cuisine de Ouverte came into view. It was like a beacon to Peter. The pretty flower pots on their wrought iron stands were a bright spot of color showing off red geraniums against a black and white store front. Momma Rose was out in front as all the other shopkeepers were, with her broom sweeping the area around her little café's tables and chairs.

She looked over and saw Peter walking toward her and let out a little chirp. She dropped the broom and rushed forward and into his arms. He laughed and kissed her on the head. She laughed, too and admonished him sweetly.

"Mon chou. I will take you over my knee the next time you leave for days on end and come back to me looking like a bedraggled, starving moose."

She grabbed his face in her plump little hands, looked for a moment, then hugged him tighter to her bosom, all while Peter wore quite the embarrassed look, especially when he noticed Maggie stifling a giggle. Rose released him and looked around at the other people present. When her gaze came to Margueritte, the smile slipped from her face and she whispered, "Mon Dieu," staggering backwards and holding her hands up to heaven. Peter reached out to steady her.

"Momma Rose, are you okay?"

Rose waved him away, clutching her hand to her heart, tears flooding her eyes.

"Naomi, can you run inside and get a glass of water for her?" Peter said, turning to Naomi.

The girl took off like a shot and disappeared inside the small restaurant.

"That's because she has seen a ghost," came the soft reply from Margueritte. "Bonjour mon petit bouton de rose…" she said softly. "I am late." Rose brought her hands up to her face and shook her head in disbelief.

"Margueritte, is that really you?" Tears made silent tracks down here face. "How is this possible?" Momma Rose walked forward until she stood right in front of Margueritte. "You are dead. I've been to your graveside."

She reached out and touched the cheek of the other woman.

Peter was confused.

"You know her, Momma Rose?" he asked.

Momma Rose turned to Peter, face flushed yet spectre-white at the same time and said through her tears, "Yes, I know her. She is my sister."

Chapter 28

Everyone gathered around her gasped. Momma Rose, seemingly over the shock, grabbed her sister in a warm hug.

"I don't know how you made it back to me, but praise the Master that you are here."

They hugged for a long time until Peter cleared his throat.

"Maybe we should go inside. It has been a long trip, and I'm sure that you guys have a lot to catch up on. Also, there has been a new development that we need your help with."

Momma Rose let go of Margueritte and said in a no-nonsense voice, "Yes, you need to update me on a lot of things, young man, but first, breakfast. Questions will keep their own company until such time as we ask."

She wiped nervous hands on her apron and took hold of Margueritte's arm, pushing Max aside in the process. Maggie stifled a giggle at Max's wounded expression. She took pity on him and took his arm. He looked down at her and smiled. Together they walked behind the others to the little café.

Peter took Tammy upstairs to his apartment to make her comfortable. He told her to put her things in the guest room, and he would send someone upstairs with food for her, then he would return later to check on her. She looked relieved to be somewhere she knew, that was familiar. She had stayed at Peter's numerous times after movie marathons or late night RPG sessions, and considered it her home away from home. Peter left her sitting on the bed in the guest room and went back down to the café.

He found the group sitting around the kitchen. Momma Rose had supplied a plate full of beignets and some fresh fruit. The others had already helped themselves to the food and were eating happily. Momma Rose had just finished putting fresh coffee on the table and enough mugs for all. The only one not eating in the room was Sam. He stood looking out the window wearing a vacant look. As much as Peter wished for a beignet at the moment, he knew that his friend needed him. He walked to Sam and placed a comforting hand on his shoulder.

"It'll be fine. We will get her back."

"The thing is, Peter, I can't remember something. It's important, and everytime I looked at that little girl, she nudged that memory a little. She was spunky and unafraid and reminded me so much of someone. Someone important to me… Someone that I can't remember." He growled in frustration. "As much as I want to save that little girl because it's the right thing to do, I want just as much to see if I can remember that someone I have forgotten. Does that make sense?"

He looked at Peter with a pleading expression. Peter felt that Sam had been resigned to not knowing what happened in his past for so long, that the first stirring of a memory sparked a hope in him that had been threatened by whoever had taken that spark away.

"Other than Momma Rose, I don't think I've known a more selfless person, Sam. I really think you should go see Dr. Jo. Do you still have the card I gave you? She did wonders for me. I think she could help you, too."

Sam smacked his hand to his forehead.

"I almost forgot."

He pulled his phone out of his pocket and dialed the number that was stored in his phone. Peter was confused for a moment before he heard Sam say, "Hey, doc. Yeah, we landed about an hour and a half ago. We are having breakfast, and we are going to discuss some things, but I can be there in a couple of hours, is that possible?" Sam listened for a moment before saying, "Thanks for squeezing me in. I'll see you soon." He hung up and looked at Peter with a wry smile. "Does that answer your question?"

Peter smiled and said, "I guess there is only one thing to do at the moment, then."

Sam looked a question at him.

"Eat."

Sam laughed and walked over to the table with Peter. The others looked to be about finished partaking, and Peter sat down, reached across the table for a plate, and started to help himself.

"Whath diid I misth?' he said around a mouthful of beignet. He closed his eyes, savoring the flavor as he waited for their response. When he opened his eyes he found that everyone was watching him, and Momma Rose was smiling at him."

"What?"

"Man, I have never seen anyone demolish anything like that," Abe said with a chuckle.

Peter looked embarrassed, but Momma Rose came around and kissed the top of Peter's head.

"Leave him be, Abraham. He is my biggest fan."

Sam had poured himself a cup of coffee and was watching the group with amusement. He gulped the last bit down as the door of the café chimed.

Time to get down to business, he thought.

"Alright, we need to decide what to do about Sarah." It was like someone flipped a switch, hushing the good-natured conversation immediately. "Ideas? Anyone?" Sam said, scanning the faces at the table.

"I can tell you who I think has her," came a new voice. They all turned to the doorway to see Joshua standing there with a pensive look on his face. "I scanned a fingerprint that I found on a piece of the broken window and sent it to my people. They put it through AFIS and the hit came back almost immediately. It belongs to a local goon by the name of Jean Scarasse. Ring any bells?" he asked as he scanned the faces at the table. After a collective *no*, he continued. "He's usually a solo small-timer, but in recent years has been working down on the docks at a warehouse belonging to a local merchant named Narcisse Olivier." At the mention of the name, Max sat up and lean forward.

"I have had dealings with him before. He works with my father." Max said, then surprisingly turned to spit, disgusted at the mere mention of the vile man being known as his father. "My apologies. That was crass," Max said, turning back to the group and looking queasy. "I cannot call him that any longer, and I will not."

Margueritte looked at her son with a mixture of pride and pity and reached out to take his hand in hers. Joshua came to the table and sat at the last seat available. He pulled a little notebook from his pocket and looked at Max.

"What can you tell me about him?"

Max looked a little uncomfortable at all the attention, and Maggie placed her small hand on his arm. He covered her hand with his and took a deep breath.

"He is in procurement and distribution. He looks harmless until you cross him, then—it is accurate to say that he has a veritable army at his disposal. It is one of the reasons that Lev uses him so often. The deals he has with him are usually for children."

Max had turned to stone once again and Maggie could tell that he was wrestling with his inner demons.

"I tried to have as little contact with him as possible, but I can tell you that with only a call, Lev could have him unleash trouble upon anyone, anywhere. He is a very well-connected man. Lev has had him work not only in the United States, but in the U.K., Lebanon, Thailand, China, Iraq, Africa—you get the picture."

"I don't know much about Olivier, but I will tell you that after our run in with him in the bayou, I had my organization pull the schematics for his warehouse, and I had a pilot buddy of mine fly over and get some thermal scans of the area," Joshua told them. "The thing is, there are people that go in and out of that warehouse at all times of the night, but we have not been able to detect anyone, nor have we observed anyone, go in or out during the day."

Joshua raised his eyebrows and scanned his audience, letting them know that what he was about to say was important, or at least he thought it was.

"Here's where it gets sort of Fright Night; when we ran night scans using a drone, there were only minimal heat signatures. Most of them can be attributed to small rodents and the occasional cat. No humans."

"What are you saying, Joshua?" asked Maggie, trying to piece it together. As the others were trying to puzzle out this new riddle, an idea popped into Peter's head.

"Whoa. What if they are like the grunch?"

Joshua turned to Peter, grinning, "I think you are onto what we thought."

"What are you two saying? English, please." Maggie was getting frustrated and tired.

"Okay, follow me for a moment. This will sound far-fetched but over the last month I have seen things that make this a definite possibility."

"Go on," Joshua said with a hurry up motion of his hand.

"Well, what if they are vampires?" Peter said in a rush. "I mean, this would make much more sense if you think about the lore of the vampire. They don't come out in the daytime. They have no heat signature, and a supply of fresh blood in the form of children would be a must."

Peter sat back and waited for the jokes to fly. He was surprised when none of that happened. Joshua instead looked at Momma Rose.

"Rose, you know our position on this. What do you think?"

Momma Rose looked over at Margueritte, paused only a moment before saying, "Oui. There is a brood that lives here," she affirmed. "Has for years. They pick off revelers that pass through our streets every night. Most do not even know they have been victimized. There is the occasional murder, and those who make that mistake answer to the Quorom. It is rare."

Margueritte looked at her sister with new eyes, "You are saying that vampires are real?" she asked in a small voice. She had unconsciously raised her hand to cover her bare throat, pulling the shawl she wore a bit tighter to her bosom. A shiver passed over her body, and Max put a comforting arm around her shoulders.

"Oui, they are very real, and in this city, very active." Momma Rose gripped her sister's hand and looked her in the eye when she said, "But you do not have to worry about them. This place is protected from them at all times."

Peter shivered a little at the thought of vampires in his city.

"What do you mean *protected*?" Peter asked.

Rose smiled lovingly at Peter and stood, motioning the group to get up and follow her. She walked to the far side of the bistro, past the shelves of old dishes and bottles, past a row of pretty geraniums, to a side door. Holding it open, she spoke to Maggie, the first one through.

"Maggie, walk to where I am pointing, cher," Rose said, pointing to the back corner of the brick building.

She waited for them all to gather at the place indicated, and she joined them, shushing them as the chatter had become significant.

"Joshua, can you hand me your key, please?" Joshua reached into his pocket and produced a small apparatus about the size of a nail, but rounded and smooth. It shone as if made of a very bright metal, like platinum. He held it up for the group to see the details. It was flat on one end, with what appeared to be a semicircle with a chevron and some dots. He tossed the key up from his palm, caught it, displaying its heft, and handed it to Rose.

"Thank you," she said, bending low and motioning the group to look at where she was indicating. About a foot from the lowest brick on the corner, she took the key and slid it along the bottom edge of the brick there, and the group let out a collective gasp of surprise when, about halfway across it clicked and stopped. Rose turned to them, smiling, and proceeded to move the key straight up from its current position, until, again the key clicked and stopped. Rose pulled the key away from the brick, and as she did, a glowing symbol appeared. There were exclamations of surprise from everyone except Joshua, who just stood watching, and Sam, who seemed mesmerized and confused in equal measure, staring at the glow. The symbol that appeared shone in a sort of alien white light, and it appeared to mirror the key that Joshua had produced only moments before: a semicircle bowed up like a rainbow over what appeared to be stars, with a chevron directly below it. The glowing symbol pulsed slowly seven times and then faded from view, with no evidence that it had ever been there at all.

There it is again. Sam thought. *Clawing at me, trying to make me remember— I know I've seen it before, but somewhere else. Where?*

It was driving him crazy. Momma Rose's voice snapped him back.

"There is a sigil on this place that marks it. This place is set apart ,and the sigil offers the protection of ARC," Momma Rose told them as they all re-entered the café, now brightly lit with morning. Maggie and Max shared a smile and then turned back to Momma Rose. It was Maggie who spoke this time, after they had all resumed their seats.

"I have run across this name before. Who are they?"

Momma Rose looked over at her curiously and asked, "Where did you see this information? It could help, more than you know, to know how you came across it."

Momma Rose's tone had grown serious. Peter knew it; he had heard it on only a few occasions. Never directed at himself, and it always left him hoping it never would be.

Maggie cleared her throat and looked at Max who nodded, then said, "When we rescued your sister, I liberated some files from Lev's underground lab. The naga we ran into took the files from me before we escaped, but not before I had a chance to rip out a few of the pages. The acronym ARC was written on one of the pages."

Maggie hesitated to hand over the notes that she had only just started to really look into.

"These notes—what were they about?" Momma Rose asked her.

Maggie wasn't certain how much she wanted to disclose, and

she was conflicted. The journalist in her did not want to opt for full disclosure, but she liked Rose, and she trusted the situation she found herself in.

"They were referring to a subject that was tested and found to be 100 percent human. It said that the subject was perfect for egg harvesting, and that the subject would never know, never be let go, and they had to make sure that ARC never found out," Maggie said.

She heard Margueritte gasp and saw Rose stiffen.

"That was me, wasn't it?" Margueritte asked, "Answer me, Maggie. It *was* me? I was the subject?"

Maggie could hear the hurt and the anger in her voice.

"Yes, I am sorry, Margueritte. That was from the first day, the day you disappeared. I'm sorry I was not able to get the other sheets from your file, but I did manage to get ten pages before I had to catch up with Max in the cave."

Joshua was more than a little lost.

"What the hell are naga? What are you guys talking about?"

"Naga are ancient monsters. Snake people. Now be quiet, Joshua, I'm working," Momma Rose admonished him.

The rebuke caused him to roll his eyes, throw his hands up, and slump down in his seat like a petulant school boy. Momma Rose turned back to Maggie.

"Maggie, can you tell me anything else about what they were doing in that lab?"

"There were cells with iron doors and chains," Maggie shivered as she remembered them. "Tons of files. I went over to the filing cabinet and found that the files were all labeled with the names of, what I thought at the time, were fictional monsters. Vampire, Werewolf—a bunch of others; and the last one was Human. I thought it strange that all the other listings had multiple files but the human listing only had one file. Margueritte's. When I skimmed through the files, I saw that they were extracting DNA from each of the creatures, and if it wasn't exactly what they wanted, they would terminate the creature."

Peter thought that Maggie had gained an inordinate amount of information under extreme stress. He could tell that there was more to this woman than she let on. Momma Rose must have thought so as well.

"What made you think to get so much information in such a stressful situation?" Momma Rose asked.

Uh oh. Peter thought. *Momma Rose is giving her the look.*

It was a look that Peter knew well from his childhood. It was a look that said, "*I know there is something that you are not telling me, and I will be extremely irritated if you don't fess up.*"

"Yes, about that—" Maggie started but Max spoke up on her behalf.

"Maggie is an investigative journalist. I asked her to look into Lev, and she has been working with me to bring him down."

Maggie relaxed a little and smiled in thanks at Max.

"Well I'm not sure mixing yourself up in Lev Avatov's dealings was a smart idea, but we will welcome any help you can give us regarding Sarah's disappearance."

"Who exactly is *we*?" Maggie asked, mimicking Momma Rose's previous look. Peter marveled at how much alike the two women were. Momma Rose paused and cocked her head as if listening to something for a moment.

"We are ARC," Momma Rose responded, as if it was the most logical conclusion ever.

Chapter 29

Maggie blinked at the announcement. She had thought that Momma Rose was going to tell her about some large scale community watch program, but this was more than she had hoped for.

"What does ARC stand for?"

She was half-hoping for some covert crime fighting organization or something equally sensational to share with her readers. She instinctively grabbed at her pendant, awaiting the revelation. It's not like the news she had already wasn't sensational, but a crime fighting organization no one knew about would be amazing. Momma Rose closed her eyes for another moment and looked to be listening a moment before she smiled and opened her eyes.

"First of all," she said, "you can turn off the recorder."

If she had hit Maggie in the head with a brick, she wouldn't have been more stunned than she was that the small woman knew about the recording device. Maggie reached up and turned it off, knowing anything she could say to try and dispel the idea of a recording device would be rebuffed.

"Thank you." Momma Rose looked at all of them in the room and said, "ARC was founded, as you can imagine, a very long time ago. We are an organization made up of specific individuals, not everyone is allowed to join, and that is by design. What we do requires a specific type of character and a very specific DNA."

"But what exactly do you do?" Maggie asked. She was getting information but not as much or as fast as she would like.

"As trite as it sounds, we fight the forces of evil."

"The forces of evil, huh?" Maggie, skeptical of the explanation, went on to ask, "What kind of evil?"

Momma Rose looked sorrowful for a second.

"Evil is evil, Magdalene. It doesn't have a type."

She knows my name, too? Did someone out me on social media or something? Nevermind, not important right now. Evil is evil, it doesn't have a type.

Maggie thought about that statement for a moment and decided that Momma Rose had a point—evil *was* evil no matter if it was small or if it was on a large scale, but she was confused about what that evil consisted of and said as much to the others.

"Ah, now that is the question to ask. Evil can take many forms. You have seen a few and probably experienced the human side of evil. Molesters, traffickers, murderers, rapists, gang members... just a few representations of evil in the world. Although we help in these instances as well, it is the non-human representations of evil of which I am speaking."

With that bombshell, Momma Rose took a sip of her tea. Peter knew what she was doing. She was allowing everyone enough time to process the information. Maggie was the first to ask a question.

"So, you are talking about those things in the caves? And vampires?"

"Yes" Momma Rose said. "The creatures of which I speak are not of this world."

"What are they, then? Aliens?" Peter asked, and laughed at the thought.

"In a way, yes," she told them. "As Michael told you before, when this world was created, the Master had a place for every creature in it. He created everything and gave everything its own space in the world. The Master had helpers. He gave them specific jobs and had them watch over his creations. They were called the Watchers. I know you know of this, but the others do not, so hush." She turned to Peter and Abe to forestall them, and raising her eyebrows, continued, "Angelic beings. They were never meant to be in the world, but over time they grew to love the creations of the Master and chose to reveal themselves to them and take wives from among them. The offspring from these human wives produced a cross-breed."

"Nephilim," Maggie broke in. Momma Rose clapped her hands and smiled.

"Very good, Maggie."

"But how are the nephilim bad? I thought angels were good?"

"You have heard of Lucifer, yes?"

Momma rose reached over and patted her hand, and Maggie got her meaning. Not all angels were benevolent.

"The nephilim were not creations of the Master and did not have a place designed for them in this world. They were abominations and should not have existed. The Master was… sad when he found out about them."

"Why was He sad?" Sam asked. "Wasn't he pleased that they were brought into existence?"

Momma Rose looked at him, and her expression softened.

"He was sad because they were not His creations. He did not have a place for them in our world. He was sad because the Watchers that he chose to protect His creations instead used them for their own purposes and created something that was not part of the original plan."

"I don't understand?" Sam sounded genuinely confused. Maybe even a little angry. "Couldn't the One who created everything find a spot for them?"

"I'm sorry, Sam. I am not privy to the Master's plans. I know that the original plan had no place for the nephilim, although the Master, in His love for the Watchers and His human creations, allowed their progeny to remain. It wasn't until later that they were found to carry an unnatural corruption. The evil of the Morningstar was in them. Nephilim all eventually became cruel and distorted. They possessed superhuman characteristics; some were taller than a two story building, some were more intelligent than the smartest person, and some could command the elements or wield magic. They possessed power through fear. They subjugated and tortured humans to get what they wanted and killed children or other family members to secure a place of power in their community.

They became men of great bearing and immense power. This is what made the Master sad. Their cruelty and corruption doomed them; it forced the Master to act."

"So what became of them, then?" Sam asked.

"There was a major battle in the heavens; the angels were forced to war against their Watcher brothers. The nephilim children were destroyed, and the Watchers were judged and condemned for their crimes against humanity and their disobedience to the Master," she said with sadness.

"If the Nephilim were destroyed by the angels, why bring them up?" Maggie asked.

"Another good question, cher. As I explained, the nephilim were not part of the Master's original plan. Since they were not supposed to exist, there was no place for them to go when they died, eternally speaking."

Momma Rose could see the confusion on the faces of her audience, so she tried to explain it in another way.

"Have you ever seen the children's puzzles where the pieces are all in the shapes of different animals or plants?" she asked and was pleased when the majority nodded the affirmative. "Good, now think of those puzzle pieces as the Master's creations. Every piece has a corresponding hole to be placed in. When they pass on, that hole is filled by another of the same puzzle piece." She gathered that this was well received and hurried on. "The nephilim were not made by the Master so there wasn't a corresponding hole for them to fit into. When they were destroyed physically, there was no place for that soul to go." She waited for the inevitable questions that would come from such a statement and was not disappointed.

"Are you saying that the nephilim were floating disembodied in the universe?" asked Maggie.

"More or less, yes. They could not go to where the other 'puzzle pieces' went." She made air quotes with her hands. "Since a soul can't exist without a body, the nephilim soul had to attach itself to something else in order to survive. Many new hybrids of creatures began to appear. The soul of the creature invaded fused with the nephilim soul, and a new creature was born, physically. Out of this came the first vampire. This was the oldest and truest form of the Nephilim."

"So vampires are related to the nephilim? I thought they fought against each other?" Peter said.

"Don't believe what you have seen in the movies," Momma Rose replied with a sigh.

"What about the other creatures we have seen? The vila, grunch, and those snake things they saw in the cave?" Peter asked her, indicating the trio of Maggie, Max, and Margueritte.

"Those are hybrids of hybrids. After the nephilim were destroyed, the bodies they were born into didn't exist anymore. They originally chose human hosts, but once their soul was fused, the new entity deteriorated within a matter of days or months. The nephilim started to look for alternatives and experimented with all sorts of creatures to find a new host body that would not die."

"So, the bodies that they snatched didn't work for them, and they decided to try to build the perfect body? Is that right?" Peter asked her, trying to follow the story. He picked up his coffee and took a long sip.

"Yes," she told him. "They tried for years to replace the bodies they had lost in the Great War but were unsuccessful. Many evil creatures were born of their meddling, though, and each progression became worse. It wasn't very long before they ended up with creatures like the grunch and the naga. They are not human, but they are not animals, either. The nephilim have not, as yet, found a way to replace what they had before. The created bodies die too easily or are too hard to control and their creations overrun our world."

"How do you know all of this?" Maggie asked her.

"ARC has been around since shortly after the holy flood." Momma Rose said. "It has been run by the same bloodline since its inception."

Peter whistled, "That is some long bloodline."

She smiled at Peter.

"Yes, it is. It can be historically traced through many kings, and there are only a select number of the pure line left. The heart wills what it wills, and through marriages and such, much of the line has been tainted over the years. We do try to find those who still are among the pure lines and bring them into ARC for protection."

"Protection from the nephilim?" Maggie asked.

"Nephilim wear many skins—vampires, werewolves, naga, grunch, and many other foul creatures. They will not stop trying to collect pure samples or complete the desired host bodies. Unfortunately, because the nephilim have to jump from host to host, we do not always know who or where they are. They will promise anything to get others to work with them, usually power or money," Momma Rose said.

Maggie shifted in her seat and suddenly stood, excited.

"So, there are differences in humans because they have been breeding with nephilim in order to create host bodies to inhabit. They have done some kind of weird genetic testing on humans in an attempt to make this happen, to the point that the majority of humans on the earth are not 100 percent human anymore. Have I got that right?

Momma Rose nodded and motioned for her to continue.

"So, the pure human descendants are so scarce now that the nephilim have a hard time finding them, and when they do find them, they mobilize, in the form of vampires, werewolves, and the like to capture them so they can continue their experiments?".

"Very good, Maggie. Yes to all the above," Momma Rose praised her.

Maggie still looked confused.

"I don't know how the pure humans fit into ARC, though. Why, other than the obvious genetic testing thing, would ARC want to collect these humans?" she said, sounding perplexed.

"I thought we would get around to that." Momma Rose straightened her apron and placed her hands on her lap. "I have been allowed to tell you what I have because we need help, and I have it on good authority that there are a couple of pure humans in this room, besides myself. However, ARC and its history are for them alone. Until I have further permission, I can tell you no more about it. Just know that ARC is all about protection of the Earth and getting rid of the things that are set to destroy it."

Maggie was disappointed.

"I know one of the pure humans, but who are the others?" she asked.

"Why, Peter of course," Momma Rose said beaming at Peter, who blushed furiously at the attention that bit of news brought him. "That is why the vila sought you out in Russia, Peter. They have a sense about these things. Many of the Shem line are resistant to the vila charms. Did you find her at all attractive?"

Peter blushed again, but said, "No," thinking back to his reaction. "I really disliked her, and everytime she used her power on some-one my aversion grew. By the end of our conversation, I wanted to strangle her."

He remembered the anger and loathing he had felt when she was around. He remembered Tammy's face.

"She didn't get to me, either. Does that mean that I am pure human, too?" Sam asked, grinning.

Momma Rose's smile faltered for a moment but Peter thought only he saw it.

"You..." she hesitated and cocked her head to the side in that listening position again, then continued. "You are late for your appointment."

Sam looked at the clock on the wall.

"Damn. I forgot all about it."

He turned and ran from the room, throwing a "See ya later," over his shoulder.

Momma Rose smiled at Peter and said, "He's going to see Dr. Jo."

Maggie waved her hand at them and said, "Yeah, that's great for him, but was he correct? Is he a pure human, too?"

Momma Rose frown at her abrupt dismissal.

"No, Sam is not a pure human," she said, equally dismissive, but Maggie would not let it go.

"What is he, if he isn't pure human?" she queried.

Momma Rose "listened" for a moment before answering.

"Sam is special, and he is also not your problem. Let's just say that there are some things that he needs to work out before he can be of further use to us. As far as the rest of it is concerned, until we can get you tested, I cannot share more information with you. I am sorry."

She looked at Peter and Margueritte and said, "As for you two, there are choices that must be made." She turned to her sister, "If you choose to join us, the rest will be revealed to you. If you do not want to know, then we will set you up and protect you as best we can, but I'm afraid they already know about you and will try to capture you no matter what. All of you," she emphasized, including Peter.

She looked sad at the prospect of losing one or many of her family members again.

"My choice was made when I was 13, so..." Peter said with a grin. He stood up and hugged her and she smiled at him in return.

Margueritte took her time. She sat tearing a napkin into small pieces in her lap. When she looked up at her sister, she wore a determined, almost angry look.

"I am not sure that there is a choice in this but, for what it is worth, I wish to join. I can stop bad things from happening to others like me. What was done was an abomination, and to know that I have been an unwilling participant in something so horrendous…" She trailed off and Max placed a hand on her shoulder in comfort.

He looked at Momma Rose and asked her the only question that was on his mind at the moment.

"Aunt Rose, I have just now found her again, and I do not think that I will be leaving her for a while. She has confessed to me that I am not Lev's son."

The shock in the room was palpable. Everyone was stunned except for Maggie and Margueritte. One sat with watchful eyes, and the other had resumed her napkin destruction.

"My father was left in Paris, never to be heard from again. So, knowing this, how do I get tested?"

Startled, Maggie's gaze swung to Max. He did not look her way ,but looked at Momma Rose steadily.

She smiled at him and said, "I did not mention it earlier, but there should be no need to test you, Philippe. Your father, Rene, was of the line as well as your mother. It is now only your decision that awaits."

Max looked first to his mother, then to his Maggie—two of the most extraordinary women he had ever known, both of whom he loved greatly. What would it mean? What would it cost? He knew that duty beyond his wants bound him, and he hesitated a mere moment before proclaiming,

"As my own man, I submit myself to ARC."

Maggie squeezed his hand.

Rose said quietly, "I will go and make the arrangements. While I'm doing that, why don't you all go over the information for the warehouse again and see if we can't get that sweet little girl out of there?"

Chapter 30

The sun painted the front of the Royal as he turned the corner, and Sam knew that he was late. He hated when he was late for things. Sam was supposed to be at Dr. Jo's office at 10 a.m., and it was now half past. He walked through the double doors to the building and was able to find her office with no problem. He walked through the door and up to the counter. The small woman behind it looked up and smiled broadly.

"You must be Sam," she said with a big smile. "Dr. Jo was expecting you a while ago but made me reschedule appointments because she figured it might be a little later than when you intended."

Sam looked down at his watch in annoyance and then back up at the receptionist.

"Yeah, there was a problem at the airport when we landed that needed some planning. Sorry to be such a pain, but I really appreciate you helping me out like this."

"It's no problem, just a little reshuffling," she said. "Dr. Jo is expecting you. She told me to let you in as soon as you arrived."

The little woman moved fast and was holding the door open to another room before Sam could ask, "Isn't there some paperwork that needs to be filled out?"

"Yes, there is, but Dr. Jo is anxious to get started. She said you could fill them out on your way out this afternoon."

She smiled and ushered him forward with her free hand. Sam carefully stepped around the petite woman and entered a large office. Despite it's space, the office was warm and inviting. It looked as though Dr. Jo had tried successfully to make the office seem more like a living room. She had a fireplace, and on one side was a large, comfortable looking couch; on the other, two wingback chairs with a small table placed in between. Against the wall was a bank of cabinets and a counter with a coffee urn and tea service. Off in one corner, Sam spotted a full bar. He smiled appreciatively. He figured that she probably was prepared for anything her clients could want.

Under the counter he spied a small refrigerator, which probably held soft drinks or lemonade. There were two other doors in the room, the open door lead to the bathroom. Sam could just see the corner of the sink. The other door was closed, and Sam figured that this door must lead to Dr. Jo's inner office.

His suspicions were proven correct when the little woman walked around him to the closed door and knocked.

"'Dr. Jo?" she called. "Sam is here to see you."

With that announcement, she turned and walked back to the front of the room, through the door, and left with a wave. Sam decided that he shouldn't stand in the middle of the room, and walked over to the big plush sofa and sank into its depths. He rested his head against the back of the sofa and closed his eyes, inhaling deeply to calm his spirit.

Sam couldn't remember the last time he had felt this tired or defeated. Unbidden, an image popped into his head. It was a young boy with electric blue eyes, smiling up at him. Sam knew the boy was important to him somehow, but he couldn't remember who he was or how he was important. With a frustrated growl, he sprang to his feet and spun towards the door.

"Good. Now I know you're not asleep, we can get started."

A sharply dressed woman stood in the doorway to the inner office and smiled broadly at Sam.

"I have had people fall asleep on me, but usually it's after we start the session, never before."

Sam smiled sheepishly. "I really wasn't asleep. I had a vision, or... more of a flashback, I think. I really am not sure what it was, but the boy I saw, I think I know him, somehow," Sam said excitedly.

"How far back can you remember?" she asked him.

"Thirty years, maybe? It feels like a lot more time has passed but I can't remember it, you know what I mean? Maybe you don't. You can't be older than I am."

He ran his hands through his hair again, his frustration building.

She raised an eyebrow.

"I can't? It may interest you to know that we are the same age."

"How do you know that? You don't have any of my information yet." He looked at her suspiciously.

"The internet is a wonderful thing, Sam," she said without hesitation. He relaxed and sat back down on the sofa.

"So, what do we do now? You said that there was some sort of therapy that you could do. How does that work?"

"Well, I do have techniques and treatments that I can use on you that should bring latent memories to the surface and into the conscious part of the brain. The only thing that you need to do is lie back on that sofa and close your eyes. Do you want to try?"

Jophiel said a silent, fervent prayer for her friend and for guidance. *Never a more important session,* she thought. *I must be perfect.*

"Lie back on the sofa," he said lying down and getting comfortable, "and close my eyes." He closed his eyes and waited.

"Now, I want you to take a deep breath—in through your nose and release it through your mouth."

He obliged, and she said, "Now, do that slower. Breathe deep, hold, and release."

She let Sam do that a few more times before continuing.

"How, do you feel now, Sam? Are you relaxed?"

"Mmm hmm," came his drowsy reply.

"Good. Without opening your eyes, I want you to listen to my voice. I want you to focus on relaxing your body. Starting with your toes, I want you to relax all the muscles in your feet, and then move on to your legs. Feel the muscles loosen and your tension ebb away. Keep breathing in and out as instructed before, but focus on relaxing your body. You should be working your way up into your chest and down through your arms. Your limbs should be heavier, it should be hard to move them."

Sam was so relaxed now that he thought he could fall asleep. He couldn't remember the last time he had actually slept, though. He knew that it wasn't natural, and he didn't share that fact with people. He usually pretended to sleep while just closing his eyes and listening. It was how he found out a lot of the information he had used against Lev.

He suspected that Abe might know, considering how many flights they had shared over the years, but he had never broached the subject, and Sam certainly wasn't going to bring it up. Sam was now finding it hard to focus on anything and just let his mind wander while listening to the doctor's melodic voice.

"Okay, Sam—I think it is time to travel a little. I want you to think of your plane; picture yourself in the cockpit. You are surrounded by all the switches and buttons on the control panel. You are going to set your coordinates to the furthest memory in your mind. Do you have that memory locked in?"

"Yes."

"Good, Sam. Now—I want you to take me to that memory. Tell me what is going on."

"I'm in Hawaii. Island-hopping in a charter Cessna 172."

"Do you know what year it is?"

Without hesitating he answered, "1988."

"Good, Sam. Can you think of anything further back?" she asked, still using the same sing-song tone.

Sam thought for a moment, but it was like the memories were blocked from him. He kept hitting the same memory, over and over again, like hitting a wall. He told Dr. Jo what he was experiencing. He started to move, but she placed a hand on his shoulder and held him in place.

"No, Sam," she said soothingly. "We are making progress. It may not seem like it, but you can break through that wall. Take a deep breath. Good. Now, let it out. I want you to get back into your plane, your current plane. This time, you are approaching a storm. The memory wall is now a wall of rain and wind, the storm, that you have to fly through. You have to make adjustments to your plane to travel through this rain. Are you ready to punch through, Sam?"

Sam took another series of breaths and mentally prepared his plane to punch through the wall of rain that was before him. He flipped switches and punched buttons, all the while breathing the way he was taught.

When he felt he was ready he said, "I'm ready when you are."

"Take us in, captain.

Sam took another calming breath and gave his mental plane the punch it would take to fly through the rain wall. His mind shot forward like an arrow and pierced the wall, and just like that, he was through. So many images flooded his mind all at one time.

The Sixties, Thirties, Twenties—further. I'm a soldier? World Wars—the American Civil War—the war for independence. He kept traveling back through time. He saw himself in the employ of Elizabeth I, Charlemagne, and Xerxes. Back further still he went. *Ramses II of Egypt.* He followed the people of Israel, and yet he kept going. *A world covered with water and one lone boat bobbing along, no shore in sight.* This picture brought a sadness with it that he didn't fully understand. The scene changed yet again.

I'm standing with a woman and a young boy. The boy was laughing and looked up at Sam. Sam gasped, and he could feel a tear sliding down his face. He knew who the boy was. Those piercingly blue eyes shining up at him with love. The boy belonged to him and the woman, his wife. She, too, looked at him with love and longing.

Another scene came to him. A lone warrior stood in golden armor looking down on the corpse of the woman he knew was his wife. *Michael, my leader and brother—what did he do?*

She had been slain and her body crumpled on the ground at the warrior's feet. He remembered giving a great cry and running at Michael, sword drawn, ready to kill or die. He remembered the anger and the guilt that came flooding to him, but the rage at seeing his wife slaughtered was all-encompassing. The warrior parried the sword that Sam had swung at him with a mighty weapon of his own. The two swords clanged, and Sam was sure that the sound could be heard at a great distance. The warrior looked at Sam with a mixture of sadness and maybe a little pity.

"I'm sorry, brother," came the warrior's strong tenor voice. "This was never meant to be."

"You killed her," Sam shouted in response. "You murdered her."

"The Master forbade it, and yet you defied him and created something that has no place in this world."

Sam could tell that the warrior was sad, but he did not know why he was sad. He swung his great sword again and the warrior deflected it easily.

"She was mine and I loved her. Isn't this what the Master wanted? The humans to flourish and populate the Earth?" Sam said, with another swing in the warrior's direction.

"No, Sam, think," he said with another parry. "The Master sent you to protect what is His. Protect. Not seduce. You took something that was pure and defiled it."

The warrior was now angry and his blows forced Sam back.

"I defiled nothing," Sam shouted back. "We were here first. Do we not deserve happiness as well as the humans?"

He thrust his sword forward, making the warrior jump back and parry.

With a sneer the warrior yelled, "You are speaking like *him*. Do you now worship the ground he walks on like the others? You are better than that. Why would you let some imposter sway you? What did he promise you that made you turn against your brothers, against your Creator?"

The warrior had locked swords with Sam and looked him in the eye as he asked these last questions. His face showed his curiosity and longing to understand Sam's motives.

"*He* denies us this, Michael. I did this for happiness. To experience love and understanding denied to us by *Him*. Is that so wrong?"

Sam was weary down to his soul. "I wanted more than death and destruction, I wanted life. And yet…"

He turned and looked at the small woman crumpled on the ground. He let out a keening sound and knelt on the ground beside her.

"Yet, all I *ever get is death.*"

He raised his fist towards the sky and shouted, "*I will never forgive You for this.*"

He turned with a steely look in Michael's direction.

"Nor you."

It was said to wound, with a finality that he could tell hurt Michael to the core.

"Do what you must, but be quick."

Sam turned back around and bent to smooth the hair away, confessing to his beloved's lifeless visage, "You are innocent in all of this. I am so sorry."

He heard Michael move up behind him, heard him whisper, and then felt the blow against the back of his head. He knew nothing until he woke up later outside a village. As he staggered into the village a farmer took notice and offered him shelter and a meal. This, Sam knew, was the start of many years' worth of memories.

They all flooded back into him, the many lives he spent with many different people. The final memories of those places and people were always followed by one person, Michael. He would always come after a number of years, and Sam would wake up somewhere else in a different time, with no memory of his previous life. He would be able to do things that he had no memory of learning.

He did realize three things, though—Dr. Jo was not who she seemed, he had a score to settle with Michael, and his son's body was not with his wife's that night. He didn't know what happened to the boy—but he was going to find out.

Chapter 31

Sam slowly opened his eyes and looked at Jo sitting quietly in the wing-backed chair. She gazed steadily at him.

"Hello, Samael. It's been a long time."

"Jophiel. I am surprised I did not notice it before. You will pardon me, but I am pissed off," he said with no pause. Sam sat up and rested his arms on his knees.

"Where is he? Where is the bastard?"

"I haven't the foggiest idea of whom you might be speaking," Jo said with an air of innocence. "I do not associate with bastards of any type."

Sam sneered. "You know I speak of Michael, Jo. Don't pretend otherwise."

Jophiel could tell that Sam was upset, but she stayed calm.

"You mean the one who saved you from your own personal hell? Trapped with that demon and his lies? You should not be so quick to condemn, Sam. Your brother saved you from a fate worse than death. He went before the Master to plead for your soul."

Now Jo *was* angry.

"You call him a bastard? The one that you should be thanking? The one who saved you from your own arrogance and selfishness?"

She stood and paced across the room.

"He killed my wife," Sam shouted at her, rising.

Jo spun around. "You think so little of him? That he relishes the suffering of others?"

Sam had the good grace to look ashamed, then angry.

"I don't know, but I know that he knew they were my family. He knew they were important to me."

"I did," came a new voice at the other end of the room. Sam spun around and closed the distance between him and Michael.

"You killed them—and then took my memory from me? For what purpose?"

Michael reached out and grabbed Sam by the arm. In the next instant, Sam found himself face down in... *Sand? Tons of sand. All around him.* They were not in Jo's office anymore, but in the middle of a vast desert.

"Why have you brought me here?" he said

He got up and brushed sand off his clothes. Michael stood with his hands on his hips.

"I thought we could use some privacy. Also, some distance from anything breakable. I didn't want to mess up Jo's office."

Upon mention of her name, Jophiel appeared, along with the other archangels: Raphael, Gabriel, and Uriel.

"Come to finish what you started?" Sam sneered at the lot of them, then turned his attention back to Michael. "Weren't you finished with me long ago?"

"I didn't start this, Sam. Neither did you. The blame lies with Lucifer and the rest in the pit. He and the others brought you to this. Although, I would have to say that you went willingly, I don't feel that you had any malicious intent. I honestly believe that you had love for Ailah and Cephas," Michael said.

With the mention of his son, Sam once again threw himself in Michael's direction, only to be stopped by the gleaming blade of Gabriel against his throat.

"Maybe you should stop reacting and start listening," he suggested in an even tone.

Sam looked at him, and then at Michael.

"Speak."

"Samael, you are special to the Master."

Sam scoffed at the prospect that he was in any way special to the Master, but he continued to fume and listen to Michael. It wasn't really hard, considering Gabriel's sword was still at his throat. He reached up and gently pushed the sword away. Gabriel raised an eyebrow but did not resist.

"If I am so special, why has the Master allowed you to keep me trapped on Earth for so long? How many lives have I lived, Michael? How many years have I been forced to forget? How many *people*, Michael? The only *special* I am to Him is a special thing to torture for eternity."

Michael sighed. "The Master has always had a plan, as you know. The nephilim children were not part of that plan. When you all rebelled against Him and created them, He was angry and hurt. The children posed a threat to His Earthly creations—the very ones they were sworn to protect as Watchers. We were sent to destroy them."

Michael looked wearily and sadly at his friend.

"Do you remember any of this? Do you remember what happened? The Great War?"

"If I rebelled, as you call it, along with the others, Michael," Sam said, "why didn't I get thrown into the pit? Did I deserve my own special hell of being shuffled around every age, doomed to forget everyone over and over again?"

He had a suspicion, but waited to hear the answer for himself.

"You were being protected all of that time. You *are* special... more special to Him than you could ever know. You have a unique ability, Sam. Gifted to you... just you. One that is sorely needed."

"If the Master has need of this ability, why did he shut me away for so long? Out of touch with all our brethren? Why now?" Sam shouted, spitting, and furious at his betrayer. "And why, after *everything* that *He* has taken from me, should I help *Him* now? Why should I help you, Michael? *Brother*?" he spat the word, murder in his eyes. "You killed my family to serve... what? Who? One that destroys what is good to further His own plans?"

He spat the last of his venom at Michael and the ground rumbled in response to his accusations. Sam looked once again to the heavens and cried out in a broken voice, spent and sobbing, "Why?"

Michael reached out to try and comfort Sam but was rebuffed and shove away for his effort.

"Sam, we did what we had to do. You know that… somewhere in you. None of us, including the Master, wants to destroy the living, but what was created did not belong. When he came, the corruption came with him. If blame must be leveled, level it at the one who lied to you, who gifted the humans and Watchers too much power. The Master watched in silence for years but when the nephilim started to corrupt the very nature of the humans with greed, envy, spite, wrath—it was the final straw. The Master had to take action."

"My family was not that way. My wife was good. My son was good."

"*None* are *good*." Michael thundered, flashing brilliantly. "You suppose yourself to be the arbiter of what is good?"

"He and my wife were murdered by you as innocents." Sam lunged once again at Michael, this time pulling a great black sword from what appeared to be thin air. Gabriel met Sam's sword with his own.

"No," Michael yelled. "This has been coming a long time. Let Sam have his piece of me."

He pulled his own gleaming blade from the ether and he and Sam squared off.

"You have accused me of a great many wrongs, brother."

"You are no brother of mine."

Sam stepped to the side and swung his great sword, missing Michael by a hair's breadth.

"Michael, be careful. You know which sword he is using," Gabriel said, standing off to the side with his own scimitar gripped in his hand.

Michael and Sam circled each other under the scorching sun of the desert.

"I am aware," Michael said, not taking his eyes off of Sam or the dark sword. To Sam he said, "I have ever been your friend and brother, Sam. I was when you chose to take the lesser path, I was when I begged the Master to spare you the fate of the others, and I am now as I stand accused by you of murdering your family."

Sam stopped circling a moment and said, "You *did* murder them. I saw you myself, standing over the body of my dead wife."

He spat at him. In a surprising movement, he rushed Michael with his sword held high and his rage behind him. Michael met his blade and held it as he looked him in the eye.

"You saw me standing over the body of a woman who had already been murdered."

Sam let go and stepped back quickly.

"What lies do you tell now, Michael?"

"*I do not lie.*" Michael shouted as he closed the distance with his great sword in hand.

This Michael was the one to be feared. He was the bringer of justice and the herald of righteousness.

"If you know no other thing, you should know that I have not lied to you. Not once. It was not by my hand that your wife was murdered, but by your own son."

Sam had taken a step backward, and at this pronouncement, sat hard in the sand. He stared at nothing, trying to make sense of what he was just told. He knew it was unfair of him to accuse Michael of lying. Sam knew better than anyone that Michael was incapable of lying. He was a master at sidestepping issues, but Sam knew that when he spoke about anything, he told the truth.

He didn't want to accept that his own son may have been the monster that Michael had accused him of being, but he had been in the world a long time and had seen seemingly innocent people do monstrous things. The others stood in a circle around Sam and let him work out in his head what this new information meant to him. After what seemed like hours, Sam finally looked up at each face standing around him.

"I do not like this," he said in a sullen voice.

"We do not like it any better than you," Michael told him. "We have watched you for eons and felt that now was the right time to tell you, to show you, what really happened all those years ago, and to bring you back."

Sam looked at Michael, squinting through the bright afternoon sun. "What do you mean, *show me*?"

Michael sighed and said, "The Master has allowed me to share my memory of that day with you, so that you may see and experience for yourself what happened."

Michael reached down and touched the top of Sam's head. Sam was immediately surrounded by light, and he felt himself falling back through time. He recognized the point in time in his memories earlier where he came upon Michael, only this time he *was* Michael. Michael walking through the streets of the city, the noise of battle furious in his ears. He felt great sorrow as he watched his angel brethren fighting one another over the abysmal creatures that had been created.

Women were screaming, running from the warriors and clutching children by the hand. Michael hurried through the street, fighting off the occasional combatant with ease. His destination was known to only him, and he felt the sudden need to fly the remaining distance. He vaulted into the air, golden wings unfurled, chanting justice and vengeance in equal measure over the battle below.

Streaking northward, he came to a small house on the outskirts of the village. He alit, and ran to the door. The house was well kept, with a few small plants used for medicines and potions planted just outside the door. Michael paused and knocked respectfully. The door was thrown open and standing before Michael was a wild-eyed youth. Michael looked the boy up and down. He didn't remember him as tall as he was now. He felt sure that the boy was on his way to becoming one of the giant men that the Master had warned him about. Sam was not going to like this at all.

"Cephas, where's Samael? Where's your father?" Michael asked him.

Cephas stood, his great girth blocking the doorway and a sword held tightly in his fist.

"Out protecting the village from attackers. Is that why you are here, uncle?" Michael winced at the term Cephas used and placed a large hand on the boy's shoulder. He was definitely named well, thought Michael. The boy was easily six and a half feet tall at only 13 summers old and was a solid mass of muscles. Michael knew in his heart that Sam had been teaching the boy how to swing a sword, how to protect his mother and his village. Why was Cephas not with Samael?

"How come you're not with him?" Michael asked him circling around to look for Ahlai, Sam's wife. "Where is your mother?" Michael made to go to the adjoining room but was blocked by Cephas.

"Mother is resting, uncle," he told him. Michael found that statement strange, considering the carnage taking place down in the city. Ahlai was one of Michael's most favorite people, full of life and light, but prone to great emotion and hysteria if she got excited or scared.

"I'll bet she is afraid. Let's check on her, huh?" Michael again made for the door to the other room when Cephas tackled him to the floor, the bulk of the two great bodies smashing a table to pieces. Michael threw Cephas off of him and stood. He backed toward the door to the adjoining room slowly, keeping Cephas between him and the door.

"Why don't you want me to check on your mother, Cephas? What's happened?"

Michael watched as a look of panic came over the boy's face. He watched the rocky countenance crumble before his eyes.

"I didn't mean for it to happen. She wouldn't go with me." He exclaimed, the unsure boy that he was resurfaced where the man stood a moment ago. "I told her that father sent me to get her out of the village and to safety. She said she wouldn't leave and that I should go back to him, that she could take care of herself."

The silent tears made tracks down his cheeks as he told the rest of the story.

"I told her that I couldn't leave without her. She was holding a small sword in her hand, and when I went to get her, she ran from me. She tripped over the water bucket and fell. The sword…"

He was crying in earnest now. Michael went into the room and found Ahlai face down, the blood had seeped into the dirt floor and made a wide stain around her unmoving body. As he knelt down, his eyes took in all the evidence around him. The bruising that was evident on Ahlai's face and body. The sword held out, away from her body. There was no way that she could have inflicted this type of injury on herself. Michael stood and turned to face Cephas, only the youth wasn't there. Instead, Sam stood looking at Michael with a face full of loathing.

The memory faded from his mind. Sam threw down the sword in his hand, and sobbing, ran a few paces, stumbling into the desert sand. He fell on his face, his body racked, lamenting "*Ahlai*" over and over until he was spent.

Jophiel approached him tearfully, laying her hands on his shoulders, wanting to soothe his pain.

She whispered, "Forbidden love is still love, and we all loved her. I grieve for her, Sam." She wept over him, then turned back to the other archangels.

"Leave him to his grief. He is ready," she said, wiping a tear from her eye.

After some time, Sam rose up, wiping the mud from his tear-streaked face, and walked back to the group. Coming upon it, he considered the sword he had wielded moments earlier.

He picked it up and looked at Michael.

"It was Cephas. My own son. I am sorry, brother, for doubting you. Can you forgive me?"

Sam sank again to his knees with the weight of the revelation.

Michael smiled down at Sam and helped him up from the sand.

"I forgave you long ago."

Sam wiped sand from his pants and from his hands and asked, "What happened to Cephas? I naturally concluded that he was dead, but when Jo opened up my memory to the past, I realized he was not in the house. Your memory showed the same thing. What happened to him after...?"

Michael looked around at all the faces present and received a small nod from Uriel.

"Tell him the rest."

Michael nodded and turned to Sam who stood waiting, his fists opening and closing at his side.

"Sam, Cephas is alive."

Sam gasped.

"How is this possible?"

Michael turned to the others and said, "Back to Jo's." In an instant they all stood in Jo's homey office. Sam sat down hard on the couch he had vacated earlier. Michael took one of the wing-backs and Jophiel took the other.

"Cephas escaped the day he killed his mother. We were unable to find him. It is our belief that he was hidden from us."

"Who would hide someone from the Master's angels?" Sam said in disbelief. "Such a person would be destroyed."

The others noticed what Sam did not, his visage flickered between that of Sam as he sat on the couch and a behemoth in black armor with the cold look of death in his eyes. They turned and regarded each other, then Michael turned back to Sam.

"Yes, the Master in his wisdom knew that the demons had taken and hid Cephas from Him. With you as his father, he is able to reside in hell for as long as he wants."

"What do you mean? I thought all the angel-born were destroyed in the flood?" Sam ground out in frustration. "Just get to the point, Michael. What aren't you telling me?"

Michael looked at the others and at Jophiel who smiled in encouragement.

"Cephas was never destroyed in the flood. He has taken up residence in Hell. It has allowed him to live on as part mortal and part angel. He is the one who is responsible for the first hybrids."

"You mean like the naga, werewolves, and the like? How?"

Sam wasn't completely sure he wanted the answer.

"He wed the daughter of Abbadon. They have produced many children, the first of which was a vampire named Alaric. I believe he is still alive and causing mayhem. The firstborn of Cephas and Addaine are said to be the strongest and the hardest to kill," Michael said, running his hands through his hair in frustration. "We have managed to get rid of a few of them, but most of them are able to return to Hell on a regular basis, thus hiding from us. This is a tragic complication that has cost countless lives."

Sam was feeling guilty.

"What is it you want from me? An apology? Fine, I'm sorry, Michael." He looked skyward and said, "Is that what You want to hear? I have wronged You and have been made to see the error of my ways."

He faced Michael and the others with pain-filled eyes. "What does He want from me?"

His shoulders slumped in his brokenness, and the others turned to Michael. Michael sighed and became blunt.

"Do you not yet remember who you are?" The ground trembled and Michael looked skyward. His gaze came back to Sam and he simply said, "Forgive me." With a snap of his fingers, Sam was gone and the five were alone.

"Has he been summoned?" Uriel asked Michael.

"Yes." Michael said with a hint of worry in his eyes.

"You have done everything you could to make him understand without telling him outright, Michael. You've succeeded. He is ready for this. The Master is gracious and forgiving, and Samael has shown that he is repentant. The Master will not make this easy. Sam has to truly want this in order to be redeemed."

She placed a hand on Michael's shoulder, trying to reassure him. "The rest is up to him."

Chapter 32

Maggie was fuming. *Isn't that just like a man,* she thought. Max and the other guys had vetoed her plea to join them at the warehouse tonight. They all assumed that she could not take care of herself, and that the situation would be too dangerous for her, never mind the fact that, except for Max, she could probably best any of the others without breaking a sweat... *or a nail.* She pounded her fist on the countertop at Momma Rose's café, attracting the attention of not only a few of the patrons of the establishment, but of Momma Rose herself.

"Come, cher. You are scaring the customers."

She wrapped an arm around Maggie's waist and tutted to herself, "You let yourself get too caught up in what they told you couldn't do that you miss what you can do."

Maggie took a moment to collect her thoughts and turning to the older woman said, "It just makes me so mad when men believe a woman cannot do something just because she is a *woman,*" Maggie air-quoted the last, emphasizing the stupidity of the argument. "Do they realize the amount of conditioning and training I have had? I have taken down members of the Yakuza, for God's sake."

She sat down hard at the table Momma Rose had been leading her to and fought back the urge to scream.

"Yes, well let's not scream shall we?" Momma Rose said, unperturbed.

Maggie forgot that the older woman could read her thoughts.

"Only when you are really upset at something, and right now you're very nearly shouting." Momma Rose laughed at Maggie's expression.

"Sorry," she mumbled. "It's just that I have spent my entire adult life in these types of situations and I have always made it out just fine. I've spent years training for just these types of circumstances. So I don't understand why I should be pushed to the side because I am little or a woman," she huffed.

"Stop that this instant," she heard from behind her.

She swung around to find Margueritte with her hands on her hips. She looked so much better, having had a good meal, a long shower, and a chance to preen. *She looks lovely,* thought Maggie. But she didn't sound it at the moment.

"I will not stand here and listen to you feel sorry for yourself. I'm sorry that the men decided to leave you behind, but they were doing what they felt was the best thing for the people that they care about, Philippe included." She softened and approached Maggie sympathetically, "My dear, sometimes it is not about what they know you can or cannot do, but about how they can better protect the people they love." She nodded to her sister and sat down next to Maggie. "Besides, now that they have left, we can figure out how we are going to help them."

Maggie laughed at Margueritte's enthusiasm and looked up to see Naomi pacing not far from were they were sitting. Maggie felt an instant kinship with the other woman and knew instinctively that she was dealing the same thing as Maggie.

"Naomi. Come and join the planning session," Maggie called to her. Naomi lifted her head and nodded to Maggie, making her way to the table.

"What do you all have planned so far? I have a couple of ideas..." Naomi settled in and Maggie noticed the tension in Momma Rose slowly fade.

"What did you have in mind?" Naomi asked her.

"Okay, so we know that the men were taking a group down to the waterfront, half to go down by the water and enter by way of the docks, and the others will go through the building with Max and Peter."

"I do not like this plan. It leaves them exposed for too long, and

Philippe will be by himself with Olivier," Momma Rose exclaimed and Margueritte nodded in agreement.

"I know, I thought it was a terrible idea as well. Peter has his SAMS suit, but what that will do in close quarters, I don't know."

In that moment, three things happened in rapid succession: Naomi, who had been listening a moment before, stiffened and gasped; Momma Rose bolted from her seat and grabbed Naomi by the arm; and a figure appeared in the middle of the table. It was the figure of a child, naked and curled into a ball. The women could hear the girl crying, but the images surrounding her were blurry.

Naomi said, "Sarah?"

The child moved her head and looked directly at Naomi, Maggie, and Momma Rose.

They heard her say, "Naomi. Naomi, help me."

Naomi shook her head to gain clarity and said, "Sarah, where are you?"

Momma Rose asked in a soothing voice, "We want to come get you, but we need to know where you are."

Momma Rose close her eyes for a moment, and little Sarah calm down a little as if soothed by an unseen force. The area around Sarah came into focus, and the woman could see that Sarah was on a bed. They could also see that she was not alone in the room. Sarah moved her head and the women saw a man in the room behind her. He was naked and busily washing himself off. They heard Sarah whimper and turn her face away from the man near the sink. They heard the girl speaking, but she just continued to lie unmoving on the bloody bed, naked and afraid.

"She isn't talking. Am I hearing her thoughts?" Naomi asked Rose.

"Shh. Sarah, go on," Momma Rose urged, shushing Naomi's question for the time being.

"They put me in this room and told me not to make any noise or they'd hurt me."

The fear coming from the girl was evident to the ladies huddled around Naomi.

"He came in and" she paused and tried to compose herself, the tears were freely flowing down her cheeks, "then—then he began to undress. He told me that we were going to play a game."

Maggie was trying very hard to pay attention to all the details the girl was telling them, but all she could think of was Susanna.

Dammit, this can't be happening again.

In her mind she was telling herself about all the things that she wanted to do the monster in the room with that sweet angel.

Maggie, you are not helping us or yourself… Focus! Momma Rose's thought snapped her back to the moment, and to the little girl that needed their help desperately.

"He wanted me to touch him. Like he had touched me earlier."

She started to cry a little harder as she went on. "I told him no and… and…" she was crying so hard now they almost didn't hear the next thing she said. "He hit me hard across the face. When I woke up he was on top of me. In me... he hurt me so bad… down there. It hurt so bad, Naomi. I want to go home."

The pleading in the little girl's voice made Maggie want to kill the man in the room with her.

"We are going to get you out, Sarah. You are not going to have to stay with that man anymore. We need to know if you remember how you got to the room. Can you tell us anything?"

"I remember coming through a dark tunnel, there were rats and water and it was stinky."

Maggie saw her scrunch her small nose as if remembering the smell.

"We passed some other rooms and there was a tall skinny man at the end of the hall, he was the one that told them to put me in the room. I remember him from the last time. He has evil eyes." The form of Sarah shivered. "He told the men to go get the client, that his surprise had arrived. Then he pushed me inside the room and told me that if I wasn't quiet the monsters would come get me."

"That's great, Sarah. You're doing great, honey. Can you remember anything else?" Maggie asked, but Sarah did not have a chance to answer as the man chose that moment to come over to the bed.

"It's time to wake up, popkin. I'm taking you home now," he said in a syrupy, creepy voice. "We will play games everyday together... won't that be fun?"

Sarah whimpered again, and the man said, "Now, I won't have to punish you if you do as your told. You were a naughty girl, and I had to punish you. That won't happen again, will it? I would much rather we have fun together."

Sarah curled up into herself even more when he touched her shoulder. When she pulled away in a bit of defiance, he raised his hand to strike her, but the door opened at that moment, and another man came into the room.

"You will still pay full price, even if she is damaged. I hope you plan on taking her now."

The oily voice was cold and unfeeling in light of what had just happened to the child.

"Yes. I plan to take this one home with me."

He placed a hand on Sarah as if protecting her from Olivier.

"She was everything you promised me she would be. I will transfer the money into your account as soon as I get out of this hole. Please make sure that she is cleaned and dressed appropriately for travel. Do you have the travel documents ready?"

Olivier snorted, "Everything is in her folder upstairs. You will follow me now, and I will have someone bring her up when she has bathed and suitable clothing can be found for her to wear. That will be added on top of your fee since you chose to cut off her other clothing. And," he added flatly, "you will transfer the funds before she leaves the premises. That is non-negotiable."

Olivier sounded a little put out at having to do anything for this man.

"Fine. I will bring a suitable outfit for her when I return. I will transfer the money then." As the two men were leaving the room, Sarah heard the man say, "I'll be back for you later, angel—you be a good girl."

Sarah burst into tears the moment the door closed.

"Please come get me. I don't want to go with him..."

"I cannot hold the projection any longer," Momma Rose said through clenched teeth.

Sarah's image began to fade and Naomi said in a panicked voice, "We're coming to get you, Sarah. Stay strong."

The image was lost. Momma Rose let go of Naomi's arm and sat down hard on the floor behind her. Maggie rushed to the older lady's side.

"Are you alright, Momma Rose?"

Concern flooded through Maggie at the pale face that gazed back at her.

"Yes cher, I'm okay. It's been an age since I worked with a projector." At Maggie's confused look she went on. "Sarah can project herself to different places, or in this case, people."

"But how is that possible?" Maggie asked in disbelief.

"No matter, now. The point is, she *is* one. And Naomi is a receiver. That is an incredible gift," Momma Rose told Naomi admiringly.

"But—" Naomi started, but Momma Rose waved her off.

"I must get word to Michael. You two need to go save that child. I will call Peter and Joshua, and they will meet you at the warehouse. Please try to resist going in before they get there. Come with me, please."

Rose hurried past Maggie toward the far side of the bistro to a door, which led to an unassuming set of stairs, possibly to a cellar. Momma Rose flicked on a light and quickly descended the stairs, with the younger women in tow. What greeted them at the bottom was so unexpected, yet entirely expected, that Maggie and Naomi didn't even question it. A well-lit meeting room with a wall-to-wall display of guns, knives, swords, spears, and explosives, as well as other types of tools spread out in front of them. Maggie would have loved to explore the racks at leisure, but they were pressed for time.

"Grab what you prefer from over there. Take what you can use. Please hurry. Now I must make some calls," she said as she rushed from the room.

Chapter 33

Abe, Peter, and Max were getting ready to load the second SAMS on the truck when Joshua came rushing up to them. "We don't have time for those anymore. Leave 'em."

"What do you mean?" Peter asked. "These are part of our plan."

"I mean there is no time. Sarah has contacted Naomi, and her life is in danger. She told the girls where she is and basically how to find her," Joshua told them.

They were all moving now. They shut and locked the doors to Abe's hangar, and jumped into Joshua's waiting Tahoe.

"How was Sarah able to contact them? Is she some sort of psychic?" Peter asked.

"Not far from it. Turns out Sarah is a projector. She can project herself places. It's like a radio broadcast—she basically can shotgun herself out to everyone and everything close to her, or even to specific people. Not her physical form, mind. Just her consciousness."

Joshua spun the tires as they left the access road headed toward the river, and he wiped a bead of sweat from his brow as he continued to explain.

"She projected herself to the closest receiver, Naomi."

Joshua looked sidelong at Abe, who in his turn, looked confused and a bit stunned. He drove through the gates of the airport at a breakneck speed with his sirens blaring. Peter was holding on for dear life in the front seat and as he clicked his seat belt into place.

"Joshua, she's like 12 years old. Are you trying to tell me that Sarah and Naomi used some kind of link? So, they both have this power—"

"Gift," Joshua corrected. Peter waved off his correction.

"Okay, gift—to contact each other?" Peter said, rolling his eyes.

"No," Joshua said, "I'm trying to tell you that Sarah used her projecting gift to contact the closest person to her with the receiving gift, which as it turns out, is Naomi."

Joshua veered left to miss a person that had turned in front of them on the road. Peter said a prayer that they would make it to their destination.

"So, is Sarah where we think she is?" he asked Joshua. He swerved around a battered Toyota with a pizza delivery sign lit up on its roof, and continued on.

"Oh, yeah. Rose was able to help the girls stabilize their connection. The women were able to see the guy who... *purchased* Sarah. They saw him talking to Olivier."

At the shocked expression on Peter's face and the gasp from Abe, he said, "It's bad, but that's not the worst of it. That man had already raped her."

Peter was quiet for a moment, and then in an act of pure emotion punched the dash in front of him. He heard Abe swear softly from the back seat, wishing all sorts of harm on the pervert that would harm a child in that manner.

"I will kill him this time."

They heard the steel in Max's voice as he vowed to end Olivier. Joshua looked at him in the rearview mirror.

"Believe me, I'm as incensed as you, Max. Just remember, there is a difference between murder and defense."

Max looked at Joshua in the mirror and replied, "I am already damned." He said it in an almost amused, yet very flat, voice.

"Are you sure about that? It has been my experience that the repentant are the easiest to redeem."

Joshua thought he saw a flicker of hope on Max's face as he saw him turn and look out the window.

"Huh," he grunted in response, "I guess we will see."

They flew through the city streets until at last, Joshua pulled the SUV over about a block and a half from the warehouse.

"Get your gear. We run from here," he said as he opened the driver's side door.

They all piled from the vehicle and went to the rear. Joshua opened the tailgate and all the others gathered around him.

"I have a few things that will help us. Backup is on the way, but we're going to be on our own in there for a bit."

He started pulling out items that he thought they would need. Abe and Max began selecting various implements, vials, and tools and stowing them on their bodies while Peter stood, taking it all in. Here it was, laid out in front of him. The dankness of the air around them completed the scene as he stood staring at, not only the classic vampire-killing stuff: holy water, stakes, and crosses made of silver, but also modern and unexpected things like night-vision goggles, bolt cutters, and flash-bangs. Joshua spoke to them as he hurriedly completed his loadout.

"It's not easy to smoke a vampire, gents."

Peter had started grabbing at things and attaching them to his carrying gear, and he was going to speak up about what he knew, but Joshua continued as if reading his intent.

"No, not because they are hard to kill. They are just extremely fast and clever. You do not have to stake a vampire through the heart to kill it, although that method works. It can be killed many of the same ways a human can. They can still be repulsed by holy water and crosses, but that's temporary. The thing is," he said, scratching his stubble, "for a human to kill a vampire they have to be extremely lucky by taking the vampire by surprise. If it knows you are coming, it will use its speed and strength against you. If it knows you're coming, you're typically dead."

He threw a Kevlar vest at Abe, who quickly grabbed it and threw it on over his LBC.

"Vampires shoot, too?" Abe asked, strapping the last side of the vest.

Joshua chuckled wryly, "Better safe than sorry. I don't know what else we will run into. Olivier may have good old human thralls and henchmen, you know."

Max quickly unbuttoned two buttons on his shirt to reveal a similar, yet more form-fitting and expensive, vest to Joshua.

"I am covered."

Joshua just smiled and whistled and continued to outfit himself. Peter could tell that Max had been, if not in these exact circumstances, at least in some that were close enough to this, and that made him curious and wary of his new Russian friend. He would have to sit down sometime soon with Max over a beer and learn more about the stoic ex-gangster.

Joshua broke in again.

"Those of us who are marked, like Peter and me, have an advantage; a hedge of protection so to speak. Max and Abe, stay out of the way when it gets thick in there, okay?"

He spoke in clear tones that brooked no argument.

Joshua is definitely in his element, thought Peter.

"Peter." Joshua called on him. Peter stepped forward and took a flat tear shaped object from Joshua. "I have been told to give this to you and show you how to use it."

The object was about the size of Peter's palm and warm to the touch in an energized way. It pulsed slightly, and it was made of what appeared to be the same shiny metal as the key he had produced earlier that day. It was marked similarly to the scar on Peter's shoulder.

"What is it?" Peter asked him, still mystified as to why the object looked like his scar.

"It is the sigil of Michael. It's your protection against the nephilim or their descendants. Michael himself has gifted you with his sigil of protection. Not to get too weird about it, but you are one of us. This," he said, gesturing to the object, "is your defense. Just hold it in your palm as you would a sword hilt and call on Michael to protect you. This will activate a weapon to manifest in your hand."

Peter was excited and made as if to speak when Joshua placed his palm against Peters mouth.

"Hold your horses, cowboy. You only use this when it's needed. Understand?"

Peter nodded against Joshua's hand, and he let go. "Good. This is powerful magic, Pete, and should only be used when you are fighting the Corrupted. It's not a parlor trick to pull out and show your friends. And don't even think about trying to replicate it for customers."

Peter was wounded by the harsh words but mollified when Joshua said, "It's really cool— don't spoil the surprise."

Peter tossed the object once, letting the glint catch the light of the day, then he caught it quickly and put it in his pocket. Peter grabbed a rope, two small flashlights and a couple of flash-bangs. He couldn't think of anything better to take when faced with a bunch of nocturnal vampires.

"Joshua, they're going to hate these, right?" Peter grinned, holding up one of the flash-bangs.

"Oh, yeah. They will get disoriented and sort of irritated when one of those goes off. Take more than you think you'll need."

"What about Sam?" Peter asked. "He was supposed to meet up with us."

"Never mind Sam. What about the FBI?" Abe asked.

"As you may guess, my agents are not equipped to deal with this threat, either mentally or physically, and knowledge is a dangerous thing, Abe. So, no."

Joshua turned to address Peter.

"Sam knows where we are and will be with us shortly. He is coming with some friends."

Joshua gave Peter a meaningful look and Peter nodded with a smile.

"Max, what about you? Are you absolutely sure that you want to confront Olivier in his shop?" Joshua asked him. "I'm not sure of the reception you will receive. I'm sure by now your father has had a conversation with him."

"I am sure. Although, at the moment, I am not sure what kind of reception he will get from me." Max clenched and unclenched his fists.

"Well, keep it together long enough for us to get Sarah and get out. I don't care what you have to do to appease him or stall him, but give us as much time as possible. Abe, are you going with Max or with us?"

Abe looked thoughtful for a moment and then said, "This is a young man's game. I will stay and monitor the AO from the outside. I'll pass along intel as I get it, and you can pass off the girl to me once you have her."

His eyes held regret that he would not be in on the adventure, but he knew that his old body couldn't stand up to this.

Joshua brought them together and they clasped hands as he said, "May the Master watch over you."

With that the men parted ways. Max straightened his tie and put on his sunglasses. He smoothed his hair and started down the street to grab a cab. Peter, Joshua, and Abe made their way toward the dock, but veered to the left before they came to the waterfront. Joshua was usually at home around here, but today it smelled worse than death, and he was all too aware of the fading daylight in the distance. It was close to three in the afternoon, and they had quite the mission ahead of them. *We absolutely, 100%, have to be done and gone before dark,* he thought. He quickened his pace, and Abe and Peter followed suit. They skirted the water line until they came to what looked like a drainage runoff from the Quarter. Peter was there first to spot the lock on the gate.

"Now what?" he said, exasperated.

"Move it," Joshua said, trotting in behind him. Joshua had the key from earlier in his hand, and held it out towards the lock. The metal sparked and morphed slightly as they watched. Joshua shoved the key into the padlock, and it gave with a click.

"Wow," cried Peter.

"Later," Joshua said, rushing past him into the darkened tunnel.

They all entered, then stopped. Abe could hear the skittering of either insects or rats off in the distance. He didn't know which, but he wasn't fond of either. He also wasn't fond of the muck they found themselves standing in inside the decrepit tunnel. They all moved forward slowly as the sediment and sludge of decades squished grotesquely under their feet.

Joshua turned to them and said, smiling, "This ain't nothin', boys."

Peter took out one of the small flashlights that he snagged from Joshua's truck and flicked it on. Abe took the small handheld from his back pocket and gestured to Peter and Joshua that they should do the same.

"Comm check."

They quickly established that all three were working as expected, and replaced them securely. Abe reached out and grabbed Peter's shoulder.

"Be careful down there. May the Master watch over you."

He gave Peter's shoulder a little squeeze.

"You too, Abe—you have us on the radio. Call us if you see anything we should know about. Be careful, old man."

Peter laughed when Abe stood up straighter and said, "Who you calling old?"

He playfully punched Peter in the arm and looked at Joshua when he said, "Look after him. He's been known to get himself into trouble."

"I copy, chief. Keep us posted."

Joshua pulled on Peter's shirt to get his attention.

"This way. Follow me and keep your sigil key in your hand."

At his blank look Joshua sighed and said, "The shiny teardrop. Put it in your hand."

Peter pulled the object from his pocket and clenched it in his fist. He swallowed his fear and followed Joshua into the darkness.

This first thing Peter thought as they walked along was how he had gotten to this point in his life. As a child, he wished for adventure. When his parents died in such a tragic way he decided that adventure was really not for him. He discovered that you can create your own adventure without leaving the comfort of your home. He was now one of the premier cosplay experts in the world and was in the business of inventing adventurers. He had studied and created characters based on what he thought were mythical creatures, only to realize that everything he thought was imagination was actually real. He was definitely living a surreal fantasy.

They walked for what seemed like hours, but was only a few minutes, in the darkened tunnel. So far, the tunnel had not taken any turns, so when they finally came upon a split, Peter was unsure of what to do. He looked at Joshua.

"Which way do we go?" he asked, concerned they would lose their way.

Joshua pulled something from his vest pocket and made a mark on the wall.

"We have been walking north so far, so if what I remember about the city and the warehouse location is accurate, we go left."

He pointed in the direction they were to follow. Peter went to go ahead, but Joshua grabbed his shirt and said, "Me first, kid. Rose would kill me if anything happened to you."

Peter wasn't happy about it, but let Joshua take the lead. They were about halfway up the new tunnel when Peter froze. He thought he heard someone snicker. He clutched the teardrop-weapon tighter in one hand and the flashlight in his other hand. They moved a little further, and Peter could swear someone tapped him on the shoulder.

What the hell? Am I imagining things? He spun around but didn't see anyone. When he turned back around he found that Joshua was quite a bit further up the tunnel than he was. He started moving faster, and once again he thought he felt a tap on his shoulder, accompanied by the smell of… *barbecue?* It was weird, and he was getting freaked out. When he started moving again, he was ready. He smelled the same smell first. He gripped the object tight. Then he heard a snicker and felt the tap. As he spun around for the third time, he whispered Michael's name.

Shoom!

His hand erupted with light. He heard a loud scream and saw in the beam of his weapon a vampire retreating into the darkness, cursing loudly. Peter could see a faint glowing through the creature's fingers that were clenched tightly around the side of his head. One side of the face was glowing and bloodied. Peter looked down, and on the ground at Peter's feet lay an ear. Peter heard someone coming up behind him and turned to confront this new unknown, only to see Joshua stop short.

"What happened? Are you okay?"

"I cut off its ear. Look." Peter said in shock, nudging the thing gingerly with his toe. Joshua looked at the ear, then at Peter, and then looked down the hallway. What happened next took Peter completely by surprise. Joshua brought his arm up from behind him and forward, saying something that Peter could not hear. Just as he did, a glowing, oxblood red crossbow appeared. Joshua took aim down the hallway and fired. A shaft of red flew from the end of the crossbow, and a moment later,Peter saw an explosion of light at the end of the tunnel, followed by a quickly silenced scream.

"What just happened?" Peter asked.

"I killed your vampire friend. How'd you manage to cut off its ear?" Joshua asked, just as surprised as Peter.

"It was in the tunnel behind me, taunting me. You know, it kept tapping my shoulder and laughing in my ear. When I swung around and said Michael's name like you told me to, this flaming sword appeared so suddenly it freaked me out. I swung out and... I cut off its ear."

He toed it again as it rolled around in the muck. Joshua grinned and slapped him on the back.

"I wondered what form yours would take. A flaming sword, huh? You do take after your namesake, Peter."

Peter was confused, which made Joshua bark a laugh.

"I'll explain later. Come on. We need to move fast and be on the lookout now. If that one managed to tell the others we are in the tunnels, then we're going to have company."

The two men walked at a faster pace, never looking in one spot too long. They came to the end of their current tunnel and had to make a decision on whether to go left or right. This time though, they could see a light at the end of the left tunnel.

They turned to go in that direction when they heard someone say, "I wouldn't go that direction if you want to see daylight again."

Joshua spun around and Peter let out a yelp. He jumped a good foot off the ground, whirling to face the voice and evoking Michael's name again. The sword burst into being and was met with a pair of blades which blocked his.

"Whoa, down boy."

Maggie smiled and squinted through the dual flashlight beams trained on her pretty face. Peter thought how weird it was that they were literally slogging through the most vile-smelling stuff he had ever been near, and Maggie manages to enter the picture looking fresh as a daisy. *Go figure.*

"Um, Joshua? How do I call this thing off? Is there a sheath or something? Down, sword." Peter looked down to address the golden flaming weapon that was still very much at the ready in his grasp.

Joshua grinned and said, "I got you, son. Just say 'Peace,' and press here," he said, indicating a small symbol near the base of the hilt.

"Peace." Peter pressed the symbol, and instantly the teardrop-shaped object reappeared in his hand. He returned it to his pocket.

"Are you nuts? Keep that thing in your hand, Peter. We are in some deep—" Joshua looked down and gestured forward with his chin. "Look, just keep your sword ready."

Peter, flustered, gripped the sigil key tightly and turned back to Maggie.

"Sorry Maggie, you're lucky to still have your ear." Peter told her. Maggie tilted her head to the side in question as Joshua barked a laugh.

"What about my ears?" Maggie asked him.

"Never mind, just be glad you weren't here earlier. Peter is a danger to ears everywhere," Joshua told her. "We'll fill you in later." To Peter he said, "Just be careful where you point that thing." He nodded down at the object in Peter's hand.

Peter nodded.

"What's down there?" he asked Maggie, jerking his head in the opposite direction.

"A whole lot of vampires. Part of them are occupied with what looks like some very willing women, and part of them are sleeping. I saw one of them leave earlier. He went down the way you came from. Did you see him?" she asked the guys.

"Peter briefly made its acquaintance. Where is Naomi? Momma Rose said you guys were together?"

"We were, but we were wasting too much time, and there were so many doors, we decided to split up and check them. My side led here, and once I saw what was in the far door, I decided to backtrack. That's when I heard you coming up the tunnel and hid. We need to go back up this way to Naomi. Hopefully she's found her by now."

Maggie turned and started back up the tunnel to the right. Before long, they came to doors that lined the hallway at regular intervals.

"Were you able to see what's inside the doors?" Peter asked as they came even with the first of many doors.

"Most of them are unlocked and are filled with boxes and crates. I didn't get a chance to look in any of the crates, but I did find a couple of the doors had high tech locks on them. I would give anything to get a good look inside," whispered Maggie. "This way."

She led them past a couple of doors then stopped before one that had a sophisticated key pad on the outside.

"I tried this one. Couldn't access it," she told them.

She made to move on, but Joshua stopped her.

"Why don't you and Peter go on ahead? I'm going to look around a bit. I want to see exactly what they are up to here."

Maggie looked torn. Peter could tell that she really wanted to stay and help Joshua, but at the same time she wanted to find Sarah and Naomi.

Peter looked at her and said, "Hey—he's a big boy. Sarah needs you right now, okay?"

Maggie thought quickly, and relented, saying, "Okay, but you have to swear that you'll tell me what you find later."

Joshua grinned. "I promise."

Maggie nodded and then took Peter's hand and led him away into the darkness. They moved swiftly and silently until they reached the point that Maggie started from.

"Okay, here's where we split before. Past here… I don't know."

The two set off up the hallway. Every so often one of them would try the handle of the many doors along the way. The first few held supplies and crates like the other rooms Maggie found, but the further they went the rooms changed. One room opened up into what looked like a nursery for a giant baby. Everything in the room was scaled up to an adult size including the giant diapers stacked neatly by the door.

"This looks like something I've seen on reality shows…" Peter shook his head sadly and said, "Still can't understand why anyone would want to live as a baby. Who is gonna change the diapers?" he asked, pointing at the stack by the door.

"Ugh," Maggie said disgustedly. "Let's get out of here."

They closed the door and moved on up the hall. The next door they opened was covered in fabrics from the floor to the ceiling and even some tacked along the ceiling draping down over an enormous bed covered in pillows. The fabrics were all in bold colors and flowed down over the floor. On the bed lay a young woman, she was barely clothed in what looked to be wispy harem pants and nothing else.

"Um, you take this one," Peter said, averting his eyes.

"Yep, I got it." Maggie approached the bed. The steady rise and fall of the girl's chest let Maggie know that she was asleep. When she reached the side of the bed, Maggie noticed that the prisoner was chained by both her ankles and wrists to the bed. The chain looked to be long enough that she could get up and walk around but not enough that she could go very far.

Peter nodded to Maggie to wake the girl up. Maggie bent close and put her hand over the girl's mouth in case she screamed. The girl's eyes flew open and Maggie made shushing sounds to quiet her down. When the girl calmed Maggie removed her hand.

"Who are you?" the girl asked quietly. "You shouldn't be here. If they catch you, they will kill you."

She was starting to panic again and Maggie shushed her.

"I'm Maggie. Here, you must be freezing," she told the girl, covering her naked chest with Peter's hoodie.

"Thanks," she said meekly.

"This is Peter. We're here to rescue a little girl named Sarah, have you seen her?" Maggie asked her.

"I haven't been out of this room in a while," she whispered.

"How long is a while?" Peter asked her gently.

"What's the date?" She looked at him steadily.

"April 17, 2019," Peter told her.

"In that case, I have been down here a year and 5 months." With that pronouncement, she began to cry. "My family probably thinks I'm dead."

Maggie looked at Peter and frowned, "We can't leave her here." Peter nodded. He turned back to the girl.

"What's your name?"

"Vicky," she told them. "Are you going to help me?" The hope that was shining in her eyes was almost too much for Peter, he turned around so that Vicky wouldn't see the anger on his face and get scared.

He heard Maggie say, "Yes, hold still and let me see if I can pick these locks."

"Oh, no need. The keys are in the cabinet over there."

She pointed to a small cabinet in the corner of the room. Peter walked over and pulled the cabinet door open. Inside he found an assortment of sex toys and devices, drug paraphernalia, a couple yards of what appeared to be silk, some vials, women's underwear, a locked strongbox, and on a tiny hook, two shiny bronze keys. He grabbed the keys and quietly closed the door to the cabinet.

Even down in these depths and having spotted no one around, he didn't want to chance them getting caught. He handed the keys to Maggie who took them from him without looking, intently working the lock around the girl's ankle.

She absently asked while she worked, "So, what else was in there? Anything that could help us?"

He shook his head, saying, "You don't want to know. And, no."

Maggie unlocked the cuffs on Vicky's arms and legs. The girl gingerly rubbed the spots where the cuffs had been only moments before. Maggie could see old scars and some bruises that were in the process of healing as she surveyed the young woman's condition.

"Is there anything else you can dress in?" Maggie asked her.

Vicky shook her head no as she zipped Peter's hoodie. *Skimpy Princess Jasmine pants and an oversized hoodie.* Maggie wanted to scream.

"Okay, well," she pulled her out the door and Peter followed. "I need you to be very brave and follow this hallway down to the intersection. Go left down at the intersection, at the end there will be..." she looked at Peter for help.

"At the end there will be daylight and a large man named Abe. He kinda reminds me of Morgan Freeman. He will help you. Just tell him Peter sent you, and he will get you to a safe place. You must be very quiet. Here, take this."

He thrust a flashlight into her hands and told her to look for arrows set in intervals on the wall.

"They'll point you in the right direction. Just make sure you turn left from this tunnel, do not go to the light at the end, understand?"

She shivered slightly.

"Vicky, look at me. You can do this. Help is at the end, I promise."

She nodded and let go of Maggie's arm. She squared her shoulders and entered the hallway.

"Oh, if you see an older man wearing a suit coming up the tunnel, his name is Joshua. Just tell him Peter and Maggie are sending you to Abe, and he will make sure you are going in the right direction."

She smiled timidly, and took a step of two, then suddenly whirled around, reaching for Maggie, and almost falling onto her. The girl grabbed her in a fierce hug as sobs racked her. Peter and Maggie completely engulfed her, both to comfort her and to muffle her crying.

"Shhh, it's alright now. You're going to be fine, and no one will ever do this to you again, okay?"

Maggie did her best to soothe the girl, but she was worried that they were taking too much time. Peter and Maggie let her cry for a few more seconds, and then looked at each other, an unspoken signal that time was not on their side and they had their own to rescue.

Peter locked eyes with the girl and said softly, but seriously, "Vicky, get going. Tell Abe what we told you, and we will see you soon, okay?"

Vicky's body had stopped convulsing with her emotion, and she looked up at the two of them, wiping her face.

"Thank you."

She turned, flipped on the flashlight that Peter had given her, and made her way up the hall. Maggie grabbed Peter by the arm.

"Come on, she will be fine."

"How do you know?" Peter asked her. "I feel bad about making her walk out alone."

"I know because she wants to live."

They stepped out of the harem room and closed the door, moving quickly further down the corridor.

"I know because they didn't break her spirit. She's a survivor and there will be time for her to process later. She has hope and her hope will get her through."

Maggie had started to chew up the hallway and Peter quickened his step to keep up. They passed a few more doors opening them as they went. They saw the inside of a castle with a large four-poster bed and tapestries on the wall, an S & M chamber with all manner of whips and chains, and the final room they came to had the door cracked and a dim light emitting from the space. Voices, one female, one male, from inside—Naomi's voice, then the sound of flesh meeting flesh, and a cry of pain. A *smack.*

"You aren't the one I want to play with, cocoa. The one I want, I have. You are old and mean, and you will pay for making me sully my hand in hitting you. You thought you could come and steal my property? Steal my fun?" Again, they heard flesh meet flesh and then they heard Naomi say, "Let me loose and I'll show you what fun is all about. I will 'fun' you until they need a dental record to ID you."

Again, flesh met flesh in what sounded like a punch.

"Oho. A whimper? You may be as fun as her after all."

Peter couldn't wait any longer. He jumped up and rushed into the room. He saw a man standing over a bound Naomi, who was protecting a small body curled into a ball on the bed. Peter flew at the man pulling him away from Naomi and planting a fist first in his face, then in his stomach. The man retaliated by throwing the next punch to Peter's jaw. He went to throw another punch as Peter recovered, but felt the blade of Maggie's katana against his throat and stopped immediately.

"You've never had a shave this close, big boy. I really wouldn't move if you want to live a little longer."

Maggie's voice had turned as steely as the blade trained on the man she faced. He was bulbous and sweaty and disgusting, and Maggie really felt like running him through, especially after seeing the condition of the room they were standing in. A concrete, blood-stained floor, an ancient brass bed with threadbare linens, twisted and bloody, a similar cabinet to the harem room that would no doubt have the same contents that Peter wouldn't discuss. She would never understand how the nobility of man, man that had walked on the moon, cured disease, did so many incredible and altruistic things, could sink so low with a child.

The man swallowed and stammered, "It-it-it seems eh-every-one wants to play today. Now take it easy with those, sweetling. I wouldn't want to see that pretty face get damaged."

He gave her an uneasy grin. Still holding one of her katana's to the man's neck, she flicked out with the other one, and within a blink it was back by her side.

The man grinned and said to her, "See? You didn't even hit anything."

"I never miss. Look at your arm."

He looked down at his arm and found that a long line of hair was missing from his forearm.

"It's not a question of whether I want you dead or not, because, believe me, I do. But it's your lucky day—because we are here for her."

Without breaking eye contact, she said, "Peter, are you alright?"

Peter, who was watching her with a grim smile said, "Yeah, I'm fine. Momma Rose hits harder than this guy."

He turned his attention to Naomi. He grabbed a lockblade and clicked it open, working the duct tape on her wrists. He freed her and said, "You okay?"

She rubbed her sore wrists briefly and looked up with tears in her eyes.

"I think there is something seriously wrong with Sarah, Peter. She was talking to me earlier as I was looking for her, and she kept telling me how tired she was. Then when I found her, I tried to wake her up. She won't wake up."

They could hear the fear in Naomi's voice as she softly stroked the child's head. Peter went to the washstand and found a small bowl with pink water in it. He picked the bowl up, and looking at Maggie, smashed it over the man's head. He crumpled to the ground unconscious.

"Let's get her out of here."

Maggie sheathed her swords and helped Naomi gather the girl into her arms. Peter picked the man up and dumped him on the bed, when he moaned like he was going to wake up Peter punched him again. He locked the man to the bed using the cuffs that were placed at the head.

"Let's get out of here, indeed." Peter echoed, closing the door quietly, then turning to throw the deadbolt.

Chapter 34

The sights and sounds of the place were really starting to get to Maggie. *And the smells—don't forget about the smells: mildew, sewage, blood, rust, and death.* She mentally shook her head in disgust as they hurried through the nasty corridors. She was used to being in situations that required her to suck up whatever discomfort or fear she may be feeling for the sake of the mission or the story, but this was something entirely new and not at all welcome, because of the stakes and those involved.

She pushed it from her mind as they moved through the complex, listening to the drip of the rancid water from the rotting pipes. Peter, Maggie, and Naomi, who was cradling Sarah, made their way quickly and quietly up the hallway, back past all the sick and twisted fantasy rooms. They were nearly even with the doors to the storage rooms when one of the doors opened. Acting on pure adrenaline, Peter whispered Michael's name. The sword flashed brilliantly and expanded as he stepped into the path of the newcomer.

"Woah. It's just me." Joshua whispered, throwing his arms up.

Peter let out the breath he was holding with a whoosh.

"Man. You scared the living sh—" Peter started to exclaim.

"Joshua. Glad you're here," Maggie cut him off.

"Where have you been, anyway?" Peter asked him, pressing the symbol and whispering 'peace' to squelch the golden blade.

"I wanted to check out what is inside those rooms. I found plenty—enough to put these guys away for life. There is so much going on in those rooms. I could lock them away and forget they existed, if this wasn't a brood den," he told them.

"So what are you gonna do? Since you can't lock them up? Or, can you? Is there a nephilim prison that exists for things like this?" Peter asked him.

"Well, yes, there is, but no, I'm not going to use it in this instance. I'm going to blow it up, of course." Joshua told him with a grin. "But first, we have to get you guys out of here. Let's go."

They continued on towards the hallway Joshua and Peter came in from. When they hit the familiar fork in the tunnel, they stopped. They could hear shouting coming from the end of the hall where the light was the brightest. Joshua put his fingers to his lips and motioned for them to wait as he stepped lightly, continuing down the hallway. Peter and Maggie looked at each other.

"If he thinks he's leaving me behind again, he's wrong," Peter exclaimed. "Girls, the way out is down that tunnel. Look at the walls and you will find the marks that will lead you back to Abe." Naomi turned and started to walk the way Peter indicated and stopped to look back at Maggie.

"You comin' Maggie?" she asked her.

Indecision played across Maggie's face until she heard someone shouting in the distance. Maggie knew that voice almost as well as her own.

"Max?" Maggie looked back at Naomi. "I'm sorry, Naomi. Do you think you can find your way out?"

Naomi looked worried for a moment, looking down the dark tunnel and then back at her two friends.

She said to them, "I would rather go with you guys, I don't think splitting up in the darkness is a good idea. I've seen what happens in every horror movie, well—ever. I can't protect her alone right now."

She looked down at the child she held. Maggie's features softened.

"Okay Naomi, we will stay together. We only want to see what all the shouting is about, anyway."

They moved as a group to follow Joshua up the hall. When Joshua flattened himself against the wall and peered around the corner, they froze. The shouting was louder, confirming what

Maggie had already heard. Max was shouting at someone on the other side of the wall.

"Did you think I would not find out, Olivier? Do you think for a moment that I am an imbecile? I was given instructions for you to receive those girls at a certain time and place. They were delivered, and you and your lackeys lost them. Then you had the nerve to call my father and tell him that it was my fault they were lost? I should kill you where you stand."

Maggie sent a look to Joshua who had turned to look at them when they approached. They all retreated back into the tunnel, away from the commotion and out of earshot.

"Maggie, Max knows what he is doing. If you go in there, you will get him killed."

At her arched eyebrows Joshua smirked and said, "I could see it in your eyes, and I get it, believe me. You want to protect him, but you would only distract him. Let him do what he went in to do. He has as much riding on this as all of us."

Maggie thought about Joshua's words for a moment and nodded her ascent.

"Fine, but I'm staying. We all are, in case we are needed."

Joshua looked at Peter and then at Naomi.

"Naomi?"

"That's fine for you guys, but I can't go through the tunnels without someone. I can't fight and hold on to Sarah at the same time."

Joshua pulled out a small device that appeared to be a radio from his vest and whispered, "Abe? Come in, chief."

It crackled for a moment before they heard a reply. In a very different voice. "Copy, Joshua."

"Who is this? Identify yourself," Joshua hissed in a loud whisper.

"Sorry, sir. This is Vicky from the tunnels. Abe asked me to man the radio in case someone called while he is on the phone."

"Glad you made it out safe, Vicky. Please let Abe know we have Naomi and Sarah here. Ask him if he could venture into the tunnel and meet them. We need to stick around here for a few more minutes."

It was a moment before the radio squawked, this time with a much deeper, more recognizable voice.

"No problem. Send her down the tunnel and I will meet her. By the way, Momma Rose called just a moment ago and told me to tell you that the cavalry is on the way."

"Great news, Abe. Thanks for passing it along." Joshua said, smiling at the others. "Naomi, it's time to get you and Sarah out of here. Come on."

Joshua went past them to the start of the tunnel leading to Abe. "All you have to do is walk down this tunnel, and Abe will meet you in the middle. Take this."

He reached into another vest pocket and produced a small flashlight. It wasn't any bigger than a pencil, but when he turned it on, it brightly lit the tunnel. "There are arrows on the walls that show the correct direction."

Naomi took the flashlight from Joshua and turned to include Maggie and Peter when she said, "You all take care."

Without another look, she turned and strode off down the tunnel, her small flashlight bobbing as she walked with Sarah cradled in her arms.

"We need to get back and see what is happening with Max," Maggie said as she hurried back to the wall leading into the warehouse.

It seemed to Maggie that not a lot of progress had been made between Olivier and Max.

"What would make you stoop so low as to call my father and tell him that I failed you? It is not my fault that you lost the cargo—" Max was saying, Maggie could picture him running his hands through his hair.

Olivier interrupted, "I am not concerned with your petty family affairs. My only concern is the cargo that was promised to me. Someone stole my property."

It was very nearly a shout. He cleared his throat and started again. "Those girls are mine. No one steals what's mine, Mr. Avatov." He said in a much calmer voice.

"That is your affair, not mine. Hire better people. It is of no concern to me, but I will not have you pawning your failures off on me or my family like a coward. No one will believe your assertion that I had anything to do with your missing cargo, Olivier," Max said to him. "I was on my way back to Russia by way of Miami. You can check with the airlines if you so choose. I left Miami in the company of a friend for a trip back to Russia and to make sure that nothing bad happened to the antiquities that were purchased. My father was rather pleased with the antiquities. They were just what he was looking for. It is unfortunate you could not keep your... possessions, secure."

"I know what it is that I gave to you, Mr. Avatov," Mr. Olivier sneered, "but I was promised payment that—"

"Was delivered as promised."

It was Max's turn for a bit of bravado, and he pointed a commanding finger at the greasy man. He adjusted his tie slightly and took a half-step back, continuing to address the man in a calm, yet menacing voice.

"Those girls were in your possession. I cannot control what happens once the product leaves the airport. We went to great expense to bring those girls to you. I cannot help the incompetence of those around you."

Max is really enjoying himself, Maggie thought. He was playing the part of the lieutenant of a crime syndicate almost too well.

"I think that you could help it, Mr. Avatov. I believe that the person who took those girls from me had inside information on when they would be moved. That meant that only two people knew when those girls would come into my possession. You, Mr. Avatov, and that pilot of yours, Sam Ramos. You both knew when the girls would be moved from the airport."

Olivier was vibrating with anger and Maggie could tell that it was only a matter of time before he exploded. Max had done well baiting and stalling the man, but this could get dangerous very quickly.

Get out of there, Max. Wrap it up—he's going to snap.

"It wasn't a complete loss. I was able to recover one of the pieces. The little one, Sarah. The new owner was very appreciative when he was introduced to her last evening. I am afraid that he was not so gentle with her. I have a feeling that she will not make it to their destination if he does not control himself."

Olivier made a *tsking* sound and Maggie could see an already stoic Max turn into granite. She could tell that he was itching to pound the man into so much dust.

Joshua heard the static on his radio that told him that someone was trying to get ahold of him.

"Joshua. Sit rep," came Abe's voice.

"Go," Joshua said into the radio.

"Where's Naomi?" Abe asked.

Joshua was suddenly struck with panic.

"Abe, Naomi should have met you by now. Are you sure that you are in the right tunnel? Look at the walls and tell me if you see some arrows?"

"I do see some arrows near the top of the wall. Are they what you are talking about?" Abe asked. A few seconds later he said, "I see a light up ahead." A few seconds later, "I found a small penlight, I don't see the girls, though."

"Okay Abe, we will find her and Sarah." Joshua made motions with his hands to move the others back toward the tunnels. Maggie shook her head and took two fingers pointed them toward her eyes and then at Max and Olivier. Joshua nodded ascent, and he and Peter moved back further into the tunnel.

"We have to find them," Peter said.

He was looking around frantically as if hoping that he would spot them in the corridor.

"I know, Peter, and we will."

They started to move off down the tunnel when a soft cry reached their ears. They rushed back to Maggie's side and immediately knew the reason that she had cried out. A large man was leading a roughed-up version of Naomi and was being followed by another man who carried the small form of Sarah. Peter could tell that Sarah was not faring well and really needed to be seen by a doctor. Her face was wan and pale, and she was unresponsive to the happenings around her.

Naomi looked like she would love to beat the men to a bloody pulp, but her hands had been pulled and tied tightly behind her back. Peter watched as the man leading her stopped in front of Olivier.

"We found *this one*," he punctuated *this one* by kicking Naomi behind the knee, dropping her hard to the concrete warehouse floor, "in the tunnels trying to take the girl away."

"Did you check the tunnels to see if there was anyone else present?" Olivier asked him. The big man looked sheepish for a moment, his grand display crushed by his lack of follow up.

"No sir, we thought only of bringing them to you."

Olivier's eyes glowed a deep red with his anger. He backhanded the larger man who had physically diminished until he was almost doubled over, cowering in front of the smaller man.

"We are sorry, sir. Please forgive us. We will remedy that right away, sir."

Peter shivered at the picture and prayed that the cavalry showed up soon. Their most immediate worry was that the two goons, having laid Sarah down on the cold and dirty warehouse floor, were moving in their direction. Joshua grabbed Peter and Maggie by the arms and pulled them deeper into the shadows and prayed that they would not be seen.

The two goons, desperate to get away from Olivier's wrath, moved past them without a backwards glance. Joshua pulled out his radio and let Abe know that they had found Naomi, and that the two that passed them would be moving in his direction.

"What are we going to do now?" Peter asked him.

"Nothing for it, I'm afraid. Now we wait for the cavalry. If we try anything else, we will be putting them all in danger."

Joshua, clearly agitated, wiped the sweat from his forehead, checked his phone impulsively as if hoping for some good news, and angrily jammed it back in his pocket when there wasn't any. He pressed his back against the darkened corridor wall where they huddled trying to stay out of sight, and slumped down to wait it out.

"Oh, and, you two?" he said quietly, addressing Maggie and Peter, "It may not hurt to pray."

Chapter 35

Late afternoon had settled on the stagnant river as it languished motionless in the fall sun. Seeing it now, no one would guess it once a lively thoroughfare. It sat as dead and wasted as the land surrounding it—a murky clump of storage buildings and dilapidated storefronts. Inside, a large young man was very angry. Max watched the two women being led into the room, and he seethed under his unaffected exterior.

Naomi looked a little worse for the experience, and Max inwardly winced when the man leading her kicked her in the back of the knees causing her to lose her balance. She fell on her knees with a moan and just managed to regain her balance before falling forward. The large man grinned at her discomfort and puffed out his chest as he said, "We found this one in the tunnels trying to take the girl away." Max saw Olivier's eyes start to glow, a faint red started to show in their inky depths.

"Did you check the tunnels to see if anyone else was present?" he asked them. Max could tell that he had not, and Olivier knew it. He was toying with the larger man. He watched as the large man almost threw himself to the floor begging Olivier to forgive him. Olivier's eyes glowed a bright red now, and Max could see the glint from his large canine teeth when he smiled at the man's discomfort.

Max didn't scare easily, living with his father all his life had made him expect the unexpected, and the beatings he took as a child gave him a hard exterior, but this was new to Max, and he was having a hard time not being afraid of what this creature may do. If there was one thing that Max was good at, though, it was hiding his feelings. He waited for the exchange to play out wearing, what he hoped, was a slightly annoyed, yet disaffected, air. Olivier watched as the second man put the child on the floor and scurried away with his partner.

Olivier went up to Naomi and reached out a hand to touch her face. Max watched in admiration as Naomi made to bite Olivier's hand. Olivier reacted swiftly, he raised his hand and backhanded her across the face splitting her lip open in the process.

"You sought to take her, girl?" he shouted to no one but the air in front of him. "Why does everyone want to steal what's mine?"

From the floor, Naomi struggled to get into a position to face Olivier. She spat the blood from her mouth before saying, "You know, you aren't the first person to say that to me tonight. The monster you sold her to was just as idiotic as you are."

Olivier smiled, "What did you do with him?"

The question was asked with more curiosity than concern. Naomi finally wiggled herself into a sitting position.

"I knocked him out and left him chained up."

Naomi looked worriedly at Sarah, who was barely breathing. Time was running out for her, and Naomi would never forgive herself if she didn't make it out of this alive.

"Hmm, I wonder why you didn't kill him?" Olivier said. "I would have."

"I'm not you. I'm not a..." Naomi thought of how satisfying it would be in that moment to let Olivier know that they knew who, *what*, he is, and that she wasn't scared of him. She had to check herself briefly to be sure, but no, she wasn't afraid.

She was angry and outraged and frightened for Sarah's health, but she did not fear the thing that stood in front of her. She smirked, bloody lip and all, and sneered at the oily man.

"I think I'll wait on the fed's to show up. They'll be here any moment now."

Naomi smiled a cold smile. Olivier's eyes glowed red again, and Max felt he had to step in before the events got out of hand.

"What is she talking about, Olivier? Who has called the authorities?"

Olivier spun around, animalian, almost feral, before he regained his composure with the large man. There was a noticeable red that receded from his irises.

So, Max thought, *I am guessing they can control their appearance and bloodlust at will? I will have to ask my aunt about this.*

Olivier smiled a thin smile and spoke quietly and without haste.

"Don't worry about this. There is no threat of police presence."

"Good," said Max. "My father would not like his name attached to any kind of scandal. Our organization does not tolerate failure of any sort. What are you going to do with that one?" He indicated Naomi casually. "I do not really care, but she is dark-skinned and attractive. Exotic-looking women are rare, and I know I could find a buyer for her in Russia," Max said smoothly.

Olivier's eyebrows rose.

"I shouldn't be surprised that you know of people who deal in humans, but this one I have plans for. She will make a fine playmate for me, I think. I want to see if I can break that spirit of hers."

Olivier once again reached for Naomi's face and before she could bite him, he had grabbed her face in a crushing grip. Naomi cried out in pain in her head, but let nothing escape her lips. Tears rolled down her face, but she wouldn't give the vampire the satisfaction of hearing even a whimper.

Max was just about to intervene when he heard a deep voice say, "Let her go, Olivier."

Max looked over his shoulder and saw Sam standing by the door. At least, he thought it was Sam. If it was Sam, he was very different in a way that Max couldn't put his finger on.

"Ah yes, the chatty pilot," Olivier said, "I would not have expected you to show your face here."

"Why not? I *love* a party."

Sam closed the distance between him and Max in a few strides and spoke to the now preoccupied vampire.

"You're stupid, Olivier. I have to tell you, you have made yourself some powerful enemies." Sam grinned. "I hope that you have the cojones to deal with the consequences."

Olivier let go of Naomi's face and moved to stand before Sarah, blocking her from Sam's view.

"I have all I need to deal with you and anyone else who cares to try me. You have no idea who you are dealing with."

Max could see the fire in his eyes light up once again.

It's finally happened, Naomi thought absurdly, and she laughed to herself. *I'm in a comic book.* She started to convulse with laughter, which puzzled Max and Sam, and infuriated Olivier.

"*What* is so funny, girl?" Olivier turned and bent to hold his face inches from Naomi's, which was still laughing.

"Ahh, I can't stop. I'll tell you guys about it later—you're gonna die."

Naomi addressed the two men across from the one who was dangerously close to doing her real damage, plaything or not. No one laughed at him. Sam's voice cut in.

"Olivier, it's over. You will let Naomi take Sarah out of here now, or else." Sam said standing his ground.

The vampire, forgetting Naomi and Sarah for a moment to deal with the new, bold challenger, sneered in his arrogance, and almost laughed.

"Are you kidding me? Coming into my domain and making demands, and worse, threats? Here's what's going to happen: the girls stay here, and I eat your liver while you watch. *Or else.* That is what a real *or else* looks like, Mr. Ramos. See, it doesn't matter how powerful your friends are, they are no match for me. I have powerful friends of my own. No human will ever defeat me, I have been around for centuries." Olivier boasted. "It would take an army to bring me down. Truth is, over the centuries, armies have tried—and failed. You had better be more powerful than the army at my disposal."

He snapped his fingers and, from the shadows, emerged at least a hundred men all with glowing eyes and snarling faces. Each one was poised as if to attack on command.

Sam grinned again. It was the grin of a man begging to be tested. Max was transfixed for a moment, but then remembered the girls. Naomi was silently trying to move closer to Sarah who lay unmoving on the floor.

"It's funny you should mention an army, vampire. That's exactly what I brought—and they're better than yours. A lot better."

In that moment Max was swept up in a tide of light and figures. They moved with uncommon grace and agility. Each figure held a mighty, glowing sword or other weapon, and like waves breaking on the shore, they swept the room. Max saw only bright flashes of light and heard the screams as the first wave of the corrupted minions fell or was in the process of falling. The second wave entered, ready to battle for supremacy and survival.

"No," Olivier screamed. "How is it that the Host know we are here?"

He turned a full circle watching as his army was annihilated. He turned, and in a rage flew at Sam. "I will kill you for this. I have spent centuries. How? How is it that you have access to the host? You must be with ARC."

Max blinked. The scene blurred, and Olivier was locked in a struggle with Sam, his red eyes glowing and his fangs bared. His face had contorted into the stuff of horrors, and he no longer even closely resembled a man. His skin had scabbed over completely with blackened and rust colored scales. His eyes became redder and more bulbous. Anyone watching this morphing take place may mistake that the man was becoming...

A dragon? No, Max thought as he watched. *Nothing serpentine about him really. Just a lot of ugly.*

Sam grabbed Olivier as if he were nothing and sent him into the nearest pile of crates. Olivier flipped at the last moment, landing lightly with his feet planted on the side of the crate. He pushed off the crate and launched himself back in Sam's direction like a missile, almost flying. The move caught Sam unaware, and he found Olivier sitting on top of him grinning an evil, grotesque grin. Max heard laughter and turned to see another man walking towards Olivier and Sam.

"Come on, Sam. Don't tell me you've forgotten how to fight."

The man plucked Olivier off of Sam. He fetched him up by the neck and turned him, face-to-grotesque-face.

"Excuse us for a minute," and sent him flying again.

"Hey. It's been a while, right?"

He hopped up and quickly surveyed himself, brushing his shirt off.

"Give me a break, Michael. I'm out of practice."

Michael slapped him on the back and laughed again while the battle raged around them.

Max saw what both men had failed to notice in their banter—Olivier had pulled himself up off the floor and, seeing his minions engaged with the hosts and no help anywhere to be found, resorted to using hostages. He pushed Naomi aside and snatched Sarah off the floor.

He stood with little Sarah held in front of him and said to the two men, "It would be a shame if something else happened to this little angel today. She's already been through so much."

No, Naomi thought. She frantically scooted around and moved until she was right next to Olivier's leg. *This is going to be disgusting*, she thought. Michael and Sam had turned in their direction, both of them wore the same expression. Olivier had the upper hand and he knew it. Max had never seen the hard expression that had crossed his friend's face.

"I would be very careful in your next move, vampire," Sam warned him. Sarah chose that moment to weakly open her eyes. Blue eyes full of pain looked directly at Sam.

"You're here. He told me..."

Olivier looked down at her, "Quiet girl." He gave her a shake as if this would keep her mouth from speaking. Max moved so that he was positioned behind Olivier and Naomi. He saw Maggie, Peter, and Joshua sneak in from the back. He stood, amazed, as Maggie silently took down two vampires from behind. Deciding he would be of more use helping Peter and Joshua, and wanting to protect Maggie, he started to move in that direction until he heard a yell from Olivier and looked around to see Naomi, whose hands were still tied behind her back, biting the Olivier-creature on the leg.

Olivier looked down towards her, shrieked, and kicked Naomi hard, sending her flying backward into a stack of crates. Max heard the crack as she hit and lay unmoving. He changed direction and moved to were Naomi lay still and quiet. He leaned over her and felt for a pulse. He found one, albeit weak, and let out a sigh. He ran his hand down the back of her head and felt a nice size bump on the back of her head, and when he pulled his hand away it came away sticky telling him that she was bleeding. Her head fell back until it rested against his arm as he scooped her up and, without another thought, took her with him to find Maggie and the others.

"Olivier, like I said before—it's over. You need to put the girl down now."

Sam's tone had grown deadly. Max looked back over his shoulder at one of the few people on this Earth he called friend. He found himself mesmerized at the look on Sam's face. He could swear that Sam's eyes were aflame, and that his friend was glowing faintly. He shook his head and continued to where he last saw Maggie, Peter, and Joshua.

"She is a transmitter, isn't she?" Olivier stared down at the child in his arms. "Who told you he would come, girl?" he asked her, giving her another shake. Sarah turned her head towards Olivier.

"The Master."

This caused Michael and Sam to look at each other and then back at Sarah who was still looking at Olivier, blank-faced. They could only just hear what she was saying over the din of the battle taking place around them. Every so often, one of them or both would have to fend of one of Olivier's minions, but they were swiftly dealt with before they would turn their attention back to Olivier and Sarah.

"So, I now hold something that is important to *the Master*? Oh, this *is* my lucky day. You boys may want to take a *big* step back." Olivier bared his fangs. The threat was understood.

Michael and Sam took a step back, and Olivier thought he had them on the ropes. Michael squashed that thought with one statement. "We didn't step back for you. The fallout from your disobedience and blasphemy will be great. Are you willing to accept that?"

Olivier, who thought that he had the drop on the two men looked unsure.

"I have the transmitter, archangel. I know that you want her, you will do as I say."

Michael looked at Sarah and then at Olivier. He smiled and stood casually observing the vampire.

"Are you that stupid?" Michael smiled wide.

Olivier looked from Sam to Michael.

"Nothing is going to happen to me as long as I have this little brat in my hands. I can think of a number of people that would pay to have her, much more than my amorous friend from yesterday, especially now..."

Sam made as if to move against Olivier, but stopped as he noticed that Olivier was transforming beyond scales and red eyes now. His body was changing its shape, growing longer and leaner with every second that passed. His hands became bony, gnarled, and elongated claws with razor sharp tips, and he now stood a good three feet taller, towering over them. The tips of the claws sank into Sarah's skin.

She didn't let out a sound or move an inch. Olivier, puzzled, took a grip on one of her ankles and dangled her in front of his grotesque face. The thing spoke to the girl suspended limply by one foot.

"*Sarah*?" He shook her hard and repeated, "*Sarah? Sarah.*" The vampire let out a sigh, and said, "*Well, boys.*" he shrugged his massive shoulders. "*It appears something unexpected has occurred. I've lost my leverage.*"

At the end of his speech he launched Sarah into the air and everyone in the room froze watching the child spin through space like a ragdoll.

Peter, Joshua, Maggie, and Max, still holding an unconscious Naomi, watched with stricken expressions as the little girl came down—to land gently in the arms of Samael. He, too, had changed and now stood at least twelve feet high, his black wings flared out behind him like a massive shield.

Peter who had seen Sam in action previously, said to the others, "Don't look at his face. Come on. We have to get out of here." Peter grabbed Max by the shoulder and turned the gaping giant around. Maggie had watched everything play out to its horrific end, and she was stunned. Vaguely, she could feel someone tugging at her, but she couldn't hear anything but the blood pounding in her head. These monsters would pay for what had happened, and it would be now. She shook off the hand, unsheathing her katanas.

"*No,*" Maggie shrieked. "No. I'm not leaving her here. We can't leave her here." Maggie took a step toward the fray—toward the master vampire, toward the archangel, toward the little dead girl, and away from the man she loved. Max shouldered Naomi briefly and took Maggie in a firm, sympathetic embrace.

Peter looked sadly back to the limp form, barely visible in Sam's huge arms, and said to her, "She's fine now, Mags. They can't hurt her anymore—she's beyond them all."

Maggie let out a loud, quaking sob, dropping the weapons from her grasp and covered her mouth with her hand. She crumpled against Max and Naomi, weeping bitterly.

Max shifted Naomi back to his arms and said to Maggie.

"We must go now, love. We cannot stay here."

Max prompted her to turn around, gestured for her to grab her discarded swords, and once in front of him, he physically pushed her using Naomi as a type of gentle battering ram. Peter was the last one from the room, and as he went through the doorway that led upstairs, he chanced a glance back into the warehouse. He saw

Michael standing in front of Sam who still had Sarah's broken body cradled in his arms.

He heard the angel say in a deep voice, "Eternity with the Master is yours, Sarah. Be at peace."

Olivier, who was standing on the other side of the warehouse near the entrance to the tunnels, shrieked briefly before disappearing.

Peter made as if to rush after him until he heard Michael say, "Peter. Sam will unleash his wrath in a matter of moments. *Get out.*"

Peter had put up his hand to shield his eyes from the bright light that Sam had started to emit. He nodded to Michael and sprinted through the door to find the others.

Chapter 36

Peter caught up with the others quickly and told them what Michael had said.

"How long do we have?" asked Joshua.

"I'm not sure, but I don't think it will be much longer. The light he was emitting was enough that I could count the bones in my hand," Peter cried. "We need to get out of here, fast. I don't think we will make the front door. Any Ideas?"

Joshua thought for a moment and said, "Well, I have one, but we can't take Naomi like that." He pointed to Naomi who had not yet regained consciousness.

"I believe I can help with that." Peter recognized the voice immediately, and he whirled around to face its owner.

"Dr. Jo.? What the hell are you doing here?"

She smiled curtly in his direction and said, "I know, Peter. Later. I promise to hash this all out later. I am glad to see you unharmed.

Peter looked confused and wary, and his thoughts turned to betrayal. He quietly invoked Michael's name and his sword blazed to life in front of him, ready to protect the others.

"It's okay, Peter. I am not with Olivier—I'm with Michael," she told him with a wink. "Please, step aside. I have work to do."

A brilliant second later Peter and the rest of their group saw a transformed Jophiel. Peter had never seen anyone or anything so beautiful and pure. If he had to describe what he saw, he would have said it was all softness and light—the softest, most comforting light he'd ever seen. He felt completely calm and enveloped by spring as a soothing pulse of pure orange-yellow, the color of citrine, shone all around.

"I am here to help your friend."

She walked over to Max who offered access to the young woman he was carrying without hesitation, a concerned look in his eyes.

"It's okay, Max. She is going to be just fine."

Max held out Naomi to Jo, and Peter was amazed when she started to glow more brightly as she gently caressed Naomi's head in her hands. In what seemed like only a moment, Naomi sucked in a sharp breath and began to cry, then to sob, shaking in the large man's arms. Peter started towards her to lend comfort, but Jophiel backed him off gently.

"That's not necessary, Peter. Healing manifests itself in many ways. Let this play out and pass. Trust me."

The girl continued to cry, though less harshly, and then finally her whimpering subsided. Jophiel reached out with her thumbs and wiped away the tears from the girl's eyes and stepped back. Naomi flicked her eyes open and smiled at the being who had just touched her.

"Thank you," was all she said, but Peter could tell the words were dear and held unspoken understanding between them.

Jo nodded.

Max lowered Naomi so she was standing on the floor.

"Can you walk?"

She turned to Max wordlessly and gave him a warm hug that lasted uncomfortably long for the stoic Russian.

She squeezed him one more time and whispered, "You are just as much of an angel to me as she is. I will never forget what you did for me."

Naomi let go of Max, turned to face the group with a deep breath and, smoothing her hair back from her face, smiled and said, "I think I could run if I needed to."

"You need to," said Jophiel. "You all do. And, if I were you, I would go that way." She pointed them to the hallway on the left and added, "I hope you know how to swim."

She ran off in the direction of Michael and Sam.

"Wow." said Peter, looking after her. "We are going to have a lot to talk about in our next session. Come on."

"Wait," cried Max, "Where is Maggie?" Peter looked at the others questioningly and saw blank looks all around.

"She was just here a moment ago. You guys go on ahead and I will look for her." Peter said.

"No," Max told him. "I will stay and look for her. I have been here before and am more familiar with this place."

Peter and Joshua nodded at him, and Peter said, "Be quick, Max. I don't know how much time is left."

Max watched the trio make their way in the direction Jo had pointed, then he turned and went down the right hand hallway. He traveled quietly and peered into the rooms along the corridor as he went. Panic started to well in him, insidious and silent. *They have her and you will never see her again.* The voice hammered at his head and his heart, and he quickened his already fleet steps. He was now running from room to room. *Why are there so many damn rooms in this place?* he thought.

He reached the last door along the hallway, all the others had been standing open as he passed except this one. He opened the door a crack and peered inside. The room was large with a massive oaken desk. Behind the desk looking through a stack of papers was Maggie. He walked into the room and Maggie looked up in fright.

"Oh, Max. You nearly scared me to death." She put a hand to her heart and grinned at him sheepishly. "I couldn't help myself, Max. I had to take the opportunity to find something on Olivier."

Max closed the space between them abruptly, and he walked around the desk. He kissed her firmly, yet briefly, swatted her on the behind, grabbed her small hand in his massive one, and said, "We are going."

As he turned to leave, she resisted, so he picked her up and slung her over his broad shoulder.

"Not a request," he said, making his way back around the desk.

"Max," Maggie yelled making a grab for anything on the desk

she could reach, "Put me down. The papers in this office could be important."

She beat on his back as he walked toward the open door.

"Maggie, you are more important than any papers, and we must get out of here now. Jophiel says we have no more time," Max told her, running for the hallway.

"Um—who?" Maggie questioned, having been absent for their encounter with another of the host.

"I am certain you will meet soon. No more questions."

He moved swiftly down the hallway, past the open doors and, as he came to the staircase, three vampires stepped into view. Max pulled Maggie from his shoulder and set her carefully in front of him.

"Maxim Avatov, if you ever manhandle me like that again..." She let the threat die off as he turned her to face their new threat.

Maggie went to grab her katanas and looked over at Max, her face fearful.

"My swords are in the office, Max. I set them down to snoop."

Max winced and stepped in front of Maggie, pushing her behind him.

"Look what we have here, boys," said the largest of the three. "Dinner," he said, sizing up Max, "and a show."

The creature's eyes devoured Maggie, and she took a step back. The other two snickered at the joke and closed in on Maggie and Max. A flash of light and a squeal and the head vampire looked down at his middle to see a flaming sword protruding from his stomach. The sword was swiftly removed, and the unlucky vampire exploded in a pyrotechnic display of light. The other two vampires reacted swiftly turning around to face the new threat. Behind them stood one of the battle angels looking for stragglers and strays from the earlier confrontation. The vampires circled around the angel who stood looking calmly at his foe.

"You killed my brother. You will pay, fledgling," The vampire cried.

He snarled and sprang at the angel, knocking him backwards into the stair railing. The other vampire took advantage of the situation and landed a blow of his own. He hit with one hand and followed the blow with a rake of his razor-sharp nails with the other hand. The angel screamed and dropped his sword. Max instinctively grabbed for the weapon to help the outnumbered angel.

Pain. When his hand came into contact with the sword, it started to burn immediately, white hot and unbearable. He sucked in a breath and then bellowed, but instead of dropping the sword, he swung out against the closest vampire who lost an arm, much to his surprise. He was even more surprised when he lost his balance and fell over the edge of the railing. Max saw him turn to dust which littered the stairway below.

The angel who was fighting against the last vampire was trying valiantly to remove the creature's hands from his throat. He finally succeeded in pushing the vampire back only to cry out sharply when the creature turned and quickly sank his long teeth into the side of his neck. A mixture of pain and horror came over the angel's face before a blinding light lit the area. The vampire screamed and covered his eyes with his hands as he stumbled backward into the sword that Max held gripped in his hand. When Max's vision cleared he saw that the vampire and the angel had disappeared as if they never existed.

Max tried to rid himself of the sword clutched in his hand but found that it had seared itself to him, as if it were surgically attached. The pain was intense; Max had never known its like, but he knew they didn't have any time left to wait around. He grabbed Maggie's hand, and pulling her with him, ran down towards the other end of the hall. They were almost free of the building, when another figure came out of the darkness. Max stopped dead and held the sword out in front of him. As he got a good look at the figure he noticed that he, too, held a the fiery weapon of an angel and, although he wasn't much bigger than Max, the sword he held was twice as long.

"You need to leave now," the figure said, then looked down at the sword Max held. "Where did you get that?" The question was asked casually but Max could tell that the answer was vital to the man in front of him. Maggie answered for him.

"He picked it up when one of the others came to help us with three vampires. I'm sorry, but I don't think he made it."

Maggie looked truly upset at the thought that the guardian was gone. The figure winced and reached slowly forward, Max held the sword out to him and the man turned Max's hand, which was still attached to the sword, around so he could inspect the damage.

"There are not many mortals who can hold a holy weapon. You must have been trying to protect someone very special."

He glanced at Maggie then back to Max. He covered Max's hand with his own larger hand, and in the blink of an eye removed the sword from his grip. The pain that Max had expected at the removal never materialized. He stared in wonder at his palm. Where Max had expected to see burns and mutilated flesh, there was what looked like a scar.

No burn scarred that fast, especially not one as intense as what he had just experienced. Max was incredulous, but as he inspected it closer he found what looked like a coin that had been seared into his skin. He felt no pain, but he knew that the coin, or medallion, whatever it was, would be with him always.

He looked up at the man and said, "Thank you…"

Max did not know his name and realizing this the stranger said, "Uriel, my name is Uriel. Now, quickly. You must go. There is no more time."

With those words came a mighty sound from below. The upper level shook like an explosion and earthquake had collided, and the force knocked the couple off balance. Uriel turned and fled down the hallway to the stairs. They watched as he disappeared below. The building was rocked again, and Max knew at any moment they would be buried and smashed under tons of decaying rubble. He swept Maggie up and flung her over his shoulder again and ran towards the window to freedom.

"Max, I can run. Put me down," yelled Maggie.

"No time."

Max reached the window as another shockwave hit the building. He flew forward as he lost his balance and pushed Maggie out of the window. She screamed as she fell down until her scream was cut off by the water below. Max tried to move but his leg wouldn't budge. His foot had fallen through a hole in the floor that was made by that last explosion. He tried pulling on his pants but the small space created wasn't large enough to get his foot out of the hole. He was trapped, and if he didn't untrap himself, he was going to go down with this disaster. Finding no other alternative, Max started to untie his boot, he was in the process of pulling out his foot when he heard Maggie screaming from the window outside.

He stood for a moment to let her know that he was coming, he was able to see her treading water and knew that she was safe. He smiled to know that she had made it outside safely, forgetting for a split-second his own predicament.

He heard it before it happened—the strange silence, followed by a hiss. The explosion sent him through the window. Part of the wall that held the window onto the building was falling with him and another part was behind him. His last thought before hitting the dark waters below was of Maggie.

Chapter 37

The news followed the story of the warehouse fire for weeks, Peter had grown tired of the coverage, the questions, and the interviews. He only wanted to get on with life and to mourn the losses. They were able to save Max from the water only to lose him in the hospital. He wasn't particularly close to Max, but when you go through what they went through, all of them, well, they were all forever connected.

Peter wasn't sorrowful, though. He was angry, almost to the point of vengeful fury.

It wasn't fair. It wasn't just or right, either, he thought.

Olivier, the master vampire, or whatever he was, had escaped. He had gotten away, and Max was dead. Max, who had done so much for so many in their short time together as a family.

*Family? Yea*h, Peter thought. *That's what it feels like... family. Max, Maggie, Margueritte, Naomi, Abe, Joshua... they were all now a part of him, forever. But Max... it just shouldn't have been Max.*

The ultimate price paid by the one who least deserved to pay it. Peter paced back and forth in his office, mulling over the events of the night. He remembered Michael telling him to get everyone out. He had witnessed Sam go all Super-Saiyan before rushing from the room. He remembered that Joshua had told him he had planted explosives in the rooms and in the tunnel, and the only thing he could figure is that when Sam finally exploded with power, he took the bombs with him.

He hoped they were okay. He hadn't heard anything from Michael or Sam since then, but angel business was not his business. He was sure they would turn up before too long. It seemed that they, too, were inextricably involved in whatever was going to happen going forward.

Momma Rose had told him they were fine, but she hadn't been herself since they found out about Max. Margueritte's demeanor was different as well, but not in the same way. She has been throwing all her efforts into helping ARC find out what Lev Avatov has been doing since his only son died.

Peter opened the large French door, and stepped out into the sweaty evening to survey Governor Nichols below. The lives of the folks that passed, laughing, drinking, and holding hands had not been indelibly marked or even changed in any way by the events that had taken place recently, and he hated them for it. He wished, more than ever, to be one of the blissfully ignorant partygoers that ambled down Bourbon Street, selfish and unaware of anything but their own debaucherous goals for the night.

He sighed and placed his hands on the wrought iron, still warm from the afternoon, and thought. Maggie was on his mind presently. She was so distraught over losing Max that the doctors had to sedate her and keep her for observation the day after he passed in his hospital bed.

It was all too much for her, he thought sadly. She had split town a couple of days ago. He knew that she had spoken briefly with Margueritte before leaving town. Her *LACE* magazine had published an article that she had submitted telling the world of the illegal activities that Lev Avatov had been involved in. She made sure that the world knew of the girls he had kidnapped and trafficked.

The Russian police raided the Avatov compound and found enough evidence to seize his property, but ARC operatives had informed their contingent in New Orleans that the underground lab and all of the genetic testing evidence had been either moved or destroyed. As far as Peter knew, they did not find the naga that Max and Maggie had found, but Max did say those tunnels stretched for miles. They could literally be anywhere.

He had thought about asking Abe if he would fly him up to

see Maggie, but he felt that maybe she preferred to be alone now. Peter surveyed the horizon as the sun sank low and melted against the Quarter's skyline. He sighed heavily, then turned and headed back into his living room, closing the door on the sunset.

He felt sure that when she was ready, she would return. ARC needed her for what they were going to be attempting, so he felt that he hadn't seen the last of her. *Especially now, she has just as much skin in this game as anyone.*

Peter's phone started singing *Where No Man Has Gone Before*, what the non-nerd collective knew as the theme to *Star Trek*, and he jumped. He had been so wrapped up in his thoughts he had forgotten that the world had gone on existing.

He walked over and picked up his cell phone from the table. Naomi was calling him. He hadn't stopped thinking about her, and he excitedly answered, "Hey, Naomi."

"Peter…" came Naomi's voice from the other end of the phone, and she didn't sound good. She sounded like she had been crying and there was an exhaustion there that made Peter instantly want to comfort her.

"What is it, Naomi? What's wrong?" he asked, softly.

She probably had a fight with Darius and she needs some cheering up, he thought. No, she wouldn't ever talk to him about something as mundane as guy problems. It has to be something else.

A deep, shuddering breath and then, "I called to tell you that my uncle…" She started sobbing on the other end of the phone. Peter was worried now.

"What about your uncle? Naomi, what about Abe? Is he okay? What's going on? Naomi, talk to me," Peter almost screamed into the phone. Naomi hiccupped into the phone as her crying jag subsided some.

"He passed last night. He's gone, Peter."

Peter almost missed the chair as his legs gave out from under him. He sat down hard, taking the blow just like it were a physical punch to his stomach.

He ran his hand through his hair roughly and in disbelief said, "What? How? He was fine when I talked to him yesterday."

He heard the sniffles through the phone that told him that she was still crying.

"He died in his sleep, Peter. They tell me it was a heart attack, that he was in poor health. That's bullshit, Peter. You know it is," she said with a conviction that told Peter that there was more to the story.

"So, what happened, really?" he asked her.

"I found his window open. My uncle would never have left the window open. He hated the smell of that river at night, and especially not after finding out about those creatures who kidnapped Sarah. The windows into his loft apartment were wide open. When I looked outside the walls had scratches in them. Claw marks, Peter. Those things were in my uncle's house." She started crying again. "And they killed him."

The thought of having those creatures crawling through Abe's home was horrible. Peter shivered at the thought of the grunch pawing through his hanger.

"But why? Why your uncle?" Peter asked her.

"I don't know. A message, maybe? I think they were trying to send a message," she said in earnest.

"But how do you know they did anything to your uncle? Those claw marks could have been from before, when they got Sarah."

He wasn't trying to get her stirred up, but it seemed to Peter as if she was trying to find some hidden meaning behind Abe's death.

"I'm not crazy, Peter. I know what it seems like—Aw, poor Naomi can't deal. Those things were in his house. *In his damn room.* I heard the EMT's talking about how creepy it was, they said the word 'exsanguination.' Do you know what that means? I had to look it up later, but it means that there was no blood in his body, Peter. They told me heart attack, but it was more like heart failure from lack of blood."

At this point Naomi was nearly hysterical, and Peter was at a loss for how to help her.

"Peter?" Naomi said snapping him out of his stupor.

"Do you need me to come over, or do you want to come over here? Momma Rose may be able to help," Peter told her.

"I'll come over there. I don't think I can be by myself right now. Would you go to my uncle's with me later?"

"Sure," he said.

Silence, then more crying. She eventually calmed and they talked a little more. He laughed weakly and said, "Hey, just sit tight, okay? I'm going to come get you and bring you back here. Pack some things and you can hang out here for a few days. I don't want you being by yourself."

"Thanks. You're sweet. I'll see you in a few," she said, and hung up.

Peter's emotions were in turmoil, and he wasn't sure how to deal with this new incident. He fidgeted briefly and then stood impatiently. He was upset and was looking for answers. He shoved his hands in his pockets and out of his right pocket he pulled the little golden teardrop that was given to him. He fingered the sigil on front of the teardrop.

"Michael, I don't need a sword right now. I need a friend. If you are able to hear me, I really need to speak with you." He waited a few moments and then shoved the teardrop back into his pocket. *That's stupid,* he thought. *He probably can't even hear me at this point.*

"Of course, I can," said Michael.

"Stop doing that. You almost gave me a stroke."

Peter sat down hard in his chair, staring at the angel who was his dear friend. Today, Peter noticed, he was wearing flip-flops, a pair of jeans with the knees ripped out, and an anime t-shirt with what looked like an angel with a flaming sword that was as tall as the angel who was holding it.

"If that's true, then why haven't you answered me before now?" Peter asked him, the hurt in his voice evident. "There have been many times that I have asked for help and I never saw you once."

Michael smiled and spread his hands out in front of him, gesturing to the young man.

"Dude, I'm always available, and I will always be here for you, but it may not be in person. You have to understand that. I may not always be present, Peter, but I always sent you help. You asked for help with the grunch—we sent you Joshua. You asked for help with Tammy and—well, you really didn't need me then." Michael laughed and said, "And speaking of Sam, what did you think when you saw him taking on Olivier, huh? That was really something."

"It was something, all right. We'll get back to that."

Michael continued, "You asked for help in the warehouse and we sent the host to help you. We have *always* been there for you, even if you can't see it. Brother, I told you when you were a kid and it's still true today—you and I are in this together. I'm not leaving you. None of us are."

Peter, mollified, relaxed for a minute. He took a deep breath and finally asked what was really on his mind.

"Why did they have to die?"

Michael looked sad and said, "I know, man. I'm sad, too. Abe was—unexpected. He was supposed to go later."

Peter looked at Michael, feeling his grief, and Michael reached out a hand and placed it on his shoulder.

"It is not a loss, Peter. He will be with us. He has been placed in another job for now."

Then Michael surprised Peter by saying, "Who is they? Abe is gone from this world, but he'll be on assignment for us. Did someone else die?"

"You don't know? How is that possible? *Max.* Michael, he died in the hospital. Why did he have to die, too?"

Michael smiled, his blond eyebrows raised in surprise.

"Max isn't dead. Would I lie? Totally not dead, Peter. He is, however… um… changed," Michael said cryptically. "Nope," Michael held up a hand forestalling any further questions. "I can't tell you anything further. What was done was done for a reason and, although it hurts to see your friends go, know that they had a purpose. Now there is still work to be done, my man. You will get a chance to help us work to rid the world of those who should not be in it. Are you still willing to help?"

Michael waited while Peter mulled over his response.

"I am willing to do whatever it takes to help out ARC, Michael, but I'm not sure I accomplished the task you originally gave me. I haven't seen Sam since he blew up the warehouse."

Michael barked a laugh.

"Yeah, he sort of imploded, didn't he? He was *mad*."

He wiped tears of mirth from his eyes and laid a hand on Peter's shoulder.

"I tasked you with getting Sam to remember who he was. He needed to remember, and I was not allowed to tell him. He had to choose to remember everything and accept that his actions, while well intentioned, were not in accordance with the Master's will for him. Sam has chosen to fight against the very thing he tried to protect for so long. His redemption is just one step in the right direction."

"I'm not sure I understand?"

Peter felt like there was a bigger picture that he was not seeing.

"Our job is not done, but you will help us on our continuing mission," Michael told him. "Someone from ARC will come for you soon, Pete. You will be trained and equipped, then you will continue to help us gather our army together. Are you ready for that?"

Peter looked at Michael with a smile, resolute and hopeful, and uttered only two words.

"I am."

Epilogue

Abe found himself wandering in a lush, vast forest. The terrain was familiar, and he realized he was in Gardendale.

Wait, no, he thought. *This is different.*

All the landmarks and terrain were the same, but this was teeming, full of life. Fragrant and vividly colored flowers crowded long, sinewy vines leading up into towering trees. Monkeys called to him from branches far above his head, and he heard the birdsong loud and clear. As he walked he ran his hands over the tall brush and verdant leaves. He wondered where he was. The last thing he remembered was pressure on his chest and a searing pain in his arms and neck. He didn't remember anything after that, only that he was here now and, although it bore a resemblance to someplace he would rather not go back to, it was quite peaceful and beautiful.

Abe thought he saw a clearing up ahead of him so he kept walking. He wondered how he was going to get out of here later, but it really didn't concern him too much. He had been camping since he was a boy, and he was not alarmed at the idea of having to stay a night, or many nights, in this place.

He remembered his first camping trip with his grandfather Lionel—the memory came back to him so suddenly, it surprised him. *I couldn't have been more than six or seven. A scrawny kid this tall.* He held out a hand to mimic what was going through his mind, but the hand he saw didn't look like his worn aged hands.

He stopped walking and thrust his hands out in front of him to confirm. These hands were young and strong. He marveled at their youthful appearance. He wished that he had a mirror because he really wanted to see a youthful face staring back at him.

Abe stepped into the clearing and noticed that he was not alone. There was another man in the clearing. He was sitting on a large stump and had his eyes closed as if he were listening to something. The rapturous expression on his face told Abe that whatever he was experiencing was quite magical. Abe cleared his throat and the man's eyes opened.

"Hello," he said, "are you here for the orchestra, too?" he asked.

Abe looked around perplexed.

"Uh, I only see woods, man. No orchestra here."

Abe searched the tree line all around for an unseen band. His voice was younger, too.

"Oh, no, my friend. The orchestra is just there."

He pointed to a large group of birds sitting on a fallen tree some 20 feet away from them.

"Aren't they magnificent?"

The large man began to sway as he closed his eyes once again.

"Chopin has always been a favorite of mine."

He gestured to another stump sitting next to his.

"Have a seat, my friend. My name is..." He looked perplexed for a moment, until a young girl with a clipboard appeared and interrupted his thought process. She was tall, maybe 20 years old. Pretty, with ashy brown hair and pleasant features, chief among them was a thin, stark white streak of hair that proceeded from the crown of her high forehead to the terminus of the ponytail that she wore. She fretted as she walked and Abe immediately felt for her—he knew she was troubled by something.

"Miss, can I—" he started but she seemed oblivious as she approached them.

"Oh, no. I am so behind. You."

She pointed at the man on the stump,.

"You were supposed to be out of here before... you," she looked down, consulting her notes while she pointed to Abe, "got here. I think I'm in trouble. They are not gonna like this."

"Who are you?" Abe asked her.

"Oh. I'm June. I only arrived here myself a week ago, and I'm behind in my first assignment." She looked like she wanted to cry.

Abe took pity on her.

"No harm done. I'll wait for you to get back from wherever you need to go."

Abe took a seat on the stump by the young man. He looked vaguely familiar to Abe, but he couldn't place him.

The young man opened his eyes again and asked June, "Where are we going?"

"Well, you were summoned by Uriel. He needs to speak to you."

June held out her hand to him, and as he was reaching for her hand, she saw the mark on his palm.

"You are a guardian? Why didn't you say so? This makes so much more sense now."

She scribbled something furiously on her clipboard and looked from the young man to Abe.

"They want to speak with you as well, so I guess there is no time like the present. Come with me."

She walked across the clearing and the two men looked at each other, then back at June.

"Uh, which one of us?" asked Abe.

"Oh, I wondered why you weren't following. Both of you. Please," she added, rolling her eyes slightly.

The two men looked at each other again, unsure of what awaited. June tapped her foot lightly and looked at her non-existent watch, as if she had been waiting forever. The picture made Abe smile and he stood. The young man stood as well, and the duo moved to follow the young girl from the clearing.

"Uh, can I ask where we are?" Abe asked.

"You are in Eden," the young woman stated grandly, spreading her arms and spinning slightly as if to take it all in at once. She turned to both men, smiling widely, "You may not know this—well, certainly you *don't* know it since you've never been here before… it is the holding area here on Earth."

She stated this fact proudly, as if she herself had thought of the idea to use it. She continued, "For a select number of people, when we die, we are sent here to be used for another purpose."

This announcement made Abe stop in surprise. The other two kept walking, and soon Abe realized that he needed to move or be left behind. He ran to catch up just as he heard June say, "Guardians are special, and you should be really proud to be one."

The young man just nodded and shared a smile with the young girl.

They walked through the forest until they came upon another clearing. Abe sucked in a breath and stared skyward; the space itself was immense, but he was utterly stopped in his tracks by the sheer beauty of the clearing. Central to the vista that he was seeing stood a large waterfall, impossibly tall and disappearing into mists and clouds much higher than any that he had ever seen on Earth. Thunderous waters tripped over protruding rocks and boulders, and cascaded down into an immense lake at the bottom. On the shore of the lake stood a group of people. They were milling about, talking with one another, and seemed to be in no great hurry.

One of the people, a man with a distinctly Nordic look—all blonde and bearded, looked over at the newcomers and smiled. He was brilliantly garbed in a flowery, long sleeve tunic like Abe used to see on vacation in Bali. The shirt was mostly shades of amber and red and yellow, which made him look like he was on fire. The figure also wore a pair of jeans, and a pair of topsiders.

Boat shoes in Eden, he thought. *Huh.* He looked like he should be out on the water in a sailboat. He walked up to the trio and smiled down at June whose face turned as pink as the button down oxford she was wearing. She moved a pretty, slender hand from the crown where her skunk stripe was to the back of her head, readying herself for… something. Abe was interested to see what would happen next. He hoped that she wasn't in too much trouble.

"I'm sorry, sir. He…" she pointed to Abe, "arrived before I could bring him," she hitched her thumb in the young man's direction, "to you, so I brought them both. I hope that's okay."

As she was explaining, Uriel's smile got wider and wider. He held up a hand when she went to explain further.

"It's okay, June. You're new, but you'll get the hang of it."

The girl looked relieved and smoothed her hair again, adjusting the collar of her pink oxford. The angel turned to the young man, "Now, let's see—you are new, and expected, but Abe here was not expected for quite some time yet."

He looked at the soldier, slightly perplexed, then shook his mane of gold and continued.

"It was unfortunate that he was sent early, but now, here he is. We'll be able to use him, I'm sure, so… no worries, right?"

She bobbed her head and said, "Thank you, Uriel. I'll just leave them with you, then?"

He inclined his head to June, smiling and said, "All in all, I would say, excellent job. You saved all of us, including yourself, time by bringing Abe along with you." He turned to some of the folks gathered there on the shore and said by way of announcement, "I like it when people can think on their feet and make smart decisions." He turned back to the girl, who was now blushing. "Thank you, June, for such excellent discharge of your initial duties." He bowed slightly, looked and winked. "You may go."

She looked at the two men, and with a nod of her head she clutched her clipboard tighter and moved back into the forest.

The young man with Abe spun in a circle and said, "Wow. This cathedral is enormous. Are the musicians playing anything else today?"

Abe looked from the young man to Uriel, who looked bemused by the other's exuberance.

"Uh, Uriel is it? What is he talking about? We are in a forest with a waterfall over our shoulders. Why does he keep talking about musicians and a cathedral?" Abe asked.

Now it was the young man's turn to frown and look confused.

Uriel laughed and said, "Eden is different to each person, Abe. Max sees a cathedral and hears musicians because he so enjoyed going to the opera and the theatre as a child with his mother. These are important memories for him. You see the beauty in the outdoors near your childhood home. You were strengthened by them. That is why you chose the woods—it made you who you are. There is great wisdom in that."

Uriel looked very pleased with Abe, and it made Abe feel good to be thought of well, especially by an angel.

"Wait, did you say his name is Max? It isn't Max Avatov, is it?"

Abe did a quick bit of reasoning, realizing that if he, Abe, were now his younger self, or at least appeared to be his younger self, in this place, then why couldn't the man he knew briefly have reverted to a younger version of *himself* upon arriving here? It made sense the more he thought about it.

The young man turned around at his name and said, "Yes. That is my name. Do I know you?"

"It's Abe," the now-excited young soldier said, gesturing to himself. "*Abe,* man. Abe Sims. Don't you remember me? The warehouse, the vampires, Sam, Peter… Any of this ringing a bell?"

Max looked confused for a moment and said, "Impossible. Abe was an old man. You are around my age."

Abe smiled and embraced his friend, held him back at arm's length and said, "Cuz, take a look at yourself, because we are *both* younger than we were a couple of days ago."

Max looked at Abe in surprise, and then at Uriel questioningly.

Uriel looked from one to the other and said, "Well, now that we are all caught up, allow me to explain. You, Max, were killed in an explosion at the warehouse. As the warehouse crumbled, you were struck from behind by a piece of the wall before you plummeted into the water. Luckily for you, I marked you as mine when I took the flaming sword from you."

"I'm dead?" Max asked in disbelief.

"Yes," was all the response he received before Uriel turned to Abe. "You weren't meant to be here for another few years, but it seems our enemies wished to send us a message. The grunch snuck into your home and killed you as you slept. The coroner is a vampire in the city, and as such, recorded your death erroneously as a heart attack."

"I wondered why the last thing I remember is my chest feeling tight and a pain in my arm."

"They drained your blood from your arm and neck," Uriel told him. "I realize that this is shocking to you both, but we have need of you and you are here to decide—Do you wish to continue helping us in our mission?"

"I'm in, for sure. My old body won't slow me down anymore, and I have a powerful need to see some justice take place," Abe told him without hesitation, turning to do a bit of shadow boxing like he did in his youth.

It felt good to have a body that was responsive and strong again. He stopped to think for a moment about what he was leaving behind, but knew that if anyone could handle everything that was to come without him, it would be his niece.

Uriel looked at Abe and said, "Great. You will stay here in Eden, then, Abraham. We need someone with your tactical knowledge to help us in our war room."

Abe beheld the angel and humbly said, "It would be an honor."

Uriel turned to Max and said, "You have been marked as a guardian, Max."

Max held up his hand and looked at the small sigil in his palm. It was circular with crosses and what looked to be triangles or pyramids in the four corners.

"What does that mean, exactly? I thought only angels could be guardians?" he asked, rubbing his thumb across his palm.

"I'm glad you asked. Rarely, mortals are chosen as guardians based on displayed characteristics in dire situations. Being a guardian means that you… er… guard something, or in this case, someone."

Uriel raised an eyebrow as if asking without words if he was understood.

"Who, or what, would I be guarding?" Max asked.

"People, pets, animals, oceans, trees, bugs… I could go on." Uriel told him. "Anything important to the mission or the Master. Let's leave that open for now, okay? I could continue to explain… you look perplexed," Uriel offered.

Max shook his head and raised a hand, "No need. I get it." He pondered for a moment and said, "I get to go back into the population? How will that work if I am dead?"

"Another great question. Two for two. You will be sent back onto the Earth to protect it, but you will no longer be… well, you," he explained.

"Then who will I be if I am not myself?"

"Ah, yes. This is my favorite part. You will not look like you, but someone completely different to those who know you. You will still act like you, but no one will know it is you, for security purposes," Uriel told him. "Do you accept these terms? Will you help us fight the evil that is in the world? Lev Avatov is still very much alive and working with an evil organization. You know how he thinks and how he works. Will you help us rid his evil from the Earth, and in doing so, strike a blow against the nephilim, and those that created them?" Uriel asked him.

He seemed worried that the young man would not accept. Max looked from Uriel to Abe who smiled at him in encouragement.

"Don't you want a little justice for your mom and Maggie?" Abe asked him.

"Maggie…" Max trailed off. "Will I get to see her? Will she know me? No, you already said that I'd be different." Max looked down, reasoning with himself. "So, the people I love…"

"Are still here and still need your help, guardian. You have to look at the end game, Max. Losses are part of war. I don't know what your future holds once you are back among your living, but if you do your job well, like I believe you will, you will become a reason, a strong reason, that many more losses don't occur. We need you, Maxim. You are one of the most selfless humans I have ever seen… the way you picked up that weapon, the way you endured the pain to protect. You are valuable to us. I hope you see how rare that is."

Uriel looked at the young man again, expectantly.

Max turned to Abe, and the young soldier smiled broadly, eyebrows raised.

"Are you ready to hit Lev Avatov where it hurts?" Abe asked him.

Taking a deep breath, Max looked at his friend and then at the angel and said, "I am."

About the Author

Michelle A. Sullivan was born and raised in Fort Myers, Florida, and is a voracious reader with a three-book-a-week habit turned author. She brings a lifetime of dwelling in the fantasy worlds she so loves, together with a vivid and clear vision of a world where ARC is humanity's only hope.

She is bound by a passion for the subjects that the ARC series addresses, and her characters are relatable, fun, and flawed—just like their creator. Unlike her characters, Michelle is deathly afraid of spiders and being bored.

She and her spider-killer/editor husband share their home with various adult children and three equally-scared pooches.

The ARC Series, Volume 1: A Pale Horse is her debut novel.

Visit Michelle online at arcauthor.wordpress.com

Also Available from

WordCrafts Press

The Siege of Sternz
Luther Salyers

Tears of Min Brock
J.E. Lowder

The Awakening of Leeowyn Blake
Mary Parker-Garner

Home
Eleni McKnight

Furious
Aaron Shaver

Made in the USA
Monee, IL
16 August 2020

38505487R00225